OLIVE PARK

BY

C. J. Booth

Copyright 2011 C. J. Bootl

For Isabel Booth, who struck the spark.
For Ambrose Short, who fanned the flame.
And for my wife, Elizabeth, who continues to stoke the fire.

The author needs to give heartfelt thanks to a number of people because, damn, it wouldn't have happened without them. First, to my Maui group, Rocky, Richard, Tori, Danni, Dawn and especially Gary B. You guys helped me more than you know. Cover by James Clark of James Clark Design, jcdi.com, Seattle - thanks for the spot-on cover art. Finally to my beta readers – Nancy Crowell, Sarah Adams, Trace Adams and Elizabeth Booth, who, thanks to a sadistic tendency shared by all of them, were relentless in their pursuit of correcting my every misstep.

Take nothing on its looks; take everything on its evidence. There's no better rule.

Charles Dickens, *Great Expectations*

CHAPTER ONE

He could see the eagles from where he sat and he watched
them hover even as the caskets were lowered into the ground.
Eagles had been an endangered species he had heard, but not
anymore. Now, they were like crows; pedestrian and common.
Still, it was difficult not to admire their ability to stay aloft and
get a big picture view of all the shit that was going on below.
Seeing what they were seeing, they must regret having to land
sometimes.

M looked from the good Reverend Pleshett to his aunt and
back to the graves. This must finally be the time to throw dirt on
the caskets. They were fully lowered. The little motors that
unwound the straps holding the caskets had stopped at exactly
the same time. That was odd. He would have thought his father's
would have kept going down further, to fucking Hell.

The flower he held, a white rose, was going to start to wilt if
he had to hold it any longer. His sister wasn't holding hers but
had it resting in her lap. Smart for a six year old. The good
Reverend was still droning on and M longed to cover the
platitudes with his ear buds and some form of caustic rock.
Anything would be better.

Still, in a sick kind of way, it was funny that the two funerals
were held at the same time. Not just the funerals but the burials
and the fact that both were being laid side-by-side in the same
cemetery. Just as if they were the same. As if they were equal in
whatever God's eyes existed. As if they now had to spend
shittin' eternity together. But, that's what you get when you buy

a funeral package ahead of time. And that's what you get when you don't have any money to change the program.

No one was happy about the arrangement, but M noticed an overwhelming resignation to the whole affair, as if everyone, from his aunt to the few that attended the funeral, wanted to put the unfortunate events behind them. Get 'em in the ground and be done with it. 'Yes, yes, it was so tragic what happened and those poor kids, what are they gonna do and it's too bad that the parents have to be buried together and well that's the way it goes. Amen.'

M looked up. It was quiet with an expectant hush. Everyone seemed to be looking at him.

The good Reverend repeated his invitation with a hand gesture to M and his sister and his aunt to come up and stand next to the gaping holes in the ground. He knew from prior prepping he wasn't supposed to say anything. Nobody expected the next of kin to speak, especially since he was thirteen and Jessie only six. His aunt nudged him to get up. She actually prodded him so hard his whole arm moved. The trembling, mascara-tracked face of his Aunt Jane bore into him and then she jerked her chin toward the Reverend. She wanted him to get off his ass as they had rehearsed and go stand by the graves. He waited until his sister also stood, then they both walked together up to the abyss.

It was dark down there, but he could make out the top of the two different caskets in their two separate holes. The only reason he could tell them apart was because he had thrown a major fit. It was the only time during this whole unending affair he had really put forth anything, but he was insistent that the two caskets be different.

He wanted his mother's to be a very light color and his father's to be dark. He would not be placated. Even after the funeral director tried to make him understand that with the package that had been purchased so many miserable years before only included the Crown Premier caskets and they were all the same, don't you see. It was not possible to change them.

Unless, of course, you have an asshole kid throwing a fit in your mortuary where the next clients were due any minute.

So, his father got the crap brown, standard metal casket that came with the burial package. His mother's was now the Heavenly Rose Petal and was, as you would expect, rose colored. He hoped his mother would've liked the color.

Now as he stared down, it was easy to see which was which.

No, neither he nor Jessie was supposed to speak. They were to remain mute. Maybe cry, if tradition held, but otherwise not hold up the proceedings. Everyone just wanted this to be done.

Once again his arm jerked sideways as his aunt nudged him. He reached over with his good hand and touched his sister on her arm. She looked up at him and while her lower lip quivered a bit, she held his gaze and then tried to smile.

They both stepped forward and, in unison, let fly their roses into the grave. With a sad softness the flowers landed on the casket and stayed on the top. By previous discussion, no additions were to be made to his father's grave.

M and Jessie stepped back, once again in line with their aunt.

The good Reverend Pleshett, looking relieved that the end was in sight, started his final prayer.

"Let us pray."

M reviewed the circle of those who dared attend the funeral. Their heads were bowed as were his aunt's and Jessie's.

"Dear Father, we are born to be the singers of your song..." and so on.

Had anyone been looking up and not at their feet they still would not have thought it unusual or surprising that M stepped forward to resume his place by the grave edges. A grieving son paying his last respects. Getting his last look. Surely the eagles who still hovered overhead thought nothing of it.

What was rather surprising was the sound of M urinating on his father's casket. Piss makes an interesting sound when it drops six feet and lands on a metal box holding a big piece of shit.

CHAPTER TWO

Jessie wouldn't go in which, thought M, was a wise idea. Actually he doubted his aunt would have let her go in. It was going to be difficult for all of them anyway and a six year old did not need to re-live the bad stuff. Jessie hadn't come out of their room that night and he was pretty sure she hadn't even come out from under her Little Mermaid comforter until the police and aide guys had come stomping in. Pretty sure she hadn't seen anything. Pretty sure.

But she'd heard everything.

M looked up and down the street. All the houses were built about the same time, probably by the same builder who had one or two so-so split level plans and stuck with them. Theirs was painted a don't-offend-anyone off-white that his mother had liked. And if you didn't know about any of this and you had to pick out the house on the block that had had the father who betrayed his family, the father who decided one night that it was better if his wife, his kids, were smeared all over the walls, well, you wouldn't be able to pick it out.

Until now. Now everybody knows this is the death house. The house where a murderer went batshit crazy.

M shivered and checked his watch as he stepped into the dark. It was now after eight o'clock, late enough according to his aunt that they wouldn't attract a crowd, or well-wishers or whatever you call the morbidly curious who insist on viewing a crime scene with the pretext of condolence. She was probably right. He sure didn't need to see any of his friends, Tommy or

Mick or Rush. He didn't want to have to explain what happened. He really didn't need to think of it anymore.

So now they were sneaking in under the cover of darkness.

"How about a pizza?" asked M over his shoulder. He wasn't sure why he said it and he couldn't see her, but he knew his aunt must have stiffened like she does when she runs into anything unpleasant. Cat pee, spilled garbage, kid vomit. Stiffens right up. Least that's what he observed in the last few days.

M had watched her check out of their motel, this morning. The desk clerk had been some Arab guy with a rug tied around his head. His aunt never said a word. Just threw down her credit card and stared at the guy as if he had been one of the pilots of the planes in New York.

Now, she stood outside of the death house and addressed M.

"No. Nothing to eat. We won't be here that long and besides your sister's waiting in the car," she said, a rough harshness to her voice.

Then, sweetly to Ralph and his son, Blake, both conscripts from her trailer park, she said, "If you both can help me with some boxes in the back bedroom, that would really help."

M heard them disappear down the back hallway to what was euphemistically called the back bedroom, always held in reserve for guests who never came. In addition to an uncomfortable roll-out bed, it now held an old dresser rescued from a second-hand store. On top was their ancient computer. Inside the dresser drawers were the jumble of papers and statements that comprised the innards of the financial past and current financial position of the Cooper family. M knew what they would find. They were broke. They didn't have scratch.

Unless you inventoried the liquor cabinet.

M could tell them all about it. About the bounced checks, the maxed credit cards, the persistent phone calls at dinnertime. But why spoil the evening. His aunt would have plenty of time to be disgusted and disappointed later.

M stopped at the entrance to the living room. The crime scene. His hand automatically found the living room wall switch in the same place it had been for the last ten years, and turned it on. Nothing happened, of course. In the past, like last week, the switch had turned on the two lamps that flanked the couch.

Those lamps were nowhere to be found. They were evidence. The other light in the living room, a fake Tiffany type lamp with a lot of stained glass in a flower pattern, sat undisturbed on a side table across the room. It was about the only thing left in the living room that hadn't been hit with the craziness.

The hallway light cast a harsh and wholly unsatisfactory illumination halfway into the living room. Still, M could make out where the couch had been and where the lamps had ended up and where his father's head had bled all over. And where his Mother had lain.

M realized someone had cleaned up, or at least made an effort. Yet the lingering sour coppery smell hung on. Whoever eventually bought the place, he realized, would probably tear the house down. At least rip out some of the interior. Do some karmic as well as physical cleansing.

Tough to let your child crawl around on the floor where months before two adults had lain in yin-yang nesting, staring at each other with lifeless eyes. That would truly suck.

His aunt stole up behind him. "M! This way. Nothing to do in there."

She turned and led the way to the bedroom he and Jessie had shared.

He took a few steps into the room and looked around. It was as if he'd left it ten minutes ago, but now it had shrunk somehow. It was if he'd grown bigger or the room had lost some of its dimension.

The *Star Wars* posters were still on the wall, but now they appeared juvenile, silly. The soccer ball in the corner sat awaiting some other boy's foot. The metal Space Needle, the postcard he'd received from Radio Moscow, the signed picture of some old comedian who had done a charity stint at Meadowwood Mall. It was all still there, parts and pieces from someone's life. The boy who had lived in this bedroom couldn't have seen his father beat his mother to death.

"Only a few things for now," commanded his aunt. "A suitcase full. Blake will help you." She pushed little ten year old Blake into the room behind M. "Blake'll help with Jessie's stuff too."

She left them both standing in the room.

After a few moments Blake moved over to the pile of stuffed animals Jessie had arranged in a tenuous pyramid at the foot of her bed. "You think she wants any of these? They're kinda beat up, a bit."

M looked over the grouping. They'd all been scrounged from church thrift shops and they did seem rather run over for sure. He reached down and lifted the blanket on her bed. Underneath was a stuffed elephant-hippo type thing with wicked stripes. It had two things going for it; it had no errant stuffing trying to escape and it was already on Jessie's bed which bestowed on it some sort of animal royalty he guessed.

"This one here." He gave it to Blake and began a search for a cardboard box, a paper bag, anything in which to cram Jessie's clothes. His aunt should know they had no suitcases. Suitcases were for families who traveled and did things together. They had no suitcases. Never had as long as he could remember.

"Here, this'll do. Use this for Jessie's stuff." M grabbed a laundry bag and dumped out a dirty jumper of Jessie's, recognizing it as one she loved.

So, do I give her shirts and pants and stuff she likes or do we start over?

He reached down and put the jumper back in the bag. There was no money to start over. May as well be comfortable.

"Grab a few of everything in her drawers, you know, a few socks and shit, whatever." He handed the bag back to Blake. "Go."

M surveyed his half of the room. The covers were still thrown back on his bed. He remembered the screaming and finding his phone and the continually unanswered 911. He remembered not being able to take it anymore and jumping out of bed. He remembered pausing at the doorway. He remembered dialing 911 over and over. Then, he wasn't sure what he remembered.

M pulled open the top drawer. His mother had carefully folded his underwear. Jesus. Folded my underwear.

He started crying. He couldn't help it. He tried to be quiet but he could tell Blake could hear him. M caught his breath and forced himself stop. He started to wipe his nose with his sore arm, then switched and ran his nose all along his other sleeve. Shit, I'm probably freaking him out, thought M. Hell, I'm freaking myself out. What the hell am I doing?

He took a few more deep breaths and then moved to the bed. With his good hand he pulled the sheet out at the corners and spread it out on top of bedspread. He didn't have a laundry bag. All his dirty clothes always ended up on the floor, and then they would magically disappear to appear later in his drawer, neatly folded.

In the middle of the sheet, he placed some pants, a few shirts, and a sweatshirt and piled on some socks and underwear. He started to fold up the corners of the sheet when he remembered the closet.

The closet was small, and neither he nor Jessie had had much to put in there. Certainly precious little to hang up. He grouped Jessie's one little plaid dress that she had been made to wear to church, with his own sport jacket, a browny-tweedy thing with fake leather buttons. He didn't intend to wear it again, probably didn't fit anymore, but he remembered the day his mother had gotten it for him. It was one of the few things she had bought new.

He covered both the dress and jacket with his one winter coat, boosted them off the rod and slung them over the rest of the pile. The corners were quickly folded up on everything and he tied them together.

Blake had finished and was waiting for M to gather up his stuff.

"All set?" asked M. His voice came out all phlegmy.

Blake nodded.

M examined his desk, actually the desk that both he and Jessie shared. Like the movie posters tacked on the walls and ceiling, the signed baseball in its stand, the half-full water glass, it all seemed so sad. He felt deflated when he looked at what he was leaving. His former life had had a shitload of energy. Now, he was just tired.

He opened the desk drawer and reached inside for the envelope. He couldn't feel it so he pulled the whole drawer out and set it on the bed. He swept his hand through the contents but he could tell immediately it wasn't there.

"Shit!"

Eighty two dollars, gone.

"What's wrong?" asked Blake in timid voice

M wanted to fight, to strike, anything. But everything was so far out of reach. How do you fight this shit? No wonder people walk off cliffs, jump off bridges.

He grabbed the top of his *Fast and Furious* poster and ripped it off the wall and left it crumpled on the floor. This whole goddamn life is a crime scene.

M didn't wait for Blake but picked up the bundled sheet with the top of the hangers flopping out and headed down the hallway toward the front door. "Let's go."

He heard Blake shut off the light and begin to follow him but then M heard him stop at the living room. He could sense the kid was searching for evidence of death.

"Blake!"

"What?" the young boy jumped guiltily and hefted the laundry bag and joined M at the front door.

"I...just" Blake stared wide-eyed at M.

"Yeah. Come on." M pulled on the front door and let Blake go out first. He could hear his aunt and her friend from the trailer park loading up boxes in the back bedroom.

Mr. Swinton, M's English teacher, loved to talk about cherishing life's events. 'Someday,' he had said, 'you will realize that you're doing something for the last time. That you'll never see that place or person again. When that happens late in life, that's called regret. When it happens early on, when you are younger, it's life knocking you upside the head telling you to please pay some goddamn attention.' Something like that.

Okay, Mr. Swinton, I'm paying attention. I'm not sure what I'm supposed to see. What the hell part of this life am I supposed to cherish? I have a shitload of regret. How's that for cherishing?

When he exited the front door he saw little Blake talking to Mick. Mick, M's best friend, lived across the street and M was sure Mick's parents had sent him over, afraid to come over themselves, to see what was going on. M came up to the two.

Mick finally said, "Leavin'?"

M nodded.

"Comin' back?"

Tears came to M's eyes again and he shook his head and walked to the pickup and dumped his stuff into the back bed. Blake followed and did the same.

M stayed with his back to Mick and held tight onto the pickup's sides

"Hey," said Mick. He had come up behind him.

M didn't want to turn around. There was too much of his old life, before all this, in Mick's face.

"Hey," was all M managed, still fixed on the side of the pickup. He tried to sniff up the tears and snot.

Mick shrugged. "We're sorry, you know."

"Yeah," M acknowledged.

"Rush and Tommy, too. They like, told me to tell you."

"Yeah."

Mick started to turn away, and then remembered. "My parents too. They said…you know."

"Yeah, I know."

They were both silent for a moment.

"Kinda the shits, huh" said Mick. It wasn't a question.

M finally turned and looked up. "Yeah." He wiped his face with his good arm.

Ralph and his aunt appeared at the front door. His aunt set down her two boxes, ready to lock up. Ralph brought his load down the walk to the pickup past Mick, who was already walking away.

"Wait!" called M. "You got a pen or pencil or something?"

Mick came back and dug in his pocket and came out with nothing.

"Here," said Ralph, handing M a red sharpie. "We're done marking boxes, I think."

M gave Mick the pen and held up his arm with the brace on it. M managed a smile. "It's only temporary, comes off in a few days, but go ahead, write something. Make it for Tommy and Rush too, okay?"

Mick's tongue slid to the side indicating he was deep in thought. Finally he raised M's arm up a bit and started writing.

"No one's gonna see it there, you know," said M.

Mick kept writing while Blake and Ralph climbed into the cab of the pickup. His aunt shut off the porch light, brought her two boxes down the walk and set them in the truck bed.

Mick finished and admired his work, then closed the pen and handed it to M who handed it to his aunt.

Mick waved and trotted back across the street. "See ya."

M watched him go. "Yeah."

Kids had no dialogue for grief.

"What'd he want?" demanded his aunt.

"Saying sorry and all that shit."

She stiffened. "No need for that kind of language."

"And he was signing my arm thing, my brace."

His aunt surveyed his arm. "I don't see anything…"

"Down lower."

His aunt raised up the brace so the streetlight gave her some illumination. She lowered it quickly and shot a glance at Mick who had just entered his house.

"What a horrid little boy."

CHAPTER THREE

Out of the corner of his eye, M watched her drive. The dash light lit up her face in a sodden green with occasional flashes of on-coming headlights. He couldn't tell if she was upset and if so, at whom.

At times, to M, she appeared to be crying, but then again, maybe his aunt was one of those people who always looked baggy-eyed and sorrowful and was ever ready to burst with some salt water.

The Honda was full to the brim and then some. His feet were crammed in under the dash wedged in by his backpack full of books and some clothes. Jessie had fallen asleep about thirty miles ago and was the smallest item in the back seat. Looming over her were the boxes that his aunt had grabbed from his parent's office. The Honda's trunk and Ralph's truck held the rest of their clothes and some disparate items that his aunt in her incredibly warped idea of what they would need, had thrown in at the last minute. Probably because she saw part of her trunk was still empty. Or, more likely, since she had never had any kids, she just had no clue.

M had asked her about his and Jessie's bikes and their desks and Jessie's wagon, which she loved. When would they be able to get those? 'Later,' had been his aunt's answer.

Later, like never.

He pulled his feet free and turned to check on Jess. His arm still ached when he moved it the wrong way, but he twisted around and looked down on his sister. Maybe it was true about little kids. They could take life's bad shit better than most. At least bounce back quicker. He hoped so. Through the back window he imagined he could see glow from the lights of San Francisco. But it probably wasn't. It was just sky glow. Maybe it was fires in Oakland.

"M, turn around now."

His aunt had her lips set tight. Her hands gripped the steering wheel. She didn't like driving at night as she had announced more than once. For a few miles they had been followed by her friend from the trailer court, Ralph and his son Blake. But evidently Ralph had given up trying to drive ten miles below the limit and had left them as a memory just after crossing the Bay Bridge.

"Can we stop and get something to eat?" He realized he was starving and tried to remember when he'd eaten and what it had been. He couldn't.

"No." Then she softened. "No, we're almost there. Another fifteen minutes. Then I'll feed you. I think I have something you can eat."

"Swell," he said without enthusiasm. He also couldn't remember ever visiting his aunt's trailer, though she said he had. That had been before Jess had arrived, he guessed.

"So, how big is this place where you live?"

She looked at him for the first time on the drive. M knew she was having trouble determining whether he was being sarcastic, sincere, insulting or just plain stupid.

Defensiveness crept into her voice. "It's a very nice mobile home park. I've been there for a long time. There are about fifty other homes in the park. There's even a small playground, of sorts."

"No, I meant your trailer. How big is it?"

"We don't call them trailers anymore. They're homes, mobile homes, if you like. And mine, it's standard size with a garage too."

"How many bedrooms," asked M, but he already knew the answer.

"Just the one…"

"So, we're sleeping in the garage then." He said it as a statement, but he knew his aunt would never let them sleep anywhere but inside the trailer after what happened. She'd sleep in the garage, he knew, before she let them sleep there.

"Of course not! Don't be silly. You and your sister will sleep in the other end of the trailer, mobile home. It's where the living room is now. The two couch sections are quite comfortable. One's a pull-out. No one's gonna say I don't care for you, that you're not well provided for, even though you aren't mine," she added.

Right. Even though I killed your brother, thought M. We'll see what kind of care you really give us. Poison cupcakes as a treat. Back your little Honda over us. Slit our throats in the middle of the night.

She looked at him with purpose. "No garage, okay?"

"Whatever."

M could see she wanted to say more, probably to reassure him that he wouldn't be homeless. He knew that was going to be a lie. Ever since that night when he heard his mother cry out, he knew things were going to be very different. And the reality was they weren't going to be better and the likelihood of things turning to major crap was pretty high. It's what happens when the normal course of things are interrupted by a psycho's craziness. He had seen TV shows before. He just had to prepare himself. And Jessie.

It's kind of what the therapist had said. The one they'd made him see right after the funeral. M didn't believe in all that psycho-counseling shit. Therapy was only for people who had gone mental or couldn't deal with their everyday life. Like forgetting to shower or staring at the wall for days at a time. Those were the ones who needed some help. They needed someone to tell them to shower up or stop staring at the friggin' walls.

Of course, as the therapist had said, he and Jessie had suffered a shock. As if someone had stuck their hands into a light socket, only mentally. Now, they had to rest. The therapist had wanted M to help Jessie. She had told M not to look back on the days behind or think of what happened, and not to look forward and try to wonder what was going to happen. Take it one day at a time.

Even considering the source, it was probably good advice.

He knew about one day at a time. His father, five or six years ago, when someone must have dumped a bucket full of guilt on him, had agreed to go to AA. For a while they had pamphlets all over the house, even in the bathroom. So when M was doing his business he got to read all about taking it one day at a time and the steps needed to get sober or get your life back on track.

Well, that hadn't worked out so well.

Still, M thought, for Jessie and himself, it was probably a suggestion that was worthwhile. Besides, the therapist had nice tits and he tended to believe women with good tits. In hindsight, he thought, she could probably have told him to swing a dead cat around his head three times and spit and he would've done it.

But not looking toward the future was not going to be an option. When the therapist had left the room, he had heard his aunt and what must have been a social worker in the next room discussing good old Aunt Janey's options regarding him and Jessie.

The lady from CPS was doing all the talking. "There are three real decisions you can make. You can keep them..." She had paused then, probably to elicit a reaction from Aunt Janey. But, no words had been forthcoming. In fact his aunt must have indicated that she wanted to hear other the options because the social worker continued.

"Okay, or you can give them both up to a foster home overseen by CPS, or, you can split them up, foster home for one and keep the other."

M listened intently, but no one said anything and he thought they were done discussing his and Jessie's future until finally his aunt spoke up.

"How soon? How soon can you take 'em? He killed my brother, you know. I just don't know what he's gonna do. So how soon?"

M's stomach knotted. Nice. So much for one day at a time. One way or another, their stay at the House of Janey was going to be temporary.

M had seen a movie one time about a guy who made it through a plane or train crash and he was completely unhurt. Everybody else was killed or injured but he walked away without so much as spilling his drink. Some horseshit like that. Anyway, he walked away from the burning wreckage and became a new man. Whether it was because he didn't die because he was lucky or because he was somehow God's gift to plane crashes with some invisible protective shield around him, he didn't know. But, the guy came away with an attitude that said, 'Screw it, I can do anything.' He was empowered, thought M.

And that was the way he was feeling. It had grown slowly. His belief that he had made it through the crashing and burning of his family gave him that empowering sense. Sure the family was in a goddamn nosedive for a while, but looking back, it was a miracle he hadn't become extra fuel for the inferno that erupted.

Sorry oh beautiful one with nice tits, I am looking ahead and I can do anything for me and my sister. Empowered. And it doesn't involve being lap dog companions to Aunt Janey.

He wished now he had paid more attention to the Christmas cards they had received. Or any family communications, actually. He would have a better idea of the relatives their family had and where they lived and what their situation was. As in, were they well off enough to pay for the upkeep of two kids? He needed to sort out his options of where he and Jessie would go. Somewhere warm if he could manage it.

In a minor stroke of genius for which he was still proud, the last item he had grabbed as they were leaving the house had been his mother's address book. It appeared to be a treasure trove of options. At least he hoped so.

"We're here," said Aunt Janey, breaking his reverie.

"Here?"

His aunt guided the Honda through the two concrete pillars capped with red Spanish tiles. The sign on the right pillar, lit by the wash from a low wattage bulb, was light blue and orange and read, 'Sunshine Vista'. That's all. Didn't mention the fact that there were fifty or so trailers crammed onto five acres.

They poked their way past a 10 mph speed limit sign. It was the speed bump that woke Jessie up in the back seat.

"Where are we?" she asked sleep laden.

M said over his shoulder, "Evidently, we're here."

She sat up, rubbed her face and grabbed the back of the seat. "Really?"

Anyplace new is new. Hell would be new. New always had a fascination because it was new. Didn't mean it was going to be good, just different. New sometimes lasted only a minute. Jessie's lasted about two.

His aunt pulled the Honda into a little tiny driveway. Even though it was dark, M could see that the driveway was lined with bright yellow flowers and there was a path that led from the driveway to the front door. Concrete stepping stones that let the grass grow up between the patterns. The grass was trimmed tight and close, like a crew cut.

They got out. M grabbed his backpack. It had enough clothes to last him until they sorted out the rest. He grabbed Jessie's laundry bag.

"What's in there?" she asked as she slid out of the back seat.

"Everything you need, I hope,"

"Let's go you two. Come on. We can get the rest of the stuff later. I need to get you fed and to bed."

M started up the walkway but Jessie held back. He turned and she came up and joined him. "We're going to sleep in there?"

M surveyed the trailer. It looked clean enough. Had a nice little miniature plastic and aluminum cover over the front door area. Large enough to cover the two chairs that sat angled together on a little concrete patio. M wondered who usually sat in the other chair or whether it was just out for an invitation to someone wandering by to rest their dogs.

There were two small clam shells on the patio. Burnt and pinched cigarette butts filled one of the shells.

"Yes, little Jessie Cooper. This is it,' M said as lightly as he could.

Jessie did not look convinced. "M…"

While Aunt Janey struggled with her keys, M knelt down in front of Jessie.

"Just for tonight, okay?"

She appeared to think about it. "Then where tomorrow?"

M shrugged. "Probably here again. We'll see. One day at a time."

"I don't know what that means."

"How about this. We can sleep touching toes, okay? You'll know I'm there and I'll know you're there. C'mon, it'll be okay."

She allowed M to guide her toward the door which Aunt Janey was holding open.

"How about some peanut butter and jelly sandwiches before you go to bed. That's good." It wasn't a question.

Jessie was quiet as she stepped over the threshold and took in the trailer's cramped space. There was the smell of a spice, cinnamon maybe M thought, and an old-lady type perfume. Frilly white curtains covered the windows. Small gold and green throw pillows with tassels sat nicely arranged on either end of the couch. Even aliens from another planet would be able to tell there hadn't been a male presence in this trailer since about forever.

M set down his backpack and Jessie's things. Neither of them ventured off the small little tile area that extended just inside the entry.

"Okay," said Aunt Janey, pride creeping into her voice. "This is the kitchen and dining area here. The bathroom is down the hall on the left, when you two have to go. My bedroom's beyond that."

M and Jessie turned their attention to the other end of the trailer. Aunt Janey moved to what was the living room. It was obvious to M she hadn't really given any thought to exactly how she was going to arrange a bed for two kids.

"The couch pulls out to a bed."

Both M and Jess looked at the living room. Big fluffy couch, a coffee table with a few magazines on it. M was too tired to acknowledge the irony of the two House Beautiful magazines on the small coffee table. A TV sat on a small buffet at the end of the trailer. That was it. It was alarmingly neat.

"It will be a little cozy, only until…Well, it'll be fine. You'll see. And you can watch TV right from your bed. How's that?"

Jessie looked up, unsure. "M…"

M closed his eyes. He felt like they were being squeezed into a can. Shit City. It could probably be worse, somehow. One day at a time. Beautiful tits.

"This'll do." He looked straight at his aunt. "For now."

His aunt gave a weak smile but couldn't hold his gaze. She opened the refrigerator and pulled out the sandwich makings.

Jessie sat tentatively on the front edge of the couch and watched her aunt's every move, as if she was going to have to run at any minute.

"Just pull off the cushions and then grab that little handle thingy and pull up on it."

M waved Jessie up and looked around for someplace to put the sofa cushions and the little throw pillows and ended up tossing them on their stuff in the corner. He yanked at the handle and the couch unfolded. There were sheets on it but they appeared to have been left by Custer before he took off for the last stand.

"I'll get you some blankets. Eat now."

M and Jessie moved to the small round table. They sat and ate their sandwiches in stunned silence.

New doesn't last very long. Once you eat a meal in a new place, it's yours. You own it so to speak. It was that reality that settled on M. He could see Jessie felt it too. No going back. Shit City.

Jessie started to whimper while she ate.

Aunt Janey looked at a loss. "We'll make the best of this, okay? We've all been through…"

M looked up sharply but said nothing.

"…and we'll make the best of it. We'll figure out some better arrangement so we can all be comfortable. You'll see."

"Yeah," offered M with an edge that seemed to frighten Jessie, "maybe we can ask the goons at CPS to send us somewhere."

His aunt looked struck.

Jessie looked horrified. "I…I don't like goons." She began to cry harder.

"That was…uncalled for, you know," said his aunt.

M stared at his aunt. Empowerment was good.

"Now, look," she said sharply, indicating Jessie who had tears streaming down her cheeks.

M put his hand on Jessie's back. "She'll be fine. We'll be fine."

Aunt Janey rose abruptly. "I know you're both tired. Finish and go to bed." She glanced at Jessie. "You'll be fine, honey." Then she turned and started down the hall to her own bedroom but stopped as if she had forgotten something.

"Oh, and starting Monday, I've arranged for someone to look after you during the day while I'm gone. A sitter."

M was disbelieving. "You're shittin' me."

She closed her bedroom door.

Empowered. Yeah.

CHAPTER FOUR

Brilliant, thought Detective Stan Wyld as he surveyed what was to be his office, a roofless glass-walled thirty by thirty foot cubicle in the center of the ground floor courtyard of the four story atrium of the old Rogers & Sons Cold Storage facility.

The irony was not lost on him. The newly resurrected cold case division of SPD, the Sacramento Police Department, was now operating out of a former furniture storage warehouse that in the late 1800s had been a state-of-the-art cold storage company. Rogers & Sons had been the massive centerpiece of Sacramento's warehouse district. Four stories, solid red brick, it had chilled almost two million cubic feet of whatever meat and foodstuffs had been dragged up from the steamers on the Sacramento River.

It was, Stan admitted, an innovative solution to the department's storage problems for the archived evidence and files from past cases. And now, some place to throw the brand new cold case division. Shove them into the 'cold storage' warehouse, bellied up to the evidence boxes and files they would need.

Stan had studied the historical plaque screwed to the outside wall which heralded the bricked-in Gothic arches and corbelled cornices. A formidable edifice, he admitted, but inside, gone were the miles of pipes that circulated the chilled salt brine. Gone too, were the boilers, steam engines and compressors.

What remained were four stories of wide-planked warehouse floors surrounding an open atrium that had, for some unknown reason, a central office made of four glass walls.

Stan could only stand in the opening to the glassed-in cage and stare in amazement. Four half walls all topped with another three feet of crystal clear glass secured at the top of the panels by a bright metal border. With the light streaming down from the clerestory it was both stunningly beautiful and totally impractical.

The entire center of the glass room was taken up with a conference table, maybe twelve feet long. Above the table, shaded fluorescent bar lights hung suspended from an open lattice that formed the office ceiling. A number of semi-matching chairs were shoved up to the table edge. Four miscellaneous oak desks, two with missing drawers, were up against the outside walls.

He didn't get it. He was used to the low-ceilinged sweat box that used to house his desk, along with those of six other detectives. The cacophony of the phones, suspects being shuttled back and forth to the two 'boxes' for interrogations, all the detective's desks back to back. Privacy was non-existent. He had known more about his compatriot's affairs than he needed to.

Here, he was surrounded by glass and with no one else around, it was completely private. Go figure.

Stan rapped on one of the glass walls. He couldn't fathom how Rogers & Sons had run an office that was open to everything and everyone. Any lowly employee walking by could see Mr. Rogers scratch his ass or pick his nose. A man could command no authority sitting in a glass house.

Given budgeting issues, Stan knew no one was going to pony up the dough to remove the glass and fence them in with conventional walls and ceiling.

This was their glass play-pen for the foreseeable future.

He searched for a few feet of open space to set down his box of personal items. Piles of evidence boxes most legal size, some stacked five tall, had been wheeled into the room and placed with no apparent care as to their order or classification. They now filled most of the remaining floor space.

The only 'new' item on the boxes was small bar code stickers that appeared stuck on at the last minute by the moving company.

He leaned in to the nearest pile of boxes, brought his lips close to the topmost and gently blew a small cloud of dust from the side.

The years 1960 to 1963 were now visible on the curled and stained label. Stan brushed more of the dust away. Precinct number followed by case numbers came clear.

He set his personal effects down and stuck his head out of the glass enclosure.

"Just who the hell did this?" he yelled the length of the warehouse. His voice echoed in the cavernous place. He knew no one would answer, but it felt good. Like a dog marking his territory.

A pair of old security guards who were moving more boxes at the far end of the atrium looked up briefly when he yelled, but they didn't work for him and so went back to moving what they had to move. More case files.

"Welcome to the department of Who Gives A Crap, Detective Stan Wyld." He began narrating his own introduction to the disarray of the new Cold Case Division.

He maneuvered himself deeper between the piles. "Nice. In addition to four million boxes of old abandoned cases, as a bonus, we have some discarded furniture." He put both hands on the nearest table. It swiveled on loose legs like a tired drunk. "In great shape. And chairs to match." The chairs were old oak and stacked seat to seat so the broken supports for the legs were easy to see.

"And looky here," He lifted the flap of the nearest storage box, getting a solid waft of mustiness, "modern mimeograph machines and the latest in Dictaphones." He picked up the microphone handle of the top Dictaphone and blew into it. "And they piled them right next to the always serviceable rotary telephones." He looked around at the mass of stuff surrounding him and wondered if HQ really expected them to use it or were they just dumping the old office equipment with the old cases.

He held the microphone head close to his lips. "You've done it now, detective. Not only are you the apparent heir to everything old and useless, you're also tusk deep in the elephant graveyard of investigative failures."

He put the Dictaphone handle down and laughed.

"Perfect."

Cold cases *were* perfect for him. No pressure. No one was clamoring for any of these to be solved by tomorrow morning.

Still, his younger partner, Jake, had resisted the idea of lobbying for a cold case division. Jake's adrenaline was still fed by Homicide's current cases and their insistence to be solved yesterday.

His and Jake's partnership was based on simple opposites. Stan liked to be first through a door. Jake liked to be first to figure out how the door opened. For ten years the collaboration had operated like the opposing pistons of a steam engine; complementary actions, yet moving forward. Stan Wyld and Jake Steiner. Like Smith and Wesson.

It was Stan who had insistently needled the younger man until Jake admitted the inherent value of working one case at a time until it was done. No more jumping from case to case like nervous fleas.

Stan took a deep breath and looked around. He felt jazzed.

If there was a place and time to strip away the crap he and Jake had had to suffer under for the last ten years, it was here in the bowels of the Rogers & Sons Cold Storage building running the Cold Case Division, now officially renamed the OID, the Ongoing Investigation Division.

Stan liked the new name. He had to give Jake credit for it, though. As Jake had pointed out, these cases were only looked on as 'cold' by the men and women of the Homicide and Robbery Division who were always busting their butts trying to solve whatever was current. And there was always something current. Time was the enemy. As if on a conveyor belt, the new cases appeared with an increasing regularity that was disheartening for an investigative staff that had been suffering under a hiring freeze for the last two years. Sacramento was no different from any large city when it came to fighting increasing crime on a diminishing budget.

But, once Jake had come on board with the idea of a new and energized cold case department, they had both lobbied hard for reactivating a group that would specifically work on cases that had been not forgotten, but been put aside. Stan had written the proposal himself. It had been grand. Instead of each member of Robbery-Homicide working on past cases as they could squeeze out the time, which they never seemed to have, Stan had proposed taking over half of the fifth floor, with five detectives, two support staff, and with all the best computers.

He and Jake had pointed out the advantages of such a group; detectives working independently, without trying to manage their current caseload and then shifting gears to wrap their brains around finding a missing child from ten years ago. Cold cases were always set aside once some whack job would beat up his wife or poison the neighbor's dog or knock down a mini-mart.

It was time, he wrote in his proposal, to rework the original evidence in the older, 'ongoing', cases, combing through them now with all the new technologies: DNA, improved access to the more sophisticated databases of NCIS, FBI and DOJ, and of course the internet.

He and Jake had also stressed the unsaid moral mandate of any police department. They were to serve all of their constituency, not just those with immediate problems, not only those who yelled the loudest or had the greatest visibility, but everyone, including those whose hurt and troubles had been yesterday's.

It was an inspiring proposal. And Sacramento agreed to fund it for two years. A pilot program.

He removed his cell charger from his box and cast around for a plug.

Sure, they funded the program, but of course, gone was the support staff. The modern computer equipment was down to two laptops. The proposed half of the fifth floor had morphed into this thirty by thirty fishbowl in the middle of a concrete fortress.

And, as expected, the detective force of five was cut to just Jake Steiner and himself.

Still, Stan knew they should feel fortunate. It had happened. Not the way they had planned, but what does?

And it only happened because the furniture storage company had been bounced out of business after the two idiots who ran the place were convicted of moving more than bedroom sets and dining room tables through their facility. The drugs had been found in everything from people's dresser drawers to antique armoires.

The city fathers had been able to not only secure the Rogers building at a bargain price just before it entered foreclosure, but they had also been able to claim some moral high ground by establishing the new Ongoing Investigation Division, as they said in the press release, '...because the Sacramento Police Department serves all its constituents. And no cases are forgotten. No unsolved cases would ever be closed.'

Whatever, thought Stan. We're here.

He took his sleeve and wiped a small portion of the glass wall near the entrance. With double stick tape he brought just for this purpose, he stuck the sign that Jake had ordered.

Ongoing Investigation Division.

No more weekends unless they wanted to. No more hustling their asses in and out of squads. No more trying to hide his bad knee from those who would retire him from active duty if they only knew.

OID. If we solve 'em, we solve 'em. We don't, we don't.

He lifted up the cardboard top of one of the boxes, myriad files and envelopes and plastic bags from six or seven forgotten missing persons cases, burglaries, rapes or murders stared back at him. He lowered the top and looked out at the looming pile of boxes beyond. The immense reality of what encircled him tap-tap-tapped him upside the head like an insistent velvet hammer.

"Wow...," he whispered.

Fifty-two years old and he felt like a new recruit again with that adolescent rush of starting something new. It had been a long time.

"So," came a feminine voice from the doorway behind him, "Is like 'wow' the best you can do?"

CHAPTER FIVE

Stan jumped at the sound. A young blonde woman, about 25, with a large leather bag over her shoulder was leaning against the glass entry to his new office holding two paper sacks that Stan recognized. He didn't need to read what was written on the side, he could smell the spicy-sweet aroma of Jimmy's Old World Deli pulled pork from where he stood.

Stan shook his head, "I didn't order any lunch." but his stomach growled in disagreement.

The girl looked disheartened and set the bags on the conference table. "It's okay. Whatever. You still owe me $12.60 for lunch. You and Detective Steiner, each."

Stan stared at the girl who, as much as she tried to hide it behind an officious attitude, was strikingly pretty.

"Name's Mallory." She cleared off the nearest oak desk and spread out the goods. "Avocado and tomato for me and pork sandwiches with slaw for you two."

She paused and looked up at Stan. "I asked around. This is what I heard you guys ate. Correct? I mean you are Wyld aren't you?"

Stan watched as she slid back on an old credenza that graced the side of the glassed cubicle and threw her hat down, a beret-looking thing. Her blonde hair was fashionably and unevenly cut at shoulder length and subtly streaked with three levels of blonde. She swung her legs back and forth.

"Hello!" she repeated, "Wyld, right?"

"Yes, I'm Wyld."

"Okay then, Eat." She jumped off the credenza and slid onto one of the conference chairs.

The smell was true Jimmy's. He'd had untold numbers of pork grinders over the years, usually with a few beers. This lunch was an old comrade and his stomach rumbled louder in fond remembrance. He guessed he had about 30 extra pounds thanks to Jimmy's.

"I had 'em put the horseradish on the side. Where's Steiner?"

Stan made his way past the pile of boxes that said 1973, took off his coat and hung it on the back of a solid, old oak chair, part of a mismatched 1950's desk set.

"You work for Jimmy's then?" asked Stan, confused.

She seemed taken aback and Stan could sense defensiveness in her as she sorted the food.

"Ummm…like, no. Do I even look like a deli person?"

"Well…" Instead of continuing he dug into his back pocket and pulled out his wallet. "How much again?"

She seemed miffed. "$12.60 each. But..."

"So, twenty five something. Here's $30." He extended the cash toward her but she made no move to take it.

Stan could see she was getting pissed. "Okay then *Mallory,* how 'bout $35?"

"I don't need a tip for crissakes, *Detective* Wyld," she said with a quiet intensity as she sat down and freed what looked like a veggie wrap from the Jimmy's bag. He didn't even know they made frou frou stuff like veggie wraps.

"What are you doing?" he repeated.

Her mouth was now full and she shrugged her shoulders and indicated the sandwich.

"Mm eetng." She shook her head side to side trying to swallow.

"Eating. I can see that, but why here? Are you on a lunch break?"

"Um wif de deparmnt," she tried to say. She held up her hand to stop the conversation and dug a diet soda from the bag. She took a big swig, waited a second, burped, shook off the carbonation, and then said, "I don't work for any deli. I'm with the department, whadya think?" She said it as if that made everything clear.

Stan examined her as she took another bite. "What? Department of food delivery?"

She rolled her blue eyes and settled back in her chair. Then with great enunciation as if she were speaking to a four year old, said, "I'm Mallory Dimante from the po-lice de-part-ment. I have been assigned to partner with the two detectives who are working cold case and one of them, the prehistoric one, is molting right in front of me."

She took another bite of her wrap.

Through a mouthful, she managed, "And I was being friendly, you know, getting some lunch. Don't worry, I'll front it. Keep your damn money." She waved at the cash Stan still held in his hand. "You and Steiner can buy your new partner a rum and coke or lots of rum and cokes or lunch or something very expensive later."

She took a swig of soda, burped again, quieter this time and resumed eating.

"Assigned to partner?" Stan hesitated, then laughed.

"Yeah, well, sort of your partner," she said. "With Steiner, of course. Where is he?"

Stan dropped his hand with the cash.

Mallory rambled on. "Yeah, well, I don't see any Steiner, so I guess right now it's just you and me." She seemed to think a second, then with a cockeyed smile, "When he does get here it'll be like a three-way, eh, detective? Out here all by ourselves."

Conflicting visions spun through Stan's brain.

A stack of boxes full of evidence files appeared on a handcart at the office door maneuvered by a weary looking security guard. "Where do you want these lady?" he sighed at Mallory.

Mallory flipped open her black case and brought out a hand-held scanner. Bracing her legs against the table, she stretched out and swiped the bar code on the top box and read the readout on the back of the scanner.

"They're 1996. I don't want 'em in here. Leave them outside the door, okay?" She turned back to Stan and smiled.

Stan watched the boxes retreat, and then he forced an answering smile. She appeared alarmingly perky and moved side-to-side when she talked as if she couldn't control her inner energy, even when she ate.

Mallory stood up and put her sandwich down. She looked as if she had to deliver bad news.

"Deal with it, detective. The Sacramento Cold Case division, if you can call us that... wait, I'm sorry, the new OID..." she surveyed the chaos that stood in varying height piles around them, "...is you, me and Steiner, if he ever decides to show. Three of us. Partners."

"Bullshit." Stan settled confidently back in his chair. "I've heard nothing about you or anyone joining us. Neither has Detective Steiner."

"Oh." Between bites Mallory lifted the leather flap of her bag, reached in and slapped two department envelopes on the table. "Forgot."

Stan didn't bother opening them. He had a pretty good idea that if she was telling it straight, the departmental notifications were just as she had said. That meant he and Jake would be playing nursemaid to Barbie for the foreseeable future. Stan groaned. Jake, the horny bastard, would probably love it. Stan could just picture Jake exaggerating his limp; stiff-legging his cast around the office dropping pencils and asking her to continually pick them up.

Stan took inventory. Cute, no ring, maybe 5'6", skinny but healthy, works out, good taste in perfume, not carrying, works indoors, kind of nervous.

Stan sighed. "Mallory what?"

She cocked her head to the side and smiled with a smile designed to make men cheat.

"Wow, memory is the first to go, you know that don't you? Mallory Dimante. Slave of the SPD."

If she had weighed her decision early in life between modeling and police work, to Stan it was obvious she had chosen unwisely.

He knew he and Jake could use the help, he just hated to be upstaged. Most of all he hated being surprised. Really hated it.

"Yeah, fine," he sighed. "Look, Detective Steiner won't be joining us for lunch. Or for the rest of September probably. He's at 15th and Madison."

"Where?"

She had stopped eating when he spoke and was looking at him with honest interest. It was unnerving.

"He's doing a week of handwriting analysis. Everyone, especially the nurses, who signs his metal cast, gets an earful; he tells their fortune based on their handwriting. And since he's got a full leg cast he's going to be a busy boy."

She nodded as she spread out the paper the sandwich came in so all the corners were flat. "15th and Madison; Sacramento General."

"We were T-boned by a bread truck over the weekend. Hit the passenger side."

"He okay?" She didn't look at him but kept at the sandwich paper, smoothing and re-smoothing it.

"Busted leg and the cigarette burn under his eye. Airbag."

Mallory winced.

Sad blue eyes, not much makeup.

"He'll live. Won't be much help for a while."

"Okay, that's good," said Mallory with simple sincerity. "I mean good that he'll be okay."

They were quiet for a moment then Stan said, "On the positive side, we now have a shitload of deli rye bread if you want any." He spread the pungent slaw on the warm pork and replaced the bun. After an awkward pause, he volunteered, "Yeah, and thanks for the lunch."

He was aware that Mallory had stopped eating and stopped trying to flatten all the sandwich paper and was staring.

He looked up. "What?"

She continued to stare then she smiled, "Yeah, they said you looked like that old actor, you know the Cape Fear guy. The original one."

Stan sighed. "Mitchum." He had heard it before.

"Robert Mitchum, yeah. Cape Fear, Farewell My Lovely and The Big Sleep and a lot of other shit I stayed up 'til two in the morning watching instead of doing homework. That guy. Yeah. You do look just like him."

"Except I'm a real detective and he's not."

"Yeah, but you've got sorta the sad eyes and streaky slicked black hair thing going on, you know, just like good ol' Mitchum."

He fished for something appropriate to say about her. "And Mallory, your actual police experience is what? Police detective novels? Too many late night movies? The love of a misguided relative who thought he'd get you into a cush job working for the city? Enlighten me. What exactly are you doing here?"

Mallory was caught with a mouthful and tried to speak through it, ignoring the sarcasm. "Computers. Data search, you know."

The light finally dawned. She was partner in her mind only.

"You're a civilian tech. Just a tech," he said.

"Duh."

Stan sighed. "And you're not going to be saying, 'you know' all the time are you?"

She appeared to think about it for just a second. "I dunno. Probably. Anyway, I'm I.T...."

Stan said nothing. This was not the way he envisioned Sacramento's cold case division proceeding. It was infinitely better. Some help for Jake and himself. And someone who knew their way around a laptop.

Mallory misinterpreted the look on his face.

"I.T., Information Technology. Been with the department for over a year now, actually almost two.

"I know what I.T. is."

"Anyway, Captain believes you two don't know shit about computers and he said you couldn't tell your boxers from your briefs, computer wise, whatever the hell that means, and you could use all the help you could get."

"Swell."

She shrugged. "I did stick up for you two. Well, pretty much. I told him you and Steiner..." She paused as Stan got up and pulled his way over to the other desk, favoring his bad leg. She saw him struggle but had to finish what she started ".... you and Steiner had limped along so far without me."

Stan looked at her then at his bad leg.

She continued, "But he was afraid with all this new stuff online, you two would be wasting a lot of time unless there was some sort of ... plan. So, I'm the plan."

Her smile showed a lot of white teeth and seemed genuine.

Dear God, Jake was going to have a field day with this. Stan just hoped they could keep her long enough to do some good. Show them a little of what she knew before she filed the next sexual harassment suit against Jake. And, thought Stan, it will be just my luck; she'll probably decide to include me too. In the long run, it would have been better if downtown had sent them someone who looked like the crone he had in second grade, dour, hook-nosed Mrs. Bauer. One old plaid dress, black clunky shoes, eyeglasses and lacking the ability to smile. Dentures too. Loose ones.

Mallory sat down and started back in on her wrap. She took big bites and swallowed. "By the way, he also said that if you two gave me any grief at all, he would personally smash your nuts and feed them to Vicious. Think that's his dog. Maybe his wife. Not sure really."

She shook off the thought, then sped on, "Anyway, last week, while you two were playing dodge-em with the bakery truck, I went over every box since 1980, bar coded and cataloged everything they sent over." Pride crept into her voice. "You won't have to dig through box after box. It's done. So Detective Steiner has a busted leg, what's wrong with yours?"

Stan found his voice. "My leg? Nothing." He rubbed the thigh in small, practiced circles. "Just 22 long years of solid police work."

Mallory accepted the dig at her inexperience, "Ahh...okay. Whatever."

They were both quiet for a moment.

"Well, that, and a pissed-off ex-wife who thinks she knows how to aim a Chevy."

"Hah!" laughed Mallory. Then her smile faded. "Not.... really?"

Stan surveyed the room. Besides the twenty or more stacks of evidence boxes and case files, there were scores more outside the small office.

Mallory followed his glance, and then said, "This is about a quarter of what's coming over."

"Holy mother." It would've taken him and Jake weeks to just sort the case boxes, let alone index them.

Mallory wasn't smiling now. She put down her sandwich, wiped her hands. "Look..." The oak desk creaked as she reached behind her and grabbed a legal sized box and set it gently next to pile of files. "I don't know who you guys pissed off, or maybe there is some serious ass wiping going on somewhere, 'cause here's what we're working first." She grabbed the top manila file from the box.

Stan waved it away. "Yeah, well I don't think so. Jake and I had already decided we would start on some missing person's cases," he added. "We thought we'd..." He stopped when he saw the box she had centered on the table. It had too many signatures on the front. The year scrawled on the box was 1997.

Mallory stopped eating, swallowed and turned serious.

"Yeah, well, I'm genuinely sorry, Stan. I am. You and Steiner weren't around and I didn't know what to say to them. I guess I didn't know how much crap we would be in if I said no to this."

She rested her hands on the box, then flipped open the top folder. "I guess it *is* sort of missing persons."

Stan sat very still. He knew what it was.

He was afraid of this. His vision of working with Jake at their pace on the cases that interested them the most had all been a detective's folly. Who was he kidding? This was politics. CYA. This was cover your ass time.

Mallory slid a few color 8x10s across the table.

"It's Olive Park," she said softly.

Stan pushed his sandwich away. This was crap. First an office assistant who thinks she's a partner, then downtown shoves the most screwed up, unsolved case of the century down their throats.

Olive Park. Dear God.

Three child victims, tortured, buried, probably alive, in a lonely wooded area outside Sacramento just below the looming El Dorado Hills. In Olive Park.

When he first moved to California and started with the department he learned from his Mexican landlady that Sacramento was a Spanish derivation of the Holy Sacrament. 'Jesus' reparations,' she'd said in broken English.

Sacramento. California's atonement for all its past sins. If any case represented the worst of what horrors man has dreamed up to inflict on his fellow man, this was it. There was no atonement for this. You could give no reparations for something like this. Jesus or anyone else.

He stared at the top picture but didn't touch it. It was a child's cry for help from the past. A plea that would not go away. An unsolvable case that had haunted all who had touched it.

It was now his turn. Unless he could get them out of it.

Mallory turned the picture so he got a better view.

Stan started to push it away but his fingers stopped at the edge and held it. Through twenty plus years in the department he had avoided it or maybe it had never before found him. Better men, far better men than he, sat deflated in the shadows, in the long years since first finding the Olive Park victims. He knew three good men who, while they wouldn't say it out loud, and would never admit it, felt mauled by failure. When the lights went out at night and they stared at apparitions on the ceiling; when they worked Olive Park over and over in their heads and nothing came, nothing ever came; when they had a few minutes alone, like a song stuck in their heads, they would rework and rework some obscure piece of the evidence.

No matter how distinguished a career, no matter how lauded their accomplishments, the lives saved, the people helped, deep down, like the last bit of mud on their boots, they couldn't shake the feeling that they had failed. A permanent plague of 'should haves'.

He pulled the 8x10 to him.

You are trained to do your job exceedingly well and for years it appears that all your training has paid off for there is nothing that you cannot solve, nothing that cannot be fixed. A growing confidence says that you have seen it all and have always been able to bring things round right every time. But, there is a crevasse in the blackness whose depth and treachery are hidden in its depravity. Humanity's humanity is a fraud for the few young, unfortunate innocents who smile with clear eyes, who give us their trust because it is human to do so, who look to us as they should for protection. And who sometimes suffer with a magnitude unimaginable.

With both hands he cradled the picture. The tiny, curled hand of the child's arm sticking up out of the shallow grave reached out in quiet supplication

Without looking up he said "Give me the rest."

CHAPTER SIX

On the low-walled roof of the Rogers & Sons Cold Storage
building someone had constructed a rickety arbor out of old 2x4s
and pieces of delaminating plywood and discarded roofing
materials with a crosshatch lattice on top, just so they could have
a shady spot under which to eat lunch and contemplate why the
hell they were working at a furniture storage company. Probably,
thought Stan, the night guard would come up here and sit
watching the stars, probably doze. Don't-give-a-shit, let them
steal anything they want. Not my warehouse. I'm not getting
paid enough to put my life on the line for someone's dining
room table.

Stan bellied up against the wall and surveyed the view from
four stories above Sacramento. He loved California. He loved
how big it was. He loved the brown furze covered hills curving
down toward the ocean. He loved knowing some of the best
wines in the world were a short drive from where he stood. He
loved L.A. and San Francisco. He loved the excitement of being
among the most innovative and creative people he'd ever known.
Everything happened first in California and Stan Wyld liked
being first.

His old partner in Minneapolis had looked at him like a
demented deserter the day Stan told him he was joining the
department in Sacramento. Had treated him as if he had a fatal
case of idiocy.

You either liked this place or you hated it, they said.
Actually, thought Stan, you could do both because it has the best

and worst of everything. It was usually only the worst that got the press.

But what he loved the most about California was the weather. God, he loved the weather. Sunny, breezy, warm, hot, some rain, fog. Living in a fertile valley, in sight of a spit-dry desert, yet some days, even from eighty miles away, he could smell the Pacific Ocean.

He inhaled and watched the fog from the valley wisp up the hillsides to the east. You either understood California for what it was and accepted it or you stayed in the humid, mosquito summer and freezing, driving snow winter wasteland that was the Midwest. Great people in the Midwest, shit for weather.

It had given him pause one day sitting on the deck of one of the Sonoma wineries underneath a waving willow, half glass of a mellow Zin in front of him. He had realized he was in love with a place. Sadly or not, it was a tug stronger than anything he had ever felt for any one person. He had raised his glass to the shimmering valley below and the hazed green and browns on the far hillside. He knew he would never leave.

"A little help here, detective," said Mallory behind him.

He turned and saw she had three boxes one atop the other in her arms. He took the top two and set them on the table underneath the arbor.

"What were you doing?" she asked, catching her breath, "Not thinking of jumping I hope. Not yet anyway."

"I was enjoying the quiet," said Stan.

"Yeah, quiet's over." Mallory looked around the roof. "But, shit, you're right. It's a goddamn blessing to get away from all that hammering."

The grating monotony of the construction grunts screwing in the sheetrock screws as they worked on the storage enclosures for the Sacramento PD archives was driving them both nuts. Every few seconds. Zzzzzippp. Zzzziippp. Never the same cadence. Just when their ears adjusted to a certain rhythm, the screwing tempo changed up or stopped or two of the drills started.

Stan took the boxes from her and set them on the table. There were official signatures and log sheets taped all over them.

"Yeah, I guess quiet's over."

In all, Olive Park consisted of thirteen evidence boxes. Stan had watched yesterday as Mallory had sorted, by way of her ever-present bar code reader, all of the various size boxes, sorting them chronologically and sub sorting by investigational areas – forensics with separate breakdowns for ME's reports and autopsies, by victim, over three hundred site photos, three boxes of detectives' notebooks, two boxes of newspaper articles, clipped and cataloged by date and publication, videotapes of depositions, plus a few boxes of uncategorized hodge-podge; inquiries from other jurisdictions regarding similarities with unsolved cases on their files, folded logistical charts, maps displaying hundreds of red and blue markings and hundreds more tiny holes, evidence of pushpins having attempted to make some logical sense of a crime that followed no sane pattern.

The bags holding the paltry amount of trace evidence, evidence collected from on and around the three children's bodies found in Olive Park, only partially filled one box and that was still locked in the evidence cage at the main precinct. As soon as the new cage was built in the bowels of their cold storage building, the actual locked evidence for this and thousands of other case would be moved

Finally, three full boxes of tip line slips, stapled to follow-up forms, arranged by date from the first received, even before there was a tip line, to the last, about six months ago

Stan had read that last one. It was from a Madge Rugen. The tip line slip, which was nothing more than a yellow 'while you were out' type message and had a case number at the top, had come in almost six months to the day. Stan was amazed that anyone was still thinking about the case. Unless, of course, they were relatives of the victims. Well, Madge wasn't a relative, wasn't even in California, but did seem to have a psychic theory that Hell's Angels, roaming the Southwest, had managed to capture young kids, and somehow tie them to the back of their motorcycles and then kill them and bury them every time they went past the spot on route 50 outside of Sacramento. Madge even said their leader was a masked rider. If it weren't for the mask, she had said, she would've been able to tell them who it was.

So, Madge had given them her 'completely plausible' 'Hell's Angels theory'. Stan had ruffled his hand over the thousands of tip line slips and their attached follow-up forms, none more than a page, and wondered how many other theories were packed away. How many other whack jobs had called in to give their ideas who killed Joey, Karen and Phillip? Still, he knew that the reason the Sacramento Cold Case division had thirteen boxes of evidence and notes and even three full boxes of tip line tips and clues was because experience has shown that often among the crazy bullshit, buried alongside the 'my mother did it' and 'I might've done it in my sleep' theories, often there was the answer. Sometimes, among the way too common false confessions was a genuine one. Sometimes, the correct theory, the missing clue, the link that tied everything together was sitting there, lost in a rush to explore the more plausible. Like a diamond someone threw into a pile of cubic zirconium, right there. Maybe. Maybe not.

Mallory had lugged up the one box that contained the Murder Books with the case summaries and notes from the last two detectives who had suffered at the hands of the case, Carruthers and Thompson. With exaggerated effort she hefted this last box up on the table between them, and then went to retrieve their coffees.

Stan ran his hand across the box, opened it and pulled out the top file. Most investigated crimes had what SPD liked to call case compendiums. Homicide called theirs the Murder Book. It had the victim's pictures, bios, crime scene photos, and report summaries. A murder book contained the essence of the case. Olive Park had three Murder Books.

This was going to be the shits. He and Jake had worked only one other case with a young victim. It was a little girl, Jeannie was her name. Eight years old. Run down by her mother with the family station wagon. He hadn't known Jake drank scotch before that case.

This was three young children.

He used to box in college. He didn't know what it was that always made him step through the ropes and bang his gloves together and stare down his opponent, but he did. He always did. And now looking at the Olive Park boxes, he guessed he would again.

"Not bad," said Mallory. "Much improved over my last office. Fresh air and a killer view." She handed Stan his coffee and looked to the south.

Stan shaded his eyes and looked in the same direction. They could see the parapets of Folsom prison and somewhere in the hazy blue distance were the humble beginnings of Olive Park. Good place to get lost and bury your mistakes. Mistakes or trophies? He didn't know.

"Okay," Mallory said, rummaging in the box and starting to sort the folders, "What's first?"

"I want to get us on a different case, that what's first."

Mallory stopped. "I tried."

"You tried?"

"I told them downtown that with Steiner out of commission we were short-handed and that it might be better to start with some other case, simpler, a missing persons cases like you suggested, just until we get back to full strength."

"And?"

"It was the captain's assistant..." began Mallory.

"That shithead Samuels?"

"Yeah, well, he started to make out like we were incompetent and why the hell did they set up the cold case division for except to work on the most important cases, not some cases no one cared about. He made it sound as if we were baby whining."

"Missing person cases no one cares about..." repeated Stan. He could picture Samuels. That dick. "I'll call the captain then."

Mallory pulled her chair out and faced the sun. "Hope you have a better reason, then, because I think they believe we're just slackin'". She raised one eyelid. "You know, just taking it easy."

Stan thought for a moment and sighed. Just step through the ropes and bang your gloves together.

"Okay. Two weeks, then screw it, we're on to a case we actually have a chance at solving. We'll send a memo to Samuels..."

"I'll do it. I'm low man. I don't mind."

"Good," said Stan not wanting to deal with downtown any more than he had to. "Maybe tell them we're working on it in tandem with some easier cases...."

"Yeah, I got it. Meanwhile, where do we start?"

Stan sighed. He already had a familiar headache. "We run it from the beginning. All over again."

"Of course," started Mallory

Stan waved the agreement away. "Of course, I know you know we'll review everything, but I want you to do something else."

"What's that?" She leaned forward, elbows on the table.

Stan sipped his coffee and turned his face to the sun.

"Well, what?"

He shrugged. "I want you to play dumb."

"Okay," She stirred her coffee. "I am a blonde and it is a stretch, but I think I can do it."

Stan ignored her. He had a point to make. "Look, I have a history with this," he said, waving in the general direction of the box on the table.

"I know all the shit that Carruthers and Thompson and all the rest went through working on this before us. It damn near killed Thompson and I know Carruthers lost a marriage by misplacing priorities. He forgot there was life outside this case. He had two young sons and all he could think about was catching this guy. Found he could never leave this case at the office. Kept saying he had a hitch in his heart every time he imagined his youngest son standing in front of the guy who did it 'cause he knew what would happen. Couldn't sleep very well. Couldn't do other things for his marriage. Wife finally left. She knew in her heart what the problem was and she considered asking him to give it up, chuck it and get assigned to something, anything else. It was destroying all their lives, including the boys. But, she knew it was because of the boys that he was pursuing it.

"She finally told him she didn't have the temperament to care for him until he caught the bastard. Said she was sorry. He said he was sorry.

"Obviously he never caught him, was eventually re-assigned and then was pensioned out last year" Stan finished.

"I don't have any kids and I have no distractions," said Mallory giving Stan a small smile.

"I read your file. You also have no real experience."

"But..." She started to object.

Stan held up a hand. "But that's good. I think."

"Really?"

Stan was almost sorry she sounded encouraged. "Maybe, I don't know," Stan explained. "Look, except for a few profilers and a couple of loony-toon psychics, Carruthers and everybody else who worked on this were cops. Experienced cops. We're good at catching crooks, forgers, bank robbers because we can understand them. They need money, drugs. They're greedy. So, they commit those crimes. And we can catch them 'cause we know why they're doing it. Even rapists, sometimes we can get a handle on them 'cause we're human. But we, as a department, struggle catching a serial child killer. Because pickpockets and bank robbers and those who commit fraud don't graduate and go on to become child killers. That sickness, urge or whatever is born in their core and burned there. Something we don't have. We only know one thing about them as a group."

"What?"

He sat forward, moved his head out of the sun under the cover of the arbor. His hands rested on the folders.

"They don't give a shit about anyone else. They're sociopaths. You don't retrain them or reform them by slamming their asses in prison or running their asses through some rehab. They're born bad. They stay bad. You squash 'em on sight if you get the chance. Then you kill 'em."

Stan lifted the folder, started to open it and threw it down.

"I don't know why in hell we were assigned this damn case. We're supposed to revisit these cases when we can utilize the DNA that was found on site with new tests. But there is no useable DNA." He stopped. "There's nothing. Been nothing new in years."

"But we're going to work it, right?"

"Yeah, sure, we'll take our time and go through this the right way, from top to bottom, some effort that'll let you report to Samuels that we looked at it. No harm in re-upping the case and no harm in shitcanning it. Plenty of other cases that have a higher probability of being busted. Plenty more."

"Wouldn't you like to get this asshole, though?" The naïve eagerness was almost too much.

Stan sighed. "I don't want to die an old man working on one case. And the only reason we were probably given this case as our first is that it made the whole department, even the whole force look like thumb sucking idiots. Even the Highway Patrol got smeared with this one. It's a dead end."

Stan held up his hand as he could feel Mallory about to protest again.

"We'll take a look at it. Just give me some fresh eyes, okay?"

"I get it, I get it."

"Good," sighed Stan. "I mean don't go overboard about it. It's only until Jake gets back and we're only into this for a few weeks and you'll be doing whatever you do on the computer mostly, but..."

"Okay, okay, good," she hurried on. "Look, I've been working on this idea, you know, about missing kids. Not just these three kids but others too. I've worked up this sort of map..."

He stopped then and looked at her as if he was seeing her for the first time. "Wait, you've no investigational experience at all. That right?"

She hesitated. "Just computer, but I have this idea..."

"Shit, I didn't think so." He settled back in the chair, shut his eyes. "Christ."

She reached over and pinched his arm.

"Ow, what are you doing?"

"I used to do that to my boyfriend when he was being a jerk."

Stan rubbed his arm. "You had a boyfriend? One who actually liked you?"

"Look, I'm here to help you and Jake," Mallory offered. "We're supposed to be a team, you know. And just so you know, just for your record, I am a whiz at finding stuff online. I worked two years being the assistant, read that as slave, to Officer Ollestad. She was lead bitch on IT. You know her?"

"Sharon Ollestad. You worked for Sharon?"

"Two years. Hard labor."

Stan tried not to smile. Two headstrong blondes working in close quarters. Points for working with Ollestad. More points for chugging it out two years.

"Sounds absolutely wonderful, yet you transferred here." Stan couldn't keep the sarcasm out of his voice.

Mallory was quiet for a moment, then, "You know the guard who was killed at Wells Fargo last year? The two guys who got away with no money but their own asses?"

Stan raised his head. "Yeah."

"Well. I pretty much caught 'em."

"*You* pretty much caught 'em?" Stan sat up and stared at her. "Think again. They were cornered by sixteen of our guys out east of Folsom. Some warehouse. They were living there, or camped out. Even Jake was nearby and helped. I'm sure he would have mentioned you. You're sure you caught 'em, eh?"

"Yeah, actually, yeah. That warehouse... I was the one who found the address of the warehouse. I was the one who after 30 straight hours of knockin' the keyboard, running partial license plates, comparing them to like twenty thousand deadbeats, finally coming up with one of the slimeball's brother who had title to the piece of shit Cadillac they were driving and where it was located, and finally after 30 goddamn hours, handing the information to Officer Ollestad and having her take credit for it...so, yeah, you know, I'm pretty sure as shit I caught 'em."

She slammed back into her chair, shook her shoulders, pulled her shirt open further, popping a button and tilted her head back up into the sun.

"Fuckin' A," she muttered. "And I do have an idea, you know, about missing kids."

Stan continued, "Look with Jake out, you'll have to do some of this work. So like I was saying, since there are no DNA samples of the perp to use, we work the victims and we work the site evidence. Basically, we'll break it down into five areas; similarities of the victims in-situ..." Stan paused, then "...that means where they were found."

"I know what in-situ means."

"Good. Second, similarities of the victims while they were alive, then commonalities of where they lived, the shared commonalities of the evidence found with them and lastly, our hunches.

Mallory hooted. "What hunches?"

Stan purposely ignored the sarcasm. "We are looking at this case from present day with fresh eyes, remember?"

"And you think we'll come up with theories, hunches? Like, aren't we supposed to be following the evidence? Isn't that what you guys do?"

"If that's so, Carruthers and Thompson would be the heroes. If good police work was the key to solving this piece of shit case then it would have been done ten times over, given the manpower they threw at it. So, weed out the wacky ideas and concentrate on those that fit with the events, not just the evidence. Decipher the picture on the canvas, not figure out what paint was used."

Mallory looked at him. "How existential."

Stan sighed. "Look, just concentrate on the victim's similarities while they were alive. They all ended up side-by-side in the woods, but there had to be a connection to all three. Some common thread that brought them within range of the guy that did it. Your job is to find the connection in their lives and that's all. Use your computer skills, or whatever."

"Whoa, you said guy."

"What?"

"You said guy who did it. Sure it's a male?"

"Gotta be male, but, okay, everything's on the table, everything open. Male, female, one perp or two, or three."

"I read in *People* magazine about the wacko lady somewhere in the Midwest who kept knocking off guys who were trying to hit on her."

"*People* magazine?" Stan just stared. "*People?*"

"Yeah. *People*. So, it could be a woman. Not likely you know, but all the crazy people out there can't be men, right?"

Stan ignored her. "I'll work the trace evidence, what there is of it, the autopsies and commonalities in their deaths..."

"Did you ever see the picture of her?"

"Who?" asked Stan.

"The crazy Iowa lady. Bitchin' ugly."

Mallory got up and moved her chair about a foot so she could be in full sun.

"Buck teeth out to here." She brought her hand way out in front of her face then spread her blouse further apart, kicked her shoes off and leaned her head back.

"Somebody even had kids with her, would you believe that? That couldn't have been a pretty sight." She closed her eyes. "Okay, let's get started. I want to tell you what I've been thinking..."

Stan just stared. "*People?*"

She shaded her eyes as she looked right back at Stan. "Yeah, *People*. I've also read *Vogue, Tattler, GQ*, occasionally *Biker* magazine, *Penthouse* and some other rags you probably keep by your bedside so don't give me shit. I scan twelve different news outlets every morning, I can summarize most of the chapters in Hickman's text on Trace Evidence, I did my thesis on the Psychology of Witness Interrogation, I graduated summa cum fucking laude from UC Berkley," she said all in one breath. "So, yes, *People*."

After a moment she added, "Online version of course."

Stan shrugged. "Another well-rounded education."

Mallory settled back again, facing the sun. "Yeah, well, I'll bet my favorite sex toy against yours that one of our three kids had stashed away a few girlie magazines or even read *People*, so I guess I am the ideal candidate to bring fresh eyes to this case, 'cause it appears I just might know something about something."

"That's so? Then who's the Foo Fighters' lead guitarist?"

"God, I dunno."

"Thought so. Let's get to work."

Mallory rose up on her elbows. "Well? Who is it?"

"Let's get to work."

CHAPTER SEVEN

Stan already had the last few sheets of the Medical Examiner's summary, the 'green sheets' as the department called them, arranged on the rooftop table. He used small rocks he found on the roof as weights so the wind wouldn't carry everything off.

Next to the green sheets were the notes from Carruthers and Thompson. He picked up the top summary sheet and moved further under the lattice roof to cut the sun from toasting his neck.

"Alright, May 19, 1997," Stan read from the case summary, "A man was observed by a CHP veteran, an officer P. Duncan. The man was seen stopping his vehicle off to the side of SR 50 at a small pulloff, near the edge of town. So close you could see the city limits sign from where he stopped. By the time officer Duncan arrived at the pulloff, the man had left his vehicle and disappeared into the woods.

"Officer Duncan, concerned, followed him in, down a small path, all the time calling out. There was no response, but Duncan heard someone pushing through the underbrush and continued further where he surprised a man in a clearing. The man had his pants around his ankles. The man retreated from Officer Duncan, moving backwards and fell over a mound of earth.

"It was then, with the man draped over the mound, that Officer Duncan noticed what was later identified as our first victim's right skeletonized arm and hand protruding from the mound. First victim found was Joey Marshall, male, age ten.

"As the charging papers state, it was Officer Duncan's contention that the man had been or was preparing to masturbate over the graves when he was surprised. He was arrested, of course.

"When Officer Duncan returned to the clearing after placing a Mr. Willy Handleman in the squad, he found, next to Joey Marshall's grave, two more graves, which were later identified as Karen Summering and Phillip Boyd.

"When do we see the site?" she asked without turning her face from the sun.

Stan paused and looked over at Mallory. She continued to sun herself.

"There's nothing there anymore."

"It would be good to get a feel, know what I mean? Besides, I thought we were going to run this from the beginning."

"I've been there."

"Good," she said with a knowing smile, "then you can drive."

Stan picked up the summary and continued. "Exhumation and forensic working of the site spread over three days until it started to rain. Results of the trace evidence, the medical examiner's report on the bodies and all the work done on the victim's backgrounds are included in the case files. After a nine month investigation into Mr. Handleman, it was concluded..."

"...concluded that while he was a scumbag, he had nothing to do with the murders," finished Mallory. "I know."

"You know?"

Mallory sighed. "30ish part-time photographer found right where Joey and the others were found".

"*People* again, I assume." Stan had trouble keeping the sarcasm out of his voice.

"No, Berkley journalism class among other things. Spent part of a semester on this case studying the effects of releasing privileged information, you know the public's right to know, versus the cop's right to withhold certain evidence to use it to catch an asshole, blah, blah. So, yeah, I feel I know Handleman pretty well."

Stan continued. "Of course, on the other hand, Willy's version stated that he needed to take a dump at the side of the road. Says he had really bad guts from an egg salad sandwich he'd eaten in Reno and he couldn't wait. Had pulled over and was squatting on a log just on the edge of the brush when he sees State Patrol coming around one of these curves. So, Willy says, he moved further into bushes till he thinks he's out of sight, backing into the woods, waiting for the cop to go by.

"Instead, Willy sees Officer Duncan stop, get out. Says he freaked out and tried to move further into the woods, but he had his pants down around his ankles and he's trying to hop as silently as he can past the bushes into the woods. Duncan of course wants to find the driver and hears this guy hopping in the bushes, so he starts to investigate. Even calls out, identifies himself, 'State Police, I need to see the owner of this vehicle,' or some brilliance like that."

"Accordingly, Willy, he takes a big hop, falls over a mound of earth and twists his ankle, He's rolling around in supposed pain with his pants down when Duncan gets to him..."

Stan set the summary on the table. "So, State Patrol says they have a guy masturbating over a dead child's grave. There was no way that wasn't gonna hit the papers." Then added, "Duncan did say that Willy seemed as surprised as Duncan was, but he was arrested and we sat on him hard. So did the media. Carruthers dragged out every missing kid report he had from the whole state and grilled him on each one.

"Nothing."

"They never gave out his name did they, officially? You know, I remember that from class." asked Mallory.

"Not officially. They didn't release anything, really. Didn't need to though. Guy's full name was William"Willy" Handleman. No, the papers bought the information from someone in the department. At the time he was just a proverbial person of interest. Nothing about doing his business over a grave. That came out later, unfortunately for Willy."

"Unfortunate name, Willy," mused Mallory.

Stan said, "The whole force had been burned by saying too much to the press on the Kerker and Fitzgerald murders a few years before, so they weren't about to say anything. I mean nothing. Just clammed up. 'Course, back then confidential information just blew out through the screen door of departmental secrecy. I don't know why they just didn't invite the reporters to the daily progress meetings. Hell, rumor was anybody with enough dough or any reporter peddling favors who really wanted to find out the skinny on what we were investigating or who was under suspicion, could find an eager stooge ready to spill it."

"So, the department was sure as shit they had their guy in Handleman?" asked Mallory catching up.

"Rousted him but good." Stan remembered those days. He also remembered Carruthers and Thompson back then - so sure and confident.

"Remember, he wasn't just a photographer. He was a kiddie photographer. Took portraits of kids at one of the malls part-time. Also had his own studio where he took snappers of kids. Specialized in kids. So, you've got kids, suspected pervert, photographer...his life was done. Wife left, took their two kids.

"First, they tore his darkroom apart, printed every negative he had on file. Spent weeks trying to match the kids' pictures with not only the reconstruction of the dead kids, but any missing kids as well. Regrettably, as a sad coincidence for Willy, he had done a portrait of a kid who eventually turned up missing.

"His computer was seized, his house was tossed for the third time, walls were busted, cellar dug up, backyard a mess. I think they even brought in a backhoe 'cause they saw someone had been digging in the backyard. Turns out, of course, it was a new sewer line and the city had to replace it after they tore it up and found nothing.

"He was without his car for about three months while forensics examined each and every piece of dust and hair in there. No kids' hairs were found.

"Anyway, they verified his alibi and he was cleared. They didn't make a big deal about it, they just let it die. Not like the first headlines which had actually generated death threats."

"Still everyone, everywhere thought him guilty, right?" asked Mallory as she fingered the cup sleeve, tearing little pieces of cardboard off it and dropping them on the roof.

Stan nodded. "Yeah, they just thought the cops were stupid, that we couldn't get enough on him to put him away, but that didn't mean he didn't do it. Why else, the editorials said, would the police have gone to all that trouble?

Stan reflected, "Funny. He should have been the most innocent man in Sacramento given all the manpower, time and dough spent trying to get evidence against him, but in reality, his life was over. His business was done. There was nobody in Sacramento, even all of California who would let him near their kid.

"The realtors had such trouble trying to sell his house; they finally gave in and advertised it as the 'torture house'. A young couple bought it and promptly ripped out all the rest of the walls looking for personal items or bodies, anything. Nothing was ever found of course.

"But Willy Handleman was critical to the Olive Park murder case for one simple reason."

Mallory turned to Stan. "Then, you *do* think he was guilty?"

"No. Not at all. His arrest was a pressure relief valve on the whole mess. But, no, he wasn't guilty of anything worth mentioning except taking a leak by the side of the road. No, his importance lay in the unfortunate fact that he took the focus off whoever did it. Any possible trail was lost in the cockup surrounding Willy. Carruthers was never able to really get it back on track. Everybody still believed Willy had done it."

Mallory shrugged. "Just goes to show, don't pee, shit or masturbate by the side of the road."

"Now you see why this case is going nowhere."

Mallory sat forward. "Jesus, are you always so negative?"

Stan shook the tightness from his neck and shoulders, stretched out and up with his arms above his head. "Do you always confuse negativity with reality?"

Mallory settled back. "Apparently so."

Stan thought for a moment. "And, for all his troubles and subsequent quiet vindication, you would've thought that time and fading memories would have let him have some of his life back. Not to be. In a final twist of bad luck, Willy, who had begun taking photographs again, this time of landscapes mostly, no people, and certainly no kids, and under an assumed name, was out taking pictures one day up along the coast highway, when he was struck by a car and thrown over the embankment practically into the sea. The driver claimed that Willy was standing in the middle of the road, probably backing up to get a better view someone said, when the driver came round a curve and hit him square.

"Camera was found smashed in the road. His body was recovered and he was buried in a quiet ceremony somewhere in upstate California. Near Mendocino I think. Anyway, the irony is that the driver who struck him was the father of a missing child."

"Really?" said Mallory in a quiet voice. "That's unbelievable."

"You'd think so, but no connection was ever made, at least publicly, and especially not by us." Stan paused. "Some of the guys working on this case always believed they had had their man in Handleman, just not enough evidence. No charges were filed against the driver."

After a few moments Mallory cleared her throat, "By the way, Handleman's name was Willy but it was short for Wilhelm, not William. Maybe you should read the whole case file."

"And I guess you did?"

Mallory sighed. "All thirteen boxes."

CHAPTER EIGHT

Stan knew why the Rogers & Sons Cold Storage building was chosen to house the Sacramento Police archives as well as OID. It was rock solid, 3 foot thick walls of concrete and God knew what else. Even the floors were thick concrete. The place was a fortress and it suited Stan.

During the day the sun streamed in the upper level windows and massive skylight. It was almost too much light. It lit up the floor like a movie set.

In the grip of a late night, when the hard, blue-white moonlight cut through, it sent the area outside the blast of moonlight into deep shadow. When you stood in the middle of four glassed walls your reflection was everywhere. Even to Stan it appeared as if his reflection moved before he did.

And there was no sound.

When working alone, late at night, the loudest thing had been the beating of his heart. Eerily quiet, yet strangely echoey. Any little noise inside would travel and bounce and dart from empty room to empty room on the floors above.

'Fleeters', what he called those amorphous shadows that you catch out of the corner of your eye, seemed to have the run of the place at night.

He speculated that it must've been a challenge to keep night security guards. They would've been easily spooked. Like working in a tomb. Or a cathedral. When standing in the atrium the ceiling was a breath-taking four floors up. At night, Stan found himself whispering without meaning to.

Reflections. Fleeters. It was the exaggerated atmosphere that made you involuntarily hold your breath, waiting for an unseen companion to emerge from the shadows.

Stan didn't mind, but he'd watched Mallory work at night. She didn't realize it, but she was always looking up or over her shoulder. As if she had just heard the suggestion of a distant voice. Once in a while, she would look up and say, 'Did you hear something?' Then go back to whatever file she was working on.

But the office was comfortable. Cool in the morning, as it was this morning, but by ten it was up about seventy degrees and never a draft.

"Wassup?" Mallory breezed through the door, two coffees in hand. Without pause she placed his double tall breve in front of him. "You know that has half and half in it don't you," she said, "Enough calories in there to make even your toes swell up."

She turned and as she moved through the shafts of sunlight streaming in from the clerestory her golden reflection was dazzling.

"So. What d'ya think?" Mallory held out her arms, admiring her work.

She had the glass walls of their atrium office covered with pictures, one wall for each victim. The last wall, the one with the doorway, was reserved for miscellaneous items, theories, questions, errata as Mallory liked to call it. Each day she would put up another question or add to her own section about other missing kids.

"This is what you asked me to do, you know," she had said yesterday as she put up question number seven. "I lie awake at night or I go to the bar and then I go home and lie awake some more and these things just come to me, you know."

Stan surveyed the list again. They were scrawled in Mallory's slanty, somewhat hurried writing, as if she could barely wait to get in the door before getting the questions up on the glass. He half expected little hearts above the 'i's.

The questions were all cogent and incisive but at this rate, they would run out of glass before any answers came.

1) What does the victim's age range (9-11) mean????

2) Trace evidence – the plastic bracelet, where from???
3) Locations when disappeared – common element???
4) Found in the fall – all taken in summer, why???
5) Why those three at that time—???
6) Two different sexes?? Doesn't care??
The seventh one Mallory had put up a few minutes ago.
7) All buried same way – alive, after being stunned
Stan sat down at the conference table and put his feet up

Mallory slid onto a chair next to him. She, too, put her feet up on the edge of the table and stared in the same direction. She wore a sort of low waterproof hiking shoe and continually clunked the toes together as she sipped her coffee. Now that neither of them had to report to any kind of authority and in fact would go days between seeing anyone from precinct headquarters, except the people working on constructing the vaults, their mode of professional dress has been drifting toward casual. Stan had abandoned the coat and tie, though they stood at the ready in the closet. Mallory was now in tight jeans and an even tighter blouse. Tight enough to indicate when the room was chilly.

Stan tried to concentrate on the board on the wall. He thought about the last item.

There had been rampant speculation from Forensics, from Carruthers and Thompson, from anyone with an opinion on how exactly the bodies had been placed or dragged or tossed into the graves. And what condition they'd been in. And what happened after they were buried.

Stan sighed. The worst aspect of this was having to let your mind dwell on what might have happened, made worse by realizing that what actually happened was assuredly far worse than he could imagine. How do you climb into the twisted caverns of the mind of the sick fuck who did this?

You don't. You work the evidence. From a strictly clinical standpoint, it was Forensics' theory, based on the actual examination of the bodies that gave them a working scenario that emerged as the one most likely. Stunned by a blow to the back of the head, the bodies were placed or dragged into the grave ending up either by sadistic design or happenstance to have enough of an air pocket that when the dirt covered them, they were able to still breathe. For a short period.

It was then surmised that upon reviving and panicking, they scrabbled, freeing their arm or arms first. That was when the torture really began, stated Forensics in their report. As an arm emerged, feeling air and trying to grab for anything, it was burned. Forensics guessed the flames or heat came from something like a blowtorch. Death was not immediate.

That was all Stan could think about. He took each child's terror and pain and panic and locked it away somewhere in his head so he didn't have to re-imagine it. It was always there and just knowing that was enough for him. Those times when terrified faces in the blackness called out to him he'd take a deep breath and gently push those thoughts away and concentrate on something, anything else.

He never discussed how he felt or how he thought about the victims with Jake. It was how he dealt with it and that was all. Jake, he knew, had his own way of dealing with the bad shit.

Not speaking of it was a mute bond between them.

But if there was uncertainty about exactly how the victims came to be in the graves, there was no speculation on how they ended up – on their side, covered lightly in dirt with one or both arms extending up out of the dirt. Any limb that made it out was burned down to the bone.

Carruthers had written a scenario where the bodies were carried in and dumped from the side. As the bodies went into the hole, they rolled onto their faces. Face down.

Face down. Yet, two had managed to scrabble through the dirt where their hands at least had felt air.

"So, what? What's doing?" questioned Mallory. She picked up a pencil and started tapping the pad before her. It was still covered with notes and words and circles from yesterday. She shook her head and large dangly earrings jangled against her head.

"I was thinking that Carruthers was wrong when he said the bodies were carried in, set next to the hole and rolled in."

Stan walked to the other end of the conference table and looked at the group of site pictures laid out in a pattern, from wide shots to close ups.

"Okay. What if the bodies were dragged into the woods instead of carried, flopped beside the graves and then rolled in or placed in the graves?"

Mallory shook her head. "Except for Joey's, weren't the bodies too far gone to see drag marks? I mean, really there was no flesh, except Joey. Besides what would it matter, carried, dragged?"

"True, there were no drag marks on the backs or fronts or anywhere on their heads on whatever flesh was left, which wasn't much of anything, but there was evidence of bruises on the back of Joey's legs...unidentified trauma said the ME's report. And if the bodies were all pretty much handled the same way, then we have to assume what evidence on Joey about how he was brought into the woods would apply to the other two. If there were bruises on Joey, most likely bruises were on the others.

"And if we're talking drag marks, shit there were enough people through the scene those three days, not to mention Officer Duncan and his struggling with Handleman destroying what evidence there was. Forensics wouldn't have noticed if a Sherman tank had been dragged through from the road, let alone a body."

Stan was warming to his theory. "Dragged. I think they were dragged."

Mallory had found the green sheets which were the ME's reports and was skimming through them. "So what, though?"

Stan turned to her. "Two things. First, if they were dragged, it probably guarantees that there was only one perp and second, whoever did this was either unwilling or unable to carry the bodies. He *had* to drag them."

Mallory surveyed the pictures on the wall. "You're right," she said in a quiet voice. "He wouldn't."

"What?"

"Wouldn't have carried them. It would be too helpful. Too personal. Too intimate."

Stan stuck one of Joey Marshall's pictures under one arm while he tried to get the sticky, gummy stuff Mallory had found to adhere to the glass. "So, that means one guy."

Carruthers and Thompson had detailed twenty pages of notes from different sources on child killers. The odds of two were highly unlikely. Serial killers, child killers didn't usually hunt in packs. They were singular, alone, lonely usually. Not really wishing to share their compulsions, their obsessions, with anyone. They would be embarrassed to do so, jealously guarding their sick thrill. Stan had read it all. Mallory probably had it memorized.

"Yeah, one guy. I mean, I could run an online scan of past cases, where two bad guys were involved in child abductions or serial killings, but my guess is pretty much zilch."

"Less than zilch."

"So we agree on one. Good. Progress. And you said this was a dead end."

Stan got Joey's picture mounted. It was the one that showed a close up of his face in death, after exhumation and after it had been cleaned, but before the autopsy. He picked up the next, the one showing the back of the head.

He turned away. "Let's shift gears a moment. Check in Carruthers's notes and the ME's report about the wounds to the back of the head."

"I just had that...somewhere..." Her blond hair shimmered as she bent over the file folders, smartly flipping each one aside as she read its tab. Stan watched her and once again wondered what she was doing here. She had the energy of a jumpy cat with few pauses between quick, intense movements. She had so much push she was making him tired.

Stan carefully placed some stickum on the two top edges of the picture and one on the bottom and pressed it against the glass. It held, but Stan didn't know for how long.

"Got it...got it. The last victim, Joey Marshall," she stopped and again waved the green sheet. "This is from ME's report,

Okay. Let's see, ME says Joey was hit hard enough that the one blow knocked him unconscious…"

Stan cut her off. "Where on the back of the head? Hard to see exactly in this."

Mallory studied the head chart included in the report

"Inferior part of the occipital bone, right side."

She pulled the notes from the two detectives in front of her. "Here's what Thompson wrote, '1) golf type shot, 2) or kid was leaning over, 3) or kid was above so blow came from below, 4)or ?'"

Stan tried to imagine a golf shot arcing upward. It would be awkward and much weaker than one from above, unless it was a last resort shot that got lucky.

"Ixnay on the golf shot," murmured Mallory.

"I agree. Low percentage. Besides, the ME indicates the blow did more damage than a glancing shot would have inflicted."

"So, to get on the lower part of his head the kid…Joey, was above the killer or leaning over? Why would he be above the killer?"

Stan was silent as he pressed the picture to the glass, hoping that constant pressure would convince the stickum to work. Scenarios played out before him of little Joey above his killer.

"What are you doing" asked Mallory.

"Holding this damn thing on and thinking."

"Well, share will ya," she sighed, "I need some input."

"Okay. Holding him up would mean two people…"

"And we agreed one," said Mallory, then went back to the ME's report. "There was fabric in the wound."

"I remember reading that, what was it?" He stepped away from the glass and watched the picture to see if it would stay where he had plastered it. It did, but the first Joey picture lost its two top wads of sticky and folded forward.

"Shit."

"It was synthetic. Black nylon with a few cotton threads."

Stan returned to the far side of the conference table and found the first missing person report. He flipped to the section where the mother was describing Joey's clothes the last time she had seen him. Running out the door and down off the porch just after 8:30AM on Friday September 13th.

"San Francisco Giants jacket. He'd gotten it when his father took him to a Giants game a few months before. Nylon material. Letters on the back where ironed on or stitched in, orange cotton."

Mallory shook her head. "Jacket must've been pulled over his head."

Stan studied Joey's picture. "Was he bending over? How do you get a kid to bend over?" he asked.

The question hung in the air.

"Trick him. Bribe him. Lure him. Force him."

Both were silent, trying to imagine, trying to breathe life into a relationship about which they could only guess. Stan sat down and tilted back, planting his shoes on the edge of the table and shut his eyes. He wanted just one more picture, just one more piece. They had so much and yet so little. How to divine what might have happened between a sick son of a bitch and an innocent child?

Concentrate on the actions of the child. Kids were unpredictable for the most part. Especially at ten years old.

"Okay, okay," Mallory said with a sigh, "maybe the kid was surprised, let's start there."

"I don't know," Stan continued, "In some ways, kids don't trick easily. It's difficult as hell to make them do something they don't want to do."

"Like bend over in front of a whack job they don't know?"

"Yeah. Still it's also easy to fool them. To trade on their 'lack of life experience' as one of the profilers put it."

Stan spread his hands apart. "It's like if I say to a child, 'Come here help me with my kitten's broken paw', or some such. The kid is going to know right away that it's a trick and an adult wouldn't need help with a kitten and so the child won't come near. But, if I say, 'Hey kid, we've got a furniture delivery for the Herbert family in a big truck in a few minutes and I gotta find a place next to the woods where I can have the truck turn around, you know, sort of an opening in the woods we can back the trailer into. You know of a place like that?'

"The kid'll say, 'sure'.

"You do?" I'd say. "Take me there so I can show the guys. And so on."

Mallory stared. "That was kinda creepy," she said, her voice soft.

"Look, every kid wants to be grown up. When he's treated like an adult, an equal, he thinks that a person who values him would never hurt him. He trusts." Stan pulled out the school picture from the file that showed Joey Marshall, a young happy student. Soft brown eyes, slight smirk, as if he had been watching the kids in his class waiting to have their picture taken, making faces behind the photographer

"Okay, so this Joey Marshall wasn't lured or tricked, he was more like groomed. Thompson said when he talked to the parents they assured him that they had taught him well to avoid strangers and shit."

"They always say that," murmured Mallory. "Aren't parents the last to know things? Look, kid wasn't tricked. And if he wasn't tricked he was in the presence of this slime on his own accord. He was there voluntarily 'cause he was really fooled, groomed as you said. And if he was there voluntarily he was on a mission, he wanted to be there, he had to be there, right? How fast can you groom a kid so he trusts you?"

"If you're good..." Stan shrugged. He continued to stare at the two Joey pictures, one still upright, one about to completely dive to the ground as the stickum loosened.

Stan flipped back to the toxicologist's report. "Maybe he had a drug that was missed in his system. Maybe toxicology..." But he knew as he said it, it wasn't true. Their own in-house lab as well as the two private labs that confirmed the findings, said there was nothing unusual, debilitating, illegal, toxic, near toxic in any of the victim' systems as far as they could tell, given the state of decomposition. The deterioration was extensive.

"You mean, make him pliable?"

Adhering the pictures to the glass wasn't working. The second Joey picture on the glass also lost its top two stickums but this time didn't fold over, but swung like a slow pendulum from the bottom hook. It swung slowly, back and forth.

Stan watched it, and then to Mallory, "What did you say?"

"I said," repeated Mallory patiently, slowly, "so is Joey in this position?" Mallory started to lean over.

"No, No, I mean about the fabric." Stan continued to stare at the picture and hairs rose on the back of his neck. "The fabric in the wound. Read it to me."

He jumped out of his chair and made his way to the swinging picture.

Mallory put aside the summary sheets and paged through the thick ME's report detailing the exact wording. "Okay. Here."

"...synthetic orange nylon fabric forced into the wound about 3cm..."

"No, no, not the autopsy stuff," Stan said over his shoulder, waving his hands in hurry-up, "the fiber notes from micro analysis."

Mallory tossed the ME's report aside along with the rest of Thompson's notes and dug through the rest on the table until she found the red bordered sheets from the Medical Examiner's micro analysis division.

"All right...the section under foreign items found in the wound. It was orange synthetic woven fibers, the type is called Nylon 6-6, there were approximately 42 fibers, approximately a half centimeter by three quarters, imbedded in the wound intertwined with approximately 13 orange cotton fibers that were adhered to the synthetic material." Mallory looked up. "We know. It's from the jacket, the Giant's jacket."

"I know, I know," said Stan. "But if the white cotton fabric was from the letters that were ironed on the *outside* of the jacket..."

His raised his hand and gently kept the photo of Joey moving. Swinging back and forth.

Mallory looked up and now saw it with a cold certainty, "and the jacket was against his head when he was struck."

The outside of the jacket was against his head.
"Sweet Jesus. He was hanging upside down."

CHAPTER NINE

M hated the thought of being babysat.

He and Jessie were not stupid, they could dress themselves, knew how to call 911, knew not to talk to anybody they didn't know well, and knew their way around a microwave. And then there was the expense. M knew they were a huge money drag and this would only add to 'the troubles'. Just what in god's name was she thinking?

M glanced over his shoulder at Aunt Janey. She had his sister Jessie's hand firmly in hers as they all trekked to the rear of the trailer park. It was not a long walk over the cracked asphalt of the common drive that connected all the trailers. Sunshine Vista was a smallish park, about 52 trailers or 'mobile homes' as his aunt liked them to be called. M never understood why people cared anyway. These trailers, most weren't ever gonna move and neither were the residents. And besides, they looked like dog shit shacks and as far as he was concerned, didn't feel like any kind of home to him.

And Sunshine Vista. What was up with that? The fog they were wading through had a soupy, metallic wetness and was thick enough to block the sun for years.

Sunshine my ass.

"Aunt Janey, do we *really*...," started M.

"Don't even."

M looked back at their trailer. His aunt had left her Honda idling with the heater on full blast, warming up. With the fog he could hear it but he couldn't see it. He knew it was still there. Unfortunately, no one had taken it.

"Aunt Janey, do witches really eat you?" asked Jessie.

M stopped and waited as his aunt reached down and rebuttoned the girl's coat.

"Aunt Janey," started Jessie again, "do witches really…"

"I heard you."

"Well, do they?'

"She thinks that the gypsy, I mean, Mrs. Ev-er-heart is a witch and is going to eat her," said M.

The Honda's idle had dropped a level. It was warm and ready to go.

"Look Jessie, you know there's no such things as witches, that's just stories that other people make up to scare little children." M saw his aunt look directly at him.

He shook his head wide, side-to-side in perfected thirteen year old innocence.

"Second, Mrs. Everheart is a kind old lady who is not a witch or a gypsy, she's just old. And cheap. Okay?"

Jessie wavered.

M felt a slight budge of sympathy for his aunt. It was obvious she was not used to dealing with a six year old.

"Look, when people have had a lot of trouble in their lives it makes them look older, all right, you see don't you?"

Jessie just stared and put a finger in her mouth.

M looked up the street to where he guessed Ruby Everheart lived. He could just make out a trailer, next to the outline of a large, older RV. Both dark undistinguished blocks against the grey fogginess.

"Just because people look different or live differently than we do doesn't mean they're bad people."

Jessie had stopped. "What's a jispy?"

M turned to his aunt and shrugged. "Just a wild guess on my part, Aunt Jane."

Janey seized Jessie's hand "C'mon."

Jessie stumbled trying to make her way in a pair of M's shoes which were three sizes too big and made her feet waggle side to side.

"And where are your shoes young lady?" Aunt Janey tried to sound nice, M thought, but he could tell she was pissed.

"They were left," said M looking at his aunt, "with most of our other stuff."

He noted she had nothing to say to that! But neither did she slacken the pace of their resumed march toward the back of Ruby Everheart's trailers.

"Whoa! What is all that?" M stopped and pointed up to his left. His aunt and Jessie bumped into his back.

"Now, what?" asked Aunt Janey. Her irritation sharpened each word.

"That!" He pointed with emphasis to the pile of stuff that filtered through the fog. It looked to M as if at least fifty carnival wagons had collided together and now sat abandoned behind a tall chain link fence. It was the last thing he expected to see.

Aunt Janey turned to look. Jessie clopped around to look also.

"Wow," said Jessie under her breath.

Even Aunt Janey seemed surprised for a second. His aunt prodded him in his back. "Let's go. It's just carnival stuff. It's closed. It's storage."

"There must be the Ferris Wheel somewhere and animals, huh?" said M trying not to sound impressed.

"Can we go to a circus?" asked Jessie.

"No!" said Aunt Janey sharply. "They're closed now. It's just junk. They don't even operate anymore, okay. And no, you can't go over there. And there are no animals and there is no Ferris Wheel. It's just run down carnival stuff. It's dangerous, probably"

M turned to his aunt. "Dangerous? It's just a circus."

His aunt and Jessie headed off without him. "It's not open and I don't want you in there. Neither of you."

M took one more look. "Cool."

"M! Now!"

M caught up to them. He could see the Everheart trailer and the closer they got it sure looked to M like whoever lived there had had some trouble. The unpainted trailer actually made his Aunt Janey's trailer look rich and respectable, if that was possible.

The RV type camper next to it was long ago weathered out, white with a badly faded greenish design. It was oriented to the highway and M could make out the small neon sign mounted atop a pole that rose out of the fog next to it. 'Fortunes by Ruby'.

Someone with no obvious carpenter skills had patched together a wooden walkway, more like a gangplank, that connected the back of the trailer with the little wooden platform that sat next to one of the RV's doors. Blackberry vines covered the foundation of the trailer and had spread, even attempting to entangle the wheels of the RV. The only path to the trailer led to shaky wooden steps.

"Is that the jispy?" Jessie slowed her pace and her eyes flicked to the smaller trailer.

M saw the head of Ruby Everheart hovering in the dim glass of the kitchen window.

"Gypsy isn't a nice thing to call someone, like when someone calls you a name that hurts. It would hurt Mrs. Everheart if you called her that, okay?" Then, more to herself, "And she'd get pissed and throw you two out."

"But M said…"

Aunt Janey had to whisper now that they were almost at the back door. "Do *not* listen to your brother or any other people around here." She turned to M. "And you, tuck your shirt in." She sighed and tried an indulgent smile. "Look you two, just a couple of weeks, until I can figure…."

The door swung open. The imposing figure of Mrs. Ruby Everheart stood back from the doorway and looked down at them. She wore a frayed house dress that looked as if it had once had a better life as a slipcover. The faded lime green flower pattern contrasted with the red and white checked apron smeared with a mottled brown doughy mix.

And, damn she was big, thought M. She reminded him of a bloated, white Aunt Jemima. His father used to call almost all women Aunt Jemimas. M finally looked it up in some old dictionary or reference book, he couldn't remember exactly where and the whole definition escaped him, but he remembered the best part, 'fat, black and happy.' Aunt Janey had said that Mrs. Ruby Everhart had been part of a carnival at one time, now just told fortunes to people who were gullible enough to suck up that crap. Well, no kidding big. She had probably been the strong man's wife or maybe the bearded lady or maybe she pulled the wagons when the elephants were too pooped. 'Course looking at the dough smeared on either side of her apron, it could just be she was fat.

"Makin' gingerbread.   Kids like gingerbread, don't ya?" When Ruby Everheart spoke, her jaw made extra movements up and down, as if trying to get started. It seemed to M the actual sound was delayed a few seconds behind the jaw action. He guessed it was because of the missing teeth.

Both kids could only watch her mouth as she spoke.

"Not sure they've ever had gingerbread actually," said Aunt Janey.

Ruby Everheart looked straight at Aunt Janey.

"See, they haven't been here very long and I don't bake much."

Ruby Everheart nodded. "Don't neither. Thought it was a good idea though, their first day here and all." She stepped aside, "Well come on in and make yourself to home."

The three of them crowded into the trailer, no one wanting to venture very far from the door. Besides, M noted, Ruby seemed to take up most of the doorway so they had to maneuver around her.

"Smells great," said Aunt Janey. M noticed his aunt's fakey voice.

Jessie hung on her aunt. She seemed fascinated watching Ruby's puckered mouth work.

"Well, here they are…" said Aunt Janey. Jessie dropped her head, her blond hair hanging down to her waist.

"…this is Jessie. She's six and a bit shy."

"Guess so," said Ruby trying to glimpse under the child's long hair. "Hi, sweetie."

M felt himself being pulled to his aunt's side. "And this is M. His real name is…"

"M!" butted in M.

"Well, we just call him M," said Aunt Janey as she glanced at her watch.

"Pleased to meetcha Mr. M," said Ruby, putting her clenched fists on her hips and not attempting to shake his hand.

"Nice place," said M.   At thirteen years old, he was determined to take the upper hand and made a point of surveying the room as if he was going to buy it. But the place was a dump. Every wall was covered with circus and carnival handbills and the divider between the kitchen area and the rest of the trailer was filled with old photographs, some in dusty black wood frames others just paper clipped to each other and taped to some part of another picture. Faded color ones were mixed in with older black and white ones. All of them, M could see, seemed to be people at a carnival. Some were laughing, but most were just staring back at the camera, ready to move on.

"So, were you like a fat lady at *that* circus?" asked M indicating the conglomeration of colorful carnival mish mash next door.

Everyone stopped talking. It took Ruby a second to realize what M meant.

She let out a laughing bark. "Oh, sure, yeah, the fat lady, and a lot of other things." She patted her stomach. "But a long time ago."

Aunt Janey started backing out the door, stopped and fished a few sticky notes out of her purse.

"Here's my numbers." She swept her eyes around the room looking for a place to post the notes. The refrigerator, the obvious candidate, was covered and recovered with some old Black Sabbath posters and STP stickers and what appeared to be brown poster paint. The phone was nowhere to be seen so she just handed the notes to Ruby.

"Sure we won't need 'em, but good to have, I guess." Ruby, too, seemed at a loss as to where to post them. "I'll just..." she said but didn't move.

"M, take care of your sister," said Aunt Janey, detaching Jessie from her leg.

"She'll be fine," pronounced Ruby. "Kids warm t'me. Always have. You run along."

Aunt Janey accepted the promise, straightened her suit and left.

Ruby caught the storm door with a practiced arm before it slammed shut.

M saw his aunt turn once to look back, but she didn't smile.

"Umm, mam, Mrs. Everheart, the gingerbread's done," said M with some urgency.

Black smoke curled up past the dirty pots on the stovetop and collected against the low ceiling of the trailer. Looking up, M noticed the smoky pattern on the silent smoke detector and figured this wasn't the first time some culinary delight had gone wrong in the oven.

Ruby pulled the oven open and in one motion made room on the stove and expertly set the hot pan on one of the burners.

M moved closer, pulling Jessie along with him. Instead of the smoking mass M expected, the pan held the most beautiful gingerbread he'd ever seen, golden brown with a firm top sloping down slightly at the sides. No visible fire scars.

And the smell. Even Jessie poked her head around to see what filled the trailer with mouthwatering aroma.

"You like whip cream, you kids?" asked Ruby. "I think I got some here."

The wallpapered refrigerator door opened. The light had long since burned out so it was only dimly possible to make out the contents. Ruby squatted down and stared in. With a grunt, she reached deep inside, grasped the aerosol cream container and pulled it out. M saw the inside of the fridge was filled with pans and pots, some with loose foil covering, some with unrecognizable contents just drying out on their own.

"We love whipped cream," said M.

Jessie stuck her head around her brother's leg and shook her head 'No'.

"We do," said M again, looking at his sister.

"All kids like whip cream," said Ruby as she turned to the gingerbread and worked on the nozzle. "I always did."

"No," said Jessie louder. "Kids don't."

M watched the struggle with the fake whipped cream can and finally said, "I think you're just supposed to push the nozzle to the side."

Ruby banged the whipped cream on the counter. "Must be stuck."

"You push the nozzle to the side," said M, louder than he intended. She could at least try what he was suggesting. That would be polite.

"I don't like it!" yelled Jessie.

At the same moment, M touched Ruby on the elbow and said, "Push it."

"What?" asked Ruby, leaning into M. Her jaw worked side to side instead of up and down. "What?" whispered Ruby, conscious again of whom she was addressing.

M said nothing.

"Can't hear so good," she continued. She smiled a toothless smile and cocked her head to her bad ear so they would understand, then turned back to the warm pan. "So speak up when you talk."

M reached over and gently took the whipped cream from Ruby. "Like this," he said in a loud voice. He pushed the nozzle to the side and whipped cream spurted in a diagonal streak across the gingerbread.

Ruby Everheart let out a hearty laugh. "Goddddammm, that's right!" She took back the can and decorated the top of the gingerbread in concentric swirls. It melted slightly as it sputtered and ran to the sides of the pan.

"I gotta be looking at you to know what you're sayin' pretty much," said Ruby, admiring her work. "Used to be able to hear the elephant fart two tents away...know what I mean?"

M said nothing. She wasn't looking at him and if he had to shout all day he was going to be hoarse by the end of it.

M and Jessie watched the drizzled whipped cream melt and spread on the warm gingerbread. Aunt Janey's breakfast of cold cereal was a soggy memory.

"You two sit here," said Ruby.

The table was covered with the morning paper open to the comic pages and M saw that a few of the astrology predictions for that day were circled in red ink. Ruby started to clear the paper, saw the circles and stopped. With the same knife that was used for the gingerbread, she sliced out the astrology section and stuffed it in her apron. The rest of the paper was left as a makeshift tablecloth.

M made sure Jessie was settled then slid into the other plastic seat. The cut and curled yellow plastic chafed the back of his leg. Well, the old bag couldn't be too bad if she made something that smelled this good, thought M. He could see Jessie was happy that the piece Mrs. Everheart was serving her was almost entirely devoid of whipped cream as it had melted and slid off the side.

"You kids eat up now, eh?" Ruby said. "I gotta work."

"We will," said M. Jessie just nodded.

"You kids…," Ruby stopped. Her gaze lingered on Jessie.

It seemed to M as if she working up to spit out some unpleasantness.

"You know. I can't be your entertainer, I told your aunt. I work at home here in the RV there. I have people in and we talk." Ruby's jaw continued to work after she stopped talking.

Jessie ignored the old woman and scraped all the whipped cream remnants from the top of her gingerbread.

"I know," said M, "you tell people what's going to happen to them."

"Well, I do sometimes."

M thought she was going to say more about what she did, but instead, told them about the doors.

"Doors lock by themselves when they close. Don't appreciate anyone snoopin' in my place you know. You kids come down to the RV when you're done. Don't bother cleanin' up or anything."

No kidding, thought M. There was no room in the sink anyway.

Ruby grabbed a large set of keys and left the trailer. Her slippers made soft slaps as she padded along the plywood walkway. M heard the keys unlock the door to the RV and the door slam shut.

"Is she a real jispy?" asked Jessie. She was already two big bites into the warm treat.

"Gypsy, not jispy."

"Is she?"

M looked at the paper and the jagged hole that was left in it. "I don't ..." He stopped and looked over Jessie's shoulder out the window.

. M saw the police car approach the back of the trailer through the thinning fog. No lights, no siren, just the soft crunch of something very heavy moving with ponderous inevitability over gravel. M's stomach tightened and he put down his fork. This was not good. He knew cops never came by to tell you what a good job you were doing with your life.

"Keep eating Jess."

But Jessie stopped immediately and turned in her chair. "Whhaah?" she asked with a mouthful of the warm cake.

"Nothin'. It's nothin'," said M. "He's just checking to make sure the neighborhood is safe."

The engine stopped but nobody got out.

Jessie swallowed. "Are they going to arrest the jispy?"

"I told you..." M focused on the windshield through the screen door. There was only a vague outline of a person. He remembered he and his father had gotten stopped for speeding one time. He had looked back at the patrol car and like now, couldn't see anyone in it. When the cop finally had gotten out to write the ticket, he could see his father was really steamed but kept trying to talk to the cop as if he was a bar buddy, joking, but not really. M had watched his father's hand while the cop stood by the driver's window and wrote the ticket. The hand had crept to the rounded front edge of the seat. All the while his father kept joking about some lady and her 'Virginia', except he kept mispronouncing 'Virginia'. Even though he'd been only ten at the time, M knew enough to swing his legs over the seat edge so the gun his father was reaching for could not be dislodged.

That speeding ticket, the last in a series, had been the beginning of what his mother had called 'the troubles'. For a while, she'd even had to drive his father to work and back. Rides to the bar were another story.

Nope, they never come around to tell you how good you're doing. And they never come when called. Even when you call 911 over and over.

"M?" asked Jessie in a small voice.

"It's fine."

M and Jess watched the cop exit the patrol car, look around and approach the three wooden steps that led to Ruby's door. He stood for a second on the lowest step with his foot on the tread and his fingers hooked in his belt, sucking on a toothpick. The cop reached up and with a fat knuckle rapped on the screen door. He retreated, looked around and waited.

M and Jess sat very still.

The cop looked to his left then right, checking the curtains in the windows for movement. Seeing none he leaned forward once again and with a little bit more insistence tapped on the screen door, cleared his throat and said, "Anyone home?"

M put his hand on Jess's arm. Both stared at the front door.

Getting no response, he leaned forward and put his head right up against the screen door. M could see the top bill of his hat pressed against the screen as the cop strained to see inside a dark trailer. His hands were cupped around his eyes. He scanned the room, saw the refrigerator, the sink full of dishes and finally with a start he saw M and Jess at the table, unmoving.

Because they were sitting so still, he had to look twice to make sure they were real.

"Hey, you kids, anybody else home?" he asked.

M and Jess sat very still and said nothing.

"Glad to see someone's there," said the cop. The smile was cardboard. M had seen it before.

"I thought I was talking to myself." The cop reached up to the screen door to open it, but it was still latched.

"Hey you two," he said in mock friendliness, "Can I come in a sec?"

Jess looked at M. M didn't move and neither made a move to unlock the door.

"Hey kids, come on now…" but he didn't finish the sentence.

Still smiling, he adjusted his night stick on his belt, reached into his shirt pocket and pulled out a piece of paper. M could hear the creak of leather from his belt and holster as he moved.

He unfolded it and read it. "All right, I'm looking for Rendell, a Mr. Rendell and a Mrs. Rendell if there is one. Are they home? Are you the Rendell kids?" The policeman leaned in again. M saw him pulling on the screen door to make sure it was still locked, testing the latch strength.

"Hey you kids, I need to know if Mr. and Mrs. Rendell are home. Can you at least tell me that?"

M pushed down on Jess's arm meaning for her to sit where she was. He got up, went to the door and stood there.

The cop looked relieved to see some action inside the trailer. He relaxed a little bit and repeated his request one more time. "So, young fella, are Mr. and Mrs. Rendell home? I've got some papers here."

M reached out, grabbed the edge of the door, and swung it closed in the cop's face.

"Kid look, I'm not foolin' around. I'm looking for Mr. and Mrs. Rendell. Now, open the door and answer me."

M's only answer was to lock the door.

"Fuckin' kids," muttered the cop. M watched him through the thin, stained curtains.

The cop reached up with a fist and was ready to pound on the door, but stopped. "Listen you kids, I just want to talk to Mr. and Mrs. Rendell." He leaned back while he spoke trying to see in the windows. "You know, if you kids are in there alone, without any supervision, I may have to report you…."

He backed off the step so he could get a better view of the whole trailer and the back of the RV next to it.

"You know what that means don't you? People can't be leaving kids all alone. Someone will come and have to take you away."

M threw the deadbolt.

"Fuckin' kids."

Putting his eyes right up to the gauzy curtains, M saw the cop return to the side of the patrol car, still looking back at the trailer, probably expecting to see a window curtain move or the door to be reopened. But M was careful.

The cop backed the patrol car away from the trailer, turned it around and headed down the street.

M watched him go. He saw the patrol car turn in one of the trailers' driveways and park. He could just see the blue nose of patrol car sticking out from beyond the hedge three trailers down.

Let him wait, thought M.

"Is he gone?" asked Jess.

M moved away from the window.

"No, he's still around, but he won't be back for a while."

CHAPTER 10

Stan stopped her at the door of their new office. Mallory was coming in and he was leaving.

He gripped her shoulders and turned her around. "Let's go."

"Where?" She had a sly little grin.

Stan didn't say anything as they headed out the heavy entry door toward the cream colored 1994 Dodge. Not a new model. Cold case division detectives exploring old cases get the old cars.

He thought briefly of holding the door open for her, but thought better of it. It wasn't the structure of the relationship he wanted to have with her. Either she could open the damn door herself and didn't care, or she didn't belong.

Mallory didn't seem to notice anyway.

The Dodge shook a bit as it started. Stan gunned it and laughed. Steiner, when he was driving, would shift into neutral and stomp on the gas pedal in whatever piece of shit they were driving that month. 'Cleaning out the carbon' as Jake used to say. It did seem to help it settle down to a rough idle.

He pulled out of the deserted parking lot where two construction workers were laboring to install an electronic gate. It would be controlled by security cards they were supposed to be able to tap on the magnetic reader and the gates would open. Stan and Mallory had already been issued the cards, months before the gates were going to be operational. Stan was sure they weren't going to work, or worse, work part of the time and he sighed as he already envisioned getting stuck in the parking lot and not being allowed to leave. He supposed he'd have to bust down the gate. He smiled.

"Any luck getting us out of this case?"

"What?" she asked. She couldn't hide the surprise in her voice.

"Your memo to Samuels. Remember?"

"Yeah. Oh, yeah." She waved her hand as if she hadn't been hearing right before.

"Well?"

"Look. Like I said before, they're going to think we're slacking, not doing our job." She hurried on, "So, where we going?"

Stan gripped the wheel tighter and looked over at her. She seemed to have moved toward her door and was looking eagerly straight ahead.

"You didn't send a memo. You didn't make a call either, did you?"

She didn't answer right away.

"You didn't do anything I asked. 'Oh, I'm low man, I'll take care of it,'" he imitated her voice.

She turned and protested, "No, I did send a memo...," she said defiantly. She turned back to look at the scenery going by.

"... and I even got a response."

"You did! From Samuels? Was he pissed then?"

"No, he was fine." She hesitated. "You know I had to couch it in terms that wouldn't reflect back on how we were doing our job. I didn't want it to come back to you and Jake..."

"...and you, too," added Stan.

"Yeah, of course. It would reflect on me too. So, I had to put it a certain way."

"Like how?" Stan had an uneasy feeling.

Mallory shrugged. "You know, diplomatically, sort of."

"So, I'm guessing we're still on the case? That's what you're saying? I'll give him a call."

"Wait. Yeah, okay, we're still on the case but, good news, we have a deadline. We only have to look at it for a while, you know, a set time like we talked about then we move on to other things if we haven't made any progress."

Stan was quiet waiting for more, but Mallory just kept looking out the window. They were moving away from downtown and the road was starting to twist and the vegetation starting to evolve toward high desert.

Finally, "So, two weeks and we're out, right?"

Mallory shook her head. "Stan," she said, enunciating as if he hadn't heard her. "I said I had to be diplomatic, you know."

"Stop saying 'you know', and how diplomatic were you?"

Mallory took a breath and let it out hurriedly, "Three short weeks. That's all. Three weeks and we're out if we can't do anything on it."

Stan maneuvered the old Dodge around the turns that were coming fast like minor switchbacks. The Dodge hesitated before it entered each one, then it seemed to screech 'what the hell' and accelerated into the next sweeping turn.

"Hell, Mallory," was all Stan said, but he smiled to himself. He half expected to be told that they were on it till they were dead or caught whoever did it, whichever event miraculously happened first. "That was the best you could do?"

Stan could see Mallory relax realizing he wasn't going to shove her out on the next outside turn.

"Absolute best, Stan. Promise."

She hesitated, but kept glancing at Stan then back at the road then back at Stan.

"We're going there aren't we?"

She reminded Stan of an old terrier he'd once had when he was first married. They'd drive to the park and take the dog along. Every turn that got them closer to the park would hype good 'ol Max up. He was turning circles in the back seat and jumping from Stan's headrest and the back seat and back again, until they turned into the gravel parking lot, then he would jump up to the back passenger window and smear his nose all over the glass, checking out the other dogs that were already sniffing the good sniffs.

Mallory, the terrier.

Stan lifted a hand off the wheel. "You wanted to see it didn't you?"

"Yes, of course, but..." she craned her neck and looked straight up at the sky, "...do we have time. I mean, it'll be dark in a few hours"

Stan laughed. "It's all the way across town, true, but we're going to take a look, not do a forensic grid and sift."

"No, I know, it's just I'd like to get a feel, you know, a better feel for the case."

"We'll spend a little while there if you stop saying, 'you know.'"

The road straightened out a bit and he accelerated up behind two Harleys. He saw them glance in their side view mirrors and slow way down. They could smell an unmarked miles away.

"Look, Mallory..." He paused, and then thought what the hell. He was getting too old for subtlety.

"Look, I don't want you to take this the wrong way..." Out of the corner of his eye he could see her brace.

"But since we're together and you've never been in the field..."

She turned and started to object but he continued.

"Your work file shows that, yeah, you're good with computers but you weren't assigned as an investigator to this division, you're an assistant and I don't know what you know about working a crime scene and I don't know how you ended up with me and Jake, and I don't really care, but two things you won't be doing..."

"What?

"What you won't do is mess this up for Jake and myself. We *are* partners. We've been through a great deal of shit together and we like working together. We don't want a newbie complicating things."

Mallory sat staring ahead.

"Look," said Stan softer, "I've got a bit of a bum leg and I want to retire here in a few years and Jake's got plenty of duty years left, but neither of us wants to do the crazy shit we used to do, keeping crazy hours, running to domestics or chasing after some carjacker."

"Okay, okay, I get it," said Mallory, "you two want to take it easy. Get cush."

"Yeah. No. What we want to do is use our brains, use what we know, instead of running all over the place at all hours of the goddamn night, running ourselves ragged. We want...we need to be the inside guys, see? We just want to take some time and try and solve some of the old cases. We're not looking for flash."

Mallory turned away and watched the Harleys pull off to the side.

Stan pushed the Dodge.

"Just that we're definitely not looking for cases like this one."

"You don't think we'll solve this," interrupted Mallory, "and you don't want me screaming to anybody that you guys are just two goldbrickers who want to kick back and relax, sip a few brews while you yak about old times and, 'oh maybe we'll try and solve this case, here. This one looks easy. This one won't make us get up from our easy chair and require us to do some actual police work.' Well, fine..."

"You know that's not what I meant."

"...but, I'll tell you this and maybe this is why I was assigned to you two 'cause they knew you were going to require a kick in the ass, but..." She turned to look at Stan. "...we will solve this. We will find this asshole. I am not wasting my time, my working life, pussyfooting around you two just because you don't want to do the tough stuff. We will sure as shit beat this case and the next one and the next one until you two bozos retire and then I'll run things and we'll *really* make some goddamn progress."

Stan saw Mallory bite her lip and he thought she was going to either cry or take out a gun and shoot him.

Great. Unbounded enthusiasm made him nervous.

"Just so you know," began Stan, "neither Jake nor I are lazy as you will find out, that is if you can keep up. What we are doing is rearranging our methods of working, redirecting our intensities. What we will want is someone..."

"...a partner."

"...*someone* who will help us with these old cases and yeah, also not go running to Command about the lack of progress we're making or not making. These cases are old and cold. They've been worked over by better minds than most of us and we will be fortunate if we are able to solve one in five that we look at. And Jake and I are good at this. Look, all I'm saying is that you may have too much energy, too many expectations about what we'll be able to achieve here. And this site is a good example."

"What do you mean?" she asked with concern.

Stan sighed. "This is an old site. It's not going to look any different just because it was a crime scene many years ago. Things change. Site may be bulldozed. It may be a housing development. Hell, I'm not sure who even owns it these days. I told Sharon Ollestad to find out and then…"

"I could've done that, you know. You didn't have to go to Sharon. That's why they assigned me to you for shit's sake." She crossed her arms.

"I just told her to find out and then if it was a local owner, to send a squad out this morning to give them some notice we'll be viewing the site. I gave her the job 'cause she could then send out a squad. You can't do that. You're civilian."

Mallory stared straight ahead.

"Anyway, we're going there just so you can get a feel, as you said. Don't expect much and don't be too much like a terrier."

Mallory stayed slumped back in her seat.

"I'm sorry you were assigned to us and not because I think you aren't an asset, or won't be someday," said Stan quickly, "but because your optimism may be misplaced. You may be better suited to working on more current stuff downtown." He glanced over to her. "Just sayin'."

"And I'm just sayin' we will get on top of this," said Mallory with quiet determination.

"Sure," said Stan with sarcastic conviction, "*if* something new turns up or the killer pushes his way through the front door of the Rogers & Sons Cold Storage building and begs us to handcuff him. My guess is the over-under in Vegas for that event happening is… well, you wouldn't be able to get anyone to lay any kind of odds."

"Why did you agree to show me the site?" she asked looking sidelong at him.

Stan watched the houses along the side of the road begin their transformation from individual single family, 1950s, cracker boxes to the perfect blend of architecture and capitalism, the modern housing development. California, it changes while you're not looking.

"I haven't been here in a long while." he looked at her, knowing how weak that sounded. "Also," he hurried on, "we said we'd work this from the beginning. And I keep my promises."

"Good. I like it." Mallory settled back again and stared out her window.

"All I'm saying is don't expect it to be...don't expect to see too much. It's been a long time."

Mallory sighed. "Not for me. You forget. It'll be all new to me."

"Fresh eyes," said Stan, "That's true. That's what I asked for."

"You know," she said, "I was thirteen years old when the bodies were found."

Stan swept the Dodge around the curves, lost in thought.

"In 1997, after Joey Marshall was found..."

"Last victim, first uncovered," added Mallory.

"Yeah, Joey. Well, when everyone heard that little Joey had been buried alive, that was bad enough, but when they heard what we had been trying to keep from the public for legal reasons, as a detail we were holding back, some detail only the killer would know, they had a shit fit. And since we had no one in custody and no imminent arrests they came down hard on us, especially Carruthers and his team and the whole homicide group. None of us could go anywhere without questions popping up about how close we were to catching the bastard. Most of us had no connection to the case, but the lack of progress was killing us. The public had no patience. And, according to Carruthers, even when the task force did come up with something that seemed relevant, they obviously couldn't announce it, they had to try to keep it under wraps, keep it from getting out. So, there was never any good news about how close we were or what new leads there were." Stan sighed. "Just nothing."

Mallory nodded. "I remember the papers. I was in college, mostly sleeping my way through journalism as a minor. One assignment was to go back and analyze press coverage on Olive Park, especially how it related to the public's right to know in serial killings where the cops had to keep some details out of the press."

"Yeah, and what did the class decide?" Stan accelerated with one hand on the wheel, skillfully weaving around the body of cars, doing about 10 miles more per hour than everyone else.

"Are you kidding? Cops lost in a landslide." Mallory gave short laugh.

"What about you?"

"It was Berkley, liberal mecca. Most privileged kids aren't touched with having to get dirty with the scum of the world. In their life, they always travel the safe streets; there are no bums, homeless, pimps, child killers on their block. Selfishly, when bad shit happens they just want to read about it for their own titillation. There's precious little thought given to anything beyond their own lurid imaginings. Sad."

Stan turned down the scanner which was spewing out a series of calls to CHP regarding arresting Mexican truckers for hauling frozen scallops up from Mexico.

"And what about you? What did you decide? "

"There were a few of us who argued against the mob. We said, maybe look at it from not the cops point of view or even the public's, but maybe from some of the families involved. Shouldn't they get some justice? I mean, shouldn't they be able to find out who did this to their kids? Shouldn't the cops be given every tool to find the assholes, one tool being to keep some of their favorite lurid details out of the papers? All of it was going to come out at the trial anyway."

Mallory turned and watched the scrub on the side of the road change. She put the back of her hand against the glass to judge how cool the outside air was becoming.

"They shouted us down. One of us, Mary Alice something, burst into tears and threw her notebook at the professor. I got a C minus."

Both of them were quiet. The traffic coming the other way had thinned.

"How much further?" asked Mallory. She watched milepost 14 go by.

Stan slowed on a curve so he could glance up the next stretch of highway, and then did a sudden U-turn. He swung around into a gravel pulloff that was big enough for two vehicles. It was guarded by a rough border of two-man rocks to keep cars from going into the woods.

"We're here? This is it?" asked Mallory. She sat forward and studied the woods in front of the car.

Stan shifted to park and shut off the engine. It shuddered, then surrendered.

"Yeah, doesn't look like much, does it?" Then he nodded and turned to Mallory. "Okay. Fresh eyes."

She nodded back.

"We're back in 1997 and we're about to come upon three dead children..."

Mallory nodded.

To Stan it almost appeared as if she crossed herself.

She tried to hide it but Stan saw her hand shake as she reached for the door handle.

CHAPTER 11

Where he pulled the Dodge to a stop everything looked pretty much as he remembered. He surveyed the area around him. Highway 50 was the same, the woods were still here, but they had passed an RV trailer park that he didn't remember. It was the same and yet it wasn't.

"I had to come here once," he said. He scanned the woods, saw the opening in the trees.

He opened the door and stepped out. The in-between area, that no-mans land, on the edge of Sacramento and just before Highway 50 climbed into the foothills of the El Dorados, can get hot, but today in the late afternoon sun, the breeze came down from the north and cooled them. Both of them turned toward the wind.

"So, why do they call it Olive Park? There's an Olive Park in San Diego but no Olive Park on any of my maps or GPS anywhere near here. Besides the San Diego hit, all my online searches came up with just this murder case, nothing else about an Olive Park. This is not a 'park' park and olive trees aren't native to this area, so why?"

Stan shrugged. "Not up on the historical stuff. I remember Carruthers saying something about Spanish missionaries finding peace and shelter under the branches of a mythical olive tree when they passed this way. Probably untrue, but that's why, when he had to come up with a name for this case, he wanted something to counteract the shitty images of three murdered kids. So, he called the case Olive Park."

"Smells... clean up here," Mallory took a deep breath.

"You're getting a good whiff of sugar pines, mostly, some incense cedar." he looked around. The sun was already behind the hill they had just rounded. "Evergreens, some aspen....c'mon, light's fading."

Mallory closed the trunk with two flashlights in her hand.

Stan saw the flashlights. "We won't be here that long."

"Whatever."

"This way." Stan stepped past the boulders and over the two creosoted logs that formed a barrier on the outside of the gravel and entered a path, mostly overgrown.

"You never met Duncan. He was way before your time."

Mallory shook her head as she tested the flashlights. "The cop who found Handleman?"

"Yeah. Helluva nice guy...really bad temper though."

"That wasn't in *People* magazine."

"Cute. Anyway, he told us a story. Funny, I remember this. Okay, he was leading Handleman out of these woods after he arrested him and cuffed him. Well, Officer Duncan fell backwards over these logs here. Landed on his ass. Lying there with Handleman looming over him.

"Duncan'd been really shook up with what he saw in the woods. He said he could tell right away it was a child's arm sticking up. It really threw him he said. Mind was going in a million directions when he fell; gotta get the prisoner secured in the car, gotta call it in, gotta secure the site. You know, all that. He was so pissed he fell and now the prisoner was just standing there..."

"Surprised he didn't shoot him."

"No," said Stan turning and looking at her. "Said the damnedest thing happened. He said he was really upset, looking like an idiot when all of a sudden Handleman turns around and reaches down with his cuffed hands and offers to help him up."

"Really?"

Stan started walking down the path. "Yeah. He said it was like instantly being able to look into the future. He could see everything that was coming. He could see that with Handleman leaning down and trying to help him up that Handleman was telling the truth. Just like that. He knew the guy had nothing to do with what went on here. He was certain."

The gravel underfoot turned to a smooth, softer base of jackstraw and pine needles. A few dying aspen leaves were already spinning off the trees and swirling at their feet. Branches had extended their arms since Stan was here last. He didn't remember having to push so many out of his way. He held them for Mallory as they approached the clearing.

It was odd, thought Stan, how the quiet enveloped you just a few feet into the woods. He barely noticed the Harleys when they passed, gunning hard heading higher up into the hills.

Stan halted abruptly and looked around.

He spoke over his shoulder to Mallory, "Here."

He stepped back and widened his arms out to include a clearing about the size of small churchyard.

"It was right here."

Mallory stepped forward past Stan and took in the scene.

The wind had freshened and Mallory shivered.

Stan had seen rape victims. He'd been with them shortly after they were attacked. He had seen them months and years later. They healed but you could tell by looking at them that something had happened in their life. It helped to look into their eyes while you held their hands. If you didn't know anything about them, you could still tell they had had a trauma that stole something but left something too, like a black hardened tumor.

As he stood in the clearing, he could tell tragedy lived here. A deep violation. And if you knew nothing about this site, this clearing, you would still feel it. A sadness borne of great pain.

The few leaves remaining lacked the will to move even in the afternoon breeze. The sun shone with difficulty into the clearing. The ground, though it had been many years, still looked raw. The area where the three mounds had been was still defined, though he couldn't say exactly how. Even if he hadn't been here before, even as Mallory was seeing the clearing for the first time, he could still walk in here and say with dead certainty that there had been three victims, laid out in a neat row, a few feet apart.

The underbrush had not advanced into the clearing; no leaves had really fallen into it either. Nature wanted to heal but knew no way to overcome what had happened. And so, three faint outlines of what had been. Red ants had taken them as their domain. They poured from their nests in the top of the mound and ran down across the clearing.

Stan remembered when Carruthers had led him in to the clearing. Stan had just made detective at the time and while he wasn't assigned to Olive Park, it was *the* case. He had bullied Carruthers to at least see the site until the man had relented.

Carruthers had brought him to the edge of the clearing and stopped and Stan had started to walk around him, but Carruthers put his arm out gently to stop him. He lowered it as soon as Stan halted.

Stan had looked down, thought he'd been about to step on something. Hadn't seen anything then looked to Carruthers.

Carruthers's lips were a tight line as he had stared into the clearing. It was then, watching the man that Stan realized what Carruthers was feeling. He was scared. He was scared to his bones. Like Duncan, Stan thought, Carruthers, too, could probably see the future. Could see the enormity of what had happened.

Three children. Carruthers could see headlines, media, pressure – all bad shit ahead. This would be the biggest case he had ever handled. This would be his career. And he was terrified he'd screw it up.

The photographers had already been there and documented the scene. Over three hundred pictures had been taken, Stan remembered Carruthers telling him later.

Forensics had already taken a cast of Officer Duncan's shoes and had confiscated Handleman's shoes as evidence. Casts had been made of every indentation in the ground around the bodies. The top two inches of topsoil had been removed in a gridded pattern and sifted through two size screens. That had been hours ago.

When he and Carruthers had stood at the edge of the leafy clearing, the forensic team had just begun exhuming the bodies. They had started with Joey Marshall, the most obvious choice because of his burnt arm sticking up at a pleading angle from the loose dirt that covered the rest of the body.

The two forensic techs used brushes and their gloved hands to begin to take the dirt away from around the arm. Stan had left when a shock of light brown hair had been uncovered.

Now, with Mallory, Stan's eyes swept the clearing. It was open and raw, as if waiting for someone to fix it.

Mallory must have felt it too.

"So, they were buried here and they were killed here," said Mallory quietly.

"Yes," Stan whispered.

He extended one hand out, pointing to the mound to their right.

"Joey."

He moved to the center mound.

"Karen."

The last

"Phillip."

Mallory stayed silent then took a few steps forward and placed her hand carefully on the first grave. She let it rest there, leaving it long enough to say a prayer, Stan thought. Or to make a promise.

"Buried here..." she said again.

She faced Stan and touched her two palms together.

"Buried and killed here."

Stan met her eyes. "And tortured here."

"Maybe. "

"Maybe?"

"You're saying that just because it was in the file? I thought we agreed to set aside everything we knew. You said, you know, think outside the box. Get creative." She touched her face beside her eye. "Be the fresh eyes"

Mallory crossed the clearing, stepping carefully between the low mounds.

Stan spoke up so she could hear him. "Except for the few small items that were found here with the bodies, there was no other evidence of anything up here except three graves. None. No blood found, no extra clothes, no souvenirs of torturing little kids except the condition of the bodies themselves. Just the three graves in this clearing and the woods around it."

Stan watched as Mallory looked around, examining the clearing. He saw her searching through the stiff, black branches, listening to the wind overhead. The clearing seemed to sigh as if it was alive and guarding this sacred site. It was alive and still had not made up its mind about these two now in its midst. The bare trees hissed in the breeze. Branches clacked together. The dusky smell of dark earth permeated the clearing.

Finally she turned to Stan.

"Why here? Why this place?"

Stan shrugged. "Ask Willy. Except that there was a small pulloff, why would anyone stop here?" He moved to stand next to where he remembered the first grave being. "In fact, that's the very reason why Carruthers and Thompson were so hot for Willy Handleman to be the perp. Why would anyone stop here, unless they planned this," he indicated the area where the three graves had been, "for this spot?"

They could hear a semi-trailer go by in the distance.

"Convenient," said Stan.

"Still, rather remote," added Mallory.

Stan tried to envision the clearing through Mallory's eyes. Someone who'd never seen it before. It was unusually open. Strange, because the woods surrounding it were so dense. 'White poplars, some aspen, some evergreens', the report had said in describing the woods around it. Of course, now the leaves were gone from the branches. The clearing had little growth, some moss, some sodden leaf detritus, and a few fallen branches but otherwise open to the sky. Mallory was right, thought Stan; it did smell clean. Earthy too.

The graves had been carefully exhumed. Stan had studied the pictures. It had taken Forensics three days to fully process the site. They worked round the clock and were able to get in a full 36 hours before the press found out. But even before the camera trucks invaded and the crews from all over California began staking out the scene, even before the tabloid headlines, even before endless days of punditry, the whole department knew even then that this case was going to be a ball-buster.

Now, what remained of the grave mounds was subtle, but once you saw one the others were easy to see, especially being all in a row. Behind them, and still obvious, was a larger mound. It had been thought to contain more than one body by its size, but, in fact, there were no bodies at all. It had been about six feet by four feet and about three feet high and its purpose was unknown.

"What are you doing?" Stan watched as Mallory moved along the perimeter of the clearing, staring up into the trees. She didn't take her eyes off the trees and occasionally stumbled but always regained her balance.

"Just looking..."

"What?" Stan took his eyes of Mallory and he too began to search the trees. "What are we supposed to see?"

She continued to move counterclockwise around the site.

"Probably nothing..." She stopped rubbed her neck, shook her shoulders, then continued on. "Just trying to put pieces together..."

"You do that. Look, SacFor was all over this site. For three very long days this was their field headquarters. They were all camped out here. One of the most thorough site exams ever by Sacramento Forensics they tell me. Finally quit when it started raining..." Stan knelt down and picked up some dirt. "...that and when three million press locusts descended on them."

Mallory stopped and turned. "I can just see them on their hands and knees, working the grid over the entire area right?"

"Damn straight. They double sifted everything down to six inches and a full foot below each grave and within a few feet either side."

Stan let a handful of dirt hourglass from his hand. "You read the report. The stuff they found that's not supposed to be in the woods was all listed."

"They did a swell job, three days crawling around in the dirt but they never looked up did they?" asked Mallory.

"Why the hell would they? Evidence falls to the ground. "

Mallory looked away, deep in thought. "Still..."

In many ways Stan was envious of her energy, but they were only up here to familiarize themselves with the gravesite. He looked up. The sun no longer hit the tops of the trees. He knew the hills lost light fast.

"Getting dark. Time to go."

"Say," Mallory said turning back to Stan, "Mr. Detective, you know Forensics, can they lift prints off tree bark?"

Stan wanted to laugh, and then realized it was an interesting idea.

He considered and tried to remember all the places Forensics couldn't pull prints from. They'd gotten awfully damn good, but tree bark that had been in the elements for years, it wasn't possible.

"Fresh maybe," he said finally. He remembered as a child playing in his own woods he could see his own sweaty palm prints where he gripped the limbs as he climbed to their tree house. It had been a huge spreading beech tree. Smooth, off white bark.

"Yeah, I suppose they could pull prints from some woody thing with smooth bark maybe, like a beech. But prints would have to be fresh. I mean really fresh, as if someone had just touched or gripped a branch. After all this time and weather..." Stan thought a minute. "Course, if they'd left blood or had some other fluid on their hands that might have dried with more visibility or lift-ability than just sweat then...." Stan stopped. It sounded idiotic. He was sure he was giving any Forensics team too much credit. Good, but not that good.

"Tree bark? I don't think so. No way."

Mallory smiled. "You sure?"

"Why....what is it?"

Stan moved quickly across the clearing. Without thinking, he side-stepped the subtle mounds where the graves had been.

Mallory held up her hand as Stan got close. "Stop. There's something on the tree here. Not sure, maybe blood, maybe not, I don't know."

"Well, shit..." Stan leaned close to the smooth barked tree and wrapped halfway around the shaft of the tree appeared a smudge, maybe a palm print, but probably just spider shit or caterpillar slime, who knew.

"Son of a bitch."

"I just wanted to make sure you didn't run up and grab it, you know, and compromise the evidence."

"I've got a knife in the evidence kit. We'll cut out the bark, take it with us. Who knows, maybe it's something."

He looked at her. "Good eyes."

"Yeah? Just wait." she said with a slight smirk. "Give me a boost, will ya?"

"A boost...?"

"Yeah. Up." Mallory was already trying to interlace his fingers with each other to form a place to step.

"What the hell for?"

Mallory shrugged. "You remember what we talked about on our roof the other day? Oh, and you have a camera and some evidence bags with you?"

"In the evidence kit." He turned. "Why?"

"I think we're going to need them for this...."

"You mean the smudge?"

"No. Look." Mallory raised her eyes and pointed straight up.

The hairs on Stan's arm rose involuntarily. At first Stan saw nothing except a large branch six feet above their heads. It stuck out at a right angle from the beech's trunk. It was the perfect branch to attach a rope swing.

And a rope was what he saw.

They both knew immediately what it meant.

Before Mallory could speak, Stan reached into his pocket and took out his phone. With one motion and without aiming, took a quick picture.

"Boost me up will you!" said Mallory.

"No, wait" commanded Stan. "Shine your flashlight on it. I need another picture. And I need a picture of the mark on the bark."

Mallory shone the light first on the mark, then along the length of the branch. The manila rope was wrapped around the branch five times and tied off nearer the trunk of the tree. Stan could see it had many broken strands that bristled out at all angles and at least ten or more knots along its length. Probably to shorten it up, he thought. About halfway out on the length of the branch, eight feet away from the trunk, the end of the rope hung down about three feet.

"That's a strong bugger isn't it" said Mallory. "Must be half inch thick."

Stan said nothing but reached over and directed the flashlight in Mallory's hand to the end of the rope which hung motionless three feet above their heads. He held the light there.

"Stan, look…"

But Stan Wyld had already seen. On the end of the rope was a loop. The perfect size to fit snugly around a ten year old's ankle.

His words on the roof came back to him.

Upside down.

It had been just words, a theory, but here it was. He turned away and let go of Mallory's hand.

He remembered that day with Carruthers when he'd first come to the clearing and how Carruthers had taken a moment because he knew the enormity of the job he had to do. And the responsibility he felt. Stan took a deep breath. Shit.

"Damn, Stan, this is bad, I mean good, isn't it?" asked Mallory. She sounded unsure. She had raised the light up to the end of the rope again. "Son of a bitch."

Stan stared at the image he had captured on his phone. It was just a digital image. He shifted his gaze to the rope itself. But, here it was. The thought surprised him. Maybe he never expected a cold case to come to life. Maybe he always expected to have silent images, 8x10s, autopsy sheets, phone tip slips, small baggies of evidence to deal with in the comfort of an office. Maybe, in the back of his mind, he expected to sit in the bowels of the Rogers and Son Cold Storage and muse about old cases. Treat them as if they were abstract and didn't really involve someone real, someone who had been alive. Like three real kids. Maybe he expected to solve these cold cases, the cases they had wanted and had asked for, by just sitting on his ass. Maybe he thought he would phone it in.

Not now. This rope. This rope hanging above his head made sitting on his ass not an option. He wanted to reach up and touch it. To feel it. To connect with what had happened here so long ago.

He switched the phone over to the video mode. Then to Mallory, "I need you to slowly move the light along the rope. Start at the base of the tree and move upward, then out along the branch and end at the loop."

He watched the light travel over the tree and the branch and the rope down to the end. The rope seemed to glow in the growing gloom.

"Again," commanded Stan. "Slower this time."

Mallory sighed but moved the light back to the base of the tree and started the beam moving up at a creeping pace, as if examining every rough edge in the bark.

"You know," she said softly, steadying the light now that it reached the branch, "You know...instead of spending all their time on the ground...your forensic guys should have probably looked up..."

Stan concentrated on the image. "That's not why they didn't find it."

"What do you mean? It's hanging down three feet. A jackass should've seen it."

"Leaves," said Stan. "These trees were flush with leaves. You could have hidden a marching band in these trees. Besides, there was no evidence then that a rope was involved."

Stan watched as the image traveled along the many knots in the rope, then he directed the camera down and let the video end on the loop at the end. He zoomed in a little on the loop, then shut it off.

Mallory switched off the flashlight.

The darkness was starting to squeeze in, the woods around them helpless to stop it.

"So," asked Mallory, asking the question Stan knew she would ask, "We take it or leave it?"

Stan examined the rope again from below. There was something about the rope, but he didn't know what it was. This thing had been such a surprise. A jolt from the past and he was having a hard time deciding. He weighed his options and tried to summon the voice of Danni Harness, the hardass who ran Forensics. 'What! You *moved* it?' Or. 'Shit, Stan, you *left* it out there?'

"Well?" asked Mallory again.

"I need you to circle the edge of the clearing once more, looking up into all the trees. Make sure we're not missing more shit that's been left here for twelve years."

Mallory wisely said nothing, but began her perimeter inspection. She used both flashlights, crisscrossing the beams, flashing into all the dead branches. By the time she made it back to Stan he had decided.

"Nada. Nothing," she said. "This is the only tree with a branch this size that extends into the clearing at all. All the other ones are wrong, you know, point into the woods or too weak looking. And no other ropes or torture devices or marching bands or anything else that I can see."

"Okay, when Jake gets back next week and it's daylight, the three of us will do a more thorough search…"

"You don't want to bring Forensics up here?"

"Not for a daylight search we could do ourselves. I couldn't take the abuse if we dragged the group up here and they didn't find anything. If we're lucky and stumble across Dillinger's fingerprints, we can get them out here. Let's see what they say about the bark first."

"And the rope? We leave it?"

Stan looked up. The loop stared back, daring him. There was still some damn thing he should figure out first but he couldn't quite get a handle on it. Screw it.

"We take it…"

Mallory did a fist pump. "Yes!"

Stan collected the largest evidence bag from the car. It was big and deep and designed to hold a whole bloody comforter off a king sized bed. It would have to do. When he got back, Mallory was dancing around like a cat near water.

"Come on, boost me up!" She clicked her gum twice as she waited for him.

"Put these on first." He handed her some gloves. "They did teach you the very basics about evidence gathering didn't they? I mean you didn't skip that day in training did you? Maybe to go get your nails done instead?"

"I'm civilian. Everything I learned about evidence collection I learned from the OJ trial, if that's what you mean. C'mon, boost me up big boy."

Stan made a step with his hands.

Mallory stepped into the stirrup he made and stood up. Her head was even with the bottom of the branch.

"Okay, now. I want you to carefully unwind it until most of it is hanging down one side of the branch with the loop side on the other. Don't drag it. Got it?"

Mallory popped her gum. "Roger."

With one hand, Mallory reached up and touched the rope lightly with her gloved hand. "You know Stan; this damn thing has been out here for God knows how long. Been rained and snowed on, it's still in pretty good shape." Mallory held the evidence bag and, while balancing, fed the rope into the open bag, carefully lifting it off the branch instead of dragging it over.

Stan re-braced his legs. "How much do you weigh for crissakes?"

Mallory closed the bag, folding the ends over and hopped down.

"Hey, I'm a mere slip of a thing, one hundred and twelve with nothing on. It's this thing that weighs a ton." She hefted the bag then gave it to Stan.

"See?"

Stan took the bag. He felt the rope's coils through the bag. It felt like a snake ready to strike.

"Let's go."

They started across the clearing and when they got to the edge Mallory stopped.

"Did you hear something?" she asked. She had turned and was staring into the darkening woods. Leafless trees and branches moved with a shiver in the slight wind. Both of them strained to hear, anything. She switched on one of the flashlights and whipped it through the trees, rapidly slashing from tree to tree. Maybe hoping to surprise someone.

Mallory looked at Stan. He shook his head.

Still, she turned back and focused on the woods at the back of the clearing and remained still for a few seconds, then broke her trance and headed toward the car.

Stan stayed and listened. There *was* something there. It was soft tears of thanks from Karen, Phillip and Joey. He was sure of it.

It did not occur to Stan until much later that the reason the rope had not been found when the three bodies were discovered was because it hadn't been there.

CHAPTER 12

M led Jessie into the darkened RV.

"This smells...," whispered Jess.

M noticed it too. A sharp, earthy smell, like dusky perfume.

"Close the door you two and sit over here," whispered Ruby.

M pulled the door shut. He hadn't been sure what door to enter; the front door where the paying customers entered or the back door of the RV that was connected by the planked walkway to the back of Ruby's trailer. He didn't feel like leading Jess all the way around to the front, so he just yanked open the back door.

What met them was smelly gloom. In the background was a black hulk that was Ruby Everheart, slightly silhouetted by the flare of a match that then lit a low candle.

M wasn't an idiot. Wasn't about to get all gaga over some gypsy's carnival trick. After all, she'd cut out the astrology section from the newspaper. You'd think a psychic would know what the astrology section said before she even looked at it.

"So, this is where you scam people by faking their fortunes, huh." He could see Ruby, a dark robed figure shuffling from candle to candle.

"Over here," she said. Her voice was a husky whisper.

M took Jessie's hand and moved forward.

Ruby proceeded to light the rest of the incense sticks and stuck them into small jeweled holders. Ashes from the burnt out sticks were draped like small gray snakes along the table.

The only light inside flickered from the two wax laden candles and M could barely make out where Ruby was pointing.

With tentative steps he led Jess over to one corner of the room. They pushed the old newspapers off the two wooden chairs that had been shoved back against the wall and sat down.

Good thing she's lighting some incense, thought M. It was barely masking the sense and smell of a cellar.

When his eyes finally adjusted to the dimness, M could see the RV had been completely closed up from the inside. The windows, while they appeared to be normal windows from the outside, with curtains and all, were actually boarded up behind the curtains. Outside he would have sworn the lights were off because all he saw was black. Now, he saw there were no lights. The boards were painted black to make it appear like no one was home. Whoever had nailed the boards in place and sealed the room had done a very good job. Small remnants of insulation attempted escape around the edges of the board, but even so, M noticed the blocked windows sealed out all light from without and hid everything that went on from within. The concealment was perfect.

The RV had been gutted of whatever had made it once a recreational vehicle. There was no miniature kitchen or fold out bed or couch, just a hellishly black room with a door to a closet at one end and a barrier blocking access to the driver's compartment.

Ruby stooped and touched a new match to two perfectly white candles on twisted iron stands, then placed them at the far end of a large black wood table. M could see the table was crescent shaped and the surface was rough, like it had been dragged out of the woods and only partially finished with some sort of black shiny polish.

"I need you guys to be quiet. If you're quiet you can stay, but if you get fidgety and such, you gotta not be around."

Both kids nodded.

"I mean I gotta work."

"Yeah," said M.

It was obvious to M that she was uncertain about whether having two kids watch her work was a good idea. She must really need the babysitting money, otherwise, why would they be here.

"So," ventured M, "What is this? Some mobile fortune wagon? If you can't come to the crystal, the ball will make a delivery?"

His eyes were now fully accustomed to the dark. M could see that Ruby had changed her clothes. She now wore a flowing purple or dark red robe with a peaked hood. Her face was hidden in the hood. He couldn't see her face

She was still busy lighting candles. Lots of candles.

Jessie's mouth was hanging open slightly, and she stared at Ruby and what she was doing.

"Nice outfit," said M. "You supposed to be a monk or something?"

Ruby brought the dying match close to the shadowed opening of the hood and blew it out. Her large hand emerged from the draped arms and pushed the hood back. She tilted her head back and gave a short, subdued laugh.

"Fun being here, huh," he whispered to Jess, trying to calm his sister who, he felt, was ready to bolt out the door.

Even he didn't believe his words. He was worried about the candles. The ceiling and walls seem to be covered with a dark thick cloth that hung in malevolent black folds. The candlelight flames flickered and waved, every breath seemed to push them toward the walls.

M looked over at Jessie. She swallowed once but never blinked.

Ruby had finished lighting the candles, turned with her hands on her hips and stood looking at the two kids from underneath the hood.

She's regretting ever saying yes to Aunt Janey, thought M.

Finally inspiration struck. She said, "You can help."

"Help with what?" asked M. He had no idea on how to tell a fortune and he knew Jess would hardly be able to move. She seemed riveted to her chair.

Ruby moved over to the side of the room. "C'mere you two."

She knelt down near the floor and appeared to be untying something, although with the heavy robes she was wearing and the dim candles, M couldn't get a good view of exactly what was being untied.

When M got out of his chair, Jesse jumped out of hers too. She would not be left alone. They followed Ruby to the corner and stood behind her as she turned.

With the hood, all they could see was one eye and half her mouth.

"Okay," said Ruby, "You kids can raise and lower the curtain." She seemed to laugh as she said it.

"What's the curtain for," asked M.

"It's a curtain that goes up to the ceiling, you see, and blocks out everything but me. Just my head pokes through."

"Yeah, so?"

"Well, look, people pay me money and they come to see me, not this RV you know. I mean, if they could look around and really see the inside, they'd know they are inside a trailer and it would spoil their experience. I make them feel they are someplace special because that's what they want. To feel special."

"They don't want their fortunes told?"

Ruby worked her jaw up and down and pushed back the hood of her robes. "One thing you should know about people Mr. M, is that they don't want to know what's going to happen to 'em. They don't want to know they are going to get old and sick or die." She paused. Jessie stood mesmerized by Ruby talking about death. M could see Jessie was convinced this was a gypsy for sure.

Ruby tried to smile but the near toothless mouth gaped open instead. Even M was transfixed.

"Ah, this shop talk is too much for you guys," said Ruby. "You can just raise the curtain or you can play outside, just don't wander past the fence into the old trailers over there," she nodded with her chin to the far end of her trailer indicating the jumble of abandoned carnival wagons inside the locked chain link fence. Maybe, M thought, because they were screened off with chain link, everyone ignored them.

"Not really safe. And if you see anybody over..."

But M interrupted. "Well, what do you tell them then, if you don't tell them what's going to happen to them?"

Ruby raised the hood again and looked down at M. He could tell she was confused about what he was asking, then she got it. With a raspy laugh she said, "I tell 'em they're happy."

"But what if they aren't happy? What if..." M searched around the room for an example. "What if something bad has happened to them, what if they lost their money or someone hurt their arm or busted their leg or ....someone died and they aren't happy."

Ruby turned away and started to uncover the crystal that was in the center of the table. "Kid, that's all of us."

But M was not deterred. "But what do you tell them?"

Ruby sat down at the table and pretended to adjust her chair ignoring M and Jessie.

M waited for Ruby but she didn't appear close to answering.

"I want to know," said M. An intensity in M's voice made Ruby stop and look up.

"You wanna know what I tell others who pay me..." asked Ruby, "...or do you wanna know for yourself?"

Before M could answer Ruby said, "Sit there." She indicated the chair across from her.

M sat, took his cap off and set it next to him. Jess followed as if on a string and stood by his side.

Ruby settled herself. "Give me a dollar."

"Why?"

She leaned forward a little and the hood slipped even further forward. M could hardly see her eyes. "Because I don't do this for free. One dollar."

M was going to say she was a fake and how dare she charge him anything, but thought better. He squirmed in his seat and brought out a rumpled dollar bill which he tossed next to the crystal. "Is that all you charge?"

Ruby reached out and slowly with strong fingers smoothed out the bill. She left it on the table next to the crystal.

"No, you're getting a special deal."

Ruby got up and went over and raised the curtain herself. M and Jess watched as the room became even darker and quieter than before. M closed his eyes. When he realized he could no longer hear the traffic outside, he opened them.

He could have been anywhere.

Ruby placed both hands on either side of the crystal and leaned forward. The hood fell even further, completely obscuring her face.

M felt Jess move closer to him, almost snuggling under his arm. Her mouth was half open and she was watching Ruby's every move.

The candles flickered and reflected in the crystal's facets, and M could see the crystal wasn't a round ball at all, but half a crystal ball. It was sitting on its flat bottom but the flat bottom seemed rough cut so as the candles flickered and their flames moved, so did the reflection on the bottom of the crystal.

Ruby held very still and said nothing. M continued to stare into the crystal, watching the images dance deep inside the glass. No one spoke.

"M?" whispered Jess.

"Shh," said M, but it was a faraway voice.

The light continued to weave colors and shards of colored reflections back onto M's face. As M moved his head slightly from side to side, the light shifted as if rotating around points that were at the edge of each of the facets which had been roughly hewn into the crystal.

From deep inside Ruby came a fakey moan that became low guttural speech. "You may ask three questions. One about the past, one about the future, and a third of your choosing."

M stayed focused on the glass. When he spoke it was to the glass and as if his words were bouncing off the crystal and up to Ruby. The crystal was the conduit.

"When was I born, what is my exact birthday?"

Ruby stayed silent for moment, and then answered. "I will answer that last."

'What a bunch of hooey,' thought M.

"Okay, then, will we have lots of money?

Ruby, again, was silent for a while. "That is a future question."

"Duh."

With a quiet certainty Ruby said, "I think money will not be a problem in your life." To M, she seemed to be almost laughing.

"Sweet."

"Your last question?"

"What happened to my father?"

Jessie looked first at M then to Ruby. "No" she whispered to her brother.

"What happened to my father?" M asked again.

"No!" Jessie whispered louder and moved around to look into his face. "No."

"Your sister's right, you shouldn't ask questions when you already know the answer."

"That's no answer," said M.

"You already have the answer."

"What if I don't?"

"But you do."

M's lips tightened. He shook his head. "I knew you were a fake."

Ruby leaned in toward M and her hands pressed the table. M could not see her face, but her voice and intentions were unmistakable.

"Of course I'm fake, this is my job," she whispered, "I peddle fake happiness inside an illusion and I do it for money."

"Isn't that like stealing?" asked M.

Ruby Everheart tilted her head back and laughed. Her right hand reached out to the one dollar bill and stuffed it in a pocket hidden somewhere in all her robes.

"February 29th," was all she said before there was a knock on the outer door.

CHAPTER 13

The knock on the door wasn't so much a knock, M thought, as a hard fist on a hard wall. Whoever was there wasn't asking to come in, they were demanding it.

Ruby jerked her head around, and then scanned the rest of the trailer.

"You kids, quick now, over here." Her arm indicated the corner with the low bench. Her eyes watched the curtain that blocked the outer door.

M saw the curtain that covered the front door move as the door was opened, then closed behind it. He pushed his sister over to the bench and sat her down. When he turned, he saw a small dark shape in front of the curtain.

M didn't think much of the residents of the trailer park. In some way he knew they never aspired to live in a weeded over back lot in a tinny excuse for a house, but here they were. His father once said that 'shit finds its own level'. Looking at what just walked into Ruby's trailer, he guessed his father had been talking about people like this.

All M could think about was a cornered dog that had found shelter. He was small, not much over four feet. M could tell there was a lot of mean crammed into him. It spilled out of the eyes. It suffused its brown cherubic face. And even though the trailer park had its share of bizarreness, the more he studied the man, the more M realized it was more likely he was a freak who had slithered out of the busted down carnival next door.

Ruby nodded to the man and he pulled himself up on the chair.

"Mr. M, would you please hand me my tarot-te cards." Ruby pointed to a worn, wooden box that held a deck of cards M recognized. She pronounced it with a snooty air, M thought, and rhyming tarot-te with karate.

"You mean tarot cards, these?"

Ruby nodded. "Tarotte. Those are special tarot-te cards."

"Whatever," mumbled M. He got up trying not to look at the man who now sat at the velvet covered table picking his teeth with a match book cover.

"Why thank you, Mr. M," said Ruby smiling.

M dropped the cards on the table. It was becoming damn irritating listening to Ruby's phony friendliness. He noticed though, that she had pushed back her monk's hood. Obviously, the little brown man didn't need the mystery of a hooded figure to have his daily astrological forecast parroted back to him.

With an unneeded flourish, Ruby removed the cards and started to shuffle them. Her fingers struggled getting them to riff so the cards remained in their same order. "Well, now, let's see what we have..."

The man across from Ruby didn't move, just stayed slouched digging at his teeth. His eyes worked around the room. He gave M and Jessie a good working over.

"The cops were here," announced Jessie. Her small, pocket-sized voice had immediate effect.

The small brown man in the chair squirmed forward and turned to Ruby whose mouth started working. Her eyes widened as she turned to find Jess in the darkened trailer.

'Great,' thought M.

"Where?" barked Ruby, "They're here? Now?"

Without waiting for an answer, the brown man slipped off the chair and waddled past Jess and M to the back door and jerked it open, but only a few inches. He took up a one-eyed position looking through the crack. M could see the stiffness in his unwashed pants. The smell reminded M of a woodsy, unflushed toilet.

"There ain't no cops...," said the man, speaking for the first time, with a deep voice that belied his size. The man closed the door with both hands so it made no noise. He shook his head at Ruby then bore down on Jessie who stood her ground.

"What do you mean cops are here? What's your name?" he growled.

M jumped in, "She means cop, not cops. A cop was here, but he left."

M saw him glance at Ruby.

"It was just one cop, that's all," said M."

"One cop," repeated Ruby. She wiped her hands up and down on the side of the black velvet robe. "That's all."

M saw the man search the corners of the room. Maybe he's expecting them to come busting through the door and arrest his sorry ass.

M continued, "He said he was looking for Mr. or Mrs. Ryandell, something like that, and that if they weren't home but we kids were home alone, he'd have to take us in for our protection."

"You mean Rendell?" asked Ruby quietly. "He's looking for a Mr. and Mrs. Rendell?" A slow smile leaked onto her face.

"Yeah. Rendell, that's it. And who are the Rendells? Former inmates of the crazy carnival?"

Ruby turned and looked at M with sharp eyes, then her face softened. "What did you tell him?"

Jess chimed in, "M shut the door in his face."

Ruby put her hand on the armrest. "He shut the door in his face," she repeated.

M glanced at Jessie, surprised to see she was liking all the attention.

"Hard" she added.

"He shut the door hard," repeated Ruby again. "Well, I reckon I don't know what to say, 'cept you seem to be a valuable person to have around Mr. M. As I said, don't like people snoopin'. 'Course nobody does."

"So, who is this Rendell?"

Ruby went quiet and stared at M. Finally, she answered him. "Rendell's the genius who put that," she hitched her thumb in the direction of the tangle of carnival wagons, "Joyland together. Put it together and held it together. Made it something. Something everyone can remember."

M was going to comment on the state of things in the whacked out carnival but the little man interrupted.

"So, he's gone?" His face looked like that of a mad baby's.

"Who?" asked M. "You mean the cop? No. He's sitting at the end of the street."

M caught Ruby and the man exchanging looks.

The man turned as if to check the door again, but instead, slapped his hand on the table, shuffled past Jess and M and brushed the curtain aside until he found the front door. After a quick check of the parking lot in front of the trailer, he exited through the door he'd entered, closing it softly.

M turned to Ruby, "Who was that guy anyway? He kinda stinks."

Ruby was staring into the crystal on the table. "Stinks?"

"Yeah, you know like he hasn't seen a shower in about forever," said M.

Jess nodded and waved her hand in front of her face.

"What, do you just let him come in sometimes 'cause he has no place to go, you know like he lives under one of these busted down trailers and it's be-kind-to-bums week?" M had cracked up when Mick had told him about be-kind-to-bums week somewhere.

"That," spat Ruby, "is my brother."

Jess moved around behind M and hugged his waist.

M froze. "I..."

Ruby's face widened into a nearly toothless grin, and then she tilted her head back and hooted. Her mouth continued to work after the laughter faded, like a dog biting at the air.

M watched her as she recovered and began to straighten up her tarot cards, whistling through what teeth were left, and then looked straight at him as if he was the most gullible kid in existence.

"He used to work over there." She indicated the carnival. "One of the freaks."

CHAPTER 14

They were silent for most of the drive back.

Stan was working over the scene in his head as he drove. There had been something about the rope he felt he should know or should have seen, but he just couldn't reach it. He mentally stepped back and pictured the whole area. What did he see in looking at the whole picture? What was it about the rope, besides the obvious, that bothered him?

He didn't want to ask Mallory, or talk it out with her, as he would have done with Jake. This was something he knew that he knew. And even though he had asked her for 'fresh eyes', he needed to do this himself.

Mallory could not sit still. Every minute or so she would turn around and put both hands on the back of her seat and just check to make sure the evidence bag with the rope was still there. She'd stare at it as if trying to see through the bag. Stan thought maybe she was bothered by the same unsettling feeling too. She reached over the back seat, grabbed his jacket and pulled it into her lap.

"You need something?" asked Stan glancing at her.

She searched each pocket. "I want to see it," she said. She fished out the phone, turned it around a few time until she was sure she had it upright.

"Shit, man, you need a new phone. This is like the rotary version of cell phones. I'm surprised this thing even has video on it."

"It makes calls. I receive calls. It has GPS 'cause I usually don't know where the hell I'm going and it can take pictures." He paused. "Actually, I wasn't exactly sure of the video.

Probably should have checked it before we left. Think I did it right."

"Let's see."

Stan kept glancing sideways, watching her pink polished fingernails tap the keys. He had been going to tell her how to access the photo and video feature when he realized she was young. The young were born with the innate ability to navigate the digital world. Still, he couldn't help himself.

"You get it?"

"'Course," she said with some distracted indignation.

By the lighted reflection on her face, he could see she had found the video.

"You did record it twice, right?" she asked without taking her eyes off the screen.

"Once pretty fast, then I went back and did it slower, remember?"

She watched the video play through and then start over, starting at the base of the tree. As the second playback started she began tapping a few keys.

"You know," she said, "you can zoom in a bit on the video…"

No, he didn't know, but he wasn't about to share that. He tried to watch her and drive at the same time so he could see what she was doing.

She noticed him weaving a bit. "Just watch the road, okay. I got this."

Still he kept glancing at her. Her intensity was complete and impressive. After she restarted it for the third time he couldn't help himself. He had to ask.

"What are you doing?"

But she didn't answer.

"What?"

Finally, she looked up with a solemn look. "Stop the car."

"What? Why?"

She never took her eyes off of him. "Stop the car. Now."

Stan started to pull over onto the shoulder. "What? I screwed it up, eh? We gotta go back?"

He stopped the car and looked at Mallory. She just shook her head and handed him the phone. He took it. She had the video paused on one spot and it was zoomed in so much he could hardly tell what he was seeing.

"What am I supposed to see?"

"Back it up a few seconds."

Stan looked at her helplessly.

"Here." She took the phone back adjusted the zoom back a little and rewound it about ten seconds. She handed it back.

"Push the 7 button to start it and concentrate on the top of the loop."

Stan checked to make sure they were completely off the road, then pushed 7.

The image panned just off the trunk and started along the branch and the rope and the knots. It was a better image than he imagined he had recorded and was immediately impressed with what he had captured. Where he could see the branch through the rope knots it was a smudged white and the black tree bolls showed clearly. Beyond the branch, the rest of the woods showed up as just blackness. The rope he knew was a dirty ochre color, but with the contrast of the video image it showed up almost as golden. It was multi-stranded and many of the strands had frayed and were poking out. He followed the image as it panned the rest of the rope, then down to the top of the loop. Then he saw why Mallory had given it to him.

Stan looked at Mallory. "Can we zoom further?"

She shook her head. "It's all the way. So, what is it? What are we looking at?"

Stan stared at the image, the dark spot above the loop.

"Is it blood?"

"Maybe," said Stan not taking his eyes from the image. "And how come we didn't see it before?"

Mallory sat up straighter and blew off his question. "Dunno. Lot more contrasty when you play it back. But, hell, least we found it, right?"

"Yeah."

"So, if it is blood, whose is it and can they tell whose it is after all this time? Shit, the damn thing has been out in the damn woods for god knows how long. Rained on, snowed, you know. I mean if the elements couldn't destroy it, can they still tell? Forensics, I mean. How long, how degraded can it be and still get a match? I mean I saw the OJ trial, first they said you could, then they said you couldn't, you know." She slapped the dashboard. "This is good, really good huh? Jesus, I gotta pee."

"I could stop and you could pull a Willy Handleman and pee on the side of the road."

"Funny, let's just get back, okay."

Mallory let out a sigh, shut off the phone and settled back in her seat. She put her arms around her as if she was cold.

Neither spoke.

Stan's thoughts ran to the nagging what-ifs. What if they hadn't gone to the site? What if the smudge was blood? What if it wasn't any of the victim's blood but someone else's? What if Mallory hadn't thought to look up? She had remembered their conversation they'd had on the roof the other day, about Joey hanging when he was hit. Why hadn't he? And, if the victims had been hanging, then they had to be suspended. Of course.

He started to twitch inside as if someone had thrown him into a vat of adrenaline. Yes, they had found something, but harsh experience had taught to temper hope that it might lead to further revelations. So much of police work for him, especially when he first started as a detective was dealing with disappointment. He'd seen cases fall apart after what everyone thought was solid evidence turned to a pile of steaming turds.

A few hundred times of that happening and he had built up a tough-ass skin. Detective Stan Wyld version 2.0 now traded instant gratification for a slogging determination to dig harder and not believe everything at first glance. Too much had blown up in his face. And sometimes it worked; sometimes it still went into the shitter

When he looked over at Mallory, her eyes were wide with innocent anticipation.

He finally laughed. "Damn."

She looked at him, smiled, then turned all the way around, placed both hands on the back of her seat and stared at the evidence bag being chauffeured.

"Wow."

She turned back around, slumped down, her blonde ends bunching around her neck. Her feet went to the dash board and started lightly tapping each other.

"Just fucking wow."

CHAPTER 15

Stan sat on the edge of the conference table situated in the middle of the room. Half of what they knew about Olive Park was spread out on the table. The rest was mounted on the three glass walls of their cubicle and reflected a summary of the case. Stan had insisted they re-do the walls that Mallory had started and Mallory had reluctantly agreed.

Now, one wall listed the three victims, little Joey Marshall, Karen Summering, and Phillip Boyd. On it was a bio of each, one picture of what they were like when they were alive and when their families knew them and one their friends could recognize.

Below that were the pictures of the site excavation of each victim, with close-ups paper clipped to the side of the wider shots. Beneath that were a few pictures from the autopsy of each. It was the practice to draw lines on the board or use strings to connect the commonalities between each child. Ages were different, gender was different, where they were from was different by hundreds of miles.

There was only one string. One commonality. All three were found in shallow mounds in the Olive Park clearing.

The next wall had the main evidence groups they were working. There were three blue circles at the top of each – one had 'Trace' written in it. Underneath was a list of the five items found at the clearing, the main guesses about their meaning and the direction that Stan wanted to pursue. The second circle was labeled 'Psych'. Stan hated this one and had trouble getting up the energy to get excited about pursuing elements that the profilers had worked up. He wanted to acknowledge the importance of profiling and if anyone had asked him, he'd say it was a vital leg of their three-legged stool of criminal investigation. But, honestly, he hardly knew where to start.

The third glass wall circle was labeled 'Clearing/Rope'. He saw Mallory had put a big question mark above the rope.

The final wall was one Mallory had come up with by herself and a line of investigation that Stan was happy to let her pursue. 'Missing.' It listed 27 missing children from all over California, even some from Nevada. Mallory had taken the hundreds of missing kids and filtered it down to the age range of the known victims; Joey was 9, Karen was 11 and Phillip was 9. She had then eliminated all the black and Hispanic children since their victims were white. She cut out all those who had had a past history of running away. She was currently toying with the idea that all the victims were from the lower middle class. Stan was not sure how she was defining that.

Mallory stopped sorting the pictures they'd taken of the tree and the rope and the clearing and looked up when Stan answered his phone.

He listened, then snapped it shut.

"What is it?"

"Gotta go." He began to gather up all the pictures not caring what order they were in, squared them up and shoved them in evidence folders.

"Hey," said Mallory, "I was working on those."

"Yeah, well, not anymore."

Mallory watched him collect the pictures, and then a smile spread across her face as she made the connection.

"That call. The rope! They have something on the rope? That was quick!"

When Stan didn't say anything Mallory sighed, "Shit, you mean they *didn't* find anything?" wailed Mallory.

He turned. "Yeah. They found something."

Mallory had her coat on and was helping stuff the pictures in Stan's briefcase before he was done speaking.

"Where you going?" asked Stan.

"Funny."

After the open spaciousness of their glass cubicle and the soaring ceilings and the relative quiet of the cold storage offices, the cacophony and the crowds of the central precinct hit him like a migraine. For some unknown reason his security card didn't work in the swiper at the basement entrance and they had to trek back to the main public entrance.

"If I'd known you were no longer welcome here I would have brought my own card." Mallory walked with her arms folded.

"Humorous," intoned Stan.

He and Mallory showed their badges at the front entrance but were still required to go through security. It took fifteen minutes amidst the throng of primarily pissed off public who were also waiting to go through metal detection. The detector had just been installed and tempers were short.

It wasn't as if those around him were waiting to board a plane to the Bahamas, they were waiting to get in to pay a fine or bail out a relative or try and fix some other aspect of their screwed up lives.

When it was his turn to go through the detector, Stan held up his badge and indicated to the thoroughly bored guard on the other side he wanted to go through and since he hadn't taken anything off his person, he was probably going to set it off.

The guard perked up, then said, "Empty everything, weapons, cuffs, c'mon, you know the drill."

"Hurry *up*!," came the shouts from behind him as he stepped back and emptied his pockets, unholstered his weapon and dug out his car and house keys and dumped them into the plastic tray.

Finally, the guard waved him through. Miraculously he didn't set it off.

"Congratulations," said the guard. "Let's see the ID."

The guard looked at him, the ID, then back to Stan. "Don't you work here?"

"Used to. I'm over at Harvey and 5th now, working cold cases."

"Whatever. Listen, next time, use the employee entrance. You don't have to go through all this shit, you know."

"What a great idea." The sarcasm came naturally.

Mallory, of course, swept through the metal detector without a beep. The guard made a point of gathering up her cell phone and keys from the tray and personally handing them back to her. He received a nice smile in return, then kept watching her as she made her way to Stan.

Sacramento Forensics was stuck in the basement of the cavernous building. He knew to not try the elevator, but guided Mallory to a metal door with a wire glass window and peeling paint, pushed it open and headed down the two flights of metal stairs. Bare bulbs that always seemed to be swaying shone the way.

"You sure…?" asked Mallory as she followed behind.

Stan grunted. "Sure."

Each year had brought promises to remedy the cramped working conditions. Now as they emerged on the lowest floor Stan could see the overcrowding had gotten worse. As he made his way down the cramped hallway he thanked whomever above for their digs at Rogers & Sons.

He came to a halt as too many people tried to pass at once. It appeared to Stan that even the water cooler had been relocated and now held a prominent place along one wall of the pale blue hallway. Its presence allowed only one person to pass it at a time. Moving on, he could see most of the kitchen stuff, microwave and all, had been removed and sequestered into the area of the second darkroom, the one that was dedicated to developing the more obscure films, the infra-red and the high speed. He had heard that some of the darkroom equipment couldn't be used at the same time as coffee was brewing – the circuits couldn't handle both.

"'Bout time," said Danni Harness, grabbing Stan's arm.

Stan looked at her as if he had been away for years. "Danni!" exclaimed Stan. "Good to see you." He leaned in and pretended to whisper. "Tits still as perky as ever?"

Danni Harness, the 30 year old forensic queen who ran SacFor pulled him further down the hallway. "That's sexual harassment you know. But, hey, thanks for remembering."

Danni let Stan open the doors to the main lab and the three of them entered. CSI this was not. What had started out as a well-designed crime lab, smart oak cabinets, glass fronts, counters underneath at the correct height running along three walls and large Formica topped table in the center of the room, now was overrun with people and equipment. Some of the equipment sat on the floor, including the photocopier and what looked like a video projector, as there was absolutely no more counter space.

Beyond the main room Stan could see the clean room, which still seemed to be clean. To his left was Danni's office, her desk overflowing with so many papers and binders that they even spilled out into the lab.

There were five techs working when Stan and Mallory walked in.

"Out! Out! Now. All of you!" shouted Danni. "Go, go, go." She shooed them away from what they were working on. "No. You two stay," she said indicating two of the youngest techs.

Then she made sure the doors were closed.

She turned on Stan. "Seems ever since you brought in that damn rope, nobody wants to work on routine stuff. We're all behind schedule and it's entirely your fault."

"My fault?"

"And don't you dress the part anymore? No tie. Not regulation at all. Still, you look good. Too damn good to be a detective." She leaned into Stan and pushed her glasses up on her head, "Is that a tan I'm seeing? Shit, we can't get out from under these goddamn fluorescents. I swear we're gonna move over with you, live the good life for a change."

Mallory spoke up for the first time. "What? And leave all this?"

Danni ignored her.

"Stan, you know my two slaves? Frank and Joe or something" She indicated the two technicians in lab coats and bad ties she had made stay. "Probably not since you've been in Shangri-La. We've had some turnover. These two managed to hold onto their jobs, so I gave them the enviable task of studying the rope you so kindly gift wrapped for us."

Stan started up in defensive mode. "Danni, that evidence bag was all we had…"

Danni Harness waved the words away. "By the way, did you ever once give some professional detective thought to leaving the damn thing in place to give Forensics a go?"

Stan glanced at Mallory then looked Danni straight in the eye. "No. Never. I looked at the rope in the tree and I asked myself, what would Danni do? If she were in my place would she want to screw around in some dank woods trying to untangle a rope from around a branch or would she like to be back in her cozy lab…"

"Cramped as shit lab you mean."

"…where she can work in peace or at least get her minions to do it for her. So, no I never thought about making you go all the way out there."

"Good call. 'Cause I wouldn't have gone. How old is this damn case anyway?"

"1997."

"Thought so." She shrugged. "Still, uncharacteristically, we gave this high priority."

"Why thank you Danni," said Stan.

"Don't thank me. The rest of the stuff we had in here was boring as hell. This was all these two wanted to work on." The techs standing behind Mallory shifted uncomfortably.

Stan watched Mallory as she opened her mouth to speak. He jumped ahead of her.

"So, what about the bark? What was on it?" he asked.

Danni scrunched her eyebrows together. "The bark? Oh, yeah. We got that right away. Well sort of, kind of. It's paint of some kind."

"It's not blood? Or part of a bloody palm print?" asked Mallory.

"Blood!" Danni looked at Mallory as if she had just crawled through the door. "Blood wouldn't last that long." She started to say something else, but turned back to Stan instead.

"Paint. Don't know what kind, maybe we'll know later." She grabbed Stan's arm. "This way," she said quietly. The whole group followed her around the center table to a light box mounted on the wall. Danni hesitated with her finger over the switch to turn it on. Stan saw the two techs roll their eyes at the dramatics. One even re-inserted ear buds into his ears.

"First, that smudge on the rope…" began Danni.

"Blood," Mallory blurted out. "You did find some blood." She looked at Stan. "I knew it."

Stan groaned.

The mood ruined, Danni tossed her glasses on the counter and turned to Mallory, but addressed Stan. "Who the hell is this bimbo?"

But Mallory answered. "Mallory Dimante. I work with Stan."

Stan wanted to limit the carnage but he knew better. He   let Danni Harness vent.

Danni turned to Stan. "Who is she? Really?" Without waiting for a reply, she continued. "I sure hope she just wandered in off the street because she sure seems to be living up to what a blonde knows, which is absolutely nothing about forensics and probably less about police work."

Stan raised his hand a few inches. "Danni. It was Mallory here who found the rope."

Danni muttered to herself, "Probably poked herself in the eye putting on her mascara and walked into it."

Stan started to object.

"No matter," said Danni. Then turning to Mallory, "Listen, we don't have time for stupid around here, okay? So, just listen." She started to tick off the points on her fingers.

"First, we can't take fingerprints off of trees, especially prints that may have been around since 1997."

"Second, blood exposed to the elements on a fibrous substance like the rope that Stan brought in wouldn't last from 1997. Just wouldn't."

When Mallory didn't offer up any further questions or gems of wisdom, Danni decided to cap it. "Got it? Babe?"

Stan had forgotten until this moment that Mallory had worked with Sharon Ollestad, the bitch of IT. Oh shit.

"Yeah, well, this babe," continued Mallory with a frozen smile on her face, "would like to know if it wasn't blood, what the hell was it?"

Danni started to speak, but Mallory wasn't finished.

"I mean did you a run a peroxidase test? A precipitin series? You eliminated both human and animal blood I hope."

Stan turned away.

The two women bore into each other in silent savagery. To Stan's surprise it ended because Danni Harness seemed pressed for time. She slowly shook her head in mock sadness at the younger woman, reached around and turned on the light box and looked at Stan.

Fluorescents snapped to life.

The light box glowed with pictures of the rope. Stan remembered Danni liked to work primarily with backlit negatives. She believed she could see details that a normal positive picture didn't show, no matter how much you blew it up.

Of the six transparencies, two pictures were close ups of the end of the rope where the loop was. Four successive pictures showed closer and closer views of a dark reddish smear near the end of the loop.

Danni picked up a ruler and pointed to the smear. "Not blood. As I said, blood wouldn't last. It's the same paint as the bark."

"The same?" asked Stan. He was tempted to press by asking if she was sure, but thought better of it.

"That's the good, the bad is we don't know what kind; not house paint, not the brittle kind like auto paint, maybe a spray on paint, I don't know. The chromatography and spectroscopy won't be back for a week or so. When we know, you'll know. So, unless you have a guess where it's from, we wait."

"No idea, "said Stan.

"Didn't think you would. Frank and whatshisname here will be working on that. It may help you, may not. One more thing and you can get your asses outta here."

Stan and Mallory moved up shoulder to shoulder next to the light table.

"The rope itself is a very odd choice," continued Danni. She pointed to the picture of the entire rope. "You probably don't know this, no I'm sure you don't, but this is a marine grade line capable of handling about, oh say, 2,000 pounds give or take." Her eyes moved up to Stan. "Odd choice to hold a 60 pound child wouldn't you say?"

She didn't wait for Stan to answer. "Of course it is. Okay, another thing about this wonderful rope that is strong enough to secure any yacht." Danni took her pen and traced the area of the rope that reversed back to form the loop, then moved to the close up of the same area.

"Look at this. See where the end of the rope doubles back on itself and then interweaves in the original so the entire end of the loop is not only hidden in the original length but is now a complete part of the whole rope."

Stan, following the weave of the strands as they meshed together disappearing into what looked like the grey braid of a widow's hair, marveled at the time it must have taken to merge the one into the other.

"How do you do that?" he asked.

She leaned back. "That my friend is called an Immelman weave, a variation of the eye splice, and how it is done, based on a quick check of the internet, is by loosening the weave, about three feet back from the end in this case, while keeping the rest of the strands intact, and then passing the partially unstranded end through and then back through and then through again until it is completely engulfed in the main body of the rope. Then it is slowly tightened so it forms a loop or noose that is three times stronger than the two ropes together."

"Impressive, no?" Again she didn't wait for an answer. Stan knew she wouldn't wait.

"Of course it is. And, you'll never guess where the Immelman loop is used the most and, in fact where it was probably invented was…?"

Mallory brightened. "Boats, ships…by sailors."

Danni acknowledged Mallory with a nod of her head. "Like I said, interesting."

"What about the multiple knots?" asked Stan

"Well, we didn't untie them if that's what you mean. But I agree with your guess. I think whoever used this just knotted the rope to shorten it up. It would be a quick and easy way to do that."

"So where are we?"

"Beats me, Stan. You brought me bark you pried out of some poor tree with what we know is a paint smear on it and a knotted rope with a loop at the end and a smear of the same kind of paint on it. You say it may have been used to hold or hang children but it could've been used to hold a whole classroom full of kids and all this would mean nothing except..."

Stan finished for her. "...for where we found it."

Danni shrugged. "You're the detective. Could be looking for a sailor who likes to paint. Could be looking for a housepainter who owned a long rope. I have no idea. Your job, not mine." And just don't expect this kind of service next time cold case needs somebody to look at their ropes and stuff." She winked.

"Of course not. And it's OID now."

"Yeah, ongoing whatever."   She handed him the folder with her summary and the blow ups.

She tapped the top of the folder with her ruler. "Good luck with that."

CHAPTER 16

M stretched his legs in front of him. He didn't think his aunt would appreciate him sitting on top of her trailer. As a matter of fact he was sure that she would shit her pants if she came home and saw him with his legs dangling over the side above the front door. But she wasn't home and wasn't likely to be for a few hours. She said her bridge group with her card-playing biddies would last until ten o'clock.

Jessie hadn't lasted long. She'd fallen asleep before he'd even finished getting to the wild rumpus part of her favorite book.

Bridge. He assumed it was what unmarried women did at night instead of getting screwed. *I mean, when there was no man around, what does a woman do?*

Fleeting visions of his mother quietly entering her bedroom with her head bowed and his father closing the door behind them as soon as he got home skittered past him until he shook them away.

He shifted position again. The aluminum roof of the trailer made a dull wrump sound as part of it moved up and part flexed down as his weight shifted. It wasn't very sturdy, but it was strong enough to hold him. Hell, it had to at least be able to handle 110 pounds. And he didn't think the noise would wake Jess. He had watched her when she fell asleep. He had watched for almost fifteen minutes without moving. He wanted to make sure she was asleep. Her breaths evened out and her mouth parted slightly and she seemed to be really asleep. It was the first real sleep she'd gotten in the last week, he thought. He wasn't making a sleeping chart, but he could sense her almost every night at the other end of the couch, shifting and pulling at the covers. Sometimes he'd heard her sort of whimpering. Each time, he'd moved his feet a bit to subtly touch hers. He wanted to let her know he was there. That she was okay. They may be in a screwed up situation, but they were together right this moment and she was okay.

She had whispered, "M?" once in the dark a few nights ago.

He hadn't answered right away. He had just wanted her to go to sleep.

But she'd asked again, "M?"

"What?"

"Is that you?"

"Course."

There was a pause and he thought she had fallen back to sleep.

Her next words caught him up short. "Where are we?" she'd asked.

Oh, Jesus. "We're at Aunt Janey's, remember?"

Another pause, then "Oh, yeah."

"Jess?"

"What?"

"You're okay, you know."

Another pause. "Okay."

M needed to say more. He needed to reassure her. He needed to do what his mother used to do. She would come into their room, sit on the edge of his bed, stroke his hair and just say, 'Good night'. Then she'd move to Jess's bed. Even if Jess was asleep, she'd sit, touch Jess's face and tell her, 'Good night'.

"Jess?"

"Yes?"

"Good night, okay?"

"Okay."

The perspective of the park was different from up here. He could see the tops of all the trailers that lined the street leading all the way up to Ruby's trailer at the dead end. There was only one streetlight, a raw, blue-white mercury light that was

unrelenting in its brightness but also caused the blacke.
shadows where it was blocked.

It was easy to imagine people hiding in the shadows, ready to
grab as you walked by. Long ago, when he told his father he was
sort of afraid of the dark sometimes, his father had cuffed him on
the back of his head. "You crazy, boy? Theys nothing but empty
space. You can't be afraid of empty space. Sure, it's black and
all, but hell, boy get a fuckin' grip. Maybe once in your life
some shit will come out of the shadows, but most likely it's
gonna be a possum that you scared or some damn raccoon. Don't
you know boy, people don't hide in shadows. And if they do,
they're hiding from you! Damn."

His father had pulled him around to face him. "Look at me.
You cannot be scared of what ain't there. None of mine should
be scared of anything. Shit, if anything, you gotta worry about
the bad shit you see, not the stuff you can't. Got it?"

M had said he got it. But, what could be worse than bad shit
that you couldn't see? Still, every time the shadow fear rose up
in him, he pushed it back and tried to laugh at it.

Now, from atop the trailer, his eyes darted from one shadow
the next.

"Street of ghosts," he said out loud to himself. "And they
aren't really there."

He took a big inhale. Smells were different up here too. The
warm breeze carried mostly city smells, some wood smoke. But
around the edge, on the periphery, M could sense a sweetish
scent festering. Every now and then he'd turn his head and pick
up a whiff of…something.

There was a funny looking Chinese lady a few trailers down
that he had seen picking dead geraniums out of her flower box.
When he walked by her yesterday she had yelled at him in
Chinese, he supposed. She sounded pissed, but whatever she was
cooking smelled like a rotting garlic's underarm. Worse, she was
always cooking her dead rat or whatever it was in the stinking oil
in the morning. It was enough to make you barf before you even
got hungry.

But, tonight, the only smell was one of old things. Not stinky. Just old. And tired, too. Old and tired. The whole place, this trailer park, his aunt, Ruby, Sacramento reminded him of some weeded over lot behind a busted down old house where the rusted farm machinery served as lawn art. Where the '60 Chevy sat with windows broken, waiting for a new transmission. Where old flower pots were stacked, waiting for some new geraniums. Where a discarded hot tub rested on its side, waiting to be righted and filled. Where nettles and chokeberries grew over and around to remind whoever owned that shit that nothing was ever going to happen with it, so forget about it.

Old stuff.

He had to get out. This place was death. This place was for those who had given up, who could see that the end of their useful lives was a helluva lot closer than their beginnings. Besides Jessie and himself, there were really only two other kids in the whole park, a kinda goofy looking kid with autism whose mother walked him on a leash like a dog, and a 16 year old biker who was only parked here between jail terms.

Last night, when his aunt had been watching TV, he had pretended to be reading a book but he was really searching through his mother's address book he'd taken. He knew somewhere there were relatives in some other state who would take them in. Someone who would recognize that they were basically good kids Especially Jessie. Whoever took them in could overlook his part in the whole nightmare and not hold it against him.

Or at least give him a second chance.

It had to be only a matter of a week or two before his aunt would start the eviction process, turning him and Jessie over to CPS. Then all bets were off.

Out of the shadows, from a trailer halfway down the street came the cat again. It was grey and white and he had seen it yesterday. It didn't appear to belong to anyone, but you never knew. It made the rounds of just about every trailer and it didn't linger at any one in particular. His aunt had given that knowing look when he asked about it. 'Feral', she'd said. 'Wild. Stay away from it.'

M watched as it headed out into the street and stopped with one paw half lifted, looking and listening. M stayed quiet, but then deliberately moved his leg against the side of the trailer. The cat instantly heard the sound and caught the movement. It stayed frozen, watching him. M stayed frozen, hoping to confuse it into thinking it was seeing and hearing things. But, he knew they could see damn well in the dark and it probably had him made easily.

It looked mean and lean. M guessed it would have to be to survive around here because when everything, cars, residents, life moved so slowly it made you complacent. You had to be sharp, on your guard so when that owl came swooping out of the tree or the car came around the corner too fast, you were ready to save at least one of your nine lives. If it stayed sharp, nothing was going to get that cat.

Once the cat realized M wasn't going to fly off the roof and catch it in his horrid talons, it turned and quick-stepped to the chain link fence, slipped through, and became lost in the carnival site, ready to dine on rodents. Maybe even other cats. Kill or be killed. That was his father's motto.

M wanted to give it a name. Everything should have a name. He remembered his father loved to tell the joke about the cat with one eye and three legs and no teeth. He didn't really remember the joke, only the punch line, 'And they called it 'Lucky''.

This morning Jessie had asked him if their father was in heaven. How can someone be funny and a monster? How can someone care enough to take him to a Giants game and the next week belt whip him raw for eating all the potato chips? How can someone cry when he murders his wife?

If you were two different people, one good and one bad, then you could let the good one into heaven and burn the other one. It was impossible, M thought, to be a Christian like his mother and forgive. Shit happens. Shit happened. You can't ignore it. You can't pretend the bad part wasn't there. You just can't ignore it and say I forgive you. You just can't. It can't work that way. You have to burn the bad person and let the good part go to heaven, or wherever it should go.

M had not answered Jessie right away, but she had kept staring. So, he told her the truth as he saw it, 'cause a kid should always know the truth. Maybe not the brutal truth, but at least they should be put on the path to knowing what the hell is going on. That's what older brothers were for he figured.

"No," he'd said. "You won't see him again."

Jess had nodded and lowered her head. She was remembering the good dad. The good part of their father.

M let her have the good memories. He just had the bad stuff roiling in his head. The bad stuff. That was what tomorrow was for. Tomorrow was going to be his first psycho visit. Dr. Avery was his name and psychos apparently were his game.

M let his head fall back and looked at the stars.

He didn't see the cat come racing back across the street with its kill.

And he didn't see the other movement in the darkest shadow either.

CHAPTER 17

M stood in front of the building and hesitated. He hated the pain of going to the dentist and he imagined this would be searingly worse. The only two things he knew about psychologists were they weren't psychiatrists and they never answered your questions. They just kept asking more questions. The thought of wasting time that way left him feeling ill. Well, that shit would have to change.

Besides, what did they want him to say? The court had ordered him to see a psychologist. For what? They said it was for his protection, for his well-being. The judge had sat up there and was perplexed. M could see it. The judge, M saw, felt he should do something, should issue an order. Something. Two people were dead. Must protect the child. Must protect society. Do something.

So, in the end, because two people had been murdered, not just died, but murdered and the lone person left was a minor the judge stepped in as *loco parentis*. Okay, six months seeing a psychologist, court will review the psychologist's report at the end of that time, blah, blah.

Who was crazy? Was anybody crazy? Was everybody crazy?

M judged that he wasn't crazy. Yeah, some bad shit happened, but what the hell, he thought, I'd do it again. Looking back, he knew he'd do it again, but this time maybe he'd shoot the motherfucker in the balls as he was taking a shower. That would fix his pretty red wagon, as his father used to say. That would've solved some serious problems and saved a bloody step or two. And saved a life, too.

Of course, if he was honest he knew what he did was only in a primal defense of his mother. Sure his father was shit, but M knew he couldn't have slipped into his father's bathroom one morning and shot off his nut sack. Who does that without a reason? In cold blood. *That* shit was crazy.

At least now he'd have something with which to grill the psychologist.

The building elevator smelled like fresh cut lemons, as if someone had just finished polishing the wood paneling. M ran his hand across the paneling as he watched himself in the mirror on the elevator's walls. He raised his hand to his face. He used to love that smell. His mother had always kept a clean house.

Avery's office appeared to be on the top floor.

Good thing I'm not paying for this, thought M as he hit the fifth floor button.

The elevator doors opened to a polished marble hallway with big globe lights and more wood paneling, and a thin, tidy man in a brown suit who introduced himself as Dr. Patrick Avery.

"Good, you're here," said Avery before M had even gotten off the elevator. Avery shooed him back onto the elevator, got in with him and pushed the lobby button. He then paused and looked at M. "Uhh, you are Mr...." He searched for M's name. "You are my three o'clock child aren't you? My three o'clock appointment?" He appeared to be only slightly concerned.

"No," said M with childish innocence, "I just came in to use the phone. Where are you taking me? Are you going to kill me? Should I call for help?"

Avery studied M for a moment, then his lips curled up a bit the ends. "A sarcastic asshole, just like your file states. Just wanted to make sure I had the right kid. Apparently, I do."

"Whatever. Where are we going?" asked M.

"Out."

Nothing more was said on the ride to the lobby.

M followed Avery across the lobby, past the building directory and out into the sunshine. Avery was wasting no time, M saw. Wherever we're going, it's probably better than being cooped up in an office, lying on a couch. He didn't know if psychologists made you lie down or if that was just psychiatrists. Maybe he sat you on a chair and they sat behind a desk, just asked question after question and tried to look concerned at some of the answers. M had seen some of that shit on TV.

M was about to ask Avery again where they were going, but Avery at that moment picked up the pace and without glancing back to see if M was following dashed into the crosswalk to make the light. M had to run to keep pace. Even so, the cars had started to go and honked at them both as they waited for them to cross.

M wasn't sure but it looked as if Avery gave the driver closest to them the finger.

After they were across, Avery said over his shoulder, "Keep up."

About mid-block Avery veered into a Starbucks.

'Jesus, he needs caffeine. That's what we're doing. Making a coffee run,' thought M.

"What do you want?" asked Avery without looking at him, and without waiting for an answer placed his own order with the barista. He stepped aside and looked at M as if he'd been waiting minutes for an answer.

M looked not at Avery but at the cute girl behind the counter. He smiled.

"I'll take something sweet."

With no hesitation she asked, "Something with caffeine or not?"

"Yeah. Of course."

"Hot or cold?"

"Cold."

"Big or small?"

He pointed his thumb at Avery, "If he's paying make it the biggest you've got."

"Done." She banged the computer register. "$11.25."

"Wait!" said M. He reached over and grabbed two peanut butter cookies. "These too."

Avery looked at him and brought out more money.

M put the cookies in his jacket pocket and zipped it up. Jess loved peanut butter cookies.

He followed Avery out of the cafe and they both jaywalked across the intersection until they got to South Point Park, at least that's what the sign said. It looked nice to M. Concrete paths led like a spider web into a circular pathway surrounding a fountain that seemed to be having a bit of trouble. It streamed upward in fits and starts, rising up six feet then falling back and dribbling over the concrete edge, then spurting back up three feet, then falling back to the dribble mode.

Still, to M, the fountain, the park, the trees, the pathways looked nice. Better than a couch.

Avery watched M survey the park.

"Pretty place, huh?"

M shrugged.

"Better than inside, right?"

"So, why aren't we in your office? You embarrassed?"

Avery looked around for a place to sit and started toward a bench.

"Well, adults when they come to see a psychologist expect to be in an office, I guess to make it official they're seeing a doctor. Kids...young adults don't really know what to expect, so why not come out here. Get some coffee and enjoy the sun, you know."

M moved over to the bench, wiped off some bird shit and sat down. The air was cool but the bench was in the sun. It was the combination he liked. Positive and negative. He closed his eyes and felt the breeze.

"You look like you've never been in a park before. They do have parks in San Francisco?"

"Yeah," said M. Of course they were mostly concrete with other decorative touches of concrete. "It's a big goddamn city."

"I've heard of it."

Avery stretched and looked around at the park. "So, you crazy or what?"

M opened his eyes. 'Here we go,' he thought. But he said nothing.

Avery continued. "Crazy by somebody's definition means that your personal reality has broken with everyone else's reality. It doesn't mean necessarily that your reality is wrong, just that you're not on the same page as the rest of the sane world. So, *have* you broken with reality?"

M turned his head and looked up at Avery who was still standing next to the bench.

"Any craziness I should know about?"

"Recently?"

Avery gave a soft laugh and turned away from M.

He sat down on the bench and sipped his latte.

"I've read your file. I've read the official version of what happened. I'm sorry. Sorry for you, what you went through. Sorry for you and your sister. Your whole family...the whole...situation. How's the arm?"

M tried hard not to listen but instead watched the ebb and flow of the fountain and the few kids that stood next to it, fascinated with its unpredictableness. He flexed his arm above his head and felt the sharp twinge that struck these days when he raised it too high but twisted it around anyway. "I'm pitching tomorrow for the Giants."

"Good luck. Anyway, I'm going to write in my report that you're not crazy. Just so you know..."

"Gee, thanks."

Avery shifted. "I'm going to report that everything with you is normal. Well, at least not abnormal."

"How nice."

"Now, since you're in the clear as far as the bullshit court ordered psycho report is concerned, we still have to meet and all." He laughed. "I mean I have to bill them for my time and everything, but, like, if there are any movies you want to see or places you want to go..."

"What?"

"...or if you want to talk, or anything. Basically, what I'm saying is that my report contents are already written, or at least outlined, and I don't believe you're crazy and I don't believe you're going to harm anyone else or take a leak on them. You did what you had to do."

M turned away and lowered his arm into his lap.

Avery continued. "I believe us meeting for however many weeks we are supposed to meet may be a colossal waste of time. Yours and mine. So...you're how old?"

"Thirteen."

"Thirteen. Okay, look...One of the things I do have to check for is clinical depression."

"Yeah? And how do you that. Take my temperature? Or do I have to take a bunch of tests with inkblots and shit?"

"Not really." Avery paused, thinking. "I could give you a bunch of tests or basically I could just ask you if you're depressed. Sad. Well, not just sad. Of course you're sad, but if that sadness is affecting what you do every day."

M was silent.

"Well. Is it?"

M felt tightness in his chest. No one had asked him directly about what happened and especially how he felt about it. How he was feeling. They either were afraid of the answer or really didn't want to know. Most who asked him how he was didn't really give a shit, M knew. Most thought him borderline nuts. If not nuts before, then probably headed to nuts town after what happened. This guy was being paid to want to know. Nice.

M shrugged. "Fine, I guess."

Avery stretched his legs out. "Fine, huh? So, I collect coins, mostly nickels and quarters and that's how we rate the condition of the coins, by the degree of 'fineness'. Some of mine haven't really been handled much at all and they are super fine, then there is extra fine, you know, kept in a drawer or wrapped in plastic, then there is regular fine, sort of rattled around in a pocket for a while, then less than sort of fine, some of the details worn off, then not at all fine, when more details and the edges have been worn down. After that, well they get into the good and fair categories..."

He turned to M and took a sip. "When you say you're 'fine', which fine do you mean?"

"Dunno."

"Would you say you're closer to good then fine? Or are you down in the dreaded fair category."

"Dunno. Good, I guess. Whatever."

Avery leaned forward and pulled some sunglasses from his pocket and slipped them on. He put his elbows on his knees and kept staring at the fountain and the activity around it.

"One of the things missing from the report was what your family life was like before. How would you describe it?"

M laughed without thinking. The question was so absurd.

"You laugh?"

"Well, what do you think? It's a stupid question."

"So, humor me, and tell me how you would describe it in ten words or less."

M got up. "This is stupid. What do you think? It was…" M tried to think of a way to describe it.

Finally, "It was a quiet house."

"Quiet?"

"Quiet, okay? We were afraid to breathe, okay?"

"We? You mean you and your sister?"

M didn't answer.

"Or did you mean you and your Mom?"

M felt the tightness in his chest again. His eyes started to water. He moved over to the trash can and tossed in his untouched drink. It was still tough to breathe and he kept his face averted from Avery. If he saw him crying that would just get the good doc to ask more questions. More shit.

"I gotta get back," he said to Avery, keeping his voice as level as he could. He started back up the path, wiping his eyes as subtly as he could. For some reason he thought about Jessie being back at the trailer park without him.

M didn't look back but felt Avery following him. They both stopped at the light.

M felt Avery's hand on his shoulder. He continued to look straight ahead. Now what?

"I think your mother would be proud of how you're taking care of your sister. I'll see you next week, same time. In the park."

M's breath hitched up tight. He hoped his mother would be proud.

His eyes brimmed over as saw Avery walking down the block leaving M standing alone at the corner. He watched him until he turned the corner and was gone.

No chance to ask Avery about the sick shit people who kill other people in cold blood.

Next time.

CHAPTER 18

"You sick?"

Mallory had her eyes shut and her head resting on her arms when Stan breezed into their office. She had heard him as soon as he came through the outer door whistling the theme from Star Wars.

"What's wrong with you?" he asked cheerfully.

She raised one hand to stop him from saying anything else and tried not to lose her still nebulous idea of how she would connect other missing kids to the Olive Park victims. But thanks to Stan, it was an idea now floating away. Staring at the back end of a retreating train and trying to remember what the engine looked like. Further and further away. Something important, she just couldn't catch it.

"Shit." She sighed and raised her head. "Since when do you whistle?"

Stan stopped midway from removing his jacket.

"Luke, I am your father!"

Mallory rolled her eyes.

"You looked sick. Or something."

"It's or something. It's called thinking." She lowered her head back to where it was.

"Ah, you continue to impress."

Mallory shook her head and gave up. It was no use right now.

"I just hope you were thinking about whatever galaxy we're moving on to next."

"What do you mean?"

Stan tapped his watch and moved over to the picture board. "Three days and we move on to some other case."

He started to grab the pictures from the wall and toss them onto the conference table.

Mallory bolted from the table and gathered the pictures he had removed.

"What the hell are you doing?" She began replacing them back on the board, straightening them as she went.

"What am I doing? What are you doing? What *I'm* doing is getting ready for the next case."

Mallory ignored him. "I can't believe it!" She continued to replace the pictures.

Finally she said, "We're not done yet. You said a few weeks. We've had two weeks minus three days and we've made progress."

"Jack shit progress." Stan settled back against the table edge. It was his fatherly pose.

"Everything we found just confirmed the facts we already knew. No DNA, no fingerprints on tree bark. Your missing kids' thing hasn't panned out; at least I haven't heard anything more from you. I've reviewed all thirteen boxes at least twice and I'm sure I could recite parts of the murder book like the Gettysburg Address, I know it by heart.

Stan turned away. "I actually contacted Carruthers and that wasn't pleasant. You'd of thought I'd stabbed him in the eye or something, just by asking him if he remembered a few details. No, we're done."

Mallory finished with the pictures and turned to face him.

He ticked off the points.

"Look, we determined Joey at least was strung up and knocked on the head while he was upside down. Probably the others as well.

"Second, in a case of looking where others didn't," he inclined his head to Mallory, "I give you that one. That was good. You found a rope in a tree at the burial site. Which, if you think about it was no real surprise. We had figured the victims were upside down, there had to be a rope somewhere. If not at the site, then somewhere else. So, we found it, but, where has it gotten us? It's been in the weather for years."

"Third, we found some information about the rope; marine grade you can buy in any of 4000 stores."

"Fourth, Forensics found some paint, which they still haven't identified and may never…"

"Yeah," interrupted Mallory, appearing ready to tear up. "Isn't all that progress? That's what you said you wanted."

Stan sighed. Oh, for a real investigator. At least Jake would be back on limited duty tomorrow, and then they could move on.

"Mallory," he softened more than he wanted to, "We gave it a shot."

Mallory shook head. "Do you ever get laid?"

Stan's eyes widened in surprise.

"Yeah, well, I thought not." She moved back to her seat opposite Stan and sat down.

"Do us all a favor and get some, or drink yourself silly, or go crazy and watch the Star Wars septology, or whatever it is. Anything, Jesus. Just lose the negative vibe, okay? I honestly don't know how Steiner stood you all these years."

She tapped her pencil against her head. It made a hollow noise. "Unless, of course, he's as bad as you are…or worse," she muttered to herself. "God, he could be worse."

"You can judge for yourself, he'll be here tomorrow."

"Here? He'll be here? He's out of the psycho ward early?"

Stan studied his phone. "He's healing, I guess. Plus, there was an issue with a nurse, plus he doesn't want to be left out of anything…"

"What do you mean an issue with a nurse?"

Stan looked up. "It's just Jake." He held out his upraised palms and pretended to try and level them. "Nurse. Jake. Nurse. Jake. You know."

Mallory rolled her eyes and sat back. "Jesus, God, he *is* worse. I can't wait."

"And I think he wants to meet on this case evidence…"

"He wants to meet about the case?" Mallory slid into her chair and started rearranging papers at random. "See? See? He wants to get to work on this case."

Stan shrugged. "I got a text. I think he just wants to see where we are, see what we didn't achieve before we bury this thing."

"Hah!" Mallory began tapping her feet together under the table. "Maybe he's not so bad. He wants to review the evidence..."

She pointed a finger at him. "Okay, so we get an extra week, now that he's here and gonna be working it with us. He needs at least a week to get up to speed."

"You'll be amazed at how fast he is. How fast he can kick this case into the shitter. And no extra week."

"Stan...!"

"Finit. Kaput. Over. Baked. We looked, we saw, we went away. Simple as that."

She held up her hand. "Let's wait till tomorrow. Better yet, wait until Detective Steiner reviews everything. Let him see what progress we've made. I'll work tonight, all night if I have to on the missing kid angle. I'll go through the boxes one more time, okay?"

Stan opened his mouth, but in the end realized he *was* curious to see what Jake would have to say. Yes, they had chiseled a small chunk out of the marble block of Olive Park, but that was all. He feared, and all his years of experience were telling him, that this case was a ball buster. Stan was determined that his career would not be defined by his failure to solve this one case.

He looked at Mallory. She was like a nervous dog that needed to be walked. Could hardly sit still.

"Okay. Two days," he said at last

.

CHAPTER 19

Mallory looked at her watch and realized Stan had left hours ago. That was the problem with this office. When the sun streamed in the clerestory you knew it was midday, but round about dinnertime, without windows, it was damn tough to tell what time it was. She started pacing back and forth between her desk and Stan's.

Stan. Damn. Mallory knew they couldn't quit this case. She wouldn't let them. Although she hated to admit it, their chances of finally figuring out who did this was probably very remote. Screw it, she committed them and they weren't quitting.

Only shit, she'd never felt this much pressure. She thought working for that bitch Ollestad was bad. Holy hell.

Stan was right, Mallory knew, Handleman had derailed the investigation. When that line went sour, when Handleman proved that he wasn't the bad guy, or rather Carruthers and Thompson reluctantly came to that conclusion, it was like the rabbit punch to the gut of the case. No one could really go back and pick up the pieces. Oh, they tried, Mallory knew. But really, Carruthers and Thompson spent half their time trying to figure out how they had screwed up the case or how Handleman had gotten away with it. It was tough to wrap your brain around the fact that you had driven your car down a dead end and now you had to back up, find another road. Worse when you realized that not just you, but a whole bunch of smart people, had all gotten lost with you.

Mallory could just see Carruthers picking up a file on this and start to study it for the twentieth time. Then without warning he would start to wonder how Willy had cleaned his car or his house so there was no evidence of any crime. The case was picked up in fits and starts, mostly fits.

She didn't want to think about Handleman. She didn't want to remember how everyone believed he was the one. Or how everyone truly in the heart believed he had gotten away with it, until he was forced over the guardrail into a 300 feet swan dive.

Mallory also knew Stan was damn correct when he talked about fresh eyes. He was talking about her, he said, but she suspected he was also talking about himself. And Steiner too. Time away from a case had a way of re-prioritizing the facts. What was assumed or not really pursued, often stuck out like a thorn.

She realized now she was pacing around the cubicle and had been for about ten minutes. Her watch read 11:35. It had been dark for three hours and she remembered she'd eaten lunch but couldn't really recall what she'd eaten and now she thought she must be hungry. Instead, she began to rework what the three Olive Park victims had been doing when they disappeared.

She stopped in front of the three pictures of Joey, Karen and Phillip.

What are they? They're kids.

She looked at Karen's picture. "What happened to you?"

Mallory thought back to the interview with Karen's parents. She'd read it three times.

"Okay, okay. First, you were playing. You were going to spend the night at your friend's house, Jane or Jan's house, whatever. But you never got there. Somewhere along the way..."

She looked up. "Then you were declared missing. Before you were dead, you were declared missing."

Missing. Missing kids again. She slid across the conference table to end up in front of her laptop, pulled it to her and studied the list for the hundredth time.

Months ago she had run the databases from 1995 to 2000. Had culled it down, weeding out the ones who had been found, who had been faking, who had run away with their girlfriend or their boyfriend, or had escaped to a relative for a few days.

She was staring at what was left. The ones who had disappeared and were never found, who never came back. Five years' worth of unsolved missings, ages 9 to 12, all from central California.

Yeah, yeah, some escaped to a different coast and were just fine, living as housewives in New Jersey, some were below the radar and were homeless or had somehow reinvented themselves. They were fine. Still listed as missing, but not lying in a shallow grave somewhere.

Mallory figured. Okay. 37 missing then minus the ones that we can't find but are still fine. So maybe half left. Eighteen families waking each day with the word 'Missing' prominent in their lives. It was the same 18 she had brought with her when she came to OID.

She got up and started pacing again.

"Missing. Not found." An idea was tapping around the edge of her brain trying to gain entry. Mallory stopped pacing and stood holding her breath. She wanted the thought to reveal itself before something happened, before the phone rang, before her mind wandered to what she was going to eat for dinner.

She jerked her head up. We need to compare the similarities in how they came to be *missing*, not their deaths. We work backwards. They all had to be missing first, right?

Mallory was shaking when she sat down at the laptop. Give me a bigger base to work from any day and then work backwards!

She looked at the evidence boxes stacked at the end of the table. That's what we know. Our three were missing and they were killed.

The names staring back at her from the computer never had their stack of evidence boxes because they'd never been found. Normally, there'd be no reason to connect them to Olive Park's three victims, but 'being missing' was the key, she was sure of it. If we could find out what all these missing were doing before they went missing, there might be a pattern that would include Joey and Karen and Phillip.

Mallory checked the clock. It was near midnight. She could do a lot before she met with Stan and Jake tomorrow. She could access many of the missing case files online. Many of the summary sheets and some of the transcripts of interviews of parents and friends had been scanned and put into SPD's database. Details that weren't easily available meant a trip downtown to pull the physical files.

She opened the small refrigerator that she'd brought with her when they moved in. She had stocked it with a few good Chardonnays. She pulled a 2007 from Raymond Burr Winery. How appropriate, she thought. Good ol' Perry Mason is going to help me tonight.

Mallory was holding up her glass admiring the color when the echo of footsteps from somewhere in the building became clear. She froze and tried to be still. Tried to hear what she thought she heard.

In the middle of this stupid glass office she knew she was lit up like a mannequin in a store window. The only lights on anywhere in the whole building were the long lights over the conference table. The rest had been shut off when the construction workers left. Even the outside entry light was off. Some kid had busted it out days ago. Whoever was in here could see everything she was doing.

She set her glass down.

"Hello?" Her voice sounded weak and desperate.

Her Mace was in her car she remembered as she scanned her desk for some sort of weapon. Nothing. Then Stan's. Nothing but office supplies. Immobilize him with a stapler. Right.

Screw it. Whoever was in the building must have had a key, unless of course they broke in. There was no janitor service yet, she knew. Damn!

She went to the opening to the glass office peered into the gloom and yelled, "Who the hell is there?"

The footsteps stopped. Then started up slowly. The gait was quirky she noticed, as if someone was carrying something heavy and was walking lopsided.

"Stan? Don't screw around, okay?"

She pulled out her cell phone.

From the darkness came a slightly mocking voice. "I don't think you'll need the phone little lady unless you're calling for pizza or some exotic form of takeout for me, I'm starved."

Out of the gloom limped a tall, well-built man with sandy hair and almost a full leg cast. He was on crutches and didn't look too happy about it.

"Who...?" Then Mallory knew.

He just stood there, wavering a bit on his crutches. She couldn't tell anything about his demeanor, but damn, she loved his eyes.

"Jake right? You're Detective Steiner I hope." Mallory slipped the phone back in her pocket. She held out her hand. "It's good to meet you."

Detective Jake Steiner hesitated then shook her hand and moved past her into the office. He went immediately to the first chair he saw and sat down, angling his cast out in front of him. He let the crutches fall to the floor and looked around at all the glass walls showing multiple reflections of everything in the office. Then he titled his head back and looked up into the three story gloom above him. "Some fishbowl."

"You were supposed to be here tomorrow."

Without moving his head, Jake brought his arm up to his face and stared at his watch. "It is tomorrow. What's there to eat?"

"Nice to meet you too," muttered Mallory. Then, "I have wine and cheese and crackers."

Jake raised his head and stared at her as if she was from outer space.

"Uh...I think Stan has some scotch."

Jake waved a hand, meaning 'yes' she guessed. He didn't appear ready to get up and get it so she went to Stan's desk, knelt down to the bottom drawer and pulled out the bottle. She knew it was not her imagination when she felt his eyes all over her as she made her way across the room. She knew her ass always looked good in her favorite jeans.

Let him watch what he can't have.

She found a Styrofoam cup and poured him a healthy slug. "Did you want me to fix you a sidecar or stinger or some scotch aperitif?" she asked as she handed him the cup.

He took a sip. "Stan said you were a sarcastic bitch."

"He did not! And I'm not."

Again, Jake gave a little wave which she took to mean he was kidding.

Mallory watched him drink his scotch.

"How'd you get in, anyway?"

He stared at her over the cup, and then smiled. "I picked the lock."

She noticed he had great blue eyes but his face had lost most of its color. At least she hoped he didn't always look so pasty. A week under the fluorescents plus having your leg beat to shit probably didn't help. The burn under his right eye seemed to be healing nicely though.

"What are you doing here? I mean now. This time of night."

Jake set the cup down and avoided her stare. "They kicked me out." He shrugged. "Anyway, it was time for me to leave. Nothing more they could do that they hadn't already done."

He shook out a cigarette and let it hang from his lips as he looked at her.

"That's attractive and there's no smoking in the building."

"Got a light?"

"No smoking."

"Who's going to tell?"

"No one, 'cause there's no smoking. I don't have a light and you're not lighting it anyway." She moved to her desk and poured a little more wine.

He patted his coat where the pockets were and when he didn't find any match tossed the cigarette on the conference table.

Mallory walked over and picked it up, broke it in half and tossed it in the wastebasket. "We work here, you know."

Jake was silent for a while and just watched her through narrowed eyes. She couldn't tell if he was really pissed or about to go to sleep.

Finally, he stirred. "I'm here aren't I? Let's get to work. Show me why you've kept Stan looking for a child killer from fifteen years ago when nobody else, not the entire Sacramento police department which has spent untold man-hours and taken a shitload of grief on this godforsaken case, cares a rat's ass. Explain to me why we should waste our time further on this hobby and not get back to real police work working on cases where we have a chance of finding who the hell did it."

"Now?"

He moved closer to the conference table and waved at her again. "Hell girl, just give me what you're working on." Then he waited until she gathered up the sheaf of printouts she'd been studying with the list of missing kids and the map of where they were from.

"Well, first I think you need to see the map…"

Somewhere around 2:30 she fell asleep, her head on the conference table.

CHAPTER 20

This was a fussy looking black woman, and not the same CPS woman who M had overheard with his aunt before. She sat at his aunt's small coffee table with an array of notebooks and a black leather briefcase full of file folders on the floor before her. She looked tired.

"I've been going since eight this morning. They keep piling on the cases for me and I just don't know how I'm to get through them all."

To M it sounded prepared, another fakey speech. A speech someone would give when they needed an excuse for not being prepared. He'd used the same thing, at least a variation of the 'tired' theme in school a number of times. It works if you can act.

Martha Simpson from CPS was good. She had a good act for a civil servant. She almost seemed genuinely tired.

As M and Jessie sat on the couch watching Martha search through folder after folder, Aunt Janey kept pacing around the trailer like a fly looking for an escape. She'd glance at Martha Simpson, then shoot a beseeching smile at M, then look away and part the curtains and stare out of the window.

Jessie was just on the verge of being bored and had no idea who Martha Simpson was and what power she held over their futures.

M knew, but was careful to not let on.

The whistle on the teapot started its scream and his aunt quickstepped to the range and pulled it off the burner. She poured the hot water into the cup with the tea bag, and then took it to Martha Simpson who gave a half-thanks-I'm-too-tired smile.

"M," whispered Jessie. "Let's go."

"In a minute."

Martha seemed to be settling down. The preliminaries were out of the way. She had secured his aunt's permission to enter the premises as was required by law as she reminded them all as she stood in the doorway. She had shown them her ID but no one really inspected it. Since she had set up the appointment with his aunt last week, it was just a formality. As was asking to be able to speak to M and Jessie.

"Mrs..." Martha slipped on some reading glasses and consulted her notes. "I'm sorry, Miss Cooper, I need your permission to speak to your children..."

"Not mine," interrupted Aunt Janey. "They're not my kids. They're my dead brother's kids," she said, as if that explained why she was saddled with these two kids. "That should be in the file."

"Oh." Martha flipped a few pages in her file. "Did I know that? Let's see." She took a minute to catch up on the latest in M and Jessie's saga, then, "Of course. Yes. I remember." She turned to M and Jessie and pulled out what look to be a six or seven page questionnaire. "Don't worry you two, we'll get you all squared away. I'm so sorry and all."

"And you can talk to 'em all you want." Aunt Janey resumed her place by the window.

Martha scanned the questionnaire as if she were seeing it for the first time or it was written in Swahili. She took out a pen and clicked it open and closed while she scanned the form.

"I don't...oh, yes, the court ordered this interview." She peered over her glasses at M and then Jessie. "Well, you two appear to be in fine shape, I must say. No, uh, problems of any kind are there?"

"Seriously?" asked M.

Martha Simpson's eyebrows raised in surprise.

"M!" warned his aunt

M turned to Jessie. "Why don't you take Mr. Bear outside, okay?"

"Okay." Jessie nodded, slipped off the couch and made her way to the door, but stopped when both Martha and Aunt Janey said, "Wait."

Jessie looked at M. He smiled. "It's okay. Really. I'll be right out. You can go."

Neither woman said anything as Jessie went out. Martha shifted uncomfortably in her chair and muttered, "I'm sure under the circumstances we won't need to speak with her."

"No. I don't think you will," said M.

He had said it with so much confidence that both women looked at him.

A few days ago when Aunt Janey had informed him that he was required to be present when the CPS worker arrived, he had sat in the dark atop his aunt's trailer, weighed his options and formulated a plan.

He wasn't normally big on pre-planning. That had never been a trait that was instilled in the Cooper household. It was more Darwinish, the fittest survive. You were so busy dealing with the daily shit that floated to the surface that it was a joke to try and plan a tomorrow. Spinning plates on sticks need constant attention. There can be no thought to starting more plates spinning. Until now.

If someone is going to try and fuck you over, it's best to get in the first lick. Advice from his father that never worked out well for his father. M guessed it was how you did it, though. He reached behind the couch and grabbed some papers. He held them over the coffee table and tamped them straight.

"When I heard you were coming, I downloaded your questionnaire at the library and filled it out. It's all done."

"What?" was all Martha Simpson could manage.

M took the top sheet off, glanced at it, handed it to Martha. "I understand that normally it would be my aunt who had to fill these out, but she works full time and she knows nothing about us. Nothing that's relevant to your forms, anyway."

"Here's section A. You'll notice we have no special needs or behavior or drug problems. Education is all filled out. I went ahead and filled in our immunization records too just cause I didn't see anywhere else to put them."

Aunt Janey sat down hard in the nearest chair.

"The section of parental involvement is obviously left blank."

Martha Simpson started to review the page M had handed her when M continued.

"All the other sections are filled out, family history, birth records, all that. I would like to say that I am currently seeing a psychologist because everyone, I guess, wanted to make sure I didn't get a post traumatic thing going on, which I don't."

M gave Martha Simpson from CPS an understanding nod. "My aunt can explain why there is no parental involvement here. How her brother, my father, came to kill my mother."

M heard his aunt stiffen up.

"The only part I didn't fill out is the financial section. My aunt will do that, of course. But I know we are a burden to her, no matter what she says." He smiled at his aunt then transferred it to Martha Simpson. He could be as fakey as anyone else.

"I'll let you two talk." He stood up and went to the door. "But, take a look at the part in Section C, that section where you have to write about long-term placement goals. I circled it so you couldn't miss it."

He smiled again. "I just want you to know that wherever Jessie and I go, whoever we are with in the future, we will not be separated."

He opened the door and left.

In the silence that followed both women could hear M laugh as he called to his sister.

Empowered. Yeah.

CHAPTER 21

It was just after nine. Stan had called them to be there for the review at nine. He'd given Jake two days back to review what they had and what they didn't have. Time to hear what he had to say.

Jake had hobbled in a few minutes ago not looking like he'd had his full eight hours. More like two. Stan knew the cast was slowing down Jake's enjoyment of his regular nighttime routines. It was difficult with ten pounds of plastic and metal strapped to his leg. The doctors had wanted him to exercise it. Walk on it, not rest idly in bed. They didn't know Jake. He was never idle in bed.

Mallory was close behind carrying a tray of three lattes and what looked like a small rattan basket full of homemade blueberry muffins nestled on a blue and white checked cloth. Stan could smell they were still warm.

Stan pulled at his belt. Shit.

He waited until they settled down and Mallory had distributed the coffee. Jake had grunted his thanks and was cradling it like the last thing he would ever drink.

"Muffins," said Stan to Jake. Jake waved a hand.

Stan watched in fascination as Mallory continued to put out little paper plates with pats of butter and plastic knives. She took pains to select a muffin for each plate. She slid one to Stan, pulled one up to her place at the conference table and reached far over to get one closer to Jake. He didn't move to pull it closer.

We're getting soft, thought Stan. Downtown, in the old days at Division a case review would have been five or six detectives, all men, slopped onto desks or draped on chairs, looking with regret at the paper cups filled with stomach-eating acid coffee, semi warm.

"Okay, let's get started." He looked at Mallory. "This is a case review…"

"I know what they are."

"The way Jake and I do them is start with a summary and then since we've all been working on different stuff, we add details or ideas as I go through the summary. Got it?"

"Right, chief." Mallory was busy with her muffins.

Jake's eyes were closed.

Stan didn't need any notes. "1997, the bodies of three children were discovered just on the edge of Sacramento, off on Highway 50. Phillip Boyd, age 9, Joey Marshall, age 9, Karen Summering, age 11. Phillip's hometown was Reedly, Karen's, Lamont, and Joey, Placerville. All California. They were tortured before they were buried. It was unclear whether Phillip was still alive when buried; Karen and Joey were most certainty buried alive as an additional measure of torture."

"From what Forensics has told us they were killed a year apart, or at least separated by a number of months. They were found in graves that were arranged in a row.

"Initially, Carruthers and Thompson's best scenario was that the clearing was used as a convenient burial site. Since we've found the rope, we know it was probably the torture site as well. Most everything that happened to our three victims appeared to have happened in that clearing."

"Oddly lucky," mumbled Jake.

Stan and Mallory looked at him.

"How so?" asked Stan.

Jake roused himself, pulling up in his chair. "Been thinking. This Handleman guy stops for just a minute to take a shit or whatever. Highway patrol is there. Handleman's only there for a minute when he's spotted. Granted it was by some chippy whose job it was to check stuff like abandoned cars, but now you're saying that our sick fuck not only had the time to bury them, he also had time to torture them and this without a single witness coming forward with all that publicity. No one came forward to say they saw any kind of vehicle stopped in that pull off at any time."

He looked at Stan. "That's damn lucky if you ask me."

"I don't know," said Mallory. "What about a vehicle someone wouldn't give a second glance to if it were stopped there; highway patrol, a maintenance vehicle, something like that."

Jake rested his head on the back of his chair. "Doesn't work for me. Sorry."

Stan and Mallory were silent, lost in thought.

Jake started up again. "Look, you guys found out, figured out that at least this Joey was upside down, and then you find the rope out there, probably the rope from which he was dangling, right? This torture dangling and torture burial thing, whatever it was, was exactly what the killer was there for. He wasn't going to be rushed. And if he's not rushed, why not? What gave him the confidence that nobody would interrupt him? Just doesn't fly time-wise."

No one said anything.

Jake waved again. "Sorry, go on. What injuries were there again?"

Stan picked up the summary sheet again.

"Forensics found damage to the back of their heads in some form or other on all three. They couldn't determine precise cause of death. It was either the head blow or more likely they suffocated in their graves."

"It was thought that the perp watched at least two of the victims try and struggle their way out from under the dirt. The two that got close, who got an arm out, got their arms burned for their attempts. Flesh was pretty much gone."

Mallory pushed the last of her muffin away from her and cradled her coffee. "I once watched a kid in my neighborhood continually pour wet sand on a big beetle. It would struggle out from under the load, almost escape, then he'd add more sand, over and over."

"The beetle make it?" asked Jake, ruefully.

Mallory looked at him. "Not the point. Thing is, the little shit kept it up for an hour. Would've kept going if I hadn't put the thing out of its misery."

"Great," murmured Jake. "Sounds like our guy."

"My point is, I agree with you about the time. All this had to take some time."

"Moving on," said Stan. "The rope is a marine type rope, used, among other things to moor larger boats. It has a loop at the free end. The paint smears found on both the bark and the rope are from the same paint but Forensics seems in no hurry now to identify it."

Stan glanced at the glass walls that had everything they knew about the case. The three pictures of the victims in happier times stared back at him.

"Okay, we've all been working on different stuff. Before I get into what I've been thinking, Mallory what about your map?"

She shoved her muffin aside, reached into her bag, and pulled out three copies of a map. It was done in color and showed California. She pulled them out of the clips and slid one copy to each of them.

"What I did, well, we'd been talking about victim's similarities…"

"Summary, please," said Jake with his eyes still closed.

Mallory ignored him. "…and I got to thinking, these three were reported missing before they were murdered. Maybe there are others that have been reported as missing too and murdered but they were never found. So, okay, okay, what if they were also victims of whoever this is, right?"

Jake interrupted again. "But, the other night you couldn't show me evidence of other victims."

Mallory nodded. "I know that, I know, but these three victims had almost nothing in common, except their ages. What if there was a pattern of missing kids that fit with these three. With more kids, a bigger database, we might be able to discover a pattern or at least a parallel between them all."

Jake was silent.

Mallory righted her copy of the map in front to her and continued. "So, what I did was to go through every missing case for the last ten years in central California and used only their ages as similarities. They were all over the map as you can see with the faded out stars. Then I filtered out the runaways, the ones that had been reported missing and eventually returned, shit that took a long time. Anyway, after all that, well, I did find a very interesting pattern. And our three victims fall right into the middle of it."

Jake opened his eyes and Stan pulled his copy of the map to him.

"You didn't have any pattern the other night when you showed this to me," said Jake, now picking up his copy of the map.

The map was enlarged so only the central portion of California was shown. The map was covered with light blue stars representing all reports of missing kids.

"What other night?" asked Stan. No one answered him.

"Yeah, well, I wasn't done."

She watched the two men study the map. "You see?" she asked.

Mallory had marked the three victims with bright red stars. The rest of the reported missing kids, excluding the runaways, were marked as dark green stars. It was immediately clear to Stan what Mallory had found.

"You see? They all, all of them, except two or three which were probably returned runaways that I missed, all happened mostly along either route 50 or 99."

The three of them absorbed the information on the map.

Mallory started again. "Similarities, you wanted. Okay." She used her fingers to tick them off.

"First, small towns or suburbs. All less than 12,000. One thing I haven't finished, yet," added Mallory, "is their exact locations in each town, but the ones I have looked at, most were from a suburban area, not from the downtown core or not from some farm out in the boondocks."

"Second, semi-main roads. Well, not the freeway."

"Third, ages. All between 7 and 12."

"Fourth. Summer or early Fall."

"Okay, four for sure and as you pointed out Stan, given the fact that two of them had jackets or sweaters on when they were found, most likely..." she held up a fifth finger, "most likely...evening."

Mallory looked back and forth to the two detectives while she took another bite of muffin. "Well?"

Stan was lost in thought and idly cut his muffin into four pieces and started to butter them. Stopped when he realized what he was doing.

"There's one other thing..." Mallory hesitated.

Stan knew Jake was thinking the same thing he was. Same thing Carruthers and Thompson had explored years ago. Long or medium haul truckers trolling for kids along their route. Except it didn't make sense, especially on route 50. Truckers avoided the curvy, irregular road and would only use it to and from Nevada if the I-80 was really gummed up. Still, it was eerie to see the line of dark green stars lining the two highways.

Jake set down his coffee and before he took a big bite of his muffin asked, "What about dates?"

Mallory looked at him. "That's the other thing that's weird. If you look at the small numbers on the stars."

Stan took out his reading glasses.

"The numbers are the dates they were reported missing. The dates and locations leapfrog. Look at the stars that say 2002 on route 99, for example. You've got a Lamont, south of Bakersfield and a Reedly south of Fresno. Then in '03, outside Tulare and Atwater. If there is a date and location pattern, it's that they are never close together in the same year."

Stan continued. "On route 50, you have Joey Marshall in Placerville in '96 and some kid named Severin from near Carson City, in 2000."

"Joey and Severin. Joey, we know what happened to him." Stan looked up. "Where is Severin?"

Jake, always the voice of reason, said "We're getting ahead of ourselves, aren't we?"

Mallory leaned back with her coffee, brought her tennis shoes to the edge of the table and started tapping the toes together. "Probably. I just thought it was interesting, that's all. You figure that some of these missing kids are still alive, maybe parent abduction, or whatever, but some are not. And if not, then this is an interesting pattern."

Jake shrugged.

Stan wrote some notes in his notebook while he spoke, "Mallory would you continue on with this, starting with the exact addresses and anything else you can find out about the missing ones on your map?"

"Sure," she said, but Jake interrupted. "I'll do it."

Both Mallory and Stan looked at him.

"Hah!" snorted Mallory.

Jake gracefully lowered his casted leg to the floor. "Look, I'm not going anywhere fast for a while. I can run the computer while she…runs errands or goes for coffee."

Mallory scoffed. "Run the computer? Run the computer, what, like it's a chainsaw? Right."

Jake looked at Mallory. "I can get close; you can teach me how to get closer." Then he smiled.

She shook her head but said nothing else.

Stan felt like the referee. "Sounds like a good plan. Spend an hour or so today with Mr. Wizard there and make sure he doesn't crash the city's computers, okay?"

Mallory gave a Steiner type wave.

"Good. Now…" Stan paused. He wasn't sure how to go on. He wasn't sure he wanted to reveal what he'd been thinking. It was either ridiculous or it was damn important. He just didn't know which. He just knew it was an angle that they hadn't pursued. And neither had Carruthers and Thompson. If he was right, the whole initial investigation had never explored the possibility.

"We done here?" asked Jake.

"No, not yet. I have… I have one other thing I've been thinking about." He looked up. "And I need your thoughts, because I think it may be important."

Neither Jake nor Mallory said anything, waiting for him to go on.

"We have always assumed that the victims were kidnapped or snatched. Snatch and grab. That idea holds some merit when we look at the map you gave us. All along two highways, all similar ages, but..."

"But what?" asked Jake. "They didn't know each other. Their similarities are their proximity to a highway, if she's right, their ages, possible similar time of year, and the fact they were victims of the same guy, pretty much in the same way. Small towns. What else is there?" He went on. "Items found on or with the victims were all dissimilar...I mean, what else you got?"

Stan pulled the interview sheets of the parents out of their folders. "After going through the interviews with the parents and the friends I believe there's an item missing from each child. Before I tell what I think it is..."

"Wait, wait" said Jake, "You think each of the victims had something similar when they were killed but it wasn't with them? Then where is it?"

Stan finished the thought. "The perp kept it."

"A souvenir?" asked Jake.

"Holy shit," whispered Mallory.

"Maybe." Stan held up his hand. "Hear me out first. I want you to follow my reasoning."

Stan took a breath. "I think there was a chance, actually a very good chance that the victims were chosen not based on any similarities they had between them, but the choice was made on the scumbag's need. A sick, yet indiscriminate need that had him choosing whoever was at hand."

"But, if just that was the case, if that's all we had to go on, random snatchings, then we are going to be as likely to find out who was responsible for Olive Park as it was for Officer Duncan to stumble across Handleman at Olive Park. Damn lucky. But, I think there was more. I think the perp specifically selected the victims, *and* they were in the perp's presence by their own accord."

"What are you saying? They went to him?" asked Malloy leaning forward.

Stan looked at her. "Yes. That's exactly what I'm saying."

He had both Jake's and Mallory's attention.

"Yes," continued Stan, "there are similarities here, but we are straining to find them. In any multiple cases like this there are always some things the same or some coincidences. Take a random group of twenty kids. At least two of them will have names beginning with A or like those same two being born in March or have two brothers. A few will have blond hair and brown eyes. I think we are looking too hard for similarities or at least ignoring two other elements: opportunity and intent."

"Our choices are, these kids were either snatched, based on their accessibility to the perp, or these kids were all trying to go somewhere or do something that must have looked harmless to everyone else, but wasn't, because they were really trying to get to the perp."

Stan looked at both Mallory and Jake, but neither wanted to stop him or argue. In fact, he could see the glimmer of recognition in their expressions.

"I believe Carruthers and Thompson missed this even though they had gone over the last day of each victim minute by minute. They had done a good timeline. But they missed it."

Stan pulled out the last day itinerary for each child.

"They verified witnesses for each location or activity each of the kids had been supposedly been doing, but, as you know, found no similarities between each child's activities."

He picked up the activity sheet for Karen.

"Karen Summering had been planning a sleepover with two other friends at one of the friend's house. She never made it there."

Then Phillip's. "Phillip Boyd played baseball in the morning and was supposed to have a normal dinner with his family that night. He never came home."

Then Joey's. "Joey Marshall rode his bike with a few friends. They got into a little trouble when one of them shoplifted a few from the drugstore. There were no evening plans for him, except maybe a delivered pizza at home according to his parents."

Stan set the activity sheets down. "Because all three disappeared on a weekend; Karen on a Saturday, the two boys on a Sunday, Carruthers and Thompson believed this lent credibility to the snatched theory. Weekend was a time when kids were more likely to be outside playing. Outside and available."

"True," said Jake. "But, it would have also been the time when it would have been easiest to see a snatching. There would have been more kids out. More eyes."

"That's correct. It would have been the time to see anything out of the ordinary. It was a weekend and if any of these three had been grabbed, had been seen talking to a stranger, or acting in an unusual way, you're right, it would have been more noticeable."

Stan grabbed the file Carruthers had done on Joey Marshall. He flipped through to the detective's summary, through to the inventory of Joey's room and possessions. He felt the hairs rise on his neck as he threw the file back on the table. The same as last night when he had discovered what was missing. When he had realized what was missing with all three kids.

"Joey's bike has never been found. Anywhere."

"Neither has Karen's. Neither has Phillip's"

He cocked his head. "You want a similarity that is rock solid. There's one."

Stan watched it sink in. He watched them process the idea as he had last night. He watched them also begin to extrapolate what that meant.

"Holy shit…" muttered Mallory.

"Thompson in his report had written about Karen Summering and Phillip Boyd. Karen's parents never mentioned a bicycle but they did say they'd seen her overnight bag for her sleepover sitting in the basket before she left. Basket? What basket? Unless it was the basket on a bike. The inventory of Karen's things showed no bike. Evidently, Thompson never made the connection and never asked about the basket again or a bike.

"Phillip had ridden his bike to play baseball. There was no mention of it after that in the report. But, there was no bike found at the Boyd home, either. Thompson made mention of the missing bike, but Phillip's parents assumed it had been left at the ball field and some other child had taken it for his own."

Stan held up his hands. "All right, follow me here. If these kids had been grabbed or snatched as the theory says, and they were with their bike and the bikes have not been found then the bikes were taken as well.

They all knew that the physical logistics of kidnapping a child and their bicycle and who knows what else, would have been a challenge. A baseball bat, balls, glove possibly for Phillip, stuff from the drugstore for Joey, overnight clothes for Karen.

Stan looked at both of them. "Where has it all gone?

No one answered him.

"What I believe is that all three intended to see the perp for some unknown reason. And they were using their bikes to get there. It means that all three were riding their bikes with a certain destination in mind. But where? They were all in different cities. What was the same in all three towns that three different kids would ride their bikes to?"

"If you're right," Mallory added, "then it also means they were planning on returning. I mean Karen had her overnight stuff, Joey his baseball glove and so on. They were coming back. At least they thought they were."

"True," said Stan. "And if your map theory has any truth to it, then whatever they were going to was the same thing in each of those places. I have no idea what that one thing would be."

Mallory was lost in thought at the conference table. Her coffee, long cold. The rest of her muffin, uneaten. Jake sat at the far end of the table, his mouth set in a hard line. He was drawing on the pad in front of him. Stan could see it was stick figures on bicycles.

He wanted the reactions from both of them, but especially Mallory. Because maybe Mallory was right. Maybe it was going to take a child, or at least someone like Mallory, someone closer to the victim's ages to get some idea of what had happened. An idea of what these kid's motivation was that made them hop on their bikes and go see someone of their own volition. They were missing something that was age specific. Kid specific.

He walked to the glass wall that held the facts they knew for certain. He took the black marker and wrote on two yellow sheets. He taped them both up on the wall.

'Bikes missing on all 3'

'All 3 Taken/Disappeared in the Afternoon'

He stood back. The wall was a big wall and it was starting to fill up. He read the rest as he knew the others were behind him.

'Taken in the late summer'

'Similar ages'

'Buried same way, same site'

One thing he was certain. One thing Mallory was sure to point out when she thought about it. One thing he almost hated to admit to himself.

They were making progress.

CHAPTER 22

"I see from the report that you were a church going family and that you attended the Faith Lutheran Church just about every week. Is that so?"

M said nothing. He remembered good old Faith Lutheran. Pale blond cinder block with a dark wood triangular roof jutting up with a glass skylight. He remembered it well. In fact he knew every inch of the church, the sanctuary, the Sunday school rooms, the bathrooms, the closets, the kitchen, everything. He and Jess had had plenty of time to explore. Time to learn the ins and outs, like how to get out of the building with no one seeing. Like how to sneak into the kitchen and grab some cookies and juice, provisions that were meant to be spread in the Fellowship Hall for after church visiting. He didn't feel bad about taking the food. It made up for no breakfast and half a frozen burrito or a slice of pizza he and Jess had been given for dinner the night before.

Didn't Jesus say, 'suffer the little children to come unto me' or some shit? Well, every Sunday he and Jess were suffering. M would have liked to have seen Jesus come and break bread and spread it around, multiply some fucking fishes, anything to give them some food.

"So, you were Lutherans, then?" asked Avery again.

M turned and scoffed. "Yeah, only because the Catholic Church was too far away."

Avery stopped to consider this. "You switched religions? Your parents decided to change faiths?"

M looked at Avery. Was he really as clueless as he made out or was he just playing mind games, screwing with my head? Or could he never truly imagine the machinations of the sick shits in this world.

Avery smiled and shrugged. "Not everything about your life is in the file, you know. So, I'm curious about how you all lived. What was your life like? And it does say your family attended church on a regular basis. To me, that would signify that you experienced some level of stability in your family life. Is that true?"

"You're pathetic," said M.

Avery looked to sky as if pretending to remember. "There was pastor or Reverend something or other, Reverend Pleshett, something like that, who said some nice things about you and Jess. Do you remember him?"

"Sure," agreed M, "Yeah. Big, red-faced guy."

"Well, he said you two were … very memorable. Always together. Looked out for each other."

"That's all he said?"

"Well…"

"Nothing in your precious report about how he tossed our entire family out onto the street when I was caught stealing did he? Nothing in there about my father interrupting a service when he came in the side door of the church one Sunday, drunk, falling down, but yelling the whole time about how Jesus was a homo? Anything like that in that precious report?"

Avery stared at M. M could see he was lost but trying to catch up.

Finally, Avery ventured forth. "Stealing, eh? I missed that part, I guess. What was that about?"

"Maybe you should ask the good Reverend Asshole."

"What would he say, do you think?"

"Do I have to do everything for you? You're getting paid. Why don't you ask him and get his side of the story." M leaned forward. "Eh?"

M shifted on the wooden park bench. He didn't know why, but he was sitting in a park and feeling claustrophobic. The air was both hot and cold. His legs radiated with a quivering twitching. He had named his leg thing the 'gotta-moves' every time it happened.

Avery also shifted on his end of the bench. With a smirk, M realized that Avery only moved when M moved. It must be some kind of mimicking bonding thing, thought M.

"How did Jessie like church?"

M widened his eyes in mock revulsion and put his hands to either side of his head and shook it. "It was tragic. She had a love affair with the choir master."

Avery pretended to write it down in his notebook. "Which church was that again?"

M sighed. "Look. She liked it, okay. She was in the silly children's choir. She went to Sunday school. Not much else to do."

Avery eyes brightened. To M it appeared someone had just spoken a few words to Avery in a language he could understand.

"She can sing?" asked Avery with what seemed like genuine enthusiasm. "Is she any good?"

"I dunno. She doesn't screech."

"Did you enjoy it?"

"Her singing you mean? Like I said, she didn't screech."

Without a pause, Avery continued. "How did she feel about your stealing from the church?"

"Screw you."

"So, what was the stealing about?" pressed Avery.

M looked away. He could still feel the big man's hand on his wrist, twisting it until the cookies fell out onto the vestry floor. Cookies for crissakes. He'd had them under his coat. Somehow they'd known he had them. The acolyte, probably. He was always a pimpled shit. They'd made him pick them up off the floor, one by one. The only funny thing about it was he was able to shove three of the cookies up his sleeve without them seeing. At least he had gotten those. He had given two of them to Jess. She had been hungrier than he was.

"We should've stayed at the Catlick Church instead of going to the Lutherans, those shitheads."

"The Catholics?" asked Avery. "What do the Catholics have to do with it?"

M gave him the 'everybody-knows-this' look. "They have the best food and the longest services. Duh."

Avery looked lost and uncomfortable at being lost.

"You don't get it do you. You still think my father had a nice bone in his body. You thought taking us to church was a great idea, a family bonding experience?" M shook his head. "He dumped us at church. He hated us. It was his way of getting rid of us for the day. It was cheap babysitting, like free. Every Sunday morning he'd drag us out of bed. No breakfast. Throw us into the backseat and deposit us at whatever church had services all day. For a while it was the big Catholic Church, about three blocks from our house. Dump us out and make us walk in by ourselves. He wouldn't return until after all the football games were over or the bar kicked him out or whatever. I don't know. I don't even know why he came back to get us."

"What would you do all day?"

"Eat."

"Eat? Didn't you have food in your house?"

"We had gin."

Avery put his notebook down. "You were stealing food."

"You know what else? We had bars installed on the windows. My father did it. He told the neighbor next door, the one left who was still speaking to him, that the bars were because the crime rate was so high. That there were so many creeps running around."

"Was that unusual?" asked Avery.

M shrugged. He scanned the sky above the park. It looked like it was going to rain. Maybe not now, but soon.

"I mean was the crime rate high where you lived?"

"You kidding? Where we lived?"

"So?"

"So, what?"

"The bars. What was the problem installing bars on the windows? Did you not think it was to protect you and your family?"

M watched the park's fountain pulse, rise and fall and spill over, wetting the concrete surround. Today, there were no little kids to watch it. Still it pulsed on its own. M felt calmed by watching it. It seemed alive and oblivious to whoever was watching or not.

"Protect us from the creeps, the bad people?" M laughed. "He *was* bad people."

Avery waited.

"You see, he also installed a few deadbolts too. Front and back doors."

"That's good isn't it?"

"Jesus," stated M. "You're always asking questions. Don't you ever listen? Did you not read the report? What are you doing?"

Avery searched his memory but couldn't see where this was going.

"You're the psychologist, right. Figure it out."

Avery equivocated. "You tell me."

M sighed. "What does nobody understand? He was Satan bad. You should know that by now. Really bad. Sure he put bars on the windows and deadbolts on the doors. And you'd think he was trying to protect us, be the responsible father...Jesus, you're an idiot. And you get paid for this?"

Avery started to speak but M cut him off.

"Idiot! The bars were only two inches apart and the deadbolts required keys to get out and he had the keys and he was always lighting matches and flicking them at my mother. You know, when a house is on fire it's a bitch to get out fast when you can't go through the doors and you can't squeeze through the bars on the windows...and you don't have the keys."

Avery said quietly, "Your father kept...the keys?"

"Not any more." M said with finality.

M realized it was obvious that they were on two different planets. "My father was a fucking psycho. There are shit people and there are psychos, for crissakes."

Avery was quiet for a while, and then asked. "You don't regret what you did, do you?"

M got up and started down the path toward the fountain. Over his shoulder he asked, "I don't really have to talk to you, do I? I mean is this really required?" He continued down the path not waiting for an answer. He was right. All they do is ask question after question.

Avery followed and they both ended up at the edge of the fountain.

M was mesmerized by the fountain. He spoke wearily.

"She's only six," added M.

"Your sister, Jessie. I know. And you did protect her," Avery continued. "By what you did."

M continued staring into the fountain. The flash of color and light was very soothing. He leaned in and swished his hand in the fountain, then looked up at Avery.

"But not my mother."

CHAPTER 23

Mallory had been putting up the twenty two pictures of the kids who were missing as she had noted on her map. She had printed out their pictures, smaller in size than those of Phillip, Karen and Joey, and now was carefully tacking them up to one of the glass walls. She took care to straighten each picture and had all arranged on three rows. When she finished she stood back a few paces and just stared at the pictures.

Stan noticed her not moving. "You okay?"

Jake looked up from his laptop.

She took another moment before she turned to him, taking a big breath. The type of breath a girl makes before she cries. She wiped her nose and blew out a big breath. Her chin quivered.

Stan glanced at Jake who rolled his eyes. He knew his partner was not prepared to deal with the emotional swings that Mallory exuded. Neither of them had worked closely with a female for any length of time. It was unnerving. Stan handled it better though, being still married to Bernice. He had long ago gotten used to the idea that there were just some things that were not to be known or understood. The working of his wife's, and all female souls, was and always would be a mystery. Blind acceptance, he believed, was part of being married.

Jake had never known the pleasure of having a steady female companion, and Mallory's palpable emotional intensity bothered him like a persistently buzzing fly that came and went. It bothered him just enough to distract him from what he was doing, then went away. But now he was distracted.

"Listen," she said, recovering a bit. "You know, I think maybe they were headed to school. You say they all had their bikes. And I think they rode them to their respective schools."

She turned to Stan who was picking his way through the thousand telephone tips that had been tossed into one of the boxes. They had been banded with rubber bands in a rough chronological order and just heaved into one of the boxes. Some had Carruthers or Thompson's or some other grunt who had been reviewing the calls notes on them

"Hmmm," said Stan looked at her over his reading glasses, "except they weren't in school. School wasn't even in session and it was a weekend."

He raised his eyebrows in a question when Mallory didn't say anything. "Right?"

She wheeled and pointed an accusing finger at him. "But, aha, school was a few days away from starting, and for two of them it was going to be a new school."

She said it as if it was obvious from her tortured logic what had happened.

"Makes sense," she said as she tapped each yellow paper on the wall in sequence with her pencil.

Jake glanced up but kept typing on his laptop.

"Makes no sense," stated Stan as he set aside a telephone message from a Mr. and Mrs. Rankin who thought they had seen Joey Marshall a few days before, talking to a stranger. It was one of hundreds of reported sightings in the days leading up to the disappearances.

Stan continued, "They weren't in school. It was summer, they were enjoying themselves. No kid wants to spend time going to his school unless he has to, right?"

She turned and climbed up on the conference table across from him and sat Indian style, cross-legged.

"Look," she said leaning forward, "I know you've never been a kid or at least you probably don't remember the 1800s when you went to a one room schoolhouse. But, in our modern era, kids go to an elementary school, then a middle school, then a high school. It's all the rage."

Stan tried to remember the last time he'd been limber enough to sit cross-legged. "Yeah, I know, so what?"

Mallory held up her two hands and raised and lowered each one in turn, showing each one of her points followed the other. "New school. New kids. New teachers. Don't know your way around. Terrified. Right?"

Stan shrugged.

"See! This is why I'm here. Damn, I remember what it was like on the first day of a new school. You have to go and check out your new school. You don't want to be the dolt who on the first day has to ask where the toilet is. You want to know where the cafeteria is, where your homeroom is. You want to walk in the first day as if you own the place. Hell, as if you built the place. You want to look cool enough to the other kids, grown up enough, mature enough that, yeah, this is a new school, but, yeah, I know my way around. Nothing scares me." She started to bob like a rap artist that happened to be sitting on a table.

"So, what you're saying is that they all went to check out their schools and they were taken at their new schools? By whom? The same maintenance guy works at all these schools? There is a traveling pedophile that each year works at a different school?"

She lifted her legs and swung around on her butt and jumped off the table.

"Look. We need the common key. We've got that with school. According to your possible intent theory, they were all headed to a destination on their bikes. And it was a few days before school started for all of them."

She turned around to Stan. "Sounds good, eh?"

"Sounds weak and desperate."

She was not deterred. "Yeah, but possible."

"I would rank it above alien abduction for sure, but..."

Mallory slumped and sat down. "Yeah, you're right it's dumb and stupid."

After a moment she yelled at the top of her lungs. "It's those effing bikes!" She turned to Stan, "Your fault! If you hadn't figured out they had their bikes and now their bikes were gone too, we could all just believe they were snatched instead of trying to look for some common place they would have all ridden to. Damn!"

Her head went down. "Your fault," she said again, studying the floor.

Stan sighed. The school theory would simmer until it was dealt with. "All right let's talk it out."

He pushed aside the box of telephone tips and pulled out his yellow pad. Mallory perked up and pulled her laptop toward her and began punching keys.

"Okay, okay..." Her mouth twisted into a concentrated grimace and she began swiping the mouse all over.

"What?" asked Stan as he put down his pencil?

"I'm looking up their schools and then I'm going to see where their houses are..."

"How do you know what school they went to? They might've gone to a private school."

Mallory typed away ignoring him. "No. None of them went to private school. And let's see, Joey was going to go to Cherry Heights Lower School and it was...is...six blocks, crow flies, from his house."

"Karen's was going to be Willard Middle School...and it is two blocks from her house."

She smiled as she looked at Stan.

"Do-able, eh?"

"It's a theory. What about Phillip?"

Mallory took a full two minutes on the internet. She sagged and finally looked up. "Well, his was four miles away. Brandon De Wilde Elementary."

"Brandon de Wilde? Wasn't he an actor?" asked Jake.

"Forget who he was. It was four bleeding' miles away. That's a good long trek for a 9 year old."

Mallory swung off the table and lay down on the credenza. "Piss on it."

"Yeah. Piss on it."

They were both quiet.

Mallory snapped her fingers. "Okay, okay. What about church, huh? They could've been going to church, right? For whatever you go to church for."

"Check the files," said Stan absently. "Joey's parents were not churchgoers. Phillip's family was Jewish, non-practicing I think. The Summerings were Christmas Protestants."

"I guess it would be too much to hope that maybe they converted or suddenly found religion in the days before they were taken."

Stan looked down at the yellow legal pad in front of him. "Remember what I said about weeding out the crazy ideas that pop into your head, well…"

He had been doodling. He had seen Jake doing it the other day and now he found himself drawing a bike with a stick figure on it. The stick figure was leaning forward as if fighting a mighty wind because he was going so fast. Stan had absently drawn straight lines behind the bike indicating its speed.

He studied it. They had something, he knew it. The bikes were the key and they showed intent.

Stan looked up and began tapping his pencil on the pad. He stopped when he realized that it was a Mallory habit he was imitating. "You know, you may be onto something," he said.

Mallory had her head in her hands and was now sitting on the edge of the credenza. "What? You mean religion?"

"No, not religion. I mean what happened in the days before they were taken. I mean we know as much as we're going to about the day they disappeared but very little of substance in the days leading up to. We know there're precious few similarities between the three kids or their activities on the day they disappeared except it was on a summer weekend and they were doing random kid's stuff. And they had plans for the rest of the day."

"And somewhere they were biking to," added Mallory.

"If you remember," continued Stan, "Carruthers and Thompson had gotten what they could from the parents and playmates about the days leading up to the disappearances, but it was always standard questions - Were the victims happy? Were they planning to run away? So forth. Then they were interrupted by the Handleman mess."

Jake looked over the top of his computer at Stan and shrugged. "As much as I hate to admit it, and I really do, she has a point. We need more about what the hell were they up to in the days before."

Mallory brightened. She looked back and forth between Stan and Jake. "So, you don't want to abandon this thing? You don't want to blow it off? You're willing to give it more days? Both of you?"

Jake said nothing but looked at Stan.

Stan sighed. "We need more."

He locked eyes with Mallory, "We have to talk to the parents again."

Mallory beamed. "Wicked."

CHAPTER 24

Mallory knew that Stan had instructed her to call Phillip's parents and conduct a re-interview with them with special emphasis on the bicycle that Phillip had ridden. Even though Phillip's parents had said that Phillip had abandoned his bike at the baseball field and some other kid had taken it for his own, now with the special emphasis on tracking the bikes, it was important that Mallory elicit what she could about the bike.

Even though she knew what she was going to do all along, to her credit Mallory did call them. She didn't let it ring long. Maybe two rings.

"Well, Stan," she'd said out loud to no one. "No one appears to be home. I'll have to go see them myself. Pay them a personal visit and just have a look around for myself. I'll have to get out in the field myself."

As she packed her '89 Toyota with a backpack and her digital recorder she continued her monologue with the non-present Stan. "I know you said I shouldn't interact with the general public on this case, that I am just to be a voice on the telephone. That I am to be heard and not seen, but, come on Stan, how do you expect me to get quality information without doing a face-to-face. Mano a mano, you know."

Anyway, what's tough about field work? You talk to people. You ask them questions. Just like conversing online only you're not in your pajamas and you're in somebody else's house. And in-person was definitely better than the phone.

"You know, Stan, they can't hang up on you as easily when you're standing right in front of them. So there!"

At the last minute she decided to throw in some clothes. She packed a small duffel with toiletries, an old boyfriend's shirt to sleep in, and an outfit for tomorrow if she had to stay over somewhere. Best to be prepared. This was probably what Stan or Jake would do. They would be prepared. Then again, they were guys, maybe they would forget.

She tossed the IPod on the seat and she was off.

She checked the address in the report as she drove. 4200 block of Gemini Rd. It sounded so New Age. It would have been nice to check to make sure they still lived there before she went on this chase. She was the computer expert after all. Stan or Jake would have at least verified where they lived before they drove an hour. Shit. Mark it up to on the job training.

She pulled out her phone and hit the browser. She'd check now. She pulled over by the side of the road and punched in the address into the reverse search. It came back quickly with the phone number and the name, but just Nathan Boyd. No wife listed.

She pulled back onto Rt. 99 and accelerated. The Toyota shook in protest but gradually hit speed and she made it to Reedley in just under 3 hours.

It was definitely a bachelor's house. In the center of the living room was one worn cloth-covered recliner with the lever on the side to kick out the footrest and two small tables on either side of it. A large screen TV was hung halfway up the largest wall. There were no plants. There was one lone picture of the three of them under the TV.

No artwork on the walls. A stack of old newspapers by the front door, waiting to grow to the appropriate height to be recycled.

And the smell of the house, while not unpleasant, reminded her of the inside of her father's bathrobe; personal and slightly gamey.

Nathan himself, now past 60, was in a checked shirt and jeans. He looked comfortable in his chair and, Mallory guessed, it was the outfit he wore almost every day. There was no one left to impress. He settled back into his chair and Mallory imagined that the swales and heaves in the chair were perfectly matched to Nathan's backside. It was his throne.

Mallory sat stiffly in the visitor's chair, a small straight-backed chair that she guessed had been sitting, unmoved, against the wall for years.

"She died. Thank God."

Mallory started her digital recorder and looked up, surprised.

Nathan shrugged. "When Phillip was taken it was the last straw, if you will. Marie's cancer was pretty advanced by then. I was down to half-time at the shop. It was as if someone was driving a stake into our life. Inch by inch. Every time we turned around or tried to do anything positive, Bam, along came the devil and knocked us back." He shrugged.

"So, yeah. I'd say it was good she died. She suffered enough with what she had to go through physically. She was headed that way and thank God she was spared waiting every day for a phone call about the boy. Spared the waiting. Just waiting, you know. It was a blessing."

"So, as I said, we've re-opened the investigation…" began Mallory.

"That was another time, back then," said Nathan. "Another time when Phillip was here and Marie was happy and we were all together. I was working then. But, I'm sorry, you said what? You opened the investigation again?"

"Yes, and I'm sorry to have to go back through some of the events around Phillip and what happened…"

Nathan held up his hand. "It's okay. It was a different time. A different life and I look at it as if we were all some other people back then. As if it all happened to some other family. Somebody else. So ask me what you want to know."

She and Stan and Jake had decided on the three areas they needed to cover and she was anxious to get going but she forced herself to proceed slowly.

"Well, we're looking at the cases of Phillip, of course, and Karen and Joey…"

"Those were the other two. I'd forgot."

"Yes, and we're looking at the case from a slightly different point of view."

"Oh. How so?" Nathan seemed interested but Mallory didn't want to go into the tortured thinking that she, Stan and Jake had gone through to get to this point, so she skipped the part about missing kids and similarities of the victims and moved right to the bikes.

"We're checking to see if there are any common items that all three victims were missing after they were taken. In other words, when all three were taken, were there any similar items they all had."

"What did you find?"

"Well, that's what we're trying to find out now." She paused. She hoped he was getting this.

"First, I want to ask if you or Phillip or any of the family had a boat or did any boating?"

Nathan looked confused. "A boat? You mean like a sailboat or a powerboat?"

"Yes."

"No. None of 'em." Nathan studied her. "What the hell you asking 'bout that?"

"Never mind. We're just checking on a few things."

Nathan continued his puzzled look.

"Okay, Phillip was going to a new school wasn't he?"

Nathan was still on the boats. "You asking 'bout boats or schools?"

"Schools. What school was Phillip going to?"

"Same one he'd been going to. Wasn't changing' schools if that's what you're thinking."

"I see." Mallory pretended to scan her pad in front of her. She took a deep breath. Interviewing people in person was tougher than she thought and old people, hell, it was, like, a different language.

She smiled a big smile. "Okay, last item. I need to ask you about is Phillip's bike. He had one, right?"

Nathan look perplexed. "His bike. Why, yes, he had one, but it's gone. A red Schwinn I think. I got it for him new. Had a horn and a light and two saddle baskets on either side of the back wheel."

"The day he went missing, did he have his bike? Was he riding it?"

Nathan settled back even further. "I can't recall specifically, but he was always riding it, so I'm sure sometime that day he rode his bike. That help?"

Mallory cut to the chase. "Do you still have it?"

Nathan raised his eyebrows. "Do I still have it? Why no." He looked off into an imaginary distance. "I'm not really sure what happened to it."

Mallory hated to, but she decided to prompt him.

"The detectives who first worked on the case reported that you or your wife said that some other kids had taken it. Do you remember that?"

Nathan was silent. He head shook slightly. "It wouldn't have been Marie who said that. I must have. That was a long time ago. I think what I said to the detectives…wait, I do remember now." He appeared to recover some animation and sat up.

"What I said, yes, I told them that when Phillip hadn't come home that night I asked one or two of his friends if he'd been to the park, if they all had been riding their bikes at the park. We were trying to think of anyplace he might have gone. They said yes, they'd been playing ball and then riding their bikes at the park. I remember, I asked them to go to the park and check to see if he left his bicycle there."

He smiled slightly. "I remember those kids being so scared 'cause their friend was missing. They would have gone to China if I'd asked 'em to."

Mallory knew the answer but she wanted Nathan to tell it. "What did they find?"

"Oh, they went to the park, searched for hours, at least they were gone for hours. Came back and said there was no trace of the bike. I remember thinking at the time, and maybe I said this to the detective who was here, that I thought maybe he had left it at the park and some other child had taken it for his own. It was a nice bike. Schwinn."

"So, the kids were riding their bikes and playing ball that day."

"I'm pretty sure," said Nathan.

"Phillip had a baseball glove with him?"

"Yeah," smiled Nathan, "must have. It was a Rawlings. A good one. I showed him how to fashion the pocket with a hardball, you know. Tie it closed when you weren't using it so it molded itself to the ball." He waved at Mallory apologizing for the digression.

"We checked the inventory list when they inventoried his room and there was no glove listed," stated Mallory.

"No glove?" Nathan was lost in thought. Mallory didn't interrupt.

"You know," he said after some reflection, "he would have had his bat too, and a ball, I'm sure."

"But, they weren't listed either," said Mallory.

Nathan hadn't heard her. He continued in a softer voice. "When we knew he wasn't coming back, well by that time Marie had passed, and I just started giving everything of Phillip's away. It was as if everybody had left and wasn't coming back and it felt silly, like an old lady, to be hanging onto stuff that could be of use to someone else. Some other kid could enjoy his stuff. So I started giving it all away. Didn't take it to the Salvation Army or anything. I found kids I thought needed a certain item and I just gave it to them."

His voice cracked a bit. "I don't remember ever seeing the glove or his bat or his bike again." He looked straight at Mallory. "They disappeared with him, didn't they?"

Mallory nodded. "We think maybe so."

"How could that be?"

Mallory picked up her recorder, clicked it off and put it away. "We don't know Nathan, but yes, it seems somehow your son went missing with his bike and his baseball stuff."

It wasn't until Mallory was almost out the door that Nathan stopped her.

"One other thing," Nathan brightened at the memory, "The glove. You would know it if you saw it. Phillip loved Jose

Conseco. He had Conseco's baseball card taped to the back of his glove always. When the card got ripped or started to wear out, he'd get another one and re-tape in place, behind the fingers. He said it was good to have Jose with him in the outfield.

"So," he said offering a weak smile, "you'd know it was my son's if you saw it."

She decided to drive past the park. It was about three blocks as the crow flies, but the development that Gemini Road was in was a wicked nest of dead ends and cul-d-sacs, so it took longer than it should have to find it even after Nathan's directions.

There was still a ball field there. It looked well used. Good to see kids were still playing baseball and not just playing baseball video games.

She got out and walked slowly to the pitcher's mound and did a 360.

Which way did you go Phillip? What made you to jump on your bike after playing with your friends and head off alone? Not with anyone else.

Which way?

And why?

CHAPTER 25

He really didn't give a crap if Avery was pissed or what. Screw him. The good doctor had even said their meetings were a waste of time. He'd even suggested they go to the movies or fly a kite instead of talking about what happened. Well, this was more important than digging into the recent past.

M looked at his reflection in the murky glass in front of him. He didn't look crazy. He knew he wasn't crazy. Avery knew it. The legal world was just covering its ass making him see a shrink.

Besides, he wasn't bailing completely, he was just going to be a few minutes late that was all. And hell, he was only a few blocks from the office.

He stood in the phone booth and looked out. Damn, it had taken a long time to find a pay phone. He had walked in and closed the door. The light had come on. Cool.

Now he stood there, reading the directions. He had never used a pay phone before but he knew somehow it took quarters. Now, looking up at the coin slots, he saw it took dimes and nickels too. Well, he'd only brought quarters.

He hefted the quarters in his hand and hoped they were enough. He had no idea what a call cost in a pay phone. He'd had a cell phone back at the house, back when he was part of a family. And even though his father bitched about the cost every month when the phone bill came, his mother always, with a gentle voice, reminded his father that it was for his safety. That M didn't use the phone capriciously, but if he ever needed to get in touch with someone in an emergency, he could.

His father came so very close each month to saying 'Screw it; I'll give him a bunch of quarters. He can use those if he has a problem.'

His father's anger was born of both the cost of the phone as well as his mother using words like 'capriciously', which M didn't actually know what it meant and he was sure his father had no clue. He knew his father had only graduated high school and then started at a community college but didn't finish the first semester. His mother had graduated from UCLA with a Bachelor of Arts, which M thought odd, since she was a woman.

M realized later that the difference in their educational backgrounds must have contributed to the problems. He also wondered, just what in hell his mother saw in his father in the first place.

Still, until everything happened, he had still had his cell phone. He had asked his Aunt Janey to re-activate it. He tried using the safety angle, for himself as well as Jessie, but it hadn't gone further than, 'Are you nuts?' He tried making the argument that he already had the phone and there would be no expense there, but it was no dice.

'When you get a job, young man, to pay for something like that, then you can have one. You know you and Jess are only going to be in the park here, either here or at Mrs. Everheart's trailer. I don't see a need.'

M hated that his aunt called it a park. It wasn't a park, just a few small acres where trailers were parked for crissakes. A park doesn't smell like fifty RV trailers dumping their sewage in the drains all at once.

M had copied the name and phone number from his mother's address book.

Now, he once again went through his rehearsed story. He had tried to anticipate the objections and the questions and he wanted to have the answers for them. He wanted to sound as if he was normal, as if he and Jessie were just trying to do the right thing by Aunt Janey.

The problem of course was he didn't actually know what the relationship of Mr. Shippen Travers of Bullhead City, Arizona was to their family. Not only had he found the name and address in the book but there was also a Christmas card from last year stuck in it. The card was very nice with buffalo grazing in a snow covered field with a bright star above. Just what you'd expect from a kindly old rancher relative. M had a vague hope that Shippen Travers was a long lost brother or maybe a favorite cousin. Hopefully, a really favorite cousin.

Anyway, he needed to be prepared.

He reread the directions again, and then lifted the receiver. He punched in the number and stood ready to load in the quarters. When the time came, he dinged in quarter after quarter. He hoped that was enough. He held six more in reserve.

The phone rang four times. Shit, it was going to go to voicemail.

Then. "Yallo."

M opened his mouth to speak but paused. The voice sounded too young. He had in his mind an old cowboy just come in off the range from punching doggies or whatever cowboys did.

"Yallo, anybody there? I hear you breathing."

"Oh, yeah, Hello, I'm looking for Mr. Travers." M finally got it out.

"Not here. Went to Phoenix. Who is this?" said the young voice.

Before M could answer the voice continued on. "Is this a joke? You sound like you're a kid. Who is this?"

"Maybe I should call back," said M trying to sound at least twenty years old.

"But who is this? I need to tell him something."

M hadn't rehearsed what to do if anyone else answered and gummed up the works. Shit. He didn't know how long these quarters would last but he decided on the 'plea' scenario he'd worked out. No choice.

"Hey. I'm the son of Mrs. Sarah Cooper. She was...killed a few weeks ago and I know Mr. Travers knows her and I need to talk to him."

There was a pause. "How old are you?"

"I'm thirteen and my sister Jessie's six."

Again a pause. "What's it about?"

M sighed big. The sigh was part of the plea scenario. "It's kind of personal, you know. I just need to talk to him. D'you know when I could call back?"

"Hey," the voice softened a little. "I'm Elliot Travers. I'm Shippen's son. Look, he can call you back. Sometimes it's tough to track him down, you know?"

"Well, that's not gonna..."

"Or hey, I know, I can give you his cell and you can call him directly. He's not always available you know, but you could try."

M looked at the quarters that were left on the shelf. "Yeah, I guess that's okay." Except it wasn't. He had nothing to write with and his memory was shitty when it came to phone numbers. "Just a moment."

He patted his pockets but that was just looking for a miracle. Outside the booth he saw a UPS guy in brown shorts loading up a handcart. He whipped open the door and still holding the receiver shouted out to the delivery guy before he took off.

"Yo! UPS guy."

The guy looked around then spotted M.

M pointed to the receiver and put on the puppy dog look, "My mother needs me to write a phone number down for emergencies, do you have a pencil I can borrow?"

In one motion, the guy whipped a pencil out of his breast pocket and handed to M.

"Keep it, kid." Then he was gone.

"All right," said M back on the phone, "What is it?"

M wrote the number on the metal shelf holding his quarters. He figured he'd find something else to write on when he was done talking. He purposely wrote the area code backwards. He didn't need some hooker or some jerk off drunk dialing Mr. Travers in Bullhead City, Arizona. No one needs that.

"Hey, listen, sorry about your mother, okay?" said Elliot. "Our mother died last year. It was kinda rough."

What the hell do I say now thought M. He settled on, "Gee, that is rough."

There was a pause. "What happened to your mother?"

M started to speak then he realized he had never said it to anyone. Never uttered the words. Thought it maybe, never said it.

"She was murdered." There.

It was Elliot's turn to struggle with a response.

He settled on a long drawn out 'Shhhiitt.'

"Yeah," M agreed. A voice came on in his ear. He thought someone had broken into the conversation but it was a robot voice asking for money if he wanted to keep talking.

"Hey, I gotta go," said M, "Tell your dad, I'll call back soon."

"Yeah, sure. Sure."

M hung up. Now what?

He dug in his pocket and found a bunged up business card for Dr. Avery. M turned it over and copied Mr. Shippen Travers' number from the metal shelf onto the back of the card. As an afterthought he wrote down Elliot's name too.

He turned the card back over and thought he might as well go see the good doctor. He was late but who cares? Maybe they could just sit down at Starbucks and watch pretty girls go by. That would be worthwhile. A good use of everyone's time.

CHAPTER 26

Jessie was riding a bicycle around in circles when he got back from another rousing session with the good doctor Avery. A bicycle! He didn't know she could ride. This was a real two wheeler, without training wheels. It wasn't a big bike. It was smallish, a girl's bike but with big tires. This was not the newest version of any bike. This was a thrift store special, but it had two small plastic pink streamers jammed in the butt end of each handlebar that, because of her jerky steering, swung wildly in joyous circles.

She was concentrating so hard, not just to stay upright but to also avoid the ruts and heaves in the trailer park's asphalt, that she didn't see M until after a few wobbly revolutions.

"Look M!" She would only glance at him for a second, then refocus on the task of avoiding catastrophe.

He watched her go round and round and couldn't stop smiling. Her single-mindedness was intense, but it was her sense of achievement that animated her whole face. Her eyes glowed, her mouth open, ready to scream should disaster strike.

"Are you sure you know how to stop?"

"I've…never…gone…this…long." She looked at him and he could see that her goal had been to get up and ride, to not crash. Stopping had never crossed her mind.

"You just let me know when you want to get off and I'll show you the best way, okay?"

"Okay. How?"

"You let me know."

"M! I'm scared. I want off now!" Her consistent circles started to wander.

"You know how to brake, right?"

She looked concerned. "Maybe."

"You just push backwards on the pedals, it's easy."

"Yeah." but there was serious doubt building.

M stood with his legs apart. "Okay, next time around you aim the bike right to me. You come right to me, okay?

"Hit you?"

"You won't. This is the easiest way, you'll see.

Her speed was dropping precipitously but she completed the last turn and straightened out and came right toward M.

"Lookin' good."

She kept her eyes glued to the ground in front of her. When she was within two feet, she reversed the pedals and the bike tires skidded to an abrupt stop. M reached out and grabbed the center of the handlebars with his good hand so they didn't move. Jessie stayed upright. She looked up at M and smiled. It was a smile for the ages. He remembered the feeling of getting a present for the first time. It was beauty.

"Okay. Hop off Niko Bellic. You make-a me crazy." M did his best Grand Theft Auto impression.

Jessie jumped off forward so she still straddled the bike, and then stepped through. She held onto the handlebar as if she was dizzy. "Good, huh?"

"I didn't know you could ride," said M.

"Mick taught me, sort of."

"Back home Mick? That Mick?"

"Yeah, sort of. He really just let me ride on his bike sometimes while he held on and he taught me how to brake. He thought that was more important. He said riding was easy."

"Really? Mick?"

Jessie went and sat on the curb. "I only did it by myself once. Usually, he just let me stand on the pedals and push backwards. He said that was braking."

M set the bike down. There was no kickstand. "Where did you get this green piece of shit?"

"Ruby gave it to me."

"Wow. She did something nice?"

"M, she's okay."

M looked it over. It had fat tires, like pictures of Schwinns he'd seen in some ancient Popular Mechanics magazines Mick's dad had. The spokes had some creeping rust and the handlebars squeaked a bit when it turned left. It also had another girls name stenciled on the inside bar.

M felt a small stab. He should have gotten it for her. He vowed to remember when he got up every day that he was a parent now, sort of. He was the last connection for a six year old who's lost just about everything. Except her brother. It was a heartfelt vow, and one he knew he would struggle forever to keep whole.

"Tires are kinda flat."

"Rides better that way."

M smiled. "Rides better. Where did you hear that?"

"Ruby told me."

M thought a moment. "She took you over to the site?"

Jessie nodded. "Yeah. To get the bike. I told you. 'Cept we didn't go all the way back to where the creeps are."

"Creeps? You mean freaks? There are no freaks or creeps there anymore."

"Ruby said some of the circus people will come back someday," stated Jessie with authority. "Even the guy who used to run it."

"She did, huh? Well, if so, they probably think they're coming back to someplace nice instead of a junk heap. I don't think anybody's ever coming back to that place."

"What about that brown man?" she persisted. "You know, the little one."

M admitted to himself he had also thought about the little creep when Jessie mentioned circus people. "Yeah, I know, but I think he's gone. Not coming back."

M looked to the end of the trailer park when he heard the car. Aunt Janey's Honda pulled into her driveway. She didn't try to put it in the small garage which was attached to the side of her trailer. She was proud of the garage and had even painted it the exact same yellow as the trailer. She was one of the few who had a garage. Ironic, M thought. She had a garage but he knew it to be full of all the stuff she couldn't fit in the trailer, including some of his and Jessie's clothes. He doubted if a car had ever been in there. He also wondered where the bike would be parked.

"I think Ruby saw him over there."

M ignored her. He pulled the bike up. "Mount up Annie Oakley."

"Who's auntie Okey?"

"She was a strong woman from the old west who could shoot a gun and hit a target while she was riding."

Jessie climbed onto the seat while M held her steady.

"What kind of bike did she have?"

M laughed. "The horsey kind. She rode a horse."

They walked in silence for a while.

Jessie held onto the handlebars and let the pedals spin between her feet. "M, can I be a strong woman when I grow up?"

"'Course. I'll make sure, okay?"

Jessie, concentrating on staying upright even though M had a good hold, kept her eyes tracing the bumps and ruts in front of her.

M stopped the bike and nudged her. "Hey. You'll be seriously strong."

Jessie smiled and nodded.

M held up his arm brace. "Brace me."

Jessie tentatively took one hand off the handlebar and slapped his brace.

It was then as he chanced to look over his shoulder that he saw the little brown man leaning up against the overgrown chain link. His features were hidden by the afternoon shadow from the fading juniper tree that had claimed the chain link as its support. He had a toothpick that he was working and M could see he was nervously bouncing off the chain link and letting the rebound propel them forward then falling back again.

M sensed he had been watching him and Jessie, but how long? Maybe he'd been watching Jessie the whole time.

The little brown man raised a hand in…what? Greeting? Friendship? Interest? Leering interest? Jackals checking out the wildebeest's interest?

M turned away. Ruby was right. Freaks they were.

He thought to ask Jessie whether she had seen the brown man again. He didn't want her to be alarmed. But, then he did. God, responsibility was a bitch.

CHAPTER 27

Jake removed the evidence bags from box 11. He set them on the conference table. Each was clear plastic with some lines for case number, date, where found, by whom. Clipped to each bag was a folded log showing who had last handled the evidence bag, when and why. The log consisted of two sheets of single lined paper stapled together.

There were three bags total. All the personal effects left from Karen Summering, Phillip Boyd and Joey Marshall. All three were nearly empty.

He sorted them as to child, spreading them out and re-arranging them so the bags were lined up alphabetically by child.

Yesterday, he and Mallory had sorted pictures taken by Forensics of all six items and placed them on the board in the same exact order. They had studied them, looking for anything that might be related, but after two days, they had come up with nothing.

Now, with the real items in front of him, seeing them, handling them, turning them over... What? He didn't know.

He picked a bag at random from Karen's group in the middle. He didn't open the bag right away but unfolded the log that was attached to it and scanned the names and dates. The beginning of the log showed a flurry of detectives and forensic techs who had examined the evidence, or done tests on them, or photographed them, or dusted them for prints, or searched in vain for anything that might harbor some DNA, some chemical trace of who might have held these items or who they belonged to. They knew from the beginning that while the items were found with the specific bodies, it didn't mean they had belonged to the dead children. In fact it was hoped for just the opposite; that the items might have been left behind intentionally or unintentionally by the killer, or had at least belonged to him.

Like a weakening pulse, the cluster of names faded with time. Six months after the initial investigation had begun, the dates stopped. At least for a time. Occasionally, Jake could decipher, there had been if not a re-opening of the case, at least a re-look, given the names grouped around dates separated by months, then years, then nothing.

The last four names were all Carruthers. From five years ago to last year. Jake had to admire the tenacity, or maybe obsession.

He had worked cases where he'd come awake holding the sheets in a death grip with a heart pounding start, realizing he'd missed something obvious. Twice he'd gotten dressed and gone to the station to once again plow through the evidence that his dream had told him he missed. It was like that with the unsolved. The worse the case, the longer they lingered.

Like poor Carruthers, he imagined. When your mental pockets got full and you got tired of carrying around the weight of a case, Jake guessed, that was when you decided to retire. Sometimes it worked, usually didn't. Alcohol helped though.

DiMaggio 340, The Babe 342, Ty Cobb 366. Two thirds of the time, they didn't do shit at the plate. Still, nobody died because they didn't get a double.

Jake opened the bag and removed the only item, a plastic wrist bracelet. It had been found on Karen Summering's right wrist and it was almost completely melted but it was still round, still connected together all the way, though most of it was as thin as a string. They'd had no trouble removing it from her burnt and skeletonized wrist.

The label on the bag, Jake noticed, unlike the picture on the board, was 'friendship bracelet.' Those were popular in the 90's. There was a notation written in the margin from someone who remembered that friendship bracelets were usually made of string or fabric in the 90s, not plastic.

Forensics had identified what appeared to be the initials KS written in ballpoint but it was all but invisible to Jake. A bluish smudge was all he could see, yet somehow they'd been able to get a KS out of it.

More importantly they'd been able to find that there had been three printed words on the worst burned section of the bracelet. There was nothing visible to the naked eye, because the amount of bracelet left was a sixteenth of an inch in diameter and charred. According to the report, using the stereo microscope they'd been able to see shiny bands in the carbonized string that they determined to be burnt ink. The best guess was eight letters in the first word. The second was seven letters, the third eight again. Forensics maintained they were all in capitals. At least they thought so.

Jake studied the bracelet. Damned if he could see anything. He was about to put it down and move on to the next when he had a thought. He'd have to check and see if actual friendship bracelets usually had printing on them, or could it have been a promotional item given out to anyone who would take them. A hamburger place, a charity, her school, the football team. Maybe she went to a concert and was given the bracelet when she went through the door. No, too young. Maybe a friendship bracelet that had some innocuous phrase on it – BFF means FOREVER or whatever newbie teens decided was important to grace their wrists back then. What did he expect, the name of the killer stenciled on it?

Finally, he wrote out 'school', six letters, then 'middle', again six letters, then 'elementary', ten letters. That didn't work.

He put Karen's bracelet aside and opened Phillip's bag. He didn't bother to check the log; he knew that Carruthers had looked at it last.

The only item was a whistle.

Jake picked it up and examined it. It was the metal kind. The kind with the hard ball of wood inside. When you gave it a good blow it would deafen those standing nearby. It had been found clutched in Phillip's right hand.

Of the few items found with the bodies, this was the most pathetic, thought Jake. He knew from reading the interview with Phillip's parents that they had given him the whistle. It was for protection. If he was ever in trouble, he was to blow it and blow it as hard as he could. They said in their interview that they had him practice in the backyard. It was so loud and alarming, the Rickers, the next door neighbors, had called the cops. They felt pretty good that their son had a way to alert somebody in case he was ever in trouble.

Some alert. Parents just cannot imagine the bad things that are out there. Jake turned the whistle over in his hand. The little wood ball was still rattling around inside. He started to put it to his lips and stopped. It somehow didn't feel right, blowing on a dead kid's whistle. But, really, what the hell, Phillip doesn't care and his parents would just as soon have him blow to his heart's content if they thought it would catch the son of a bitch who did it.

He blew, tentative at first, then ramped it up. Once he got it going from the low rattle notes to the full-blown scream it was ear-splitting. The wail echoed upwards to the fourth floor walkway and bounced around the hard walls until it died away.

Two of the workmen who had been building the new evidence storage areas came running.

"What?" They appeared at the doorway to the glass office, out of breath, adrenaline pumping. "What is it?"

Jake held up his hands. He couldn't help but smile. "It's okay, really, okay. I was just…"

But, by that time they had drifted away with a mild look of disgust on their faces seeing firsthand that no one was dying or in major peril. He imagined they had been prepared to do battle with someone or something like an out of control blaze or an escaped felon, of which there were none in the building.

Jake wiped off his spittle and set the whistle down. Either Phillip didn't get a chance or he wasn't near anybody else. Jake thought about that for a while. What did that mean? Phillip still had the whistle with him, so the likelihood that he was able to blow it was pretty good. Maybe nobody was there to hear it.

He put the whistle back and opened the bag for Joey. As on the other two bags the last log entry had been Carruthers.

He already knew what he would find. He didn't know why he bothered to take them out. Two more generic items he couldn't imagine. He tipped the bag sideways and two quarters fell into his hand. Still, he knew where they had been found and he swallowed hard. He had seen the worst acts one human could enact on another. But, if the theory that Carruthers and Thompson had postulated was true, this had to be the most heart wrenching.

Unlike the other items, the bracelet found on Karen's wrist and the whistle clutched in Phillips hand, these two quarters were found just below Joey's outstretched arm. The arm that had pushed out of the shallow grave in desperation and was burned to the bone. The quarters were lying there as if they had been dropped.

Jake knew that Carruthers had written in his report that it was his conclusion that Joey had been offering the two coins as payment for his freedom. That he had been covered in the shallow grave, still alive and had thrust up the two coins, all he had, in a desperate hope of saving his life.

This was such bad business. He knew he couldn't work too much longer on this stuff tonight. Jake turned the coins over in his hand. Two pieces of silver.

He started to close up all three bags and stopped. He realized Stan was right. Carruthers and Thompson and everyone else were so intent on working on the evidence that was found with the bodies that they overlooked half of the evidence. Stan had discovered that with the bicycles.

It wasn't what was found, it was what was missing. What should have been found.

Jake got up and moved down a chair at the conference table so as to not disturb the layout of the evidence bags. He pulled out his spiral bound notebook. He opened it to a clean page and began. He realized he could've used his laptop, but he liked old school. He liked to be able to see it; to scratch thoughts out in an instant, to relate things on a page with a quick glance. He liked to be able to doodle, to draw circles around roadblocks that had him stuck, to underline some word, some passage, multiple times if necessary, that he deemed important. Very illuminating to see your thinking graphically displayed. Old school. You go with what works.

Besides, you could flick a pencil up and down when you couldn't think of anything to write, when you were stuck. Nothing to flick, really, on a keyboard.

At the top he wrote: Items missing that should have been found.

Below that, he started with Karen. What should have Forensics field team found? What was conspicuous by its absence?

Shoes. No shoes had been found in the shallow grave.

Socks. He realized that the absence of shoes was mentioned in their report, but no one had bothered to note the socks. He knew young boys went without socks sometimes, but it was rare for girls to skip the socks.

Shoes are easily removed compared to socks. Shoes can be kicked off. He sees kids all the time just walking out of their shoes. Some wore oversize shoes, partially laced, but that was not the case with Karen. She seemed to be well dressed. She didn't seem to be leaning toward slobbery. Socks were a different story. Somebody had removed them. Karen? If so, why?

He got up and studied Karen's picture again. What else wasn't there that should have been. He went back to the table.

Hair barrettes. She had two barrettes in her hair in almost every picture. They were not found with the body.

Karen had been fully dressed when unearthed. Contrary to earlier reports, even her underwear was there. Nothing was in very good shape, but it was all there in some form.

Jake spent a few more minutes studying what wasn't with Karen. Did she have a bag with overnight clothes with her? Did she ride off to a mystery location still planning to end up at her friend's for an overnight? If she did, and if she had all those clothes, well, they were missing too. He added those to the list.

He moved on to Phillip. He pulled out the coroner's report and checked the inventory to determine the missing items.

Shoes. Again.

Socks. Again.

Glasses. Phillip had always been pictured with black plastic framed glasses. They were not listed in the autopsy report, nor were they noted in the forensic field reports.

Joey. Last seen with baseball bat and glove. Did he ride off with them?

Jake pulled the inventory from Joey's room. No bat. No mitt. Maybe they were just missed. Maybe they were not thought important enough to list. It's only a boy's room. You would expect a bat and glove. Either they weren't there or weren't thought important enough to note down.

Three kids on bikes. Some with stuff with them. All with some personal items that disappeared.

Jake sat back and looked at the list. Before Stan had convinced him to work cold cases he'd been hot to plow down the latest cases, the newest ones, the hottest ones. That's where adrenaline flowed.

But now in looking at the list, he saw how Carruthers and Thompson had been so hot, so hopped up on this biggest case of their career that they had done a full court press on the stuff that was found. It was only with time, by stepping back from the immediacy of the case, that he saw what they hadn't, that what was missing was as critical as what was found.

Jake poured one more finger full from Stan's special bottle of Ballantrae then closed it up. He hoped Stan and Mallory made some progress with the parents because he had that good tingling feeling he always got when they were getting close.

And he lived for that shit.

CHAPTER 28

Stan wished it was Mallory who was talking to Karen Summering's parents. It was almost always preferable to have two detectives, hopefully a male and female, do interviews of the parents of missing children. When he and Jake had done them, they were always aware that one parent was the de facto spokesperson and always responded to one detective better than the other. There was often a bond, tenuous though it may be, that evolved between one of the interviewers and one of the parents. With a male and female interviewer, they always had a better chance of rapport.

In this case, there was only the mother left home. When Stan had called, Harriet Summering had been very friendly, even effusive, thanking him for calling, until she heard he was a detective. Then it was obvious she couldn't really care who he was. When she realized it was about her daughter, she must've felt some guilt, Stan thought, because her manner softened. Still, she'd insisted that she be given the precinct number to call him back to verify that he really was who he said he was.

He'd given her the number and she had called back within ten minutes. There had still been suspicion in her voice and an edginess that reminded Stan of a farmer's wife, holding a shotgun at the ready as the traveling salesman approached the door.

The house was small, a single story with a covered porch in front. It was grey; grey siding, grey trim and mostly grey shingles on the newer roof. Stan pulled into the driveway and saw why she had been so happy when she answered the phone.

The metal 'For Sale' sign was prominent in the front yard. It was obvious that Harriet Summering was trying to sell the house herself, 'For Sale By Owner.' It was also apparent that the sign had been there for some time. Tufts of taller grass embraced the two legs of the sign.

Stan surveyed the house and property as he got out. The house was clean; it looked as if it had been painted a few days ago. There was a solitary tree in the yard, held up by wires with rubber hose protecting the trunk. The covered porch had no furniture. There were no flowers or shrubs anywhere along the front of the house. If it was the clean look she was going for, she'd gone slightly past that, projecting an almost unhealthy sterility to the place.

Stan knocked on the door and noticed it was a security screen door. It had been painted white, but it was difficult to mask the heavy metal criss-crossing that latticed the door.

First thing I'd do, thought Stan, would be to replace the security door with something friendlier. An entry that didn't scream that the neighborhood was a hotbed of break-ins.

The inner door opened. Stan knew it must be Harriet Summering standing before him. She bore only a shadowy resemblance to the one picture they had in the file. To Stan, it was obvious she was not well. The woman before him had the same face but she'd lost at least thirty pounds and much of her health. The skirt and blouse looked a few sizes too large. Her hair, once a vibrant auburn, was now a thinning grey.

"Detective?" Her voice was dry and whispery.

"Yes, I'm..."

"Can I see some identification?"

Stan produced his SPD ID card.

She appeared to study it, so Stan tried to find a better opening between the cross hatching so she could see it.

"That's fine," she said at last, and flipped the latch on the screen door. "Please come in."

She led the way into the living room which seemed to be part of the entry and the dining area.

"I live alone," she said as way of explaining her cautiousness.

"I understand, of course."

"Please sit down. I have coffee if you want some."

Stan sat on the couch. "No, thank you. I have limited time…"

"Of course." Harriet Summering sat across from him in a high back chair. The way she settled in it was obvious that's where she'd been sitting when Stan had arrived and probably for hours before that. Maybe waiting for someone to call or stop by to look at the house.

Flyers with a few pictures of the house and detailing the property's attributes lay on the coffee table between them.

She folded her hands. "This is about Karen, you said on the phone."

"Yes…"

"There's been new information?" She asked, but Stan could tell there was little energy behind the question. If she cared anymore, she hadn't the strength to show it.

Stan decided to keep it general. "We're re-investigating Karen's case, among others, yes."

"So, it's open again."

"Well, really, it's never been closed. As time goes by, new techniques of investigation come into use and we try as best we can to go back and apply those techniques to some of the cases still open."

"You mean DNA?" She smiled but it was weak with the sides of her mouth quivering with the effort. "I watch the detective shows, too."

"DNA is one, but in this case it really isn't… it won't help us as much as some of the other things we do. In Karen's case, and the other children who were involved, we have access to computers and computer databases that access networks that are much more extensive than we've had before."

"Computers?" She looked and sounded disappointed.

"Well, in addition to reworking all the leads, we're now able to compare the evidence at the scene as well as similarities between the three children and their activities. It's as if we have many more detectives and officers working on the case."

"I see, but is there new evidence?" She shifted in her seat. Stan wondered if she was in pain.

"A few new pieces of … evidence may have come to light. May I ask where Mr. Summering is?"

Harriet Summering shifted in her chair again and tried to raise herself up again. She brought her hands back to her lap and folded and re-folded them. "Frank is not with is us anymore."

Stan sat up. "Mr. Summering is dead?"

"Dead?" Harriet leaned forward. "He's dead?"

"Isn't he…didn't you say…"

"Dead? Frank's not dead, unless you know something I don't. Though it would not surprise me one little bit."

"I'm sorry. Then, where is he?"

"Well, he's in Lompoc."

"Prison?"

"Yes, he's in Lompoc prison. Will be there for another five to eight years, God willing. And I have nothing to do with him. I haven't seen him since his arrest. I didn't even go to the trial, thank you very much." Her mouth was set tight as if she didn't want to discuss her husband anymore, but her eyes now held some distant fire.

"We'd not heard, Mrs. Summering, what happened?" Stan took out his digital recorder, set it on the coffee table and turned it on. "I'm going to record this if you don't mind."

Harriet eyed the recorder, shifted so she was angled away from it.

She shook her head. "You…police must have the specifics somewhere, in much more detail than I do."

"Can you tell me?"

She gave a big sigh. "Frank was one of the deacons at Redeemer Baptist over on York Avenue. He ran the youth program…" She turned to Stan expecting him to fill in the rest.

"And…there were what? Sexual improprieties?"

"I think, and not to make excuses mind you, but I think Karen's disappearance affected Frank. He was a normal husband and a decent man before that…happened. But, after, well, he just changed. He must've changed, at least toward kids. Least, that's what they got him for."

"Exactly what was it?" asked Stan.

Harriet Summering looked at Detective Stan Wyld as if he'd just walked through the door and hadn't heard a thing she'd said. "Why, he was hauled out of this house under arrest for diddling the little boys of the church. What did you think?"

"We didn't know, Mrs. Summering, we had no notice," said Stan. "Was this before or after Karen's disappearance?"

"Like I said, of course, this was after what happened to Karen." She spoke as if Stan was uncomprehending.

Stan pretended to write some extensive notes in his notebook to give himself time to think. Instead all he really wrote next to his scribbles was 'Mr. Summering after little boys?' He really didn't think this had anything to do with Karen or Joey or Phillip, but it was just another nasty bud in a case that kept growing branches.

Harriet Summering seemed reluctant to interrupt his writing, but leaned forward anyway. "I divorced the son of a bitch soon as the trial was over," she said in a quiet, assured voice, nodding as if to put an end to the discussion.

"I see," said Stan. He looked at the withered, dry woman before him. Only the eyes seemed alive. Years of uncertainty after Karen disappeared, living with a parent's guilt. Finding out she was murdered and how she was killed and with no one to account for the crime. Finally, husband and supposed ally, a closet sexual predator.

When do we know our life will change?

"I'm sorry. This has been a tough time...with everything that's happened."

Harriet Summering nodded, her eyes moistened. She blinked a few times.

"Maybe," continued Stan consulting notes, "Maybe we can make some progress with Karen's case."

Harriet sighed. "Why are you here detective?"

Stan put down his notebook and sat back. He wanted Harriet Summering to be as comfortable as possible.

"You and your husband were very forthcoming and helpful with detectives Carruthers and Thompson years ago. You both provided those detectives with an excellent description of Karen and what she did that day. It was a good foundation and now I need to build on that."

"You didn't really answer my question about new evidence, detective."

Stan locked eyes with the woman. "There is new evidence…"

Harriet Summering stiffened her shoulders and inhaled quickly but said nothing.

"I'm…I will fill you in after…" Stan smiled. He wanted her to understand. He wanted her to accept the evidence they had and he wanted her not to use that evidence to fuel her imaginings of the last day of her daughter's life. Coupled with the torture that she knew that Karen suffered before dying, the additional details, about hanging upside down, about a knotted rope that nobody had found until fifteen years after the fact, was going to be too much without some equivocating.

"First, though, before I review what we've found, and I promise you will know what we know, I must ask you some questions."

Harriet settled back in the wing back chair and accepted the plan. "Go ahead."

Stan started quickly. "When Karen was here, did you own a boat?"

Whatever Harriet Summering had been expecting as a question, this was not it. "A boat?"

Stan nodded.

Stan could see her considering the question, not so much to come up with an answer but primarily to try and figure why Stan was asking.

"No," she said after hesitation. "Never had one and we never even spoke of getting one. Couldn't have afforded it anyway. Why?"

"Karen ever go boating with friends? Ever have friends that had a boat?"

Harriet shook her head, rewinding her life to a better time. "Karen was a serious girl. Oh, she had her fanciful side, I guess, but, really she had only a few friends." She looked at Stan, "...all girls I might add. So, no, she never went on any sailing date with a boy and I don't believe any of her girlfriends' parents had a boat." She looked back to Stan. "So, no, no boats in her life."

"No trips to Folsom Lake, no outings on the rivers?"

"Detective, I don't think Karen had ever been on a boat in her life. Sorry."

"No matter," said Stan dismissively. "All right, I need you to think back to the last time you saw Karen."

Harriet's eyes fluttered. "Okay."

"Karen disappeared on a Sunday, but let's talk about the few days before that. That weekend."

"Before Sunday? Before that Sunday?" She looked perplexed as if it was a new, unexplored territory. Sadly, to Stan, he thought it might be. It should have been extensively covered by Carruthers and Thompson, but it was given scant coverage, at least based on the notes he had.

"First, regarding that Sunday morning, you said..." Stan opened his notebook to the page where he had copied some of Harriet's and her husband's comments from their interviews conducted right after the bodies had been found. "You or your husband said, 'Karen was excited at breakfast'. Again, this was referring to Sunday morning," Stan explained. "You also said, 'she danced around while I fixed breakfast.'" Stan looked at Harriet.

She shrugged. "I must have said it. She was flitting around getting in the way. This wasn't really normal. Normally she would drag herself to the kitchen and have a glass of orange juice. But that morning, for some reason, she kept moving around and grabbing pieces of bacon that I was cooking."

Harriet smiled a wry smile. "I think I scolded her or asked what she was on. She was...happy, I guess."

Stan smiled and leaned forward a bit. "That's one of the things I want to know. Why was she excited? Why was she not herself? Why was she flitting, as you say, around the kitchen?"

Harriet's eyes widened. "I have no idea. I just remember being annoyed."

"In all her excitement that morning, what did she say her plans were for that day?"

"They asked me that over and over," Harriet sighed. "Besides planning a sleepover with two of her friends later that night, I don't know. She never said anything about what she was going to do in the morning or even later in the afternoon, or where she might be going, or who she might do something with. Nothing. She said nothing. I already said so. I remember after breakfast, she went up to her room to pack for her overnight."

"Okay. Now I want you to think back to the night before she disappeared. What were you and husband doing?"

Harriet shook her head. "The night before? I have no..." She stopped, prisoner of a ragged memory.

Stan didn't move and didn't speak.

"Well, I think, the night before, we, the three of us, played Scrabble or some word game." Her eyes sparkled suddenly and her face softened into tenderness. She laughed at the memory. "I do remember now... Karen, she was a smart girl, she had a good vocabulary, she was always good at those games, you know, but I remember that she kept trying to guess the tiles before she turned them over and putting them on her tray. She'd pick up a tile, hold it tight up against her forehead, close her eyes and look as if she was trying to divine what it was, and then she'd turn it over and look at it. We got to laughing because she kept saying she was right. It was very funny."

She shrugged. "Stupid. But we had a good time. I remember thinking; it was a good family night." She looked at Stan. "I'd forgotten that."

"And before you played that game, the three of you had had dinner?" asked Stan.

"Well, we often..." Harriet paused. "No. Not that night." She seemed captivated by the memory. "I'd not thought of this in forever. Anyway, we didn't eat together as a family. That night Frank and I waited for Karen, waited for her to get home so we could all eat. I'd made her favorite, lasagna, and it was getting cold, so Frank and I decided not to wait. We joked that there may not be any left when she got home."

"She got home, when?"

"Oh, she wasn't too late. We hadn't even cleared the dishes. She sometimes lost track of time, you see, and so it wasn't much of a surprise when she came in a bit late. That's why on that Sunday, the next day, we weren't really worried, for a while anyway, when she didn't come home."

"And did she say where she'd been on Saturday? Why she was late?"

"No, never did. I don't think we even asked. We just assumed she'd been out with her girlfriends."

Stan made a note to review the interview with her friends, though Carruthers's notes had indicated that none of her girlfriends remembered doing anything with her on the Saturday before.

"Who would those friends have been?"

"Who? Well, I'm sure it's all in the report, but let's see, there was Amy Sinclair, Jessica what's her name...Evans, I think. And, Maria Martinet. Those were the three she would hang around with and I'm sure if she was out then most likely Maria was with her."

"Do you know where Maria is nowadays?" Stan tried not to sound too hopeful.

"Vanished," said Harriet with a conciseness that caught Stan off guard.

"Vanished vanished? Gone?"

"Oh...no, not like that, dear no. I mean she took off, not vanished, really. Lit out with some boy when she was still a senior in high school. Didn't even finish school. Just left one day. Her parents had no idea where she'd gone. I guess they finally got a postcard or letter from Philadelphia, of all places, after about a week. S'far as I know, she hasn't been back."

Stan glanced at the open page of his notebook. There was very little written down. What did he expect?

He sighed. Time to float Mallory's theory. "Karen was going to go to a new school just before she disappeared, is that right?"

Harriet looked concerned. "I don't...let me see."

Stan waited while she figured out the answer he already knew.

Harriet was counting on her fingers. "Yes, you're right. She was going to be starting at a new school on that next Tuesday. She disappeared on that Sunday before."

"How was she regarding school? What was her mood?"

"Dear me," said Harriet Summering. "Her mood. I don't really know. She liked school. She did well in almost all classes. I don't think she was very good at math...I should remember..."

"No, what I meant was she looking forward to school? It was going to be a new school."

Harriet looked away. "Well, she was shy that's true and she didn't make friends easily. She wasn't the gregarious type, the cheerleader type, you know. But her friends would be attending with her, so I guess her mood was fine."

"So she wasn't apprehensive?"

"I don't believe so. What..."

"Might she have gone to check out her new school? Gone there to maybe get comfortable with the layout?"

"I don't see why she would have," answered Harriet. "She knew the school layout. She already took combined band practice there all the year before. Flute. No, she knew the school pretty well, I would imagine."

Stan closed his notebook.

Harriet sat up straighter and addressed him. "You said there was new evidence."

Stan nodded. "It may be nothing. It may be important. We can't say for certain. Our Forensics department is going over it this week, so we're not sure."

Harriet waited for him to continue.

Stan cleared his throat. "Recently, when we reviewed the site where Karen was found, we discovered a piece of evidence that had been missed in the initial investigation…"

"Missed?"

Stan felt he didn't need to go into detail about the dedicated Forensics team who had spent three miserable days working a site and had not bothered to look up, and an amateur who seemed to enter the site practically looking for the rope.

"I'd say overlooked the first time, but this is an on-going investigation, never closed. So on a subsequent examination of the site, this new evidence was found. A rope."

Harriet's' expression didn't change. Neither did she move.

"A rope we think may be of a type used in sailing or maybe by someone who is or was a sailor or used to working with ropes, with loops and knots."

At the word 'knots' Harriet jerked her head toward Stan and looked at him dead on. Her voice was unsteady as she asked him, "So, you think it, this rope with knots, may have been used on my Karen?"

"We're not sure at this point. Our hope is that we can eventually use it to find who did this. That's why I asked about Karen and sailing or boating. But it appears, as you said, there's no connection."

Harriet Summering softened her expression and gave a nod. "I see. Thank you. Thank you for telling me," she said.

Stan knew he would never tell her or any of the parents, at least face-to-face, about the deaths of their children in grisly detail. The parents of the dead children needed to be alone when they found out the whole story, if they ever did. They didn't need an old cop gauging their reaction to what he could tell them.

Harriet leaned forward with her elbows on the armrests, ready to rise and see him out.

"One more thing Mrs. Summering…"

"Do please call me Harriet.

"Harriet." Stan paused. "When Karen went out on the Saturday before, probably with her friends as you say, and when she left on that Sunday morning, how did she go? Did she walk or get a ride from someone? Did maybe someone's parents pick her up?"

"Walk!" Harriet gave a sad, remembering laugh. "She never walked. She always took her bike. Always. She rode that bike everywhere, detective. Even if she was only going half a block away, she'd jump…she had a way of sort of slinging the bike around and kind of jumping on it as she started to move. All in one motion. She did it all the time. No, detective, she and her bike were almost joined together. She never went anywhere without that bike."

As soon as she uttered it, Harriet caught the import of what she said.

"Her bike…" whispered Harriet. She paled and looked away.

Stan continued with care. "Yes, her bike. Harriet, where is her bike?"

"Her bike…" Harriet Summering's hands trembled a little. She didn't notice but kept staring past Stan, finally turning to him.

"I don't know."

CHAPTER 29

The dream comes on hard. He never remembers the beginning of it but Jess is in it and she's standing in a train station next to a steam train...

...and the steam is billowing all around her. She's dressed in her red coat that his mother had made for her. It has a large hood that Jess never wore, except she is wearing it on the train platform.

There is a conductor wanting to take her ticket. The person in a uniform is bothering her and starts to search her pockets. She struggles. M tries to get to her to help. He wants to push the person away, but before he can get there, more uniforms arrive and surround her.

He grabs the nearest uniform, and with all his strength, pulls him away from Jessie. It takes all his strength and yet the man in uniform moves so slowly. M pulls as hard as he can, yet the man moves at a glacial pace, falling in exaggerated slow motion back toward M.

As he falls, he turns and faces M. Suddenly, there are more men in uniform and they are looking at him. M can see Jessie disappear between the growing numbers of men that seem to be crowding around him.

They continue to press him. He can't breathe. They're pressing on his chest. He tries to call out to Jessie, but he can't see her and he can't hear her.

He calls out to his mother, and as he turns, he can see her on the floor. She looks to be asleep but he knows that's a lie.

Still they come. Still they press. They seem to be asking questions. Everyone is asking all at once. He can't understand. He can't breathe. He can't... He calls out for his father.

As soon as he does, all is silence.

The men pressing on him stop, frozen. They look over his shoulder. They just freeze. They stare at whatever is behind him.

He doesn't want to turn around, but he has to. He looks down and somehow a mallet appears, a heavy mallet, like they use in a circus to pound in the stakes that hold up the big top. It is a massive mallet. Chrome gleams off a chipped metal head as it makes an arc around. Then it melts. It just melts.

He tries to stop turning his head. He knows he doesn't want to see what is behind him. He feels it whatever it is. He hears the breathing. A raspy, chugging breath. Like a bull just before it charges. He looks down. There is a bed sheet or white expanse in front of him. It is perfectly flat. He lowers himself until he's at eyelevel with the white plain. All around him is white. Across the white coming toward him rolls a silver ball like a bright ball bearing, making a slight hiss as it rolls. It is coming in a straight line. He looks forward to where it's going to go and he sees a wrinkle in the white. He knows the ball bearing is going to hit the wrinkle. For some reason he's afraid to let the ball bearing hit the wrinkle. No, he's terrified. It gets closer and closer, rolling, hissing like metal across damask.

It takes all his energy to drag his eyes from the wrinkle to the approaching ball and back to the wrinkle, and back, and back. He holds his breath. He waits for...what?

The ball gets to the wrinkle and goes over the wrinkle and he exhales.

M woke up sweating, suffocating, doubled over in a tight fetal position and trying to catch his breath.

His mother was dead. It was the thought that he shouldn't think. He tried to stop himself, but as much as he played his fingers over the nubs of his aunt's couch and pretended tiny cars were racing between the nubs, as much as he tried to force his thoughts somewhere else, it didn't work. It never does.

The screaming.
Punching 911 on the phone over and over.

219

His mother's voice calling his name. Again and again.

Jessie terrified.
Putting the phone down carefully and slowly. Creeping down the hallway.
His mother's plaintive voice. Begging now. His father's back. Hunched over her lying on the floor. What? Shadows on the ceiling. His father turning on him like an enraged bull. Drunk grinning.
What was his father doing?
Swinging the lamp.
Lamp cord, like an obedient snake, whipping past M's head. The lamp base cracking into his arm, spinning him around, knocking him down.
On the floor. On his side. Can't breathe. Pain takes all his breath.
His mother whimpering.
He watches, helpless, as his father raises the lamp to do more.
Do something!

Like the bright ball bearing, its sick black intent was inevitable. It would hit the wrinkle. It would crush what it hit. It would go over the wrinkle and he would only watch. It would crush and he would only watch. He sees his mother's eyes. He is the last thing she sees. He watches. The ball bearing does its work.

The lamp comes down.
Her eyes plead. Forgives him. Loves him.
The scream is his own.
Now his hand is on another lamp, gripping, launching up. Swinging all the way around. The heavy mallet. The chrome mallet. Stopping when it hits bone. Once more. Swinging round again, faster, crushing, crushing, crushing the face of the beast.
The bull would not charge again.

He wiped his arm across his face and tried to forget what he could not stop remembering. But the knife that was regret bit deeper still and would not go away.

"I'm sorry," he whispered, turning to face the wall.

Then, at last, unashamed, he cried.

CHAPTER 30

Mallory pulled into Placerville, guided the Honda into the first gas station she saw and stopped. She didn't really need gas, but she could tell by the smell that her car sure needed a rest.

She spread the map out on the hood of the car. She didn't really need it either. She had GPS and she knew the address where she was headed, but she also knew herself and knew she had to orient herself to the whole town. It was easier for her to see on a map.

The conversation with Stan kept coming back to her. She thought he meant to sound fatherly or at the very least, a senior partner giving advice to a junior partner. But what he'd really been saying was, don't screw this up.

*How little you know about m*e.

She spread the map out another fold. She compared the map to the hills and the lake and found the street she was looking for, Douglas Avenue, not too far from downtown.

The house was easy to find, on a corner lot across from the railroad track and beyond one of the rivers that ran into the lake. It was a kid neighborhood, one like she always wanted to grow up in. She always heard her parents talk about the baseball games behind the tract houses and playing in the woods with the neighborhood kids, throwing rocks at the yellowjacket nests and hiding from their parents on Sunday morning when the family was supposed to go to church, and instead playing kick the can in the woods with 'the boys'. The girls playing with the boys. It sounded so quaint. So nice. She'd never experienced it but she missed it.

516 Douglas. The sidewalk and the walk to the front door was cracked concrete all the way. The picket fence had been

white at one time, but was now faded and flaked and the vines that had covered it were still there but were half withered as if they were trying to decide whether to live or die.

Mallory had called yesterday to verify someone would be home. Joey's mother said she would, though she had sounded unsure if she really wanted to open an old casket of memories. Mallory had assured her that she would take very little time, but because they had reopened the case, it was important that she retake her story.

Margaret Marshall had acquiesced, sounding to Mallory weary and resigned.

The knock on the door seemed to echo throughout the house and the sound of shuffling footsteps came with regret.

"Yes?"

She hadn't opened the door or even parted the curtains, but Mallory could see she had just approached the door, turned and leaned against the jamb.

"What do you want?"

Drunk?

"Um, I'm Mallory Dimante... we spoke earlier about... your son. "

There was no answer.

"I...I'm here because we re-opened the case, remember, and I asked if we could speak to you about it?"

Mallory could see Mrs. Marshall unmoving against the jamb.

"You said it was okay."

The door opened as Margaret Marshall walked away. "Sure. Come on in if I said that."

Mallory stepped inside and closed the door. It smelled of pine and old blankets and warmth.

"You want something...?" Mrs. Marshall's arm rotated as if she was encouraging her brain to continue on with its thoughts. "...like coffee. 'Cept I don't have any at the moment. Water, though. Water, I got."

"No, ma'am I'm fine." Mallory hurried to catch up with her. She had disappeared down the hall as if Mallory knew the way. The house was neat and tidy but time bound. Today's newspaper sat atop a *People* magazine from 1997. Fresh flowers, daisies, sat on an undusted side table. A ripped and faded area carpet sat atop waxed floors.

The hallway was filled with pictures of a little boy Mallory could only assume was Joey. She stopped and stared at a picture when, she imagined, he was about 4. She and Stan had only the one photo to go by and it had been a typical school picture, pale blue background, a sweet smile, tooth missing, and a sweater with a knitted moose across the front. The wall before her was a testament to Joey's life and parent's pride. Coming home from the hospital, the whole family posing in front of the new Ford, Christmas knee deep in paper, a birthday in the backyard. A dog with his best friend. Finally, Joey with just his Mom. Leaning his head against her shoulder, both smiling, together. About 4 years old, Mallory guessed.

"You got kids?"

Mallory turned. "No ma'am." Then, indicating the wall and the whole house in a soft wave, "this is nice."

"Yeah," said Mrs. Marshall as if seeing a friend she hadn't seen in a while but still liked. "It is, ain't it?"

She moved to stand by Mallory. "This here is all him and what he was about. His activities and all. I got tons more, but I had to pick the best to show."

Mallory thought she had chosen well. She could tell a lot about Joey. She could tell she probably would have liked him as a kid. She didn't run into many kids she liked.

"This here one is the last one before..." She shrugged. "Before he was...gone, left, ran away or taken or something," she said lowering her voice. "Least that's the last thing the police said, their last theory." She stopped and looked at Mallory.

"That what you think happened?"

She didn't wait for an answer but turned and walked into the kitchen.

"This is my husband, Erle."

"Erle, this is..." But, she had already forgotten.

"Mallory," Mallory finished. She extended her hand to a graying slumped figure in a red checked bathrobe, nursing a steaming glass of water.

Erle Marshall cocked his head and gave her a dismissive wave. He turned back to his water and the sport section spread out on the table.

"Erle is not too partial to the cops. He just didn't get along with them, you know, through all this."

She reached over and put a teabag in his water.

"We both think it's real nice you re-opening this thing up and still working on it though, don't we Erle?"

Erle stirred the tea. The spoon went round and round and the words came out in a slow steep.

"Can't say I really care one way or the other. What's done is done and no amount of effort on your part and no amount of me thanking you to do more is gonna fix things. Just so. So I say forget it. Catch him or don't catch him, it's all the same. The curtain's been drawn and ain't nobody gonna pull it back. That's all."

Mallory turned away and pretended to study the stove and the teapot and the small decorative tiles with little Dutch kids pretending to garden that arced over the back of the range. This was life after death. The life that goes on when someone else's stops. A quiet roiling wake of bitter left behinds. She shifted her bag from one arm to the other and glanced back down the hallway full of pictures. Tough to move forward when you're always looking backward.

"Come sit down please." Margaret Marshall turned and touched her arm. "Tell us what you have and why you came all this way."

Mallory pulled out the chair, set her bag down alongside her and folded her hands.

"I don't want to give you hope by my coming here. Erle, you're right, no amount of anything can fix what was done, but," she shrugged, "this is what we do. This is our job and we try to do it as best we can."

"And now we're both blessed and cursed by time. A lot of time has passed that will make what we are now doing that much more difficult. Procedures that could have been done earlier obviously are no longer viable. For much of our reopened investigation we must rely on the good work done by those who went before us. And for the most part what they did was good. Even though the case remains unsolved, it also is one of the most investigated cases in our force's history. We have mountains of evidence we may never have gotten on any other case."

"Whether you know it or not, what happened to Joey and the others touched many, many people. They worked very hard to solve this, partly for Joey, partly for you two and partly for us. This is what we do and we want to be good at it."

Margaret Marshall turned her head a bit and smiled through moist eyes. "You're nice, I can tell. Not every cop was so nice to us..." She looked at Erle who remained staring into his tea. "I mean, there were all kinda accusations, you know, like we had something to do with it or something. They didn't understand, Joey was our life. He was the best thing Erle and I ever did. Ever."

An hour later Mallory let herself out and closed the door with a quiet click. She shook her head. No new school. No boat or sailing or rope work. No memory of what happened to Joey's bike. He had had one, but no idea where it was now. The only new information she had gleaned, and that came from the tenuous memory of Margaret Marshall, was the day before Joey disappeared he had been with his Cub Scout troop. As usual.

She stood on the Marshall's porch and watched what passed for normal life in Placerville, California. She could see two boys playing with a radio controlled police car, a man washing his SUV with a bucket of suds and a chamois mitt, two teenage girls in what looked like prom dresses were trying to keep their dresses from flying above their waists as they waited for their dates to open the doors for them.

All Mallory could think about as she made her way down the steps and out the gate to her dirty Honda was what happens when very bad things happen to ordinary people living ordinary lives in your everyday small town. The wind pushed some fallen oak leaves around the street and through the flurry of leaves came the radio controlled car careening side to side. It made a sharp left turn, bounced off the front tire of Mallory's car and spun to her feet.

The two boys came in hot pursuit.

"I told you you didn't know how to drive it," yelled the bigger kid with dirty brown hair to the smaller one who looked like he had been punched.

"Sorry lady."

The big kid picked up the car off its side, cradled it and began exercising all parts testing its turning range and the strength of the drive wheels. The smaller kid, with big brown eyes and a worried expression, stood a few feet away, watching the whirring of the wheels.

It was obvious to Mallory that even though the car seemed to work, she was sure the big kid would exact some sort of retribution when she was gone.

"Is it okay?" asked the smaller one. He could see the wheels moving and said it with the hope that he would escape serious harm.

"Maybe," said the big one. With a quick glance at Mallory he started back down the street. "Let's go."

The young one looked at Mallory.

"Its fine, I'm sure," she said.

The boy with the brown eyes didn't leave with the big one, but cocked his head and asked, "You a cop?"

Mallory hesitated. "I am."

"You here about Joey?"

Mallory was surprised. "Yes, did you know him?"

The boy shrugged, then, "No way, I'm too little, but my older cousin did. He was his best friend. We all thought you guys had forgotten about Joey."

Mallory smiled a reassuring smile. "We never forget."

The little boy seemed satisfied with that and started to run off but turned back to Mallory.

"My cousin always said you'd find him, after all you can't really get lost at a circus." He turned then and ran off.

Mallory opened the car door, tossed her notebook on the seat and started to get in.

Circus?

It took her almost a block to catch up with little Stevie Ashcroft, the cousin of the next to last person to see Joey Marshall alive.

CHAPTER 31

"What would you think about living in Arizona?" asked M.

"Where is Azona?" asked Jess. She was busy dressing Mr. Bear with some paper dresses she had colored and cut out.

"Arizona," corrected M. "It's a different state, but it's not far."

Jessie continued to work on getting Mr. Bear's arms into the paper jacket without ripping it. Her tongue slid sideways indicating her level of concentration. She didn't say anything.

"Well?"

"Huh?"

"I said, shall we move to Arizona? What do you say?"

"No," she looked up at M. "Why do you want to leave? I like it here."

"You like it here?"

After a moment, Jess said, "Ruby's nice."

M started to walk around in a circle in front of Ruby's steps. Sweet Jesus. If Jess were older she'd realize we're living with a relative who not only hates me but wishes we had never been dumped on her doorstep and we're being imprisoned each day by a fat old ugly fake fortune teller who fleeces people out of their savings by telling them what they want to hear.

He looked at his sister who was now dancing Mr. Bear around the step, showing off his new jacket.

She is happy here, because she's not hungry and she has a place to sleep and no one is mean to her and no one is yelling at her. The lack of negatives does not make a positive.

M tried to think what his mother would say. How would she approach them if they were moving to a different place? How would she convince us to not bitch our way all the way to the desert southwest? Land of warmth and sun.

If they had been the near perfect family, she would have sat them both down and explained what a great opportunity they had as a family. She would tell them that their father had a new job and she was going to be able to find a job too and there were a lot of nice neighborhoods with lots of kids and the sun shone year round. She would have gone on about the good schools and lots of shit neither he nor Jessie would have cared about.

He and Jessie would have said it sounded great. In a near perfect family.

But of course, that wouldn't have been the case. The only way she would have come to them about moving to Arizona would have been in the middle of the night. She would have woken them by opening their dresser drawers and putting their clothes in cardboard boxes. She would have made them dress quickly. It was important that they blow town before the creditors knew they we're gone. Vamoose. We have to vamoose. She would have made it an adventure. She could have done it many times until they ran out of states to flee to.

"Jess, have you seen the cat?"

"What cat?" she asked

"I call him Ambition," said M. He scanned the road down to Aunt Janey's trailer. He expected it to dart out of the underbrush or from between two trailers just because he mentioned its name. Maybe carrying a recent kill. Something for lunch.

"What's a 'Bitchin? Why'd you call him that?"

"He's grey and white. And his name is 'Ambition'."

"Is he ours? Is he our cat?" she asked, suddenly interested in finding the cat.

"Naw, he's nobody's cat. He sort of wanders. Doesn't really have a home. You know, like us."

Jessie pouted. "We have a home." She pointed down to Aunt Janey's trailer. "I can see it. But, can he be our cat?"

"You two have a cat?" The voice came from behind them. The little brown midget that had seemed so scared of the cops when they saw him in Ruby's trailer waddled around the corner of the trailer toward them.

M didn't know why, but he wondered how long the little shit had been just around the corner. Had he been listening? Damn. It creeped him out knowing the shithead had been lurking around.

Jessie turned and smiled proudly. "His name is Bitchin'."

"What d'ya want?" challenged M.

The fat thing shuffled toward them. "Hey, we ain't met, I'm Pitic." There was greasy smile slicked on its face and a little pudge of a hand was extended. When M didn't take it, Pitic raised the hand and turned it into a wave of greeting. He took his place in front of them.

Then he looked at Jessie. "Scared me the other day when you said the cops were around, did you know that." He shook a mocking finger in Jessie's direction. "Had me scared to death." The smile was small but lit up white teeth in a round, mocha colored face.

Jessie tilted her head to one side. "No, I didn't."

"Oh yes, you did, you did," Pitic said to Jessie, then turned to M.

"That grey and white bitch you call Bitchin..." Then laughed at his own joke. "I've seen it around. Someone tried to kick it the other day. Missed. Don't need more animals 'round here. There's plenty here now."

"It's just a cat," said M.

"Yeah," echoed Jess, marshaling a six year olds defensive stance.

"Whatta ya got there little lady?" asked Pitic as he sat down next Jessie. "Is that a bear?"

M moved in closer to the steps. He watched how Pitic stared at Jessie. He noticed how close he sat to his sister.

"Come on Jess, we gotta go," said M angling his head down the street toward Aunt Janey's trailer.

Jess picked up Mr. Bear and was dancing him along her leg toward Pitic.

"He's *Mister* Bear and he has a new jacket, see?" She raised up Mr. Bear.

M could see Pitic switch his gaze from the bear to Jessie.

"Very nice," whispered Pitic. "Very nice indeed."

"Jess, come on!"

"I gotta go," said Jess to Pitic with a politeness M felt Pitic didn't deserve.

"Ya gotta go, ya gotta go." Again Pitic laughed at his own joke.

M put his arm around Jess and they started for Janey's trailer. Over his shoulder he said to Pitic, "Tell Ruby we're leaving."

Pitic kept his smile. "She's with a customer."

"I know," said M, "just let her know."

Pitic said nothing but M could sense they were being studied as they walked away. He wanted to turn and demand to know what Pitic was looking at, but he didn't.

Jessie danced Mr. Bear on her arm then made him jump to M's sore arm. M raised it a bit so it would be a level dance floor and Mr. Bear did his best imitation of a dancing bear with a new jacket.

"So, what do you think about Arizona?" asked M, forgetting how he believed his mother might have approached the subject. "Sound good? We have relatives there. Pretty sure."

Jessie jumped Mr. Bear back to her arm, then lowered him to her side and continued to walk without saying anything.

"Well?" M pushed.

Jessie shrugged. Her little girl shrug. A quick up and down of her shoulders. "I dunno. I kinda like it here, M. okay?"

She looked up at him. "Okay?"

"Fine." He didn't want to sound resigned and defeated. He knew the day was coming. It was good just to plant the idea for now. Maybe that's what his mother would do. He hoped so.

"We have to leave sooner or later, you know." He raised his head nonchalantly and looked around at the other trailers as if it didn't matter if they left tomorrow or next year.

Jess brightened. "Okay. Later."

M couldn't help it. He smiled then raised his head and looked over her head toward the chain link fence. Somebody had posted something on the fence. It was tough to see in the shadows of the juniper tree. Why would somebody post something on the fence? Maybe it was some sort of 'No Trespassing' sign. Kind of looked like someone had found a doll and stuck it up on the fence.

"Take Mr. Bear in. I'll be right there. I want to see what's on the fence." He started toward the fence.

"I want to see too," said Jessie, following.

"Okay, but…" M stopped short about fifteen feet away. His eyes widened and hairs stood on end. He spun around to Jessie. "It's nothing, let's go." He stayed between Jessie and the fence.

"I want to see what it is."

"Just an old rag somebody stuck in the fence. Quick, let's get back to the trailer and get a snack. Before Aunt Janey gets home, okay?"

M corralled Jessie and turned her around. They quick-stepped their way to the trailer, each pretending they weren't racing.

It wasn't until after midnight, after Jessie was asleep and after M knew his aunt had fallen asleep in front of the late night version of Wheel of Fortune, that he carefully opened the front door and crept down the steps. He felt exposed and vulnerable as he made his way back down the street under the harsh streetlight. He angled over to the fence. He didn't think his aunt owned a flashlight and the streetlight light didn't reach under the juniper. He had brought what he could find, some matches and an old dishrag from under the sink.

It was still there. He couldn't see it clearly because of the shadows, but he could see the shape.

He took out the matches and struck one. It was a moment before he looked up.

Ambition's dead eyes stared back him.

M took a deep breath and scanned the dead cat. It was hanging on the fence because someone had run a wooden spike all the way through its neck and then jammed the spike into the openings of the fence. Blood had run down the spike and spilled onto the ground.

Using the dishrag as a shield, he grabbed the spike and pulled it out of the fence then caught the cat in the rag as it slipped down. He tried to remove the spike from the cat, but it wouldn't budge and while he wanted to remove it to make cat look close to normal again, in the end he left the spike where it was and wrapped up the cat as best he could.

There was no question of burying it, he had no shovel. He thought about taking back and depositing it in Aunt Janey's trashcan, but it just didn't seem right. And what if she opened the trash. That wouldn't work.

In the end he rationalized that it was a wild cat and should stay in the wild.

"Sorry girl," said M to the bundle in the dishrag, "this is the best I can do."

With that he turned his back to the fence and with both hands held the cat at arm's length and launched it up backwards over his head and the fence. He wheeled quickly and heard it thud a good ten feet on the other side of the fence, landing amongst some sort of brush.

"Sorry."

Later, as he was lying in bed, he wondered why it didn't bother him more. He had realized with that much blood that had run down the spike and ended up on the ground that good old Ambition had probably been dispatched right there on the fence. The cat had seen whoever had done it.

He closed his eyes, knowing that he wouldn't sleep for a while.   He still remembered Ambition's eyes and he still remembered his mother's eyes. Both dead.

CHAPTER 32

She knew it was a bad idea to talk on the cell while she drove. Illegal *and* a bad idea, but she was jazzed and wanted to tell Stan about her talk with the older Ashcroft boy. And she wanted to get back to the office.

She wheeled out of the service station alternately grabbing the wheel, her cell, and her coffee and headed out, almost clipping the back end of someone's fifth wheel travel trailer.

"Sorry. Sorry." She waved. They returned the finger.

"Pick up Stanley you old goat. I have a goddamn lead!"

'This is Detective Wyld, leave a message.'

"Stan, I talked to ..." *beep*   "shitfuck, Stan I talked to Joey's parents then I ran into this little kid and he's the younger cousin of the kid who knows where Joey went. Stan, I know! He went to ..." *beep* "Damn!"

She punched her cell off and threw it on the seat. She made sure the Honda was straightened out, set the cruise and reached for her coffee.

Okay, okay. He went to the carnival. Thanks for telling us now, you prick. Where were you fifteen years ago? She knew the answer to that too. He was also at the carnival.

She didn't want to be driving. She wanted to be slamming on her laptop. She wanted to be reviewing her notes. She wanted to re-listen to the tape she made of the Ashcroft boy. Well, half a tape. She'd forgotten to turn it on until she was halfway through her interview. She had made him repeat most of it anyway.

What a scene. Her heart was still pumping.

Not only did Joey go to the carnival, but he rode his bike. Stan, you were right, you bastard. It has to do with intent. Unless he was grabbed, bike and all, while on the way to the carnival. Possible. But it didn't feel right.

What it felt like and what it sounded like listening to the Ashcroft kid was that Joey had planned to go back to the carnival...Stan he was going *back* to the carnival, which means he went before, which he did with his scout troop. But why go back?

Whatever happened, happened at this carnival. Has to be.

Mallory pushed a bit on the accelerator but Route 50 was increasingly winding and she had to back off again.

She really needed to pull over and work her notes, get online.

She tried to calm down and plan what she would do when she got back.

Damn Stan, you would have probably handled this better. Actually I know you would have.

She laughed to herself. Halfway through talking to the Ashcroft boy, trying to keep it light, trying to get as much information as she could without looking desperate, she really did think to herself in a moment of panic...what would Stan do? What would he ask? Would he be a hardass and push, or be the friend of the family, the genial uncle, just stopping by for a chat?

Her admiration for Detective Stanley Wyld swelled as she realized he had, by some convoluted detective-type elimination, come up with the plausible idea that the three kids had been headed somewhere. That they hadn't been grabbed randomly. Damn!

A carnival, for crissakes. What was up with that?

Mallory began to tick off the questions she needed to follow up.

Were all our victims going to a carnival?

Yes. Why? Because it fit. It felt right. It answered the question of what could be the same in all the small towns. It explained so much.

A carnival with freaks and stuff. Moved from town to town. Something all kids would want to go to. Stan, it fits. It fits!

She had to verify there was even a carnival in town at that time, on those dates? God if there was. Holy shit, if there was one in each location where these three kids were....that would clinch it.

She tried to remember the 'who, what, where' scenario, like a reporter. She had an idea and reached for her digital audio recorder. She turned it on and began dictating...

Who. Who exactly did Joey go with the first time? Scout troop. Who's in that troop? More important what did they do? Who did they see?

Why. Why the hell did Joey plan to go back and why alone?

What. What carnival was it? Was it the same one where each kid went? What was the main attraction?

Where. Where was the carnival in each location and more important, where is it now?

When. If this is right then we know the 'when'. Dear God, we surely know the 'when' now.

Then there's the 'How.'

Mallory punched off the recorder. With one hand she hit the rewind, and splitting her view between the winding road and the digital readout, found the beginning of her session with Ritchie Ashcroft.

She concentrated on the road for a minute, making sure she was in control, that she wasn't driving erratically. Then she hit the play button.

'... I'm with Sacramento PD...and as I said, I want to tape this so I don't have to take so many notes...that okay with you Rich?

(mumble)

... And your parents?

...Sure go ahead. I guess. What's this about again? Joey?

Right. Yes. Now Ritchie...let's see, first. You remember Joey right? Your younger cousin... Stevie said you knew him?

Yeah.

Okay. Well, what was Joey like?

He was okay.

Okay. You were friends, right. I mean you did stuff with him. Hung out...

Yeah, pretty much best friends. Hung out, I guess, did some video games....played baseball...kid kind of stuff."

Mallory stopped the recorder.

She remembered how she felt when Ritchie Ashcroft was describing his best friend. Joey's parents had told her the parent stuff. Their memories were gilded with the best; Joey's smile, his laugh, his friendliness.

But Ritchie Ashcroft was painting a different picture of Joey. They were dealing with a little boy who had been viciously murdered. He wasn't a picture on a glass wall. He wasn't his school picture; he wasn't just the nice things his parents said about him. He was a little nine year old who hung out with his friends, who played video games, who had wanted some unknown thing so bad at a carnival that he went back there by himself...for what? For whom?

She felt a hitch in her throat.

That's the answer they needed and the one she came to ask Ritchie Ashcroft.

She pulled down the visor to block the setting sun and hit Play again.

"....Ok, you were what eight then?

Yeah, think so. Eight. Joey was nine, I think.

And you're twenty three now?

Yep

Do you remember when Joey disappeared? The day he was gone?

'Course

It was 15 or so years...

I still remember.

Good...good. Then, would tell me about that day?

(long silence)

Ritchie...you remember?

Of course, of course, who could forget...I mean he was my best friend, one of 'em anyway. We were buds, you know.

What did you do that morning? The two of you?

Nothing special, I guess. You know, school hadn't started. We just did stuff.

Did you ride your bikes?

Sure. All over. I don't remember whether we did that morning or not.

What about the afternoon? You guys went to a circus together?

Hell, no. That was the day before. With our scout troop.

Day before...?

And it wasn't any circus, more like a carnival with freaks and stuff. I don't think there were any animals there.

So, wait a minute. The day before Joey disappeared you guys both went to this cir...carnival? You guys didn't go on the day he disappeared?

We didn't. (long pause) Joey did.

On his bike?

Sure, on his bike.

Hairs stood up on her neck. She turned the recorder off. It was enough to hear it again. Stan had been right. This was more than a random abduction. Joey was chosen specifically or, by his actions, he ended up selecting himself.

Either way, there was intent on Joey's part. He intended to go back to the carnival. Unfortunately, Ritchie Ashcroft had been less than helpful when it came to the reason why Joey did what he did. Maybe he knew and wasn't saying. Maybe he had no idea.

She remembered Ritchie's parents looking nervously at each other. It had been fifteen years, but they didn't seem to recollect what Ritchie was saying. This did not seem to be the way they remembered that day.

She hit the play button again.

Why? Why did he go back?

Dunno...

And why didn't you go with him?

Me? I wasn't planning on going back.

And Joey was?

Yeah. He...After we went on the Saturday, you know the day before, to the carnival, he was all excited. He started to tell me what had got him so riled up, but... he never did, really.

He never told you or you don't want to say?

No. I dunno, we got involved with other things. But, you know, I could tell he was kinda keyed up.

He didn't say anything?

Well, yeah, he did say something kinda funny, kinda weird, well not weird for Joey; he was a bit out there sometimes...

What?

(Ritchie laughs) I remember him hooking his fingers into his shirt like he's got suspenders on, you know, and says 'there's lots of opportunities back there, you know. Lots of 'em'. I thought he was quoting a movie or something. But when he said it, he pointed one thumb backward toward the carnival.

That's it?

Well, then he said, 'And I'm gonna get me some!' (Ritchie laughs again).

Why is that funny?

Because we must've said that line all weekend, every time we'd see some goofy thing we wanted, it was 'I'm gonna get me some!' Just funny, you know.

Why did he think there were opportunities there? What was he talking about?

Got me.

What did he see there? What did you see there?

(Silence)

There must've been something. What did you guys do, that you can remember?

I dunno, jeez, let me think. We bought our tickets. We got some food. We didn't go on many rides. Joey used to get queasy on things like the Tilt-A-Whirl or the Scrambler. And we'd just eaten.

So what did you do?

There was this long line of tents, some of them big, some smaller. And they all had different kind of shows, or freaks. Let's see, there was a hairy, bearded lady, a palm reader, some guy with a sword... there were a couple of freaky animals...some large rat thing. Joey said we had to see them all. Every one. And we did too. Went into every tent, even the ones with the hootchie ladies dancing with not much on, as I remember.

Ritchie, I'm trying to understand what it was that Joey wanted...what he saw...what he wanted to go back for.

Her fingers found the buttons and she shut off the recorder. Most of the rest was Mallory asking what she thought she should ask. 'What would Stan ask' she kept repeating in her head.

She'd tried to ask Ritchie in three different ways what it was that attracted Joey to the carnival. It wasn't until she was about to leave that she had some success with Ritchie. She thought, though she wasn't sure.

She checked the milepost as she went past. With a start she realized she was approaching Olive Park, the same pulloff where the bodies were found. She checked her mirror, signaled, and pulled off, cozying up to the large rocks that prevented anyone from driving into the woods.

She fast forwarded the recorder a bit, hit play. Her eyes searched the woods before her as she listened again.

...Ritchie, do this for me. Close your eyes and pretend you're at the carnival. You're with Joey...

I...

No...Really close your eyes. I know it seems stupid, but you never know...and this may help.

I don't know, I think I've remembered all I can.

Anyway, try.

Okay...we're at the carnival...

You've just gotten something to eat...

Okay...we're going down the line of tents. We peek in the tent with the alligator boy, I think, but you can see it's just going to be a kid with some rubbery tail attached, you know with scales and such...

Then what?

Okay, then we go across to where you bang the thing with the mallet, you know so it goes up and dings. We try it, don't do so good. Joey heads for the palm reader. I'm not interested and I go next door to see their version of the strong man. At least he's lifting some weights but it's with his nipples if you can believe it...

Keep the eyes closed. Where was Joey?

I had to go get him from the palm reader...

So? You went to get him and...

(Long silence) Yeah...I had to get him. I poked my head in the tent. Huh...

What?

Just remembered something sort of funny...I dunno, maybe...anyway I poked my head in and Joey was sitting with his back to me and he and the palm lady...huh...

What?

Well... they weren't reading palms; they were leaning over some crystal ball. Soon as I poked my head in, they both turned because I let a lot of light in. They both turned to me like...

Like what?

Like I'd interrupted something important...almost like I'd caught them at a dirty thing, you know....Huh...they almost looked guilty, now that I think about it.

Then what?

Nothing. Joey plunked down some money and got up and came with me.

But, it's funny...

What is?

I asked him what she said his fortune was, what did his future look like.

What did he say?

(Pause) Said his future is taken care of. Something like 'money is not an issue'. That's what he said. I remember because he said he'd pay for everything else we did that day and I let him and he did. Funny thing.

Yeah...

Mallory shut off the recorder for a moment. She was tempted to go into the trees again, find the clearing and explore some more. But after they had found the tree, even in the growing dark, she and Stan had circled the clearing, examining every tree and bush around the perimeter. There was nothing else. No reason to go there.

She fast forwarded to near the end and started it playing again. She needed to hear the confirmation.

So, it's now the next day after the troop went to the carnival, right?

Yeah, okay.

What did he say to you?

Nothing. Not really. I had to go eat lunch and then I had to go somewhere, don't remember exactly where but my parents had something planned.

What about Joey?

He said he had someplace to go too.

Where?

No idea.

The carnival?

(Pause) Maybe. I do remember he had a backpack on. He never hardly ever had one while he rode his bike. He had this bigger mountain type bike with big wheels and flames on both the front and back fenders. He sat up so high, that's why he didn't want to wear a backpack. He said it threw him off balance.

Did it?

Usually. He was a smallish kid you know, always had trouble adjusting the backpack so it was tight enough. Kept slipping.

So, he biked away from you?

Yeah.

What was he wearing?

Hah. What he always wore. The damn Giants jacket. SanFran Giants baseball. Always wore it.

Which direction did he go?

South. Sort of south east, down River Road.

Which direction was the carnival?

The same, I guess. Southeast. They set up in one of the lots past the storage centers. But...

What?

The carnival left the night before. He'd have to do a lot of biking to catch up to it I'd guess. If that was what he was thinking.

He would. Unless someone waited for him.

She stopped the recorder and picked up her phone. No one had mentioned the backpack before. And no one had mentioned the bike before. And no one had mentioned the direction he left before.

Unless she believed Ritchie. He claimed he gave all the information to the police when they questioned him about Joey. But, that was when he went missing. No one ever came around after they found the body. Until now.

Mallory stopped tapping on the steering wheel. A sudden thought struck her and she shivered. She remembered the little radio-controlled car hitting her tire. She saw so clearly the youngest Ashcroft asking if she was a cop.

Was she here for Joey he had asked?

Was she here for Joey?

What if she had come tomorrow? What if no kids had been playing in the street?

Are you a cop he had asked?

What if.

It all had to work out for her to find out about Joey and the carnival. That meant it would all work out. She was sure.

She picked up her phone and was about to dial Stan again when she saw she had a voicemail.

She listened then shut the phone. "Good, 'bout time. I'll be there."

The Honda actually spit a little gravel as it pulled back onto 50. She pretended she had Stan's car and gripped the steering wheel with a death grip and grimaced the way she imagined Mario Andretti would. She wasn't exactly sure who Mario Andretti was but she was pretty sure he had something to do with race cars, or maybe it was motor oil.

Leaning back in the seat, she hit the accelerator as hard as she could. The fan belt in the Honda shrieked in annoyance.

It felt damn good to be getting somewhere.

CHAPTER 33

It was bad enough that his aunt had set him to cleaning out her garage, a job which had taken most of the day. After the cat incident last night, he hated to leave Jessie alone, even if she was at Ruby's. He had that crawly feeling that he should keep an eye on her.

There was no one in the trailer which meant they were in the fortune telling RV.

He found them like rats huddled in a dark corner. At least that's the way he felt.

When he yanked open the RV door, the sunlight streamed in. Both Pitic and Jessie held up their hands to shield their eyes. Ruby stared straight at him, oblivious to the blast of light. The candles fluttered with the sudden rush of air.

Jessie and Pitic were side by side on the double chair across from Ruby.

M wasted no time. "Time to go Jess." He didn't like the fact that she was sitting so close to Pitic. Pitic had his arm around her shoulders. What happened to thinking that Pitic smelled? That he was disgusting. 'He's digesting,' she'd said. It was cute then.

Now, he didn't know what was going on. Relationships were changing and he couldn't keep up and didn't understand.

"So, is your aunt home?" challenged Pitic. He stared straight at him. "It's not even four yet."

M held his gaze. He was shaking but he didn't know why.

He raised his chin. "She's early."

No one said anything, and then Ruby said softly. "You might be mistaken, Mr. M. Don't you think so Jessie? Don't you think he's mistaken? You don't want to go yet until you finish our game do you?"

Pitic backed up Ruby. "We have to finish our game." He turned to Jessie. "Don't we sweetheart?"

Jessie finally lowered her hand so she could see M standing in the doorway. "M, we're playing Reds and Blues." She said it as if he was supposed to know what that was. He had never heard of the game and he felt even more left out. And now he got a closer look at her face.

"What's that on your face?"

"What? Oh, it's my 'chievement paint!"

"Close the door M," suggested Ruby. "We must finish the game. I'm sure your aunt will be home by the time we finish."

Pitic softened. "You want to play too? We could start a new game."

M ignored him and moved behind Jess. Pitic slowly removed his arm.

"Finish up Jess," said M. "We can go home and wipe that shit off your face."

Jess turned around to the table. "I'm winning M," she said with pride.

The table was covered with a strange, colorful board. There were cards, larger than playing cards, scattered about. There were game pieces shaped like sickles and ravens and tridents all in black onyx in various squares on the game board.

"Don't you have customers?" challenged M.

Ruby smiled a toothless smile and shook her head.

"Where are the dice?" asked M hoping to move the game along.

Pitic didn't turn but stared at the board. "No dice."

Jessie concurred. "We move by just telling something about ourselves M, it's fun. Then, I get a 'chievement mark on my face."

M looked at the other two. "Nobody else has any marks Jess."

"Told you. I'm winning."

"Yes," said Ruby, "Jessie told us about moving to Arizona."

M tightened up.

Jessie picked up a card. "Yeah, and cause I did I got to move six places and now I'm still winning, M."

M tried to make sense of the board. "You're almost done Jess." It was a proclamation.

Her tongue slid out to the side. "I think so, M. I think I'm going to win."

"Oh, I'm sure of it," said Pitic. He then turned and looked at M. It was the coldest stare M had ever seen.

This was wrong. This was all wrong. He didn't know why exactly, but things had changed. Worse, he didn't know what to do about it.

"Really, Jess, we gotta go. Now."

No one said anything.

Ruby's hand came up and tapped Jessie's arm. "Time to go my dear. We give up. You win."

Jessie jumped up. "Yay, I beat you! I'm the winner!"

She turned and smiled the biggest smile M had seen in a long while from Jessie. It was radiant. It was the Jessie he remembered, and he hated Ruby and Pitic for getting her to smile. He hated that she liked them and he didn't and he didn't know why.

He returned her smile, and held the door open for her.

She held up an arm against the bright afternoon and went out in front of him, holding on to the railing for support until she got to the bottom of the steps. Then, she turned to M.

"That was cool, 'cause I won!"

"That's great, kid. I'm proud of you."

They walked for a bit then Jessie said, "I'm proud of me too. Can I keep the paint on 'til Aunt Janey gets home?"

M turned and looked back to the RV in time to see the back door jerk close the last few inches.

"Don't think so."

"And guess what?"

"What?"

"Ruby says, he's coming back."

"Who's that?"

M looked down at Jess who looked perplexed. "Not sure. But I think he owns this whole place."

"Can't wait," said M without enthusiasm.

Jess laughed and skipped ahead. "Me too."

CHAPTER 34

Stan checked his watch as he angled his truck into the parking space next to Jake. Just barely 6:30, as usual

He got out and stood admiring how the morning California sun dazzled off the truck's paint job. He loved his truck. Three on the column, Sheridan Blue '51 Ford pickup. Fully restored with all chrome replaced and original paint with a luster coat finish he touched up every weekend.

It wasn't that he liked old as most of the crew from downtown had insisted, it was he loved reliable. He could work on the flathead V8 himself. He understood it. He knew how to maintain it. 1951 and it still ran and ran well. Lot to be said for reliable.

And it looked good next to Jake's vintage '60 Corvette, still a shiny beautiful Roman Red. And, he observed as she pulled into the other side, it looked extremely cherry next to Mallory's beat up piece of shit.

6:30. No one had said anything about getting here early but after yesterday, after hearing Mallory's interview with the Ashcroft boy, it was like the horses sensing the barn. They couldn't wait to press it home.

Stan watched as Mallory stuck her ass in the air, leaned into her trunk and dragged a suitcase to the back and started to lift it over the trunk edge.

"Wait. I'll get it."

She cast Stan a glance as if she were looking over imaginary glasses. Like you waited until now to help me.

Stan smiled. He knew she knew she had a good ass. He knew she knew he knew. Whatever.

He grabbed the suitcase handle, lifted it out of the trunk and set it on the ground then re-adjusted his handhold. "What do you have in here?"

"A few overnight things."

"What?" he lifted. "Like an extra pair of horseshoes, a tire jack, and a small safe?"

"A few dainties. Case I have to stay overnight."

"What? Here?"

She didn't answer as she opened the door and held it for him.

Mallory swept past him and her shoes echoed in the cavernous building. He noticed that she was wearing high heels. Women should be required to wear high heels. Damn, they were invented for a reason. Women just didn't know how good they looked. Forget the fact they were crippling. Those were some damn nice calves.

"Why are you dressed up?" he called out to her.

Mallory continued walking and ignored him.

"And you have a skirt on!"

She got to the doorway and waited for him.

"Really, you didn't have to dress to impress me. You had me at 'Fuck you.'"

Mallory took the suitcase from him and staggered into the office.

The onslaught of morning light slanting through the clerestory lit up their glass office in the middle of the atrium like a jewel. Stan looked up the four stories. It was so big and open it sucked the breath right out of him. Sitting in the middle of the glow, like a male model out of a GQ ad, was Jake, the shiny metal braces from his cast catching the sunlight and bouncing it off the glass walls.

Detective Jake Steiner looked comfortably relaxed with his laptop on his stomach and a steaming cup of coffee in his hand.

Jake did a slow take as he looked from Mallory, to Stan, and then the suitcase. He smiled. "So. You two have a good night?"

Mallory smirked. "In his dreams."

"Darlin', you're in everybody's dreams," said Jake, deadpan. But his blue eyes sparkled.

"In your dreams too, asshole."

Jake gave a wave. "Yeah, well, while you two we're fooling around…I've been digging."

"No!" mocked Mallory. "Not on your little computer?" She slid her suitcase behind her desk.

Jake kept his cast on the table but leaned past the printer and retrieved two sets of papers he'd clipped together. "This computer shit is not that tough if you just think of it as an idiot partner. Have a look." He held them out for Stan and Mallory.

Stan scanned both pages then looked at Jake. It was a rap sheet summary for some guy in Florida.

Jake perused his own copy. "So, in your travels you two ever run across this guy? Ever hear mention of him?"

"R. E. A. Rendell," read Mallory. "I need more initials in my name I think."

"Who is this guy?" asked Stan.

"Neither of you have heard of him? Doesn't ring a bell?"

Both Mallory and Stan shook their heads.

"Well, good. Pleased I'm not repeating what you guys have already found." Jake smiled and put his hands behind his head. "I didn't see any mention of him in any of the boxes Carruthers and Thompson had put together, but then again I haven't had time to go through them all."

"So, I ask again. Why are we looking at a guy in Florida?" Stan kept flipping back and forth, from front page to the back page, when something caught his eye.

"And what does this have to do with carnivals?" Mallory threw her pad on the conference table, tossed down three #2 pencils and kicked off her shoes. She started to peruse the two stapled sheets.

Stan pulled the two pages apart and set them on the conference table side by side. He put both hands on the table leaned over and studied the second page. He felt a shiver down his spine. "Holy Shit."

"The holiest of shits, my friend," beamed Jake.

"What? Somebody tell me. Explain!" demanded Mallory. "What am I looking at?"

"Damn." Stan slowly raised his head and looked at Jake. They both smiled.

This was their guy.

"What!" exclaimed Mallory, her voice rising. "I see the guy's name and address and I see he owns property near here and I see in Florida he was arrested for but never convicted for a… 288, whatever that is. And then he was charged with an indecent something or other number." She looked up helplessly at Stan then Jake. "And he's got a shitload of initials. What?"

Stan pointed to the fuzzy picture of Rendell. It showed an older man, heavy with jowls, with light thinning hair. Not only was the picture twelve years old, the police photographer had not done a great job. Rendell's eyes were cast down slightly where, with a proper booking picture, he should have been looking straight into camera. The profile picture showed a tired looking man with pasty skin and a slightly hooked nose.

He looked at Mallory. "This is him. This is our guy."

"What? Him?" She dropped her copy and moved to the table with Stan. "No way. You sure?"

Stan nodded to Jake. "I feel it." Jake smiled back. "I've got the tingle."

"Nice," beamed Stan.

"But he's in Florida," continued Mallory.

Jake piped up. "Maybe. Maybe not. But, we'll find him."

Mallory leaned over the table. Stan could see her palms were sweating. She left moist imprints every time she moved. She picked up the paper and stared at the picture. "How do you know though?"

Jake lifted his leg off the table and winced. He set it down gently on the floor and stood, gripping the back of his chair and the edge of the conference table.

"We know," he said, "because a 2117 is reckless endangerment of a child and the other arrest was for public exposure to a child."

"And how?" asked Mallory, still not appearing to understand. "How did he do these crimes up here by long distance from Florida?" Before Jake could answer, she went on. "And besides, treating kids like animals is a damn epidemic. There are hundreds of pedos in every city."

Stan could see Jake was relishing the find so he let him continue.

"No, my dear girl. If you'll notice on the second sheet, along with about twelve acres and a small trailer park, the one thing Mister R. E.A. Rendell owns is the site where you found the tree with a rope that probably held the ankles of three children whose bodies were discovered in 1997 by an Officer Duncan."

Jake couldn't stop smiling. "And, because part of what's on that twelve acre site is, get this, an abandoned circus or carnival. That's why."

Mallory slumped into the nearest chair as if sucker-punched. "No shit,' she murmured, "I don't believe it."

"So, where is he?" asked Stan.

Jake looked down. "Well, to tell you the truth, I'm going to need help." He raised his chin to Mallory who was still in her own funk. "I found out about him about an hour ago. And actually that part was pretty easy."

"I don't believe it," said Mallory, gaining conviction.

Jake studied her now. "What is it you don't believe? That I could use the computer or that we've actually made some major goddamn leaps in the worst piece of shit child murder case in California history? Which?"

"Yeah, well, I was the one who found out about the carnival in the first place, so leap over that," Mallory snorted. She was not going to be left behind.

"So, where is he?" asked Stan again. "It was easy to find him?"

Jake shook his head. "Easy to get the ID. Whereabouts could be...tough."

"How so?" asked Stan.

"The whole property just went into foreclosure. The twelve acres. The tree site, the RV park and the carnival site. Turns out Mr. Rendell's been remiss in his payments."

"So let's get him!" Mallory was up on her feet. Like the terrier Stan knew her to be, he could tell she was ready to launch them out the door with most of the Sacramento force or fly to Florida, whatever it was going to take.

Before either Stan or Jake could speak she erupted again. "Wait! Wait!" She gave a big series of air punches while dancing around the room. With one hand on her hip she wagged her finger at Stan. "It means I was right! I knew we'd get the bastard. I told you."

Mallory spun to Jake. "And if you had been here on time instead of playing grabass with the nurses at the hospital, I could say 'I told you so' to you too. Hah!"

She stopped gyrating, out of breath. "Damn, I'm good. My carnival!"

"And, something else," said Jake. He waited until he had both their attention.

He reached down and pulled over the evidence box that contained the few pieces found with the three victims. He sorted through and pulled out the plastic bag that held the items found with Karen Summering, opened the top and moved the bag across the table letting the one item slide out. His fingers picked up the blackened wire ring that had been found on Karen's wrist.

He looked from the wire to Mallory and then to Stan. "This is what's left of a plastic ID bracelet."

Mallory tendered the connection. "From a carnival? Really?"

"How so?" asked Stan.

Jake shrugged. "Circus and carnivals use these to identify who's paid and how much at the entrance. Shows what shows or places or attractions a customer can get into. A visual indication of how much they've paid."

Mallory looked at Stan, then to Jake. She looked sympathetic, as if Jake was reaching.

"Yeah, but lots of places give those out, and besides kids can buy them anywhere. You know, 'Jody hearts Ethan' and so on. Lots of places."

Jake said nothing but smiled.

"What?" asked Stan.

"Yeah, you're right, anywhere. You can get these things anywhere. A carnival or wherever, a grocery store…except for one thing."

He opened a file on his desk and held it in his hand.

"If you remember, our good old Forensics department could make out some letters of some of the words, or at least, could identify how many letters were in each word on the bracelet. I summarize. Eight letters in the first word. The second word is shorter. The third word is longer, probably 8 letters again. Second word for sure is in caps."

He looked up.

Mallory started counting on her fingers. "Circus has six letters and how would you do R.E.A. Rendell?"

"You wouldn't," said Stan. "It would have to be 'Rendell something' or 'Rendell's something'."

Mallory counted again. "Hey, Rendell's has eight letters!" She looked at Jake. "So does 'carnival'. What did you say, eight, less than eight and then what?"

Stan jumped in. "Eight letters in the last."

"Rendell's something Carnival, maybe," said Stan, starting to gain momentum.

Jake held up his hand. "Stop, okay. I already have it."

Mallory and Stan both stared at him.

"This is from 1999," said Jake, handing them both a white letter sized sheet of paper with a picture of a newspaper ad printed on it. "Found it in the Sacramento Bee, from a '99 advertisement in the entertainment section. Sorry, it's printed on regular paper, all I had. And, I had to blow it up a bit. Cheap bastard only bought a small ad."

Both Mallory and Stan studied the picture. Across the top of the ad in a blazing arc was 'Coming Sept. 22 to Sept. 30'. Below that was a picture of the entrance to a small circus or carnival with smaller letters, 'Not To Be Missed!' The next to last line at the bottom was 'Admission Only $2.00, Kids 12 and under 50 cents'.

It was the next line that held Mallory's and Stan's attention. The name of the carnival.

Rendell's JOYLAND Carnival.

"Son of a bitch!" whispered Mallory.

"You've been busy," said Stan.

"I should have found this," muttered Mallory.

"Eight, seven and eight and the second word is all caps. Damn." exclaimed Mallory. "I really should have found this," she said looking up at both of them. "I really should've."

Jake lifted his leg off the table, sat up, and rested the laptop on the desk. "You found out about the carnival. That was good."

"Don't throw me a bone, Steiner. I'm the computer person. I should've gotten it." Mallory bit her lip.

"Important thing is we got it," said Jake, placating.

Stan slid the picture onto the conference table. "Okay. 1999. I get that. This circus or carnival or whatever it was, was two years after the bodies were found. Two years. You say there's a carnival on the site somewhere. Well, it couldn't have been there when the bodies were found. Carruthers would have searched it, would have torn it apart looking for shit. At least would have noted it."

"Wasn't there, you're right," said Jake, beaming. "Neither was the RV park. But what Rendell did use the site for at that time was to store this sideshow stuff during winter layover, before they went back on the road in the spring. Evidently, it wasn't until two years after the bodies were discovered that he had the brilliant idea to have a last show of the season right there before they shut down for the winter."

"On the same site."

"The same," noted Jake.

"Well, what's there now?" asked Mallory.

"From what I can ascertain, a lot of the stored carnival stuff, though I'm not sure, yet. It's been there, unused, for a while."

"Shit," said Mallory.

"And no Rendell?" asked Stan.

Jake shook his head. "I'm working on it. Also, Florida SP is working on getting us a better picture. Funny thing. First address I have for him in Florida was right after the bodies were discovered here in California. Last I have is a PO Box in Clearwater, Florida. But, I'm working on it."

Stan nodded at Jake. "Still, good make."

"Thanks. Her too."

Mallory leaned over the table and studied the sordid record of R. E. A. Rendell. She pointed to the area at the bottom of the sheet that held his fingerprints and looked at Stan.

"Yeah," he said, "I was thinking the same thing. It's too damn bad there wasn't a fingerprint on anything, the evidence, the site, nothing. No prints. As it is now, we need to connect a lot of dots. This guy our illustrious Detective Steiner found has two tenuous connections to this case. He has a history and he owns the property. We may just be looking at some coincidences."

"My ass," blustered Mallory. "He's the guy. You said so!"

"Probably. Still, we don't want to pull a Mrs. Jameson," suggested Jake.

"Who's that?" Mallory perked up looking for a new bad guy. "Are you guys trying to shit me?"

Stan smirked. "She was the lady who owned a downtown brothel with underage Mexican prostitutes."

"Really?" asked a wide-eyed Mallory.

"No. Not really, but that's what we thought." Jake took up the story. "We went to lower Parkland to arrest her. We'd done all the leg work linking her to the building where all this activity was happening. Stan and I. We considered taking backup, but we figured we could do it ourselves. And that type of arrest didn't warrant calling out the troops."

"What happened?"

"We got there, and were a bit surprised. It was a nice neighborhood. We knocked. No answer. We figured, again assumed, that she had been spooked or whatever. I'm not sure what we thought but we came up with the bright idea of busting down the door. We were new. We didn't want this one to get away."

Stan added as an aside. "He, Detective Steiner over there, keeps a handy pack of all the tools to gain access, shall we say."

"Anyway, Stan tried the knob first. It was unlocked and we opened the door and announced our presence. We were sure she'd seen us coming and was scrambling like a rat for a hole."

"Did you get her?" Mallory was full into the story.

Jake looked at Stan. "I'd forgotten how painful this is to tell." Then back to Mallory. "Yeah, we got her all right. Mrs. Jameson was eighty-five years old. We found her sitting in the living room knitting. She was stone deaf and never heard us knock. Or call out. The first thing she knew was there were two strange men in her house. Needless to say she freaked as much as an eighty-five year old can. She grabbed her chest and slipped out of her chair to the floor."

Jake looked at Stan. "I think it only took the ambulance about twelve minutes to get there, right?"

Stan nodded.

"So you busted into the wrong house?" asked Mallory.

"We busted into the *right* house. We subdued Mrs. Jameson. Actually she subdued herself when she fainted away. She was a feisty bitch for as ancient as she was."

"I don't get it. What the hell. You did or didn't get the right house and the right person? Did you arrest her or what?"

Stan sat down at his desk and put his feet up. "Well, first we broke into her house, and then we damn near killed her by giving her a heart attack. Then when she came to we subdued her as she tried to attack us. She mistook Jake's CPR for sexual assault..."

"And, who wouldn't," exclaimed Mallory.

"Anyway, it was a mess. She actually tried to stab me with a knitting needle."

Jake continued the story. "You see, we were new and stupid. We assumed some things we shouldn't have. Yes, Mrs. Jameson was the owner. But she was the owner of the house that *housed* the brothel. She didn't own the brothel. She didn't know about the cathouse she was supposedly running.

"Seems like her attorney, who was managing her affairs, had rented out the house for her and was looking the other way when it was obvious he knew what was going on. She never had a clue."

Nobody said anything.

Finally Jake offered up what sounded to Stan like father to daughter advice for Mallory. "We pulled a Mrs. Jameson. We don't want to do that again. Instead of jumping in the car and speeding to her house our heads full of glory shit, we should have stopped and had some patience."

"Glory shit?"

"Patience. Olive Park is a cold case and it's been that way for nearly fifteen years. We have some...pieces."

"These are pieces, but aren't they good pieces? I'm not stupid, you know."

Jake rolled his eyes, then leveled his gaze on Mallory. "You are if you go off like a jackrabbit with a firecracker up her ass." He pointed to all the glass walls that displayed everything they knew about the case. "This is how we get things done. This is what it takes to get convictions. This is how we find the bad guys. We don't call out the troops. We don't go running out the door."

"I wasn't going to do that," said Mallory defending herself.

Stan moderated. "Look Mallory, between what you and I found at the site and the carnival thing, and this..." Stan picked up the top sheet again, "...Rendell guy and the fact that he owns that site, we've got a place to start. So, we work it. We make sure we have the goods on Mrs. Jameson."

Stan and Jake were quiet and let Mallory think about what they had said. Stan didn't want her to be bummed out. He knew they needed her. As much as he regretted admitting it, her skewed perspectives gave them an important angle of attack. Who would have thought it when she had walked in the door toting deli lunches, how long ago? Days, a week. He had lost track.

"Not stupid," persisted Mallory. "You know."

"Does she always have to say 'you know'?" asked Jake.

"It's her mantra," said Stan.

"Damn." Jake sat up suddenly and pulled the printout of the ad for JOYLAND toward him.

"What?" asked Mallory.

Jake reached down slowly and pulled up the evidence bag for Joey Marshall and turned it over.

Out rolled two quarters. The child's admission price for JOYLAND.

CHAPTER 35

M saw her moving from house to house. He always thought it a myth that you could tell a cop was a cop from a distance. But, damn, this was a cop. She was pretty. Nice ass and nice hair, from what he could see half a block away, but still a cop.

He sat on his aunt's steps toying with his knife. He was practicing throwing it into the small stump that his aunt had placed in the middle of her miniature landscaping area. The area had two rose bushes, a birdbath and this funny little stump that his Aunt Janey hung a lantern on. Anyway, it made good target practice.

Jessie rode in front of him on her bike. She was becoming an expert at not falling off and better yet, now knew how to stop. M had filled the tires up with a pump he'd found in his aunt's garage and had even oiled the handlebars. The bike was pretty beat up. It had been out in the weather for awhile he could tell. It still had the name of the previous owner written in black marker. He couldn't get that girl's name off. Jessie had a smile on her face and her blonde hair blew in the breeze as she whizzed around and around, her eyes glued to the ground studiously avoiding the potholes.

Now, he watched the cop make her way down the street. M could see she hadn't gotten much response from the rest of the residents of Sunshine Vista. He guessed that just about everyone in the trailer park had plenty of experience smelling a cop from a distance and so avoided the front door when they came calling.

She was now at the crazy Chinese lady's house and it looked like she was holding out a piece of paper for her to take. The Chinese lady was having none of it and was advancing on the cop.

I wouldn't if I were you, thought M. No telling what the crazy Chinese will do. Of course the old lady never seemed to venture past her own fence, but on the other hand, she does have a rake and it's raised over her head.

M watched the cop retreat and head his way. Cops. They seemed to have plenty of time to walk around the trailer park harassing all the neighbors, but they don't care enough to come and help when you need them.

He sat still. He didn't want to call attention to himself. He thought if she got closer, he'd make himself scarce. Except for Jessie. He needed to hang around and make sure the cop didn't bother her.

M saw her wave at Jessie, then come down the little concrete block walkway towards him. He closed his knife.

"Hi," she said.

M nodded in return.

"Hi," she said again.

Again, M nodded.

"I'm from the Sacramento Police Department." She held out the stupid lanyard that hung around her neck and held a plastic covered collection of official looking IDs.

To M she seemed strangely proud of being able to show her ID to someone.

"What's your name?" she asked brightly. She had really nice eyes.

"What do you want?"

M could see she was surprised, and the smile faded a bit. She was probably trying to decide if she was going to be talking to a juvenile asshole or whether she'd be able to win him over with her smile. M's gaze strayed to her chest. Nice.

He waited to be won over. Chances were 50-50.

"Do you live here?" She tried.

"My aunt does," said M. In the background M could see Jessie watching him with the cop. She still went in circles but they were more like uncertain ovals now.

"But you don't?"

"Sometimes."

"Funny." She had made up her mind. Juvenile asshole.

She raised a manila folder and tried to pull out a page from inside. She ended up yanking out the entire contents which spilled and fluttered down at all angles. Some of them bounced off his leg and further down the steps.

M looked to see what they were. They were pictures of kids. He gathered up about five or six and started to read them. Each sheet had the word 'Missing' at the top of it. There was a description of each kid below the pictures. They all seemed to be young, like seven or eight. A few maybe older. He stared hard at the last one he picked up. There was something familiar.

She reached out and grabbed them from him. "Sorry. I'll take those." She studied him for a moment then smiled again. "Thanks."

It was now 60-40.

She stuffed the flyers back into the folder and found the one sheet she had been looking for originally. She scanned it to make sure it was in fact the right one, and then turned it to M to see.

"Have you ever seen this man around here?"

M looked at the picture. He looked hard at the picture. Those eyes and that nose. What the hell. Maybe she did have a brother and, if there was, this guy was probably it.

"Who is it?" asked M. "Not a very good picture."

"Never mind about the name, just do you recognize him?"

"Maybe I know the name," said M. He decided he'd try and keep her talking to him as long as he could. Why not. Nothing else to do.

"And what would that be?"

M hesitated. "Can I see it again?"

She held the picture up to him, closer this time.

Damn. Gotta be one of Ruby's freaky relations. He decided to find out what how much trouble the guy was in before he spilled the beans. He couldn't wait to drill it into Ruby that one of her family was probably on the 10 Most Wanted List.

"What's he done?" asked M.

He saw the cop hesitate but then she lied and said, "We're just trying to find him."

M looked at the picture again. "Is there a reward?"

"Then you do know him?" M thought she looked way too hopeful based on his question.

"Well, no, but if there's dough involved, I could start to look."

The cop withdrew the picture. M could tell she was pissed, not so much at him, but more at not getting any kind of information on the guy.

She handed M her card. "Here. My name and number are on it. Call me when you remember him, okay?"

M took the card and stretched out on the steps. "Sure."

He watched her turn and walk away. It was nice watching her walk away. When she got abreast of Jessie she stopped and watched Jess go round and round for a few moments then started down the street. She'd only gone a few steps when she turned and went back to Jessie.

M stood quickly.

Jessie stood on the brakes and came to a stop and jumped down, straddling the bike.

M moved through the little yard and approached Jessie and the cop. The cop saw him coming, smiled at Jessie and resumed her walk down the street.

"What did she want?" asked M.

Jessie shrugged. "She wanted to know about my bike. She asked where I got it. I said it was a present."

"Good," said M.

Then Jessie said proudly. "She said it was kinda old. I said my brother fixed it up for me."

M watched the cop try a few other trailers with no luck. She was just getting to Ruby's trailer when M said, "Jessie! Time to come in, okay?"

Jessie hesitated before answering, "Aw, I want to go around some more."

"I'll let you watch the Simpsons."

"Yes!" shouted Jessie. "Deal!"

Before she got to the last trailer, Mallory turned and watched the boy take his sister inside. She knew he was a bit of a smartass. It came with the age. You couldn't be a hormonal powder keg and male without having an attitude. It would be unusual if he didn't have one. She also knew he seemed to react to one of the kids pictures or maybe not. Still, he had looked at Rendell's picture for a long time. And she had watched his eyes. She had remembered to do that from her training. When she had shown him Rendell's' picture, he had glanced over her shoulder at the last trailer at the end of the street before he looked back at her.

Maybe he knew something, maybe not. It was hard to tell with kids. There was so much going in their heads. That plus the attitude. Then there were the hormones. The little bugger had his eyes glued to her chest when he wasn't looking at the picture.

Yesterday, after Jake had uncovered Rendell and all the information and connections she kicked herself for not making, they had split up jobs. Jake continued tracking the property records and anything else he could find about Rendell's JOYLAND. Stan took Florida. He actually knew two fellow officers, one from Robbery-Homicide and a sergeant from 6th precinct, who had both retired to the Sunshine State. He was planning to start there. He was going to be on the phone for hours.

They all agreed Rendell's picture had to be shown to everyone in the trailer park. Mallory volunteered. She felt twitchy and needed to get out of the office rather than sit around and study a computer screen or make phone calls. What the hell, she'd done that for two solid years. She knew what Jake said was true; this was a cold case, so patience. Take your time. Do it right. Make the case. And while both Stan and Jake were proceeding slowly, she could feel their excitement building.

Someone was stoking the fire and those two were trying to hold the ship on a steady course. But they could feel themselves moving faster. No one acknowledged it, like not mentioning the imminent perfect game to the pitcher in the last inning. Just keep it steady.

Nowadays, punching the keyboard felt like death by paper cuts. Like running in place. She needed to be out actively searching for this bastard. So far though, the Sunshine Vista was turning out to be a bust. She knew not to expect to be welcomed with rose bouquets, but shit, it was as if everyone believed her to be the IRS or giving out free cases of the flu. Even the kid and his sister. If they had been inside when she arrived and knocked at their trailer she was sure he wouldn't have opened the door either.

Before she headed to the last trailer at the end of Sunshine Vista she glanced over at the chain link fence. Behind it she could see a collection of carnival wagons and some piles of other junk, looked like plywood fronts tossed in a pile. Jake was right. The whole conglomeration had a don't-give-a-shit-if-I-ever-see-this-again loneliness to it. The chain link gate had a large padlock. The whole place smacked of abandonment. If Rendell was around, he wasn't bothering to check on his precious carnival sideshow crap.

As she approached she noticed the last trailer seemed to be an older mobile home hard up against the back of an RV camper connected by some rickety porch. There was a worn area in the weedy grass leading to a set of steps to the trailer. She went up and stopped when she got to the top step.

The door to the trailer was open and seemed to be moving in the light breeze. It was solid dark inside past the slash of light at the door.

In the doorway was a child's sneaker resting on its side. Just one. Red, with blue and silver laces. The shoe had come off without first being untied. The laces were still tied in a nice bow.

Mallory reached out and rapped lightly on the door frame.

"Anybody home?"

There was a noise, she thought, from somewhere inside the trailer, but it may have come from somewhere else, maybe the RV next door.

"Sacramento Police," she called into the trailer's interior. For a brief moment she felt a fraud identifying herself as a cop. Two years she had been sequestered in with Ollestad in data acquisition. A dark room with computer screens as the main source of light. She had rarely, as in never, seen anyone from outside the department. She wasn't a cop but she was part of SPD.

She felt a flutter in her stomach as Jake's words came back to her about domestic violence calls. Really? Why? A door open. Nobody home. A child's shoe with no child around.

"Hello?"

Hell, why bother to call? She was just here to get information, she wasn't threatening anybody.

She stepped back and looked down the walkway that led to the RV next door. She wondered whether she should go down there or not. Try and bang on the camper's door. She tried to remember the procedure. She looked back at the half open door and took out her pencil. She tapped it in her hand a few times then deliberately took the eraser end and pushed the door open a few more inches. The light from the opening door revealed more of the interior.

That was when she saw the other sneaker.

This one was untied and in fact, Mallory saw, had been partially unlaced, or at least one of the laces appeared to have been ripped out of the purple ringed eyelets. It was three feet away.

"Hello? Is everybody okay?"

No answer. Just the dull drone from the highway. She leaned back and looked behind down the length of the trailer court. No one was about. And no kids playing.

Kids. What do kids do? They come running into a house, leave the door open, step out of their shoes, maybe unlace them, maybe not. That's what they do. Probably, Mallory thought. Probably what happened here.

Then why did she have this creepy back of the neck feeling?

Screw it. She stepped inside careful not to touch the door jamb or disturb the first sneaker.

"Sacramento Police, I'm coming in. The door was open."

She let her eyes adjust and scanned the trailer interior. To her right and almost in front of her was a small kitchen; further right was a sitting area with a room divider. She couldn't see much past the room divider.

To her left was a hallway. A half open door at the end of the hall revealed what appeared to be a stuffed couch or maybe a bed with a large comforter on it, or just a pile of dirty clothes. Who could tell? The place was a mess. Cardboard boxes lined the hall, some filled with clothes, some with what appeared to be kitchen utensils and pots and pans. Some filled with magazines or trash. Who knew?

There was another door that led off the hallway. The bathroom. If someone was here and not answering, that's most likely where they were. Probably appalled that someone would come in while they were doing their business.

Mallory took a few steps past a pile of boxes to the bathroom door and knocked.

"Anybody here? Sacramento Police."

Nothing. No hurried movements, no flushing, nothing.

Mallory moved back to the entry door.

Okay, parents not home, kid went out to play. Don't freak her out when she comes running back into the trailer.

Her. Why is it a her? The shoes. Too frilly for a boy.

Mallory took a step deeper into the trailer. Beyond the crowded and messy kitchen with the stove piled high with what appeared to be seldom washed dishes, was a divider wall that screened off what the trailer's designers had meant to be a living area. The left side of the divider was covered with a faded poster about five feet high and four wide. It was thumbtacked up. It showed a stylized and exaggerated version of the insides of a carnival midway and surrounding that, caricatures of the freaks that worked the sideshows. Mallory could imagine it on the side of a building facing a vacant lot, advertising what was coming to town. She looked up to the top of the poster. 'Rendell's JOYLAND Carnival' was in arcing letters across the top.

Bingo. Rendell's.

The poster was old and torn in a few corners. The slash banner across the front announced the dates when Rendell's would next be in town. But the dates where ripped away and missing.

The whole right side of the divider was covered with pictures. Hundreds of color pictures, mostly 3x5 size, were tacked, stapled, pinned, and taped in a hodge-podge accumulation that could never be called a display. It was as if whomever was in charge of exhibiting the pictures had just slapped up the next picture. There seemed to be no order and most overlapped their neighbor. Some were in black plastic frames but most were unframed and unbordered. Just a raw collection of photos showing years of the jumbled history of Rendell's JOYLAND.

Kids, families, dogs, displays, exhibits. It was all there.

Mallory peered closer. It was hard to see in the gloom, but she scanned the board looking at faces. Looking for Rendell.

Interspersed among all the faces of customers enjoying themselves, were semi-posed portraits of the freaks of JOYLAND. They stood, hunched or twisted, their bodies giving shape to their name and title.

'Alligator Boy' on the ground, back arched upward, 'Giant Rat', a very unhappy hairy dachshund with a rat tail, 'The Ferocious Fireball', a big guy who held a flaming baton in each hand and 'Strong HercuMan', the obligatory guy in a jungle outfit leaning with his booted foot up on a barbell. All there. Just what you'd want to see after you paid your admission to JOYLAND.

But no Rendell.

Mallory straightened up. Enough. She backed away from the divider toward the door, tripped over the shoe and landed on her butt. Her folder of pictures landed intact in the shaft of sunlight from the doorway.

She reached for it and a shadow fell over her hand. A large shadow.

Mallory looked up but the sun was behind whoever was there and she couldn't see.

"Whatdya want?"

Mallory scrambled to her feet and faced a sizeable lady draped in a dark velvet robe and hood with a sour pissed off look. From what she could see under the hood, this woman wasn't going to win any beauty prizes.

Mallory started to comment on the hooded outfit but thought better of it. "I knocked and called but no one answered." She gestured to the door. "Door was open."

Ruby Everheart never took her eyes from Mallory. "Don't leave the door open. Ever."

"Well, I'm pretty sure it...it was..."

"Never know who or what's gonna get in."

Screw being polite, thought Mallory. "I'm with Sacramento Police. Mallory Dimante." She held out her plastic ID cards. "Are you Mrs. Rendell?"

Ruby bristled. "I am not. There is no *Mrs.* Rendell. There's no Mr. Rendell around here either." She moved to the door, opened it wider and stepped aside. "Mr. Rendell lit outta here five years ago and most people will tell you 'good goddamn riddance'."

Mallory didn't move.

"We're investigating some missing children and we need to find Mr. Rendell."

Mallory saw the lady's eyes open a bit wider, but she said nothing.

"Just a person of interest right now," added Mallory.

Ruby said nothing.

Mallory pulled out the picture and held it in front of her. "Have you ever seen Mr. Rendell?"

A slow smile crept across Ruby's face as she turned away and moved to the door.

"I know what he looks like."

"And you haven't seen him around here?"

Ruby kept looking at the floor, and shook her head. "Told you, he's gone."

Mallory looked out at the abandoned circus lot. "So, were you part of Rendell's circus then?"

"Ain't no circus and Rendell is gone, bankrupt. Ain't nobody I know a part of it. And that's all I know." She opened the door an inch wider. The invitation to leave was obvious.

"And who are you?" Mallory had already guessed she was the fortune teller from next door, obviously decked out like a medieval soothsayer.

"I own this trailer." She jerked her head toward the top of the trailer, still not looking at Mallory. "You've seen the sign. That's me. That's what I do."

"So you're Ruby and you tell fortunes. That's fascinating, I..."

"I'm busy right now, I got customers waiting." She kept her grip on the edge of the door.

"Of course, well, no idea where Mr. Rendell is...?"

"Told you, no."

"Maybe some idea, though, of someone else who might know?"

Bounding up the steps and partially filling the doorway was a greasy dark little man.

"Hey, shouldn't leave the door open, you never know..." Like a deflating balloon the little man blanched when he saw Mallory.

Mallory saw he made her for a cop.

In one motion, he was backing up, backing down the stairs,

"Sorry, sorry, sorry..." Mallory watched as the ugly sausage of a man turned at the bottom of the steps and disappeared around the corner of the trailer.

Mallory leaned forward after him. "Was...was that your customer or just some escaped felon?"

Mallory saw Ruby pause then answer. "Not my customer."

"Right, okay." She took a step toward the door. "Well, so who then owns the site next door?"

Ruby shrugged, looking at the abandoned site. "City probably took it over."

"Weren't you a part of the circus at one time? That circus?"

"Carnival, ain't a circus." Ruby worked her mouth again and Mallory thought she was going to spit somewhere. "If you gotta complaint 'bout that property, go see the city." She jingled her keys in her pocket. "Now, you gotta go."

Mallory made a move to step over the small sneaker. "You have kids?"

"No kids." Ruby fit her key into the lock, preparing to shut and lock the trailer.

Mallory indicated the sneaker. "Small feet, then."

Ruby kicked the shoe further into the trailer. "I babysit."

Mallory had to move to the small wooden landing outside the door as Ruby started to back into her pulling the door shut. She watched Ruby lock the door and check the knob, turning and pushing to make sure it was secure.

"She won't be able to get in now," said Mallory.

Ruby turned. All but her mouth was hidden in the shadow of the hood.

"Who?"

"Whoever you're babysitting."

Ruby's mouth worked a few times and ended in a crooked smile. She slipped her keys into her robe and padded down the walkway to the RV, her velvet rippling black in the bright sun.

"She knows where to find me."

CHAPTER 36

Before M had left Jessie at Ruby's, he had impressed upon her to stay in Ruby's trailer and not be persuaded to play any more games in the dark with Ruby or Pitic or anyone else. Not unless M was there.

He could tell that she really hadn't understood why but she had shrugged her agreement, especially after Ruby had kindly set her up with some of her famous gingerbread and a slate of afternoon cartoons in front of Ruby's crappy TV. M had checked the TV listings. Jessie could leave it on this channel and have her head filled with old, and benign, Bugs Bunny animations and avoid the late afternoon soaps and reality judge shows, while Ruby worked.

Now, instead of heading to Avery's office for his appointment, he was sitting on the couch in Aunt Janey's trailer and wiping his sweaty hands on his jeans.

He didn't believe his aunt would ever notice the call to Arizona on her bill. So, instead of schlepping down to the phone booth by Avery's office, he decided what the hell. With Jessie safe at Ruby's with hours of cartoons ahead of her, it would be okay to use Aunt Janey's phone to call Shippen Travers. Once again, he'd be late to Avery's office, if he decided to go at all.

Last time, when he'd been late, he had suggested to Avery they go hang out and look at girls and they had gone to the Starbucks, ordered coffee and waited for some cuties to parade by.

He had done some further digging on Shippen Travers. He could've gotten further if he had had access to his old computer, but that had been confiscated by the police. He wasn't sure why they took it. Maybe they suspected his father of some other crime besides murder. Like it mattered now?

He pulled out the old Christmas card he'd found in the back of his mother's address book. The one from Shippen Travers. The one that started, 'Dear Cuz'.

The card had had a short note inside. It made Mr. Travers sound friendly, at least. It also sounded as if he wasn't really up to date on what his cousin's life was like or what kind of mess it was in, but he sounded warm and genuine, both of which were positives as far as M was concerned.

He thought Jessie deserved some warm and genuine about now.

He'd overlooked the specific address when he'd found Travers' name originally. He'd only focused on the fact that it was Arizona and the phone number. Now, he saw that under Shippen Travers' name was written, 'Frog Creek Farms, RR 3, Bullhead City, AZ.'

He thought RR stood for railroad so it must be by a railroad. But, a farm. Sounds nice. Chickens and pigs and goats, or maybe he had cattle. Horses to ride. He knew Jessie would love to ride a horse. He was more excited about moving to Arizona than he had been about anything in a long time.

He gathered paper and pencil by the phone. He was going to be prepared this time if he had to write anything down.

M looked around before he picked up the phone. His aunt was at work and would be for another few hours. Still, he got up and checked the driveway just to make himself feel better. He called the cell phone number Elliot had given him. The call went straight to voice mail. God, why wasn't he ready for this stuff? What was he going to say? Call back or leave a message? Things were easier when you didn't have to sneak around.

He left a faltering name and number and lamely tagged on that he's the one who had talked to Elliot and he was the son of Sarah Cooper and to please call him back.

Holy hell. He hung up then slid down to the floor.

What was he thinking? How stupid to have given this number. He should have just said he'd call back. Now, if rancher

Travers didn't call back 'til later when his aunt was here and answered the phone he'd be royally screwed.

But the phone rang right away.

M knew he needed to sound confident as if there was a real plan and it was workable, not just a 13 year old's crazy plan. Not just wishful thinking. He took a deep breath.

"Hello." He made it a statement not a question.

"Hey there, this is Shippen Travers, is this Sarah's son?"

"Yes sir, it is. Thank you for calling back." He already liked the sound of Mr. Travers' voice, like the man had a permanent shit-eating grin on his face and was bullshit-free.

"Pleasure to do it. Should have called before this, but I didn't know…about my cousin. Did my son tell me right, Sarah has passed on?"

"Yes sir." M didn't know whether he should go into the whole thing unless it was going to help his cause. He was still deciding when Shippen rolled on.

"Well, dang, I'm sorry, son. Truly am. Hadn't seen your mother in years, lotsa years. But, we still sorta kept in touch. Not every year mind you, but when we thought about it." He paused, then went on. He sounded ready to wrap up the call. "I do thank you for letting me know about the passing and all…"

And then he said it. The words M had been hoping he would say.

"…and if there's anything I can do son, you sure let me know, you hear."

"That's why I'm calling sir."

Shippen Travers hesitated. "Oh?"

"Yes sir. You see the thing is I need your advice."

"My advice! Well…"

M hurried on. "You see, I'm 13 and my sister Jessie is six and since both parents are now gone, we have to decide…"

Shippen interrupted. "Where's your father?"

M tightened his grip on the phone. Where he belongs. But he said, "He was killed at the same time Mr. Travers."

"Huh? No just call me Shippen. You say your father's dead too?"

"That's right, and…"

"Well, son I *am* sorry. How are you two managing? You're not out on the street are you for heaven's sake?"

M hesitated, just enough. "No. We're not. We're…okay. We're in temporary quarters with Aunt Jane."

"Janey!" Shippen sounded relieved. "Of course, Janey. She's looking after you then. That's good."

"Well, yes and no," said M. He hurried on. He knew he'd have to get the next part out quickly. "You see she won't be able to keep us because of the cost. She's too proud I think to say so, but it's a struggle. I heard her crying the other day."

It was true, he equivocated. She bawled at the funeral.

"And, we have to decide whether it would be better to go to a foster home together, my sister and I, or whether we should split up. And I'm asking you because, unlike Aunt Janey, you have experience with kids and all."

And then M shut up. He remembered what his father had told him once. If you're trying to convince somebody to do something they don't necessarily want to do, then give it your best shot and shut up. Don't talk. Don't run on at the mouth, just shut it. Anything more you say only makes you look weak. It was too bad his father rarely followed his own advice.

There was a serious pause on the line. M could imagine Shippen shuffling his feet and looking at the phone as if it were a hot branding iron or whatever the hell they used to burn the mark into the cattle's skin.

Finally. "Well, son. Listen is your aunt there? Can you put Janey on the phone and let me talk to her?"

"Well, I think it would embarrass her if you knew that she couldn't support us."

Shippen coughed. "I understand, son, but I still…"

"Anyway," continued M, "she's not here. She's working second shift." Okay. Now, that was a lie.

"Oh."

M could tell Shippen Travers wasn't used to being boxed in and he didn't like it and wasn't sure how to get out of it, given that it was family and all.

276

M decided to give him an out. "Anyway, if you could give it some thought about the foster home question, I would really appreciate it. You could talk to Aunt Janey. I wouldn't mention her financial problems, you know."

Shippen took it. "No, no, that wouldn't do to make her feel…this is a vexing situation son…"

"For me too, sir."

"Yes," said Shippen distraction permeating the line. "Yes, well, we'll think of something. I'm sure I could help out, you know; send her something from here…"

Shit. Shit. M hadn't considered he'd just plan to throw money at the problem. Being family and all.

But M stuck to the script. "Your advice is all we need, sir. You being the most experienced family member I know, having raised kids and all."

"Yes, well. We'll see what we can do."

He didn't sound like he was smiling anymore.

"Thank you and say 'Hi' to Elliot for me. He sounds like a nice person."

Shippen Travers rang off. "We'll be in touch."

M put the phone down and sat back. He was sweating. His heart was pounding. He got up and shook his arms.

All in all, he thought it went well. The fact that Shippen Travers wanted to send money instead of immediately inviting him and Jessie to bunk down in Arizona was a problem. He'd have to think on that. It was gonna take some convincing to get Shippen Travers to suggest they move to Arizona. Probably a bit of truth bending too.

He almost wished he still had time to talk to Dr. Avery, but it was too late today.

Still, in the back of his head he kept thinking about Jessie and her bike and how much she liked riding it. He had seen her smile. She hadn't been anything approaching happy for a few weeks. He wished he'd been the cause of her smile, but, hell, he could remedy that today.

M glanced up at Ruby's trailer as he left. He felt a little guilty about leaving Jessie, but it was only for a short time while he did some shopping. Besides, maybe he could just say his session with Avery went long. Avery wouldn't mind. Would probably even laugh when he heard about M playing hooky.

He wondered as he left the trailer park whether lies in the adult world were just considered part of any conversation.

CHAPTER 37

Stan watched Mallory pace nervously. She had not stopped talking about the old lady in the trailer park. She would pause halfway around the conference table, lean over, and straighten whatever papers she happened to be near.

"Look, Stan okay, I'm not field trained. I know you know. But, damn I have a feeling about yesterday. Shit, just bugs me. There was this kid and his sister and then that old bat that lives in the last trailer. She had a camper next door and claimed she told fortunes and she probably did, but she had this JOYLAND poster and all these pictures, and then there was a slimy slug of a man...."

She flopped down on her desk. "Damn. I know it, you know..." She looked at him imploringly.

"Don't look at me. And no, I don't know. You say the old lady never worked for Rendell, just bought her trailer from him."

"That's what she said, anyway."

"And she doesn't know where he is. So, what else is there? If she'd been a regular carnie, well then she woulda seen something, right?"

After ten minutes of watching her scurry around the office tidying up everything, he noticed that she had changed clothes again. The clingy jeans were still in place however.

"Would you sit the hell down and quit fussing or whatever you're doing. It's...unprofessional," was all he could think to say.

Mallory looked up. "What?"

She stopped arranging papers on the conference table. "Well, what are *you* doing?"

Stan had pulled three plastic cups from his desk drawer and set them in a row. Next, he broke the seal on a pint of Speyburn he'd rescued from the liquor store bag, and twisted the top.

"I'm preparing. I'm getting ready for Detective Steiner who I have failed to properly welcome to our new digs here at OID. It's been a week and we haven't inaugurated this whole operation yet. Jake doesn't always relish working with new people."

"Why? I mean, why doesn't he like new people? He doesn't like me, is that what you're saying?" She indicated the three cups. "And isn't it a little early for...?"

Stan poured the liquor and smelled the Scotch aroma settle around him. "Settle down. Jake doesn't take to many people. Sometimes he doesn't even like me and I've worked with him forever. And it's almost four o'clock and besides it's always the right time for a toast with a special single malt."

He topped off all three cups so they were even.

"And this will help."

"He doesn't seem to be a hateful person," Mallory ventured.

Stan looked at her. She looked worried.

He put the bottle back in his desk and sat forward.

"Detective Jake Steiner is an excellent detective but he's also a cautious person. That sometimes comes across like he's a bit of an asshole."

Mallory stood twisting her hands together until she realized what she was doing. "I've got work to do." She disappeared behind some file boxes.

Stan was leaning back in his chair as Jake came stumping into the house of glass. Stan raised his index finger in greeting.

"Hey."

Steiner looked around; his metal brace glistened in the shafts of the late afternoon sun. "Whatever. Where is she?"

"Me?'" Mallory came out from behind a pile of boxes near her desk. She brightened.

Jake took one cold hard glance and limped past her. He went to the end of the conference table and turned to face them both.

Stan could tell he was in a bit of pain, but this was more.

Then Jake turned to Mallory. "Who the fuck do you think you are?" he shouted.

Stan snapped forward. "Hey, man, take it easy. What..."

Jake held up his hand in Stan's direction then turned back to Mallory. Balancing on one good leg, he reached into his pocket and slapped a piece of paper down on the conference table. His eyes never left her face.

Stan looked from Jake to Mallory. She had turned ashen after she looked at the paper.

"What...?" asked Stan. "What?"

Jake spread out the wrinkled sheet and pointed to it. He looked to Stan. "Tell me you didn't know about this?"

Stan tried to play catch-up. "I don't know what the hell..."

Jake held up a hand. "Didn't think so." He turned to Mallory. "Well?"

Her smiled had hardened into death stone.

"What do you mean, 'well'?" she asked.

Jake flicked the paper by an edge. It danced across the conference table, spinning. Mallory stopped it with two fingers.

She didn't bother looking at the paper. It was obvious to Stan she knew what it was and that gave him a very bad feeling.

Jake shifted on his good leg and addressed Stan.

"That," he said, pointing at the letter, "appears to be a letter from Detective Stan Wyld and Detective Jake Steiner to our good Captain, requesting, no..." He turned back to Mallory. "...not requesting, insisting, that for the good of the department we be given Olive Park as our first case."

Stan felt the color drain away. He looked at Mallory who was now staring at the letter on the table as if she could see through it. He turned away. It made crooked sense. Why would they have been assigned Olive Park as their first case? He knew it hadn't been right. Downtown would have wanted them to settle in, get up to speed. At least move in for crissakes.

Jake continued with unbridled sarcasm in sing-song, "Oh, how did I put it to the Captain...oh yes, I remember...something about the victim's families and blah, blah, blah...oh and to help restore the dignity and credibility of the department. When we solve it, of course." He looked at Mallory.

Stan too, turned and waited for a response. A denial. A rebuttal. Anything. Anything to forestall the overwhelming betrayal he felt. The parade of lies returned as he remembered Mallory's promises to try and get them out of Olive Park.

Mallory walked her fingers along the letter until it read right side up to her. She continued to stare at it. Finally, after re-reading it, she raised her head and said to them both, "Yeah, it's a nice letter. What about it?"

"Well, Mallory, we didn't write it," Jake turned to Stan, "Did we Stan?

Stan shook his head then found a quiet voice. "Why would we do such a thing? Crazy, plain crazy."

Jake looked at Mallory. "So, *are* you crazy? Besides being a forger, I mean?"

Mallory said nothing. She pushed the paper away and sat down, put her feet up on the edge of the table and started tapping her shoes together. She shook her blonde hair and looked at Jake defiantly.

"Look," said Jake, hating the silence. "Get her the hell out of here. Before I kill her."

Mallory continued to stare. There was no contriteness in her look. Almost pride.

Stan stood up to head off whatever was going to happen when he could see there was no apology coming.

But Mallory took them both by surprise. Her voice was tight and controlled as she addressed Jake.

"Look around you, you lazy shithead. Look what we've done with this case," she said indicating the board behind her. "Look at the progress we've made."

She let her feet drop to the floor.

"You had how many other so-called detectives and suits and grunts who worked on this since it happened. 'Oh, it's too hard. Oh, I can't do it. Oh, what if we fail.' Well, screw that."

She jumped up and went to the map of missing kids the turned on Jake. "Well, we're not failing if you haven't noticed.

We're making headway where no one else did, if you haven't noticed. Open your eyes. We might solve this thing."

She turned and stared out of the glass cubicle. Stan could see her reflection in the glass.

She continued in a determined voice. "Who the hell cares how we got this, anyway? We're winning this thing. We're gonna solve it." She turned back and faced them both. "So, what's the big deal?"

Jesus, she hadn't a clue. Stan wanted to intervene. Needed to, but this was all Jake's.

Jake swung his casted leg off the table and rose up, swaying a bit.

"It's like this missy. Here's the big deal. Here's the problem and it's simple. You went rogue on us. You fucked over your partners. You screwed us."

She turned from Jake to Stan. Stan couldn't hold her glance, but shook his head and looked away.

"Think it's no big deal?" continued Jake, taut with fury. "We're gonna solve this, you say. It ain't about solve or no solve or reputations. You don't quite see that yet."

He picked up the phone and started dialing.

"When I'm out on an ugly domestic call with my partner," he continued without looking at either Stan or Mallory, "and dispatch says some husband is beating the shit out of his wife and they want me to break it up, cool things off....Judy, give me the Captain please...yeah, I'll wait."

Stan got up and stared out at the darkened atrium. He couldn't watch. It was bad enough to listen to the steely control in Jake's voice.

"You see, on a domestic, you never know what you're gonna get. Could be a big mother humper come storming out of the house. He sees me. He stops, gives up. It's okay, then. Or, it could be some milquetoast type of guy's real quiet, but when my back is turned, he runs at me with a knife I've forgotten to check him for..." Jake re-cradled the phone. "No, I'll wait."

He stared hard at Mallory. "When that dick comes running at me, I want to be able to rely on my partner to shoot him in the balls to get him to stop. Because that's what partners do. Regardless of what else they do, no matter how they really feel about each other, the one thing they know is that when that guy comes running at them while they're not looking, their partner will be there."

Jake and Mallory stared at each other.

"He knows his partner would give his life to protect him. That's what partners do. They don't forge their signatures. They don't lie to their face. They don't stab them in the back. They have their back."

Jake raised the phone, never taking his eyes off Mallory. "I'm here. Yeah, I'll wait."

He lowered the mouthpiece again. "You might have fooled Stan here. He's one of the nicest guys on the planet. Not me. He's the one I want behind me backing me up. He knows what's important. He's a cop."

Stan turned back and watched Mallory grab the back of her chair. She addressed both of them.

"I know all about the partner shit, I get it. I understand if this…this Olive Park is just a job to you. It's just another case. You're pissed because somebody tricked you into doing some real investigative work. Somebody who caused you to get your lazy asses off the bench. Somebody who spoiled your plan of taking it easy. Well, this is not another job to me…"

She turned and reached the wall with all the missing kids' pictures on it and carefully removed one of the young boy's picture from the wall. She smiled at it, and then set it on the table.

"This case is my only one. There isn't another case to me. This is the only one…."

She touched the photo.

"Sam Dimante is my brother. Was..." She held up the photo so they could both see it.

"He was taken on a warm June night, twelve and a half years ago. His birthday was the day before." She straightened up and took a deep breath. "See, he fits the profile of Olive Park. For five years, I was sure he'd turn up. So did my family. For a while, I hoped he might be a runaway, you know, but we were a happy family. Sam was a good kid. I knew in my heart he wouldn't have run away. I believe he was a victim and after the Handleman debacle broke, my father was convinced of it." Her voice got quiet. "I gave Sam a silver ID bracelet for his birthday. He really liked it. He was 11. And he was beautiful. Sam. My brother."

She looked from Jake to Stan. There was a softness to her look, but her voice was strong with resolve. "And I will find him. With or without either of you. You see, *this* is why we have this case. This is why we will find and fucking kill whoever took him. This is why I wrote the letter."

No one said anything. In the silence they all heard a tinny, insistent voice on the other end of the phone that carried throughout the room.

Stan got it then and it took his breath away. He turned from the glass. "Oh, hell. Dimante? Dimante?" His voice was high like he was being choked, as if he couldn't get any air. "Holy shit."

"Yeah. Dimante," said Mallory, her mouth a tight line. "You get it now? Dimante. It was *my* father who ran down Handleman. It was my father who killed him thinking he was the dog who got away with it. The dog that he was sure took his son, my brother."

Jake ignored the phone, looked at Stan, then back to Mallory, and then back to the letter that still sat on the conference table.

Mallory shrugged. "I know about partner shit, and I know I'm not your partner. I guess I never will be. So I screwed you guys over. So grow up. You're so smart detectives. Deal with it."

She pointed to the letter in the center of the table. "I'm not sorry about...this. You wouldn't have agreed otherwise, I know. I know you both."

No one said anything.

Mallory picked up the 8x 10 of her brother, held it against her chest so Stan and Jake could see it. She looked like a refugee from a disaster, a flood, an earthquake, holding up a picture of a missing relative. A down and outer begging for change at the off ramp. Tears started down her cheeks.

"Vowed I'd do this before I even entered USC. I did all I could working with Ollestad. But I needed help, some guys who knew their way around. When OID came along...well, here we are."

She raised up the picture a little. "So, now, I ask that we stay on this case because I really need your help."

Jake didn't let her finish but slammed the phone down. "Shit!" He stomped his way over to Stan's desk, grabbed up one of the scotches, drained it in one swallow, threw the cup in the trash and stomped out of the cubicle.

Stan and Mallory looked at each other. Mallory was smiling and crying.

"Stan, you understand, right?"

Stan was overwhelmed with the simple, yet inadequate thought that kept steaming through his brain. How simple men were and what a complicated bunch of humanity were women.

CHAPTER 38

M had memorized the number of the police car that had been to Ruby's house the first day he and Jess where there. 2858. He held back in the shadows now that he saw 2858 sitting in front of Aunt Janey's trailer. Stinging sweat ran down his arms.

Along with 2858 was an unmarked, all blue sedan with black walls, the kind of car that screamed I'm really a cop but we didn't want to spend the money on white walls like the rest of the world so our unmarked car can now easily be identified as being a cop car, not a prowler car, but one that housed more important cop people, like detectives.

Detectives. *Shit, now what.*

He lingered outside for a few moments. He and Jess couldn't live like this. *He* couldn't live like this, anyway. They needed their country uncle, Shippen Travers, from good old Bullhead City, Arizona to rescue their sorry asses. Or they needed to take off with Ruby. She kept saying she was leaving soon, planning to move to Vegas or someplace warm for her 'rhumetiz', which he thought for awhile sounded like female trouble but he realized later that it was just bad bones. Bones that cried when the weather was bad, she'd said. Swelled up like cement filled baggies. Stiffening her up, she'd said. She needed sun, warm sun. All the time.

Maybe, she had said, when Jessie and I got things worked out, we could come visit.

M took a few paces along the unmarked car. He was just delaying confrontation. He hoped they weren't here to hassle him about what happened at Ruby's trailer that first day. The cop was a dick. Okay, maybe he shouldn't have shut the door in the cop's face.

He took a deep breath. It was that feeling in his gut that the police weren't here about that. Or about anything that happened in San Francisco. We are all past asking questions now, he thought. We're supposed to be in the healing mode. The grieving time is past, blame time is past, now it's just time to forget, at least that's what Dr. Avery says.

So what is this?

He felt like the sucker in the barrel about to go over the falls. No one was visible in Aunt Janey's windows, but it looked as if every light she owned was on full blast. The shafts of yellow light lit up the area in front of the trailer where Aunt Janey had spent a few hours last Saturday planting geraniums. She had made M help. 'These are for my brother, your father; least you can do is help.' He did help plant them but when she wasn't looking; he cut off the roots before slapping them in the ground.

'Only natural there would be some resentment on her part,' Dr. Avery had said, 'given what happened.'

'Hope she likes dead irises,' M had shot back.

Avery had had no comment then.

M surveyed the whole of the trailer. Jess was probably in the bedroom, he hoped, with the door closed.

Instead of opening Aunt Janey's trailer door he thought about heading to Ruby's instead. He looked down the length of the park and could see the cars going by on the highway in the distance. The neon light was on above Ruby's red trailer but inside it was dark except for a small light in her kitchen. He stared harder and thought he saw someone standing in the window of the backdoor. Maybe Pitic watching the cops.

He set the brand new handlebar basket he'd gotten for Jessie's piece of shit bike down next to the little stump in his aunt's garden, vaulted up the two steps and swung open the trailer door.

His entrance had an immediate effect on the assembled group.

Aunt Janey jumped up, the detective in the suit turned and stared, the uniform from 2858 tensed, his leather holster creaked, and his hand naturally fell to the butt of his revolver like a tiger in a crouch.

"Hey," M said as casually as he could. 'What's up?

Aunt Janey started to shake. "Where's Jessie?"

"What?"

Aunt Janey flew around the small dining table and, as if he was hard of hearing, yelled, "Where is she!"

The uniform cop seized her arm so she couldn't physically lay into him

M extended his hands out toward the rest of the trailer, "She's here... here..."

Aunt Janey looked surprised. "Where? Where exactly is she?"

M started to speak, and then stopped.

"Where?"

M looked at the two cops who were staring at him watching his reaction. They wouldn't be here if she was fast asleep in her bed.

Shit.

"Where is your sister!!" screamed Aunt Janey. She turned away and searched for her cigarettes. "I take you in, after all that has happened and all I ask is that you look after your sister, Christ, I've got a goddamn babysitter for you six hours a day and you can't take care of your sister for a coupla hours 'til I get home? You can't do anything right." She put a quavering match to the end of her cigarette. "You fucked up your family, got my brother killed, and now your sister's gone and I sure hope you had nothing to do with it or so help me, by God, I will fucking tear you apart, I'm so sick..."

She collapsed into her chair.

"Jesus..." was all she muttered as she dragged on her cigarette and shook her head.

The uniform remained staring at M. The detective, acting as if nothing out of the ordinary had just happened, said, "Well, son."

"Jessie's not here?" He tried not to stammer.

Aunt Janey slung her arm over the back of the chair. "...Oh Christ, what are you deaf too..."

The detective put his hand on M's shoulder. "Outside."

"What is it...?" M started.

Aunt Janey rose halfway out of her seat. "You make him tell you where she is by God or so help me..."

The detective closed the trailer door and they both stood there at the bottom of the two steps. The yelling went on inside.

"What is it? She can't find my sister?" M indicated Aunt Janey.

The detective looked down at the notebook he carried. "Where were you this afternoon?"

"Forget me. Forget 'Where was *I*', he mocked the detective. "Where is my sister?"

"Where were you?"

"Is my sister missing? What's going on?"

"Where were you?" repeated the detective.

M hesitated. "Look, my aunt will tell you, every Wednesday I have an appointment with a doctor, Dr. Avery, down in the Medical Arts building, downtown...4th and Stewart. Why aren't you looking for my sister?" His voice started to rise.

"And that's where you were from...when?"

"Look, appointment time is always 3:45."

"Then where did you go?"

M licked his lips. "Kind of took the long way back, kind of wandered..."

"Anyplace in particular where you wandered?"

M rolled his eyes. *Screw him.* "No. Look, where…"

The suit's voice was calm, his stare unwavering. "Where was this... wandering?"

"Over along the Strand."

"Was your sister with you?"

"What...Jesus. No."

"You're sure?"

"I'm sure. She was here."

The suit didn't hesitate. "And how do you know that? How do you know she was here, exactly?"

"I left her at Ruby's, the babysitter, up there." He indicated Ruby's trailer. Our deal is whoever gets home first, me or my aunt, gets my sister. My aunt obviously got home first so she must've brought her home. That's how."

"You're telling me that you didn't come back and get your sister from the babysitter's? That's what you're telling me? Your aunt got her and you didn't, that's your complete statement?

M fidgeted at the mention of a 'statement'. This wasn't right. Besides the fact that his sister couldn't be found there was a feeling, an undercurrent he couldn't read.

"I just told you, yes."

The suit just stood there looking at M.

"Look," M continued, his voice rising again without meaning to, "if my sister is missing, we need to be looking for her and you...Christ, you should be investigating leads or something."

"I am," said the suit. He didn't take his eyes off M.

"Bullshit! You're not doing anything...you're not writing down anything I say...."

"You haven't told me much that's true, yet." The suit turned away and headed back to the trailer. "Stay out here," he said over his shoulder.

"Screw you. I'm going to go look for my sister."

The suit stopped with his hand on the knob, his tie fluttered against the door and he shifted on the steps.

"You stay right the fuck here and when I come out you better tell me what happened to your sister and where you were when you skipped your appointment with the doctor. Got it?"

M said nothing.

"Got it?"

Before he could answer, another squad rolled up behind M, lights flashing. The suit waved and pointed out M to the officers just getting out of the squad. He turned and entered the trailer. Through the open doorway M could see his aunt. She jumped out of her chair, "Well, what did he say? Where is she?" The last thing he saw before the door slammed shut was his aunt, both fists on the table staring straight at him.

The squad stopped at an angle, tight up to his aunt's fence. Both officers jumped out.

"C'mon, kid, have a seat."

"What?" M turned. The officers had cornered him up against the detective's car, still standing three feet away, but poised, M saw, to probably knock the shit out of him if he didn't plan on doing what they said.

"Take a seat, kid." One of the officers, the fat looking one, had opened the back seat to the squad.

M had seen enough cop shows to know that the backseat had no handles to open the door. If he got in and if he sat down on that leather seat and the door closed, he wasn't getting out until they let them out.

M smiled. "No that's okay. I'm supposed to stay right here. He said so," indicating the detective that had just gone into the trailer. M slumped back against the detective's car in the most casual way, folded his arms and kept his eyes on the trailer.

His innocent shtick usually worked on people. Not these guys. Obviously they were used to coming to the trailer park and dealing with punk assholes who lie for a living. And, with him, they had no idea what they were dealing with. Even though he was acting polite they knew he could be anything from a drug pusher to a crazy lunatic. They'd seen it all in Sunshine Vista, guessed M.

"Yeah, well you could wait right in here just as well." The officers moved to allow him to slide into the backseat.

M feigned surprise at their insistence. He knew he had only seconds to make a decision. The last place he wanted to be was in the back of a squad car, with his fingers intertwined in the cage between the driver and the felon's backseat. He never wanted to be at anybody's mercy. He had to be looking for Jessie. He didn't want to be with Aunt Janey. He didn't want to be in a trailer park. He didn't want to be standing in front of these two officers with blue and red lights flashing in his face, slumped against the detectives' car. He wanted his life to be anything than what it was right now. 180 degrees from the shit he was looking at. In fact if he could take back the last month, no make that the last week, even the last few days, everything would be all right. Maybe not all right but a B up from a D minus.

"How 'bout you let me finish my cigarette first, eh?" said M.

"What cigarette? What are you talking about?" asked the beefy one. Then when he realized he was being had, "How 'bout you just get in the goddamn car."

M sighed. "Well, I could use a smoke if you boys have one."

The skinny one just smiled and turned away. The beefy one put his hand on M's arm. M let him guide him around the door. Just before M pushed the cop's arm away ready to run like hell, the trailer door flew open and the sound of Aunt Janey screaming again drew everyone's attention.

And that's when M ran.

Mr. Beefy had turned to see what the commotion was and if he was going to be needed in the trailer. The skinny cop had started to light his cigarette.

When the big cop did look into the backseat and realized he'd been had, he spun around and scanned the rows of mobile homes of Sunshine Vista.

M, having bolted for the shadows between two of the closest trailers, was well gone.

CHAPTER 39

M shifted from one leg to the other. His shoes were wet. He needed some more clothes. Needed to get warm. Needed a place to think. He inched his way closer to the front of Ruby's trailer and could hear them talking. Why weren't they talking inside? What was going on?

When he'd bolted an hour ago, he'd done it on impulse. An act of last resort.

He was cold. He hadn't eaten, but even so, there was no way he could force food with Jessie gone. He tried to think of anything, anything but what might be happening to her. Imagination, a wild, terrified horse that would not be reined in.

She was scared. She was in a dark place. Someone was touching her. God, he knew it. Knew it! How scared she was. What she was thinking? He knew. Why had her brother left her alone? Why hadn't he been there to walk her home? Why wasn't he with her? Why didn't he come get her?

There was no question of guilt. None at all. He'd royally screwed up. He'd skipped out on Avery and gone shopping for Jessie. Screwed up, and now he needed to fix it. The cops thought he had something to do with it. How could they think that? None of it made sense.

Of course, now that both he and Jessie were missing, then maybe the cops *would* be looking for both of them. Actively looking. Somebody would find someone. They'd canvas the neighbors, make them answer their doors. Bang on some aluminum until someone came to the door and answered their questions about a pretty six year old, missing, last seen walking in front of their trailer. What did they know? What had they seen? Goddammit, where was she?

They'd search the carnival site eventually. But M had seen the TV shows. The odds of finding a child who has been taken, finding them nearby, not so much. Taken meant taken away. Far away.

But, somebody had seen something. A license plate on a car that didn't belong. A man lurking. A door to door salesman, if they even existed anymore. Someone taking a survey. The mailman. Cable repair guy. Even the crazy Chinese lady. Somebody had to know something. Somebody would find someone. Before a bad thing happened.

He couldn't shake the revulsion of entering Ruby's trailer yesterday and seeing Pitic with his arm around Jessie. Ruby yanking her hand off the table, putting something in her pocket. The three of them in the dim candlelight, playing. What? Was it a flash of guilt in Ruby's eyes for letting Jessie play with Pitic? God, the smirk on Pitic's face. Jessie not aware of anything. Just having fun.

Stupid, stupid, stupid.

Now he huddled alongside Ruby's trailer waiting for the cop to leave so he could meet up with Ruby and find out what the hell happened. Yeah, she was crusty and had the compassion of a rock, but he knew she'd at least take him in. She was an adult who would help him find Jessie.

It was that pig faced Pitic.

He'd thought about calling Shippen Travers this morning but his mother's cousin, sitting in his Frog Creek ranch, couldn't do a damn thing about Jessie. And he sure as hell wasn't going to jump on a plane and come help find her.

Dr. Avery. That was useless.

He needed to talk to Ruby. She must know. She was the last to see Jessie. Ruby. She was the one harboring that brown little shit. Ruby knows. She must know. She could help. She would help.

She jerked her hand off the table and slipped something into her pocket.

He started to shiver. The hydrangea bushes that flanked her trailer made a good cover, but every time he brushed against their branches dew sprang off and ran down his shirt. When he'd gotten away from the cops, he'd circled around the outside of the park and headed to Ruby's. They'd be waiting for him to return to Janey's. They wouldn't be expecting him at Ruby's. But, now he was starting to freeze his ass off.

The more he thought about it, Ruby had to tell him where Pitic was. Because where Pitic was, there might be Jessie. He didn't want to think about that. And he especially didn't want to think that he let her down. He hadn't been there to take care of her. His aunt was right. Shit. May have let her down? He had. He wasn't there when she needed him. And where had he been? Leisurely shopping. Damn.

M rested up against the side of Ruby's trailer. The aluminum was cold, but he was so tired, and even though his legs shook he couldn't lie down on the cold grass. He knew the minute the cop left he would have to knock on Ruby's door. She'd have to let him in. He had to trust her. His options were down to shittin' nothing.

He re-examined his decision to run. It had been impulse. What choice did he really have? The tide had been rapidly rising against him. You had zero credibility as a kid. And if you'd had some unusual tragedy in your life that was partly your own making, well, that just took you down another notch. No, he was looking at serious lock up time because the cops didn't appreciate being sandbagged. He knew he looked like a big loose cannon to them, and, now guilty because he ran.

Easier to lock up first and ask questions later.

He peeked around the corner of the trailer again. He could see they were still standing on the little front porch. She had just turned the outside light on. The cop had his notebook out.

"I know the other detective went over some of this with you a little while ago, so I'm just following up."

Ruby continued where she'd left off. "As I said, they talked about it all the time." She stood with her arms crossed, but with a stupid smile on her face and her busy mouth working overtime.

"So," the cop said looking up from his notes, "your opinion is the brother ran off with his sister?"

"Well, now, never want to be accusatory and all, but they were hot to leave. They'd talked about Arizona like I said. They even wanted to go with me when I retire next week to Nevada."

M shook his head as if the words he was hearing were not registering correctly in his brain. What kind of bullshit was she spinning? Next week? What the hell? And shit, Arizona was a secret. What was she doing?

"You're retiring? Leaving all…this?" The cop indicated her business trailer. His sarcasm trickled just below the surface.

"Oh, I still have my skills. I can still tell fortunes and there are plenty of people who need their palms read in Florida. The warmth'll do my bones good, you see."

"Florida? I thought you said you were going to Nevada," said the detective sharply.

Ruby tilted her head back and hooted. "Got good golden opportunities in both places and I'm gonna get me some. Need to go anywhere there's more sun than here. Whatever, yeah, Florida or Nevada."

The cop brought them back to Jessie. "So, can you give me an accurate timeline of what happened?"

Ruby pretended to think a minute. M had seen that pretend pondering before. It usually preceded a bald faced lie.

"I believe I can, officer. Let's see, both kids arrived about eight in the morning. Their aunt usually walks them up here, though sometimes they come alone. But, yes, today she brought them up here about eight."

"And you stayed with them all day?"

"Well, I do have a business to run, but it's next door. So, sometimes I was next door and sometimes I was here. So, yes, you can say I was with them all day."

"Both children were here?"

"Oh, yes. They're always together. They almost never go anywhere by themselves."

M knew what Ruby was saying was correct in the words, but not her meaning. She was making it seem as if they were tied together with a rope. The cops were going to believe then that if Jessie was missing, she was with him. It was all he could do to keep from stepping out of the bushes and putting everyone straight.

"Now," began the cop, reading from his notes, "I understand that the boy had a doctor's appointment with a …"

"Psychologist. He was seeing a psychologist," said Ruby. Then as a seeming afterthought she added, "It was court ordered. He had…problems, you see."

"And what time did he leave?"

"His appointment is for 3:30 I think, so he leaves about 3:00."

"And, he left at 3 today?"

Ruby hesitated. Again, M could tell she was play acting. She was pretending to be uncertain. Ruby was never uncertain about anything, even if she was wrong.

"I believe so. Didn't check the time, but I would assume so."

"And the girl…" he checked his notes, "Jessica was still here?"

"Oh, yes. Little Jess was with me until her brother came home from his appointment."

M snapped his head up. What?

The cop also raised up his head from his notes. "So, the brother comes home. Then does he come back up here?"

Ruby shook her head. "Hardly ever. You see their aunt gets home about the same time as he gets back from his appointment on his appointment days, so I usually watch out and when he gets home, he waves and I send little Jess back to spend a few minutes with her brother until their aunt gets home. They aren't without adult supervision much longer than fifteen minutes."

I wave? She sends Jess down to me? What a load of crap. I always come get her. At least until today.

"So," said the officer. "You don't keep them until the minute their aunt gets home?" He consulted his notes. "Until Mrs. Cooper gets home?"

"Uh… I believe it's Miss Cooper. I don't believe she's ever been married."

"But, you don't keep them here until she arrives?"

Ruby looked down. She pretended to look sheepish. M couldn't believe the performance. She was covering for that little brown scumbag, Pitic. He was certain.

"Officer, I'm a…not married either. And those kids are okay kids as kids go, but they're kids and it ends up being a long day, if you know what I mean. With work and all."

The officer nodded and pushed his hat back on his head. "I have two of my own. Yeah."

Ruby nodded knowingly. "Then you know."

"But, you watched as the little girl walked down to their aunt's trailer after the brother waved?"

"I watched her all the way, yes," said Ruby with a believability that made even M question whether he had been there or not.

"And you're sure it was the brother waving, indicating he was home?"

"Of course. I have good eyesight. I know him when I see him, sir."

"I'm sure you do. And what time was that. When you sent the girl down to her brother?"

Ruby shrugged. "It must've been the normal time 'cause I was looking out for him. So, probably about 5 or so."

"And that's the last time you saw her?"

Ruby looked straight at the cop with an unwavering gaze. "With her brother, yes. That was the last time"

The cop relaxed a bit. "Okay. And when did you know she was missing again?"

"Well, when their aunt, Miss Cooper, came up here about 5:45 looking for both kids."

"What did she say?"

Ruby huffed a bit. "She was a little upset and rude. Oh I understand that of course. She wanted to know where the kids were. I told her everything I told you. About the brother waving and me watching her walk down to their trailer. Just like a normal day. Just like we did every day that he had his appointment. That's all."

"Then what?"

Ruby paused. "She said a few bad things about the boy and left."

"And that's all you know?"

"Well…this is a tragedy, pure and simple, but, look, there's one more thing." She held up her hands. "I don't think it means anything and probably has nothing to do with little Jess, but…one of the residents of our little park here, I understand, found a mutilated animal pinned to the chain link fence over there." Ruby pointed to the exact spot the cat had been hanging.

"I don't know," continued Ruby, "I'm sure it has nothing to do with anything, probably neighborhood boys, you know, but I wanted to mention it 'cause it was unusual and it was only a day or two ago."

The officer started writing again. "Did the boy, the brother, ever show any animosity or violence toward his sister? Did you see him bother any animals? What was it?"

"A cat. Pretty grey and white. We called it Ambition. It was sort of a neighborhood cat. The whole thing was downright traumatizing."

"And you never saw the brother demonstrate…"

Ruby shook her head slightly, then stopped to consider. "I don't believe so. But, you know kids. Maybe he hid it well."

M tried to stop his shivering. He was screwed. He knew now that to reveal himself would assure that they never found Jessie. He knew he'd never have a chance to look. He knew that with the hole Ruby was digging for him, he'd never be believed. They'd work on him and work on him believing he knew where she was, instead of looking for her. Shit and goddamn.

Ruby caught the officer as he turned to leave.

"Oh! Officer?"

The cop threw his notebook on the seat and turned. He didn't expect to hear anything new. He'd been listening to her story for half an hour already.

"The more I think about it, I do believe they would have tried for Arizona, the way they were talking."

"Well, we should know tomorrow whether they're around here or not. We'll have the dogs out here. Woulda been tonight but those dogs aren't as good at night. If those kids are here, or nearby, dogs will find them." He started to get into the unmarked. "Have a good evening."

But Ruby would not let go. "Officer! Dogs? Tomorrow?"

"That's right." He slipped into the unmarked.

Ruby continued with more insistence. "Like I told you…they're not around here anymore!" She shouted over the noise of the unmarked's engine. "Find the boy and you'll find the sister. I'm sure of it!"

The full impact of what she was doing hit him. For an hour she had been sandbagging his sorry ass. She was selling him down the river. A favorite phrase of his father's. Now, he felt the sting with everything she said.

Totally screwed.

M slipped around to the front of Ruby's trailer, along the highway, ran blindly and hid behind one of the old entry pillars to the carnival. He held on with both hands and rested his head against the crumbling concrete.

He heard the unmarked back slowly away from Ruby's trailer, turn and make its way to the exit of Sunshine Vista. He straightened up and stepped back. His eyes went to the arcing sign above his head. Someone had taken a black spray can and scrawled over JOYLAND.

It now read, Rendell's OLIVE PARK Carnival.

He grabbed on to the chain link fence, yanked on it a few times, and let his eyes search the deserted remains of the carnival of freaks. He had never felt so alone.

Where are you Jess?

He pushed away from the fence. He had to think and he knew where he could go.

CHAPTER 40

Ruby closed the trailer door and kept her head centered in the window as she watched the cop drive away. She gave a short, serious wave, then turned and picked up her keys. She checked the window again and made sure the cop had completely left the park. She switched off the kitchen light and opened the door, closed it quietly and padded down the walkway to the camper.

She pulled out her keys for the RV and opened the back door. Before going in, she reached out to the power box and pulled down the heavy handle. The neon sign above the trailer went dark.

Fortunes by Ruby was closed. For good.

Satisfied, she slipped inside and addressed the blackness of the room. Only one candle was burning in the center of the table. The crystal ball picked up the flickering flame and sent sprinkles of light around the velvet covered walls.

She raised a fist and pounded on the RV's closet door three times.

Jessie Ann Cooper didn't answer.

Ruby settled her bulk in front of the back door of the RV and opened it a crack. And waited.

Finally, at about three in the morning, when all lights were off everywhere in Sunshine Vista, when traffic on the highway had dwindled to the occasional truck making the run from Sacramento to Reno, only then did she pick up the small pair of white underwear with the pink flowers on them, and Jessie's Mr. Bear.

Looking straight into Mr. Bear's glass eyes, Ruby Everheart tilted her head back and gave a guttural laugh that was as much a release as it was an acknowledgement that the fun was about to begin.

CHAPTER 41

Mallory slammed the big metal door behind her. It echoed in the atrium. Even though their glass enclosure was lit up in full streaming daylight and she could see no one was there, and even though the ringing phone was going unanswered, she still called out.

"Hey! Stan! Jake! Where are you?"

She moved quickly to her desk. The phone had stopped.

She looked around. She was on different ground. She knew it. All three of them had been on the same road heading in the same direction for the same destination, but she had split it. She had jammed a fork in the road and she was no longer with them.

She had wandered about until almost noon before she decided to brave the office. She had held out a small glimmer that they would be there in the office when she arrived. That when she walked in they would maybe not rush to greet her, but would at least acknowledge her presence, acknowledge that she had a good motive for what she did. Make a joke. Not say it directly, but indicate that all was forgiven or some such horseshit. Just so they could get on with the case.

She knew what they were pissed off about. She knew how men thought. Well, sometimes. Simple creatures with egos the size they wish their penises were.

They were hurt. Hurt that it was she who had made progress on a case they never wanted and to which she had inexorably tied them. They were stuck and they knew it. No backing the shit out of the garage. They were moving forward from now on.

The phone started again.

At first she thought it was her cell. She had seen Stan had called earlier. Actually she had watched the phone as it rang and vibrated across her kitchen table. She followed it around the table so she could read who was calling on the face of the phone. She didn't pick it up. No way. She needed to register a little bit of 'fuck you' by not answering. She'd take the second call, she knew, but there hadn't been a second call.

That was four hours ago.

But, this wasn't her cell, it was the office phone. "OID, Mallory Dimante." She held the phone pinned with her shoulder, and started to change her shoes while she listened.

"What? Actually that was me. I put out the request. Why?" She nodded out of habit.

"Wait. Wait just a minute, will you." She put the phone down, kicked off her other shoe and found a pencil.

"Where? In Sacramento?"

She listened for a second, and then set the pencil down. She regripped the phone.

"Where did you say?"

She listened for a few seconds, then said, "Yeah. I've got it. I know where it is."

She set the phone back in the cradle.

"Hell, yeah, I know where it is because I was there yesterday."

She swept her notebook and phone off the desk into her bag and slipped her shoes back on. She thought for a moment of leaving Stan and Jake a note, then didn't. Let 'em stew. They could just wonder where she was. Different roads. Same destination, but different roads.

As she fired up the Honda, she had a twinge of apprehension. She hoped that the response she just got to her missing children query wasn't the cute little blonde girl she saw the other day riding the bike in wobbly circles at the trailer park.

But in her gut, she knew better.

CHAPTER 42

The white and orange barricades were stationed across the whole of the entrance to Sunshine Vista. One empty squad sat behind the barricades with its blue and reds flashing. Mallory looked down the entrance to the park as she drove past. She could see a variety of residents standing out in front of their trailers, the yellow police tape fluttering in the breeze and about six uniforms standing with their backs to everyone, but all looking in the same direction, down the length of Sunshine Vista.

She angled the Honda off the road, up against one of the Sunshine Vista pillars and hopped out. Behind her she saw the first of the TV trucks turn the corner. She hustled past the barricades, wanting to get inside before the uniforms had to manage the press herd.

She passed the K9 truck. There were three of the trackers inside, one was still barking and constantly turning inside his cage demanding to be let out.

She held up her red bordered ID to the first uniform she met.

He looked at it skeptically. "OID? Cold case?"

"Long story. Cornell called. I had asked to be alerted to any new missing kids."

"Well, you've come to the right place. We got the guy, but kids still missing."

"You what?"

"Yeah, they're bringing him out in a minute. Took us a few hours to convince him. Bastard said he was holding his mother as a hostage. Turns out mother died years ago."

"You said him?"

"Yeah. Guy was on parole."

"Thanks."

It didn't make any sense. What guy and who was the kid?

Mallory moved off toward the long arm of the 'L' of the trailer park. When she got to the corner she saw everyone's attention was focused on a dingy white and green, molded over mobile home halfway down the block. More uniforms were just outside the front door, which was propped open.

Crime scene tape surrounded a small area on the driveway. Inside the perimeter Mallory could make out something white. A cloth maybe.

Another circle of tape encompassed one of the scraggly boxwood bushes next to the front door.

Most of the uniforms hurried past her back to the entrance to try and corral the press. She moved closer and then spied a Homicide detective she'd dated once, last year.

"Hey, Duggan. Who is he?" asked Mallory, moving alongside.

He glanced at her, raised his eyebrows in surprise, then turned his attention back to the trailer's front door.

"What are you doing here?"

"Cornell called me about the kid this morning. I had an alert out for missing kids for Wyld and Steiner. So who is he?"

"Druggie, out waiting for trial."

"And he took a kid?" Mallory couldn't hide her disbelief.

"Guess so. We had the dogs out first light this morning searching for the kid. Like a cannon, right for this place."

"Really?"

"Underwear in the driveway there. Found the kid's teddy bear in the bushes near the door."

There was a swell of murmuring from the crowd, and Mallory saw activity at the front door. Two uniforms emerged with the suspect between them. He shuffled along, hands bound behind him. His hair was askew as if he'd just woken up. Ripped jeans, T shirt and light brown leather jacket.

"Don't hurt me!" was all Mallory heard from where she was, as they pushed his head down and he tumbled into the back of the squad.

There was sudden wailing from behind her. Mallory saw a slim middle-aged lady slip from the passenger seat of one of the squad cars. She held her hands to her face and was now slumped on the ground and an officer moved to help her back up.

"The mother or aunt, I think, of the kid," said Steve. He reached into his coat pocket and pulled out a picture, opened it so she could see it.

Mallory sighed when she saw the cute face of little blonde Jessie Cooper. It was the little girl she had seen riding the bike a few days before.

"I saw her here."

"You saw her?"

"Couple of days ago, here. Her brother was with her."

"Yeah, the brother. They're still looking for him."

"He's missing too?"

"Ran off when they tried to question him."

Mallory watched the squad drive slowly out of the trailer park, parting the curious and the camera crews like a slow ship.

"What about the babysitter? They question her? She's a queer duck."

"I just came on this morning, and what I heard was they talked to everybody, but hey, we've got underwear and the teddy bear." He said it as if 'what more do you need.'

Mallory nodded but it didn't feel right. There was something about this…place. Not far, maybe half a mile as the crow flies, three children were found murdered fifteen years ago. Now another child is taken, but the guy who takes her is a young guy, early twenties probably. And Stan and Jake are certain that the guy they were all looking for is some guy named Rendell from Florida. He must be in his fifties or even sixty by now.

The squad, with the aunt in the front seat, pulled out and followed the suspect. The neighbors started to filter back into their trailers.

"Is this something cold case is working on? I mean, you coming downtown?" There seemed to be a glimmer of hope in his question.

"Huh? No. Yes. Maybe. Probably. I've gotta call Jake and Stan first."

"Maybe see you later, then." He lingered for a few seconds then went to check on Forensics busy photographing the underwear.

Mallory took out her cell and called Stan and got voice mail. Same with Jake.

Bastards.

She watched the activity of the forensic crew for a few minutes, then swung around and studied the pretty yellow and white trailer where the brother had been sitting the other day.

Mallory fingered her car keys and started to drift back toward her car but stopped and stared back up the length of Sunshine Vista. She studied the trailer at the end. The fortune teller's. The babysitter. Maybe one of the last to see little Jessica.

It was the white venetian blinds at the far end of the trailer that caught her eye. Someone had separated the blinds in the middle. They stayed that way for a few seconds, then like the lazy eye of a wary dog, they closed.

CHAPTER 43

"Jesus Jumpin' Johnnycake! I don't give a damn how you got this case or who asked for what or who did what to whomever or who's related to whom or who screwed who over. Look, she found a goddamn tree with a rope and that's more evidence than anyone's found in fifteen years, right? And is this what you had to see me about? This shit?"

Stan held his ground. He'd made it sound like an emergency when he called to get into see the captain. Jake, Stan knew, would not be placated unless they could get Mallory assigned to someplace, anyplace else. It was a matter of trust, or lack of it.

By tacit agreement Stan was elected to plead their case while Jake inveigled his way into Sharon Ollestad's office and hijacked the services of the best computer person in the IT office, a young 20 something guy with red thinning hair and a high squeaky voice.

Now, standing in the captain's office, Stan knew it was a lost cause. "I know...but we…"

"Open your eyes, Wyld, you're sounding like a whiney schoolgirl."

He nodded to his secretary who stuck her head in the door, "Danni needs to see Detective Wyld soon as you're done," she whispered.

"We're done."

There was a hard pause as Stan rose and stood before the desk.

The captain looked at him levelly. "Don't fuck this up."

Stan exited without closing either the captain's door or the outer door. He met an agitated Jake Steiner who was just limping up the dimly lit hallway.

"Well?"

Stan shrugged. "He told you to not fuck it up."

Both men looked at each other for a moment.

"What you got?" asked Stan

Jake sighed. "They're working on it. Trying to link Rendell with anything. I told 'em to go back as far as they can, but I dunno, we may be done."

"C'mon." Stan led the way to the elevator.

"Where to?"

"Dungeon. Danni wants us."

"$2 Rendell died in Florida when some gay Cuban smoked his sorry ass."

"Maybe."

Both men watched the elevator's numbers. Stan knew they were both feeling as if they were spinning their wheels.

"You don't think Danni suddenly got her department off its ass and they found some DNA?" Jake mused. "Something we can actually use?"

Stan shook his head. "After all this time with all the people dumped on this case. Not a chance. $2 it has to be something about the rope Mallory found."

"Speaking of, where is she?" asked Jake.

"Didn't answer her phone."

Jake scoffed. "Didn't or wouldn't?"

"Does it matter?"

"Not to me," said Jake, trying for some indignation. But Stan could see there was no real heart behind it.

In truth, they both shared a grudging respect for her devious ability to maneuver around the formidable tangle of bureaucratic bullshit and get what she wanted. It's just neither man had expected a pretty, young woman to get the best of them. It rankled. It damn rankled.

The elevator hit bottom and the doors jerked open. Danni Harness stood by the elevator, one hand extended to the frame as if she was holding the whole thing up.

"Danni!" Stan exclaimed.

"Where's the girl, Melanie? She should be here"

"Mallory," said Jake quietly. "And we've no idea where she is."

"Too bad," smiled Danni. "With that rope she found, she just opened up your case like a can of bad sardines."

Jake started to dig out $2.

"I'll show you. C'mon." She pushed through the doors with both arms and made a beeline for the center table, Stan and Jake behind. The room was in darkness except for the table where the rope, now unknotted, sat in a carefully arranged spiral under six lights that were severely bright. You could see every detail of the rope. As before, it seemed to glow with a golden hue, looking almost new.

Jake got his first glimpse of the rope. "So this is it. This is what you found in the tree?"

Danni jumped in. "Don't look to Stan. He didn't find shit. It was the girl, eh Stan?"

Stan nodded. "She was looking up," was all he said.

"Damn good thing, too." Danni smiled a grim smile. Stan didn't like it when Danni smiled.

"Okay, so you brought me this rope. Your girl found it…"

Stan nodded.

"…and it had some paint on it."

Stan nodded again. "Yeah, what about the paint?"

Danni gave a dismissive wave. "I dunno, some kind of face paint, we think. Rest of those tests will be back next week. But, forget the paint, this is what she really found."

Danni Harness turned and flipped a switch. In sequence, one by one, each of four light boxes sputtered to life.

"You are not going to believe this."

CHAPTER 44

Where was everybody?

M knew his aunt would leave only if there was a cop car left on duty in front of her sunny yellow trailer, in case Jessie came wandering back by some miracle. They would be covering all bases; she goes to Janey's, bingo, she goes to Ruby's, bango.

Or, if M happened to walk into the trailer park. Either way, whoever showed was going to be sequestered; Jessie to the pampering and guilt-free arms of her loving aunt; M to the graybar hotel until they could figure out that he had nothing to do with Jessie being gone. And who knew how long that would take.

Unless, of course, he found Jess first. That was the absolute best of all possible worlds – Jess back and she vouching for his innocence, except for the fact he'd left her alone.

He prided himself on remembering that the Catholic Church almost always had some sort of meeting going on every night. Committee for the Homeless, Men's Bible Study, whatever. There was always food out and he knew his way around enough that it was easy to find a warm classroom to curl up in. That was last night

M had called anonymously from the church this morning to see if the 'little girl from the trailer park' had been found. She hadn't, so he had expected a shitload of activity; dog teams running around, or cops searching every trailer or, God forbid, groups of searchers walking shoulder to shoulder. But there was nothing.

Not even a cop car out front. His aunt was gone, the trailer dark. All of Sunshine Vista seemed more depressed than normal, especially now the sun was setting.

He placed the plastic pail upside down below the kitchen window that Aunt Janey always kept open a crack, and boosted himself up to the transom. It wasn't easy with a sore arm. Still, he was able to hook one leg over and crawl in backwards. He ended up with his two feet in the sink, straddling the faucet.

M paused and listened. Nothing.

He jumped down and crept to the window, keeping fully hidden behind the lacy curtains and peered out at the rest of the Park. Nothing, but the Chinese lady out attacking the ground in her garden with a hoe by the light of her porch light.

Beyond her trailer at the very end lay Ruby's. Even though it was almost full evening, there were no lights on.

Satisfied, he went to the front door, unlocked it and opened it a crack. He wanted to be able to hear his aunt coming home and give himself another avenue of escape.

Now, he needed to work quickly. First was food. He wasn't especially hungry but he knew he'd want it eventually and he didn't know how long it would be before he could steal some more. He made three PB&Js, protein and some sugar, and wrapped them in plastic. He hoped he'd be able to offer Jess one when and if.

Clothes were next. He needed some layers and he had to shuck the wet ones he was wearing. After he changed he found his backpack and stuffed some underwear, four pairs of socks, and a sweater and a jacket. He hadn't brought the best wardrobe selection with him when they left SanFran, but at least he wouldn't die from the freaking cold.

After checking the street again and finding everything the same, he went to the couch and dumped all of Jessie's clothes out of her laundry bag. He sorted through them, what there was, and separated them into piles, shirts, pants, underwear.

M stood back and examined the assortment. He felt it was important to know what she was wearing. He knew all her clothes by heart since there were so few. He knew that she was wearing her yellow Little Mermaid sweatshirt and her red jeans. He couldn't find her green jacket-windbreaker so she must have it with her. Plenty of color. She'd be easy to see if...

Forget that. He put everything back except a sweatshirt and a pair of socks, stuffing them into his backpack, and then strapped it up.

He took up a position behind the curtain and grabbed the backpack, ready to run, because a beat up reddish Honda was cruising very slowly past the trailer. He didn't need company.

M moved to the front door, closed and locked it. He took the backpack and maneuvered it through the kitchen window. It fell and he could tell by the sound that it knocked over the pail. Shit.

He debated bailing now but decided to check out the car again.

The Honda had stopped halfway down the block facing the other way, pointed toward Ruby's.

M searched the small living room and found what he was looking for. His aunt didn't own a pair of real binoculars but had what she called opera glasses. They were shiny pearl plastic on the outside and you couldn't zoom, but they weren't bad, he thought, as he focused in on the Honda. His field of view gave him Ruby's trailer in the background.

Whoever was in the Honda was just sitting there looking at Ruby's trailer. A dead trailer. No lights. No movement. Except.

He refocused the glasses so they brought Ruby's trailer into sharpness. There. The back bedroom window. The blinds moved.

CHAPTER 45

Mallory left her car a few trailers away. She had coasted to a stop and sat watching Ruby's trailer from a distance.

The file sat on the seat beside her. She reached out and touched it. The picture was inside and she was certain that they would match. She felt like her body was spinning forward, propelling her toward an end she knew just had to be. She could feel her heart going and her hands sweating. She took some deep breaths. Ever since she had returned to the office she had known why she needed to go back to the fortune teller's trailer and just how she would do it.

What the hell. Her ass was probably done career-wise. But, six years of working to this point meant everything.

A head appeared in the trailer door's window. Ruby Everheart. She seemed to stare out at the street Mallory was on but Mallory was hunkered down and was sure she couldn't be seen, especially now that it was getting dark.

Mallory saw the door open to the trailer. Ruby Everheart backed out, pulled the door shut, twisted the knob and pushed on the door to make sure it was secure. She turned and Mallory watched as she went to the RV, opened the door and went in. There were no lights on. Mallory could see the door close on blackness.

Mallory opened the folder and removed the picture. She looked again at the figure of the little girl. It was a full-figure shot, probably taken in her front yard by her proud parents. She was standing next to her bike and according to Raellen and Herb Duffy, their daughter Miranda's picture was taken just before she went missing.

Mallory slipped the photo into her jacket. From her purse she took out the 'third hand' that Jake had shown her one day last week, back when they were on speaking terms, when she was one of them. She had known where he had all his 'field equipment', as he called it, safely stowed in one of the cupboards in the office. It wasn't locked. Cops trusted each other.

She hefted it and looked at it closely. It was similar to the pocket set of Allen wrenches her father had given her. She never knew what Allen wrenches were for and never ran across anything in her life that needed them, but her father had considered them part of an essential toolbox so she had kept it. Jake's third hand looked exactly like it, but instead of little graduating sized Allen wrenches that flipped out, this had straight picks of differing sizes, ones that had one bend, one that had two reverse bends, a two-pronged thingy that resembled a tweezers; everything a modern girl needed to break into some place and get into a shitload of trouble.

She started to get out of her car but stopped and tried to remember what she was forgetting. She paused for another few seconds, but still couldn't remember. 'If I can't remember, it must not be important,' she thought.

The car door squeaked a bit when she opened it further and as she shut it. She told herself, two minutes tops. That's all the time she would need.

The steps to the trailer were solid and made no sound. She crouched at the door and pulled out the third hand and tried to remember what Jake had taught her one day when they needed a break.

'First, look at the lock. It will have a vertical rectangular slot and at the bottom of the rectangle will have a few jagged edges. The bottom of the rectangle often has a depressed circle around it. That's the key to which pick you use.'

Yeah, well it sounded simple.

There was not much light to see by and she didn't want to use her flashlight out here. She shifted her head so there was nothing blocking the light. She studied the lock, saw how big the circle

and slot were at the bottom of the rectangle and pulled out the
two-prong pick. She slipped it into the lock and eased it right
then left. She could feel the give to the right, but not the left. She
slid the pick out, turned it over and re-inserted it.

A dog barked in the distance. She looked down the length of
the walkway that ran to the RV, and then the other way. No one.

She re-gripped the pick and turned it to the left this time. She
moved it up and down, twisted it harder to the left, was about to
pull it out and try another when she heard a click.

'Holy shit', she thought. 'How does anyone keep anything
locked up?'

She held the pick tight between her two fingers and with her
other hand reached for the knob and stopped.

She remembered what she had forgotten. Gloves. A pack of
brand new surgical rubber gloves sat on the back seat of her car.

With her free hand she reached down and untucked her
blouse. She tried to hold the pick still.

Using the blouse as a cover. She gripped the knob and turned
it. The door popped open, almost as if it hadn't been locked at
all.

She pulled out the pick and with her elbow pushed the door
halfway open.

There were no lights in the trailer. Only the occasional
headlights from the highway came through the far curtains.

Staying low, she crabbed herself inside and pushed the door
almost closed. The smell of bad cooking pervaded the close air.
Whatever it was it had been scalded or burnt and then left to sit
on the stove or in the open garbage.

She stood up to one side of the door and looked both ways as
far as she could see. No one.

She turned and surveyed the rest of the inside by the dim
light. It seemed to be the same as when she was here before. A
mess.

Mallory took out the pencil flashlight and clicked it on,
keeping it pointed to the ground. She raised it slightly to shine
on the bottom of the carnival poster she had seen. It was still in
the same place as were all the pictures. Just like before.

The picture she needed to see was at the bottom and was almost fully revealed. It was small, 3x5, in a black frame. It showed a little girl with a balloon. And she was at a carnival.

Rendell's JOYLAND Carnival.

Mallory felt a flutter of anticipation as she removed the photo from her jacket and held it up to the picture in the frame. She concentrated on what first caught her attention, the shoes. The girl in the frame had sparkly tennis shoes with one pink lace and one purple lace.

The shoes of the girl in the photo she held had the exact same shoes.

Mallory raised the flashlight beam to the face in the frame. There was no doubt. It was six year old Miranda Duffy. Missing two years.

"Stan you wanted proof, here it is."

She started to remove the picture when one of the pictures in a black plastic frame dropped off the room divider. It didn't break but clattered along the floor.

Mallory stopped everything, even breathing, and listened. She turned halfway around so she could see the door and light coming through where it was not quite closed. She listened for padded footsteps coming down the outer walkway. She stayed frozen for as long as she could. She knew what a lot of shit she would be in if she were caught. But she'd found what she wanted.

She pulled off Miranda's picture and another picture in a black frame caught her eye. It was partially covered by the carnival poster.

She pulled at the poster. It strained against the remaining thumbtacks, but she pulled anyway. She could just make out two legs in the picture. The poster started to tear at the tacks. She pulled further, leaned under and let the beam of the flashlight travel up the figure in the frame. The poster came completely away and crumpled in crackly waves in front of her.

Her heart pounded. The rumpled jeans the way they bunched around the knees. *No.* The hands in pockets the same shirt with the Tasmanian Devil on it.

Please, God, No.

She found herself looking at her brother as he was ten years ago, when he'd disappeared. Tears welled up as she reached up to take her brother's picture.

She didn't register the growl behind her and the cry that came from the hooded figure that had stepped into the light.

"No!"

She fell back toward the room divider. Her flashlight jerked. It lit the ceiling. She grabbed it. It lit a raised arm. It caught the harsh glint of a hammer's claw. In that instant she saw with certainty how the points of the claw had scraped along the bones of Karen Summering and Phillip and Joey.

Her arm came up in defense, but the metal connected full force above her right temple and raked its way down the side of her face.

The sick, hollow sound was her head slamming onto the trailer's floor.

CHAPTER 46

M waited.

He had seen the girl go in. It was dark now, but from this distance, she looked to be the same cop that was walking around the other day with that picture. He wasn't sure.

She had appeared to have a key to Ruby's trailer; at least she seemed to fiddle with the lock and went in. Which was odd. She'd been watching the trailer. She must've seen Ruby leave.

Why didn't she…?

It was then he saw Ruby walking with a purpose down the walkway from the RV. She didn't hesitate but pushed open the door and went in.

Then nothing.

It was all very strange, and M was about to put down the opera glasses and get the hell out of there when the trailer door opened again. He brought the glasses up and saw Ruby at the door. She hesitated and looked back, then closed the door.

But the girl cop hadn't come out had she?

What the hell?

It took him only a few seconds to realize what the orange light was coming from inside the trailer. That was fire. He waited for the cop to come out. It was on fire, why wasn't she coming out?

He picked up the phone and hit 911 but stopped before he hit send.

She didn't set the fire and she didn't come out because she can't come out.

He dropped the phone, threw open the door and sprinted toward Ruby's trailer. He'd get Ruby and have her...

Shit. You dumb shit. Ruby started it. She's burning her own place down. She started a fire in her own place and there was someone in there when she did that. And she knows that.

Maybe Jessie too!

M sprinted up to the landing and twisted the knob hard. Locked. He looked through the glass in the door. Smoke was everywhere inside, like a black hurricane trying to find a way out. It was all he could see except for what looked like two legs on the floor. He banged on the door, then the glass. Then without thinking he took a rock from Ruby's yard and tossed it through the glass. It broke the first time and with the splinters of glass came the flash of heat and smoke. The fire had more oxygen now.

The knob was already hot.

Don't screw with me screamed the fire. Go ahead; open that door and I'll cook your face.

He ducked down, reached up and turned the knob and pushed the door open.

Even low to the ground the heat sent him back on his heels and he almost tumbled backwards down the stairs.

With his arms ahead of him, he pushed forward, even lower this time, his cheek scraping the transom.

He could only keep his eyes open for a few seconds at a time, the heat was searing. Billows of smoke rolled over and engulfed him, thanking him for opening the door.

Mallory coughed, hard.

She raised her head. "Whaaatt?" She took a deep, full breath, inhaled thick black smoke and began to gag.

Her head dropped and she covered her nose and mouth but the smoke was sucked into her lungs anyway.

She needed to move, now, had to move, but all she could do, all she had strength for, was to try to find some good air to breathe.

She couldn't...find it.

This is what it feels like to drown in a roiling black death.

M had made his way on his stomach, eyes closed so he was even with the room divider. It had taken what seemed like forever to make it this far. It had taken the flames only half a minute to envelope the ceiling.

He knew you were supposed to stay as low as possible, but the smoke kept blasting down to the floor. He couldn't see shit. Could barely see the carpet three inches from his face.

Every roll of black, he held his breath. Then at the top of his lungs he called out, "Jessie!"

"What?" He thought he heard someone and had started to crawl to the back of the trailer where Ruby's bedroom was but he stopped when he saw through the smoke, more flames behind the small frosted window in the door to Ruby's bedroom. He turned around and scrabbled the other way.

This is shit. Impossible to see and there was no way to call out anymore.

He made it to the room divider and Jessie wasn't there, and then he felt all along the top of the couch. Nothing. He turned to crawl back and his hand brushed on something smooth and flat. He picked it up and brought it to his face. It was the lady cop's plastic ID He swept his hands in wide arcs until his finger smacked against her thigh.

Behind him the back of the couch erupted in flame. It blew out the two back windows and lit up the end of the room. The explosive rush of air drew the smoke straight up to the ceiling. For a few seconds it was as if someone had sucked all the smoke out of the room. He rose up on his knees to get a breath and he was face to face with the room divider that had all the pictures that Ruby had collected. All were scarred and covered with soot.

But in the middle of all the rest, he saw it. His throat tightened. He was held motionless.

Then the heat and smoke shrieked back to the floor searching for his lungs. Every breath he tried for came with the stink of burning plastic and foam rubber. He started crawling again toward the door and as his hand brushed the cop's foot he stopped. He could still see the bottom of the door. He could still make it alone.

And then he heard the cop say something.

He knew he had to try this. He knew he didn't want to regret shit again. Suffering death by fire was torture.

Lying on his back and covering his face with his bad arm, with his other he grabbed her pant leg and pulled it as hard as he could. Then he crabbed back toward the door and did it again. He closed his eyes and tried to breath to the side like a swimmer about to go under water.

It became a battle. A battle he thought he might win. But, damn she was heavy. She hadn't looked as if she'd had weight, but she was doing nothing to help him.

When he got to the door he arched his head out, took a deep breath, braced his feet against the jamb and pulled. He didn't know whether she was alive, whether she was breathing or what. It may be he was pulling a corpse to safety.

The two front windows on either side of him cracked and popped out spraying him with glass. The flames that had been feeding on the ceiling blew out in vicious licks.

It was only the smell that told him his hair was singeing.

He leaned his head back and took a full deep breath, then two.

He had her legs out onto the landing and felt bad as her head banged along the steps as they made it to the ground. He fell next to her, splayed over on his back. His arms shook from exertion and his chest heaved, gasping for any breath.

Turning his head sideways, he could see her now. She was breathing, sort of coughing. Her face was slashed from her temple to her chin. She was a mess but goddamn, she was alive.

Suddenly the whole trailer park was alive with people he had never seen. Hovering over him and staring down at him was the Chinese lady. She still carried her hoe in her hand. Arms were reaching for him. Some were trying to lift him; others were urging him to stay down. He saw that a young girl was ministering to the cop.

He took a deep breath and rolled over onto his side so he was looking away from the fire. If he was gonna throw up he didn't want it all over him. He had the Chinese lady down in his face talking to him in Chinese. She didn't smile but reached out and touched his forehead. She shrugged and got up. As she did so she cleared his vision and he froze with what he saw.

Backlit by the fire, slouching away from him and just disappearing into the carnival area was Ruby dragging a lifeless form. He was positive it was Ruby and she was dragging a rag doll with no pretense about holding it up off the ground. The doll's legs bounced along unfeeling. The head lolled side to side.

But it was no doll.

M shot up on wobbly legs, bent over double. Arms grabbed him as those surrounding him realized he was standing up. He tried to shake them off and given his weakened condition it would have been impossible if Ruby's trailer hadn't exploded, driving glass shards and aluminum shrapnel in all directions.

The blast pushed him sideways but he stayed on his feet and used the momentum to propel himself toward the chain link gate. He tried calling out, but nothing came from his raw and seared throat. All he could do was stop and suck air.

Jessie!

He had gotten a few steps when everything went black. White stars exploded in his head. He dropped to his knees and let his head fall to the ground.

Behind him M heard voices and sirens. He didn't know and didn't care who was yelling or at whom. He ignored it all.

He pushed to his feet, deliberately forcing himself to go slower. He started moving forward, begging the shooting white lights behind his eyes to stop. The wracking sobs he heard were his own.

M grabbed at the fence for support when he stepped on something. In the weak light of the flames he saw what it was. A small sneaker with red laces.

He pushed off and staggered into JOYLAND.

CHAPTER 47

The fluorescents in the main light box had flickered on and Jake had moved over to it and was studying the backlit image.

Danni looked down at the table in the center of the room and spoke in a low voice.

"Stan, I know the answer to this because you know I'd ream your ass if you did otherwise, but tell me, did you and Marlene take some precautions when you pulled that rope from the tree?"

"Danni, it was black as a camel's asshole out there, we were stumbling over each other, but, yeah if you're asking if we were careful? Yes, we were. Did we use gloves? Yes. We used gloves and we barely touched the damn thing as we, well…Mallory, lowered it into the bag."

"Okay. Mallory, not Marlene. So, you used gloves and you were careful?"

"I just said so. Come on, Danni, what is it?"

"This." She took one of her rulers and pointed to one of the knots of the rope. "The rope's frayed, yes, but when my boys finally got around to examining the knots, this is what they found."

Stan and Jake leaned closer into the light box.

"Don't strain your eyes boys. Over here." Danni pointed to another light box. "I've blown it up 100 times."

It was easy to see now. Amongst the sharp, frayed ends of the rope was what was undeniably a blond hair caught in one of the knots.

Stan looked at Jake, then to Danni.

"Whose?"

"I made the identification an hour ago. I mean I didn't have time for any DNA, but we matched the hair with the sample we had. It's…"

"Karen Summering's," finished Stan.

"Exactly. But, there's more."

"More hairs?"

Danni didn't answer but asked a question of her own.

"This Karen Summering. She was victim number…?"

When Stan hesitated, Danni finished for him. "She was victim two. I looked it up."

"Okay."

Jake turned and studied the first light box and then he understood. "Oh. Shit," he said quietly.

Danni continued on. "Karen was victim number two. Her hair was found in the second knot."

Jake stopped counting and turned to Stan. "Twelve. There are twelve knots."

No one said anything for a moment.

Danni Harness sighed. "Look, I'm sorry Stan. We…I should have found this earlier. It's a mistake. A bad one. I'm sorry."

Stan shook his head. He looked plaintively at Danni but his mind was focused in the woods of Olive Park. He voiced the question they were all thinking.

"Twelve. God, if there *are* twelve, who are they?"

Jake's voice cut the resulting silence. "If there are twelve, *where* are they?"

Before anyone else spoke, Danni cleared her throat.

"One more thing."

Detectives Stan Wyld and Jake Steiner stopped and turned.

"This rope and these knots. I examined them all myself. No way has this been in the weather for fifteen years. Someone has been keeping this out of the weather. And the one thing I know for sure is that the last knot…is fresh. It was tied in the last month."

Danni uncharacteristically raised her voice. "This rope is still being used."

Stan turned to Jake. "You asked where are they."

Jake nodded.

"Where's the best place to hide a body?" It was an old Forensics joke. The punch line never varied.

"Cemetery, of course," said Jake.

Stan shook his head. "No. The best place to hide a body, or twelve bodies, is not a cemetery. It's a killing ground that's already been searched."

"We gotta go."

CHAPTER 48

M woke up with something very wrong. His leg hurt, his mouth was scratched and one eye was swollen shut. The blood had rushed to his head and now it pounded so hard it made his good eye see stars with each beat.

And he realized he was upside down.

He swung slowly, turning like a struggling calf. His father had made him watch that hunting show all the time. His father, his mouth half open, had always gotten excited when the hunters had their prey dangling from a rope. Struggling and turning and dangling. His father hadn't been able to stop watching until they gutted the animal. Then he would jerk back and a quiet 'Yes' would escape his lips. He'd turn to M. 'See! Now that's hunting'. G'wan! Gut the damn thing. Damn!'

M swung the other direction. It was still night. Through his one good eye he could see the woods lit with harsh blue moonlight.

He arched his neck and looked at the ground. His head was about five feet off the ground.

"Well, well..." He heard another voice. His head was slapped hard and the hand also raked across his good eye, stinging. The momentum spun him around faster. He kept his eye closed. The spinning vertigo was nauseating. He just wanted it to stop. His ankle twisted against the rope and his free leg

His head was grabbed, wrenching his neck. Two rough hands held it still. He kept his eye closed. He didn't want to see what was in front of him, but he felt its breath. Could smell it.

"What are you little boy, an acrobat?" The voice was scratchy and its breath stank.

"No?"

M heard it breathing very close to him.

"Stole my rope didn't you, you little shit. Didn't know I had a few more did you?"

M finally opened his eyes. There was an arm across his face. It moved and he saw what after a second started to make him sick. The arm was covered with long scratches, close together. He looked away and closed his eyes. Cat scratches made from an animal in agony.

"Maybe," it continued as if it was having trouble breathing, "You're just a kid who can't do anything right. Can't walk a tightrope. Can't juggle. Can't swallow a sword. Can't do anything! You're fucking useless!"

Rough hands stopped the spinning.

M's eyes half opened. His stomach roiled. He was facing into the shadows of a black hood.

"How's your fucking mother?" It rasped.

The hood slipped back and the moonlight exposed with sickening certainty what he should have seen from the first day Aunt Janey dragged them up to the trailer. What had been cooing to Jessie. What had touched Jessie. What had taken Jessie. The build, the stance, the power...the now bald head.

Oh God.

He fluttered into unconsciousness.

CHAPTER 49

Mallory, too drained to move, had seen the kid leave her and run off toward the carnival's entrance. She had tried to call out to him to wait. Wait for help. He had stopped, but just for a few seconds. When he had looked back she had seen his face. Then he'd staggered through the gate and was gone.

Toward Olive Park.

She turned over and pushed herself up until she was standing. Everything was chaos. She could see around her but the ringing in her ears would not stop.

The trailer she'd been in was gone, or rather scattered all around her. The trailer's door lay at her feet. She had somebody pulling up on one of her arms trying to hold her up and a Chinese lady kept trying to get in front of her face and was yelling something in Chinese.

The fire from the trailer was hot against her face and then she remembered and brought a hand up to her right cheek. The gash was raw and still bleeding.

Then a sanitary pad was held to the side of her face. It was offered by a teenage girl. The girl shrugged as if that was all she had.

Mallory wasn't sure what had happened in the trailer. She didn't know why it was on fire or how she'd gotten out. But she remembered why she'd come to this trailer. She remembered the pictures and she remembered the missing girl and she remembered the boy had been her brother. And she had just seen him run to Olive Park.

And now she understood the answer to Jake's question - why no one had ever seen a car at the pull off at Olive Park. She knew now why the sick shit had had all the time in the world to torture and bury three children. Why there were no obvious drag marks except the thrashings made by Handleman leading into the clearing from the road.

It was because no one had come from the road. They'd come through Rendell's JOYLAND Carnival.

She shook off the person supporting her, held her forearm up against her cheek and moved unsteadily after the boy.

In the distance she heard sirens, but they sounded so far away.

CHAPTER 50

Stan and Jake were just getting into the Dodge when they heard her.

"Hey, Detective Steiner, you ignoring me?"

The commanding form of Sharon Ollestad bore down on them from across the parking lot with the skinny red-headed kid in tow.

"Here." The head of I.T. reached through the car window and slapped a file against Jake's chest. "Better picture of that guy you're after. That Rudolph Rendell."

"Thanks," said Jake. "Florida came through, eh?"

"Florida didn't do shit. It was all me, buster. Yeah. Don't thank me. But you two might want to take a glance in there if you're trying to find the guy. It's got his address and he's here, in Sacramento, detective."

Jake opened the file.

"Yeah. Take a look at page 3. Middle."

Jake found it, ran his finger down the page and then looked at Stan.

"I don't know where you dig up these guys, but the best part is the picture. The last page."

Jake turned to the last page. Stan leaned over to look too. It was the cover of what appeared to be an insider type magazine for circus and carnival people, owners and managers and even regular carnie folk, from 1990. He had no idea such a periodical existed. But under its ornate top banner, taking up the full cover, was a full length picture of a man dressed as a magician on half his body, the other half as woman gypsy fortune teller.

There were only three words at the top.

Rudy and Ruby.

Sharon Ollestad laughed. "Calls himself 'Ruby Everheart'. Your Rudy is really a Ruby. He was here all the time."

Without another word, Stan closed his door, slipped the Dodge into gear and accelerated across the lot, bottoming out as he turned onto Sixth Street.

"Jake, call it in. We may need some help."

But Jake had already picked up his phone when it rang in his hand.

"Yeah?" Jake listened.

Stan flipped on the dash beacon and pushed down hard on the Dodge's accelerator, pushing as fast as he dared through two intersections and bottoming out again at the entrance onto Route 50.

Jake closed the phone.

"Seems like our girl has been busy. Few days ago she put out an alert to be notified of any kids reported missing. Got a hit this morning. A Jessica Ann Cooper, age 6. That's where she went."

Stan glanced at Jake to get more information, but he stared straight ahead.

"Well," asked Stan. "Where is she?"

Jake's voice was low and unsteady. "Same place we're going."

CHAPTER 51

His hands felt all puffy from hanging upside down and his head expanded with each beat of his heart.

M raised one hand and touched the outside of his jean's pocket. It was still there. Carefully he worked the bone handled knife out of his pocket. The exertion made his head pound harder and spun him around so he rotated through a full circle, and that was when he saw them through the trees.

With panic rising in his throat he reached up with all he had and began to saw at the rope. The knife was sharp. As sharp as his father had made him keep it. But the rope was thick.

Exhausted, he flopped back down. It took a full minute before he could raise himself back up to try again.

The moonlight sliced through the trees and lit up the clearing in iridescent blue. The large hunched figure sat slumped on a pile of dirt. It was completely robed in red velvet that shone and rippled like stale blood in the cerulean light. With a seemingly ponderous effort, it raised its head enough so just the chin was illuminated in bright blue, the rest in shadow. One arm on one of its knees, the other, with wide draped velvet sleeves, reached out and beckoned. With crooked fingers in a flowing draw, it called to her. The head gave an encouraging shake.

"Come to me. Come here now. I'm here to… save you."

Only the drool from the chin dropping on the ground belied its intentions. And the quick silver glint from under the velvet folds.

"Come here. It's all right. You're safe now." The head shake again. "You're safe with me."

And Jessie rose and stood before it in the moonlight. And she believed.

"Come here my child. Did you enjoy my carnival today? What was your favorite part? The clowns, the animals, the jugglers, the gypsies…?"

Its lips parted to a slit. "Did you collect a souvenir?" It gave a harsh laugh.

"Or did you prefer the fortune tellers or the fire eaters or maybe you especially liked the bearded lady?"

Its head went back suddenly and it laughed a hoarse and crooked laugh. "Me too… I liked it all", it said to whatever circled above its head and in its head. "I liked it all. And I loved the kids who liked it all…."

And the woods were still and did not answer it for there was no answer.

And still Jessie stood there, her eyes barely open and unfocusing. She didn't know what the yelling meant. But this was the person who took care of her and now her arm hurt and her head hurt and her shoes were gone. This was strange but it had to be all okay because there was nothing else.

And still she believed.

The hood slipped off and the head came forward and the wig was gone. Its eyes settled on her. And the eyes would not leave her.

The drool from the slitted mouth pooled on the ground.

"Ruby?" Jessie asked so as to not make it yell again. "What's wrong?"

The curled hand came out from the folds and it beckoned again with mesmerizing slowness.

"Did you… did you ever play dress up?" it murmured.

Jessie nodded.

"Come here then."

Jessie rested on its knee. Through heavy lids she searched its face and head and slowly her eyes widened and a look of alarm froze her face.

"Where's... your hair?" she asked of it. "What's on your face?"

It tilted its head back and brayed to the moon. Then the head came back down and looked at Jess. The wispy sounds of distant sirens danced in the air.

"Little girl..." Its eyes glistened in the moonlight with sick anticipation. "No time left. Show's over. And you didn't do so well. Didn't do what I told you to do, did you?"

Jessie stared, uncertain. In a quiet voice she said, "My name... is Jessica."

It ignored her and picked up a bottle of yellow liquid, filled its mouth, brought a flame from somewhere and spit the liquid, blowing instant flame past Jessie.

Jessie slid off its knee and fell into a soft pile before it, then started to back away.

"I want to go."

It stood now, full height looming over Jessie and cutting off the moonlight to her face.

The small voice persisted. "I don't like you. I want to go...home."

It paused and looked straight ahead, staring, but seeing something unseen, something of the deep past. Its hands spun behind its back, turning the blade over and over.

"Home." It looked down on the face at its feet. "You are home. This is your home when you don't do well."

It indicated the freshly dug hole next to them. "You know that." It raised its head and shouted into the night.

"Home! Now and forever!"

Behind its back the blade slapped faster and faster into an open palm.

With a terrible eagerness it brought its hand to the front and slipped the blade up a bloused sleeve.

"Get up. Now!" It commanded.

Tears rolled down Jessie's cheeks as she stood, hands by her side looking up.

It towered over Jessie and trembled with excitement. This was the crest of the wave. That trance-like moment before something bad happens. Jessie felt it and took a deep breath.

And then she opened her mouth and began to sing with a clear voice.

"Jesus loves the little children,
All the children of the world..."

Its eyes widened, then narrowed.
"You little bitch...."

M had heard the crazy animal-like shriek. He sawed faster with the knife but he could only do it for ten seconds at a time because he had to lift himself up to reach the knot around his ankle. He could hold the position only until his stomach muscles began to spasm and he had to slump back and hang. When he did, the blood rushed to his head and a feeling like his school backpack was twisted around his neck and pulling him straight to the ground, ripped through his head.

The next time he hauled himself up, he grabbed for his ankle, began to slip and barely grabbed the toe of his sneaker with two fingers. He held on longer this time and sawed as fast as he could.

He was about a half inch from freeing himself when everything stopped. The night crickets vanished. The wind paused.

Jessie had started to sing. It was a hymn she learned from being captive in church and Sunday school for so many years. Her tiny voice carried everywhere in the clearing.

He sobbed and sawed faster, his fingers digging into his shoe. When the rope gave up its burden he wasn't ready, and he crashed to the ground, landing on his right side and knocking all air from him. He gasped, then panicked, completely incapable of drawing a breath. He managed to roll over onto his stomach and sucked until he could get some air. He pushed himself up until he was on all fours. Tears streamed down his face.

On the far side of the clearing, Mallory regained consciousness. She lay there and wondered where she was.

When had she run? When had she fallen? All she knew was her head hurt like hell, there was dirt in her mouth and someone nearby, a child, maybe, was singing.

"Precious in his sight," she whispered.

She set her palms down on either side of her and pushed. Her shoulders came up. She briefly closed her eyes and tried to will away the swirling as she slowly raised her head and opened her eyes.

It was dark but in the dreamy blue light stood a little girl standing before the hulk of a man in dark, blood-red robes. And the girl was singing.

Mallory's movement drew the little girl's attention and she looked right at Mallory. Mallory could see her eyes get bigger as her hymn trailed to silence.

In slow motion, the wave began to break.

The man reached down and grabbed a shank of Jessie's hair and pulled her up off the ground. Her scream was choked by the surprise of her head being yanked back, her neck exposed, alabaster white in the moonlight.

She hung there, half off the ground, held by one meaty hand while the other let slip the blade to its grasp, then raised it up so it caught the full light of the moon, showing its pristine edge.

Mallory could see the future, where the knife would go, where it would slash. It was all too clear. She took a deep breath to shout a warning but instead the heaving sound she made sounded demonic, like a drowning person trying to get a breath, and came out in a raspy, naked "Noooo".

The man hesitated. The knife dropped to his side and his head cocked as if he had heard something. Something not right. Something bad.

Before Mallory could move she saw a form rush from the bushes at the edge of the clearing, running full into the moonlight. With both hands it grabbed the shovel and came running.

He swung as hard as he could. From somewhere M remembered what his father had said about hitting a baseball. Swing through it. Swing as hard as you can, but swing through it. Don't just hit it.

Fuckin' kill it, he'd said.

He swung with the same swing he'd used on his father. When the lamp base slammed into his father's face he'd heard the crack, saw the blood gush from his ear, watched him crumple and fall with only a feeble 'Oh'.

Now, in these dark woods, he came on a run and swung with full extension of his arms, and as if someone else was doing it for him, helping him, he watched as the dirty shovelhead came round in a full screaming arc and sliced into Ruby's neck, gristling hard when it hit bone.

The shovel handle splintered in half, the momentum sending M backwards into the freshly dug hole.

Like a shrieking animal, Rudy Rendell contorted in perverted agony and ripped the shovel head from his neck. Blood, black in the moonlight, arced up, sprayed Jessie, and spilled on the ground.

M saw Jessie's face and coveralls covered in black drops, her drugged eyes widening with fear.

Rudy pushed Jessie and charged for M.

M backed away, heels digging into the soft dirt, getting no traction.

Rudy's eyes rolled back and for a brief hopeful moment M believed it was over. But with a low growl and singular fury, Rudy charged at him.

M grabbed the splintered end of the handle and raised it in pitiful defense as Rudy slipped on the edge of the grave and landed full weight on the jagged spike. It buried itself deep into the soft middle and M could feel the damage being done by the splintered wood.

Rudy Rendell's carnival painted features contorted with crazed fury and pain.

M sobbed and bucked, kicking away. Then, half out of the grave, he screamed.

"You said you knew what happened to my father... well this is what happened to my father..."

He drew his leg back and kicked the handle in deeper.

There was an inhuman cry.

"This is what it feels like."

Rudy staggered back out of the hole and sat down hard. The broken shovel handle rose and fell with Rudy's labored breaths.

M climbed from the hole and stood in the moonlight, his legs braced against falling backward. Racking sobs punctuated his breathing. With deliberate slowness, he reached down and picked up the rest of the broken shovel, wound it back and slammed the shovelhead onto the end of the handle driving it further into Ruby's chest.

"You....." again.

.....Sick...." again

....Sack...." again

....of Shit."

Red saliva ran down onto the handle. Ruby's head lolled to the side, then tilted slowly and smiled. The moonlight caught one eye.

Slow words gurgled from the twisted mouth.

"You like gingerbread....don't you little boy?"

M swung hard a final time and crushed the face of evil.

CHAPTER 52

Stan rested back on the hood of the Dodge and closed his eyes. He was dog tired. Good tired, but damn dog tired.

Both he and Jake had joined in the search as soon as they got to Olive Park but neither of them were dressed for a tramp through the woods and so left it to the scores of both SPD and CHP uniforms who materialized seemingly unbidden.

The boy and his sister were still being evaluated by the paramedics so interviews there would be a few minutes yet.

Jake was sitting in the Dodge filling out paperwork.

Stan had listened to Jake recount what happened at the fortune teller's trailer, the fire and explosion. He'd heard about the little brown man strung up on the fence under a juniper tree, same exact spot where a dead cat had been reported by some Chinese lady a few days before. He'd taken the call from Sharon Ollestad, now warning him about the violent tendencies of one Rudy Rendell, based on the history she'd just uncovered. A little late.

Still, for a crime scene that involved twelve victims it was respectfully quiet. Olive Park was no longer a frantic manhunt and all who were now working the site felt it. It was a memorial. A place for whispers. Even the searchers, who had now spread out from the main clearing, spoke in quiet tones.

The road was closed in both directions by two squads, half a mile in either direction, angled toward the center of the roadway, lights full on. Press was being kept far away. This time, early morning, there was little traffic waiting to get by. He'd counted at least three other vehicles at the pull off, mostly CHP squads, plus Forensics' van which had pulled up a few minutes ago.

Through the trees a quarter mile away Stan could still make out the faint glow from the trailer fire. Even from here he could see the red and blue flash of fire and rescue dealing with it.

He looked up. The stars were still out, the night air held a calm he hadn't felt in a long time. And that's when he saw the figure standing next to the Dodge.

Retired Detective Carruthers answered Stan's unasked question.

"Danni called me. She thought I'd want to know. Plus, heard it on the scanner."

Stan nodded and slid off the hood. Jake joined him

"C'mon," Stan said to Carruthers.

Jake, with Carruthers behind, followed Stan to the clearing, but Stan stopped them with his arm, like Carruthers had done to him so many years ago.

"What?" asked Jake. "What is it?"

Stan ignored Jake and nodded to Carruthers. "This," he said quietly. But then he could say no more. He nodded to the ground.

Stan felt a whole lifetime of frustration slip from him and he was infused with a feeling he hadn't felt this completely in as long as he could remember.

They stood and, with eyes too experienced, surveyed the scene.

Neither Jake nor Stan mentioned Mallory's name, but that's where their thoughts were. Thinking about amateurs, thinking what trouble they can get into, what disasters they can cause. What insight they can bring.

It was a love/hate, good/bad, lucky/unlucky.

Stan smiled to himself. It was just like her to barge ahead without caution, without the trained perspective of knowing how bad things could get and how fast they could turn to disaster. Amateurs. She had no feel for the danger. She had no sense of it.

"She just has no sense," said Stan out loud.

No one contradicted him.

"Like a damn terrier..."

Jake gave a quiet laugh. "Still, and I'm the last one to defend her God knows, the absolute last one, but ... here we are."

Stan looked at Carruthers. His face was grim.

After the tree had been found and the rope and the knots, no one had dared speak about the "what ifs".

What if the Forensics team led by Carruthers had just looked up from their three days of scrabbling around in the dirt of Olive Park to see a rope swaying slightly in the breeze?

What if there had been only three knots there at the time.

Stan could only imagine Carruthers' pain. And there was nothing Jake or Stan could say to ease it.

Carruthers had been right to be scared to enter the clearing that first time with Stan. He should have been terrified. Because not solving the crime of one's career had always been a possibility and one you accepted when you took the job. Not solving it in time to save nine other children was never in the imagined scenarios and was such a gut-punch that it could not be considered. You do the best you can so at the end of every day you can look at yourself in the mirror without looking away. So that you can sleep. So you can look at your own kids and know that you're trying.

Stan knew the pain, felt it. Homicide works as one amorphous organism. No one detective can exist by himself; he is part of the whole. The relay team that loses a race doesn't lose only because one runner's arms didn't pump hard enough or another's lungs couldn't gulp the air fast enough or because someone's legs went quivering the last quarter mile. No. The relay racers win or lose the race, not because of any one thing or any one runner. Cases were solved or not solved not due to any one person.

None of the forensic techs had seen the tree or rope. Neither did Thompson or Carruthers, but Carruthers kept digging on the case long after he left the department. Forensics did find the words on the bracelets. Jake discovered what they meant. It took Mallory to spy the tree and the rope. He surmised the victims were headed somewhere on their own volition and had not been snatched. It took Mallory to find out about the carnival and Jake to find Rendell's JOYLAND and the secret of Ruby Everheart.

You live and die trying. Best you can.

From where the three of them stood, they could see the draped figure of Rudy Rendell sprawled atop the mound of dirt. The tarp covering him was tented upward.

"Ruby Everheart?" asked Carruthers. "That was her name?"

"No," said Jake. "No. It was Rudy Rendell. He turned himself into Ruby Everheart. This was all Rendell family property. For years, when the little circus or carnival or freak show or whatever it ended up being, whenever it went on the road, Rudy would bring back a…souvenir from the trip."

"Then," added Stan, "when the economy went into the shitter and things started to go bad, Rudy Rendell ran off, or so everyone thought, but he really became Ruby Everheart, the fat and kindly old lady living off telling fortunes to the unsuspecting.

"We may never know what he promised all those kids to get them back to his carnival."

Carruthers murmured, "In plain sight. The best place to hide." He left the rest unsaid.

"Detective?" The SPD officer had approached the three of them but was looking at Stan.

"Yes? The two kids okay?"

The officer nodded. "Fine mostly. Sister and brother. Sister was drugged but she's all right. Boy's got a bad ankle and some cuts, hair's a little singed, but…"

"Mallory Dimante?"

The officer shook his head. "Detective Dimante looks like shit, sir. Not sure how she got out of that fire, but she'll be okay. Nasty cut to her face."

Stan didn't bother to correct the impression that Mallory was a detective.

The officer then touched his arm and pointed him away from the clearing.

"What?" asked Stan.

"You need to see this. We found them."

The officer guided Stan and Jake back into the woods. Over his shoulder he declared, "You know, actually, it was Detective Dimante who found them."

As they brushed past eucalyptus and ducked under the low hanging pine boughs, Stan saw a few flashlights moving further into the woods.

They came to a second clearing.

Without a word the officer shined his light on three piles of dirt, three graves, slowly, with deliberation, moving the light and holding on each pile, then sliding it to the next and the next.

"And over there..." He raised his light to another clearing in the woods, shining his flashlight further in the darkness ahead, "...and there, three more...." he moved his beam to the right where another flashlight bobbed among the trees.

"And Detective Dimante," he turned his light once again, "is over there."

"Thank you," said Stan quietly.

They separated and Stan and Jake headed toward the light that wasn't moving. As he entered the third clearing, there was just enough emerging morning light to begin to see the two additional mounds.

Stan entered quietly. For all the savagery that must have occurred, this was a reverent place. The mounds in a row, neatly laid out.

Mallory was on her knees with her back to Stan and Jake. She didn't move at all as they approached.

"Mallory...?"

And then he saw. As he moved around her, he saw her hand cradling a small, delicate, skeletonized hand that had poked up through the top of the nearest mound.

She raised her hand and with two fingers lifted a small silver chain bracelet. It was scorched, but Mallory had rubbed it hard enough so that 'Sam' was clearly visible.

Stan knelt down and put his hand over hers. He could feel her whole body trembling.

Jake, after a slight hesitation, leaned down and kissed the top of her head.

CHAPTER 53

"What's your name son?

M looked past the detective. He could see Jess sitting on a stool next to the ambulance. She was answering questions and while she wasn't smiling, she seemed pretty much okay. He'd tried to wipe most of the blood off of her so now only her ripped jeans gave any indication that anything bad had happened. He hoped she didn't get all weird about this when she was thirty eight or something.

But now he felt so tired he needed to sit down. He reached out and sat on the nearest rock he could find. His breath came hard and his eyes started to water.

"Son, you okay?"

Stan Wyld knelt down in front of M and put his hand on his knee.

"Son? I'm Detective Wyld."

M stared at the ground. He didn't want to cry in front of anybody and so focused on his shoes which were still coated with bloody mud. He knew if he just concentrated hard enough, the feeling of wanting to bawl would pass. He took deep breaths to steady his quivering chin. He wasn't going to look up at the detective until he didn't feel like such a baby.

The detective stood and put his hand on M's shoulder. "Stay here for a few minutes will you?"

M nodded without looking up.

The picture M remembered had been in a small black frame. The flames from the fire in the trailer had lit it up so there was no mistake. He remembered it because it had been a newer frame, not as dusty as the others, and it had clean glass. He wasn't sure when she'd taken it, but it must've been only a few weeks ago and it had been Jessie. And it had been taken and mounted in the small black frame and she was so small, sitting like a small adorable ball on Ruby's front steps. Behind her was Pitic. M didn't think that Jessie knew he was even there behind her. But the thing that had scared him the most was that the picture had been taken without him.

He also remembered it had been mounted in the center of the wall with all the other ones surrounding it. The wall had been full of pictures, and the pictures had all been of kids. Kids he recognized from the cop's folder. Those were missing kids. Those were kids who had never been found. Kids whose parents had somehow lost them. Kids who hadn't been protected. Kids now gone. Their pictures were on the wall in the trailer and Jessie's had been on top. Hers was the last one.

M wiped his eyes, stood, and looked back at the series of clearings. The headlights from the ambulance and the police cars were aimed into the woods. The trunks of all the trees were brightly lit. It was hard to tell what had happened here. He supposed in a few years that this little clearing and the ones beyond it would look like they always had, like they should. Maybe, he thought, it would be nice to come back up here and make sure everything was all right. Kids can do that for other kids.

M turned and approached the detective. Their eyes met and M extended his hand.

He felt strange doing this but it seemed important to acknowledge that sometimes the cops show up when you are doing something right with your life.

M smiled.

"Michael Alexander Cooper, Jr. They used to just call me..."
He stopped.
"I used to just call myself M."

Author's Note

'Humanity's humanity is a fraud for the few young, unfortunate innocents who smile with clear eyes, who give us their trust because it is human to do so, who look to us as they should for protection. And who sometimes suffer with a magnitude unimaginable.'

Children – their naïve openness and stunning vulnerability takes your breath away some days. As good and responsible parents, we nurture and feed their openness with a personal morality, enduring opportunities and an education that is, hopefully, even better than the one we had.

We also fiercely protect their vulnerability. Every day. Probably forever.

Yet, sometimes, the unthinkable happens or threatens to. If you or your child or someone close to you is in that situation, start here – The National Center for Missing and Exploited Children – www.missingkids.com. Good people doing good work.

And, if you can, give your child an extra hug tonight.

C.J. Booth

CPSIA information can be obtained at www.ICGtesting.com
Printed in the USA
LVOW011521180413

329845LV00017B/735/P